Dear Parents:

Congratulations! Your child is taking the first steps on an exciting journey. The destination? Independent reading!

STEP INTO READING® will help your child get there. The program offers five steps to reading success. Each step includes fun stories and colorful art or photographs. In addition to original fiction and books with favorite characters, there are Step into Reading Non-Fiction Readers, Phonics Readers and Boxed Sets, Sticker Readers, and Comic Readers—a complete literacy program with something to interest every child.

Learning to Read, Step by Step!

Ready to Read **Preschool–Kindergarten**
• big type and easy words • rhyme and rhythm • picture clues
For children who know the alphabet and are eager to begin reading.

Reading with Help **Preschool–Grade 1**
• basic vocabulary • short sentences • simple stories
For children who recognize familiar words and sound out new words with help.

Reading on Your Own **Grades 1–3**
• engaging characters • easy-to-follow plots • popular topics
For children who are ready to read on their own.

Reading Paragraphs **Grades 2–3**
• challenging vocabulary • short paragraphs • exciting stories
For newly independent readers who read simple sentences with confidence.

Ready for Chapters **Grades 2–4**
• chapters • longer paragraphs • full-color art
For children who want to take the plunge into chapter books but still like colorful pictures.

STEP INTO READING® is designed to give every child a successful reading experience. The grade levels are only guides; children will progress through the steps at their own speed, developing confidence in their reading.

Remember, a lifetime love of reading starts with a single step!

 Published in the United States by Random House Children's Books, a division of Penguin Random House LLC, 1745 Broadway, New York, NY 10019, and in Canada by Penguin Random House Canada Limited, Toronto, in conjunction with Disney Enterprises, Inc. Random House and the colophon are registered trademarks of Penguin Random House LLC.

Step into Reading, Random House, and the Random House colophon are registered trademarks of Penguin Random House LLC.

Visit us on the Web!
StepIntoReading.com
rhcbooks.com

Educators and librarians, for a variety of teaching tools, visit us at RHTeachersLibrarians.com

ISBN 978-0-7364-4195-7 (trade) — ISBN 978-0-7364-9003-0 (lib. bdg.)
ISBN 978-0-7364-4196-4 (ebook)

Printed in the United States of America 10 9 8 7

Random House Children's Books supports the First Amendment and celebrates the right to read.

STEP INTO READING®

DISNEY · PIXAR

LUCA

Friends Are Forever

adapted by Natasha Bouchard
illustrated by the Disney Storybook Art Team

Random House New York

What are friends?
Friends are special.
Luca and Alberto
are friends.
They are
sea monsters!

Friends are fun.
Luca and Alberto
build and ride
a scooter.

The two friends
have an amazing
time together!

Latteria
PIAZZA
CALVINO

Friends are exciting!
Luca and Alberto have
a thrilling adventure
in a beautiful seaside
town called Portorosso.

Friends are different.

Giulia is not like

Luca and Alberto.

She is not

a sea monster.

She is a human girl.

Friends are brave.

Giulia stands up

for her friends.

She protects them

from a bully

named Ercole.

Friends are supportive.

Luca learns how
to ride a bicycle.
It is not easy at first.
But his friends
cheer him on.

Friends inspire.

Giulia points
to the train that is
headed to her school.
She tells Luca that
he can go to school, too.

Friends are ready
to help.

Alberto is trapped.
But Luca is there.
He is ready
to rescue Alberto.

Friends are loyal.
When Giulia gets hurt,
Luca and Alberto
go back for her.

Luca and Alberto are
the Portorosso Cup
champions!
The three friends
make a great team.

GENOVA

Friends sometimes
need to part ways.
And they may not see
each other often.

But friends will
be friends forever.
Luca can always count
on his friends.

His mission was to destroy her.

And yet from the first moment she walked—a simple word for such a heavenly movement—across the bailey toward him, he sensed a serious breach in his defenses. An open gate in *his* wall.

Unwillingly, Gunnar recalled how she had grasped Arno's arm, the familiar intimacy of the gesture, and jealousy twisted in his gut. He, Gunnar Olafson, was jealous. He was *never* jealous; he had no reason to be. Women came to *him*; it was they who were jealous—of one another. But now he pictured dark eyes so large and beautiful, skin so fine and soft, a mouth so moist and ripe, and a firm, full body. The possibility of another man possessing all that . . . He clenched his jaw, hard. It was as if, he thought in disgust, he had never had a woman before.

"Wonderfully written and rich in historical detail."
Denise Hampton

Other AVON ROMANCES

A Chance at Love *by Beverly Jenkins*
A Game of Scandal *by Kathryn Smith*
His Scandal *by Gayle Callen*
Lone Arrow's Pride *by Karen Kay*
The Maiden Warrior *by Mary Reed McCall*
A Necessary Husband *by Debra Mullins*
The Rake: Lessons in Love *by Suzanne Enoch*

Coming Soon

All My Desire *by Margaret Moore*
Cherokee Warriors: The Lover *by Genell Dellin*

And Don't Miss These ROMANTIC TREASURES *from Avon Books*

An Affair to Remember *by Karen Hawkins*
One Night of Passion *by Elizabeth Boyle*
To Marry an Heiress *by Lorraine Heath*

SARA BENNETT

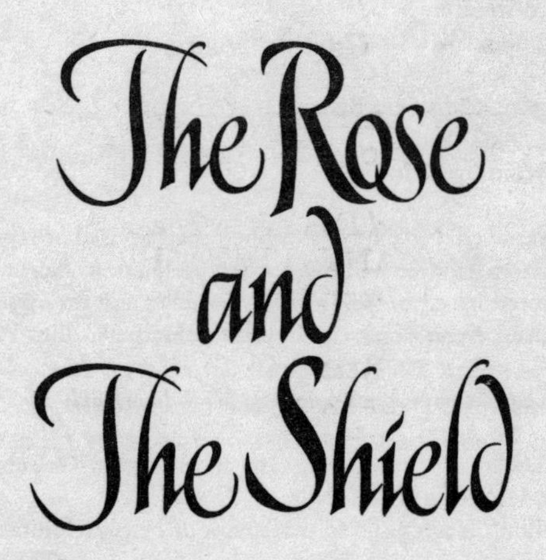

AVON BOOKS
An Imprint of HarperCollins*Publishers*

This is a work of fiction. Names, characters, places, and incidents are products of the author's imagination or are used fictitiously and are not to be construed as real. Any resemblance to actual events, locales, organizations, or persons, living or dead, is entirely coincidental.

AVON BOOKS
An Imprint of HarperCollins*Publishers*
10 East 53rd Street
New York, New York 10022-5299

ISBN: 0-06-000270-0
www.avonromance.com

First Avon Books paperback printing: September 2002

Printed in the U.S.A.

10 9 8 7 6 5 4 3 2 1

Prologue

Somerford Manor, the Southwest of England
1072

Rose leaned on the sill of her solar window and gazed out into the darkness. Lonely and alone, four years the Lady of Somerford, one a widow, she stood in the night and felt the trappings of her position slip from her. Here, now, she was simply Rose, a woman waiting . . .

There was no moon tonight, not even a hint of one, only the starlight to see by. Dreamily, Rose's gaze followed the faint, silver curve of the river Somer, to the ford that had given her manor its name. Then on past the village, past the meadows and cultivated field strips to the woods that covered the hills curling in a protective arc around Somerford from south to west. But as usual on nights like this, Rose's gaze soon strayed northward. Away from solid land, to the pale shimmer of water and the white breath of mist lying in the hollows and damp places.

Somerford Manor was situated on the edge of the Mere—a vast salt marsh fed by the sea—which covered much of central Somerset. In some parts it was called Avalon, and in others the Levels, but around Somerford it was called, simply, the Mere. Here, sedge and rushes and furze thrived and the merefolk lived on low islands, growing their crops in the tenuous soil and traveling in boats. Sometimes they made trackways above the mud with stout poles and sods, hoping the winter floods would not wash away their efforts and isolate them once more.

A strange, watery existence.

When morning came across the Mere, Rose knew she would see the islands, but more particularly the high, mist-shrouded knoll of Burrow Mump, rising from the waters like some strange, mythical beast. It was rumored to be an old Briton burial place, although the Somerford villagers' superstitions had furnished it with a far more romantic tale.

On dark nights, they said, like this one, when the Mere lay still and quiet and mist swathed the land, on such nights as this a great legion of the old gods sprang up from Burrow Mump. From the earth itself they would rise up and ride out on their warhorses over the treacherous, marshy Levels. And they never sank in the mud or stumbled, for the hooves of their magical mounts never touched the ground. They rode in a great cloud, like a coming storm, and sometimes rumbling could be heard as they approached. On their heads they wore horned helmets, like the Viking raiders of old, and their chests were bare and gleaming, and their eyes were shining with a hot and frightening glow. And if, 'twas said, anyone should be so unwise as to peek out through the shutters to see them, then the old gods would swoop down with a great rush and snatch up that foolish and curious person.

And carry him away.

To what? Rose wondered, with the cold night air on her face. A life of slavery in their dark underground hall? A fearful death? Or a long captivity as wife to one of them? For, she reasoned, if they were all men, these wild creatures from Burrow Mump, might they not long for the soft arms of a woman? Just as Rose longed for the arms of such an imaginary man—a strong man, a man who would love her and none other.

Real love, flesh-and-blood love, was something she never allowed herself. But she could pretend . . .

Lady Rose, widowed, lonely, burdened by worry for her manor and people, often found herself thinking of Burrow Mump. She was not overly superstitious, but sometimes on dark nights like tonight she found herself opening her shutters and leaning out—as if daring the old gods to find her.

And often, alone in her bed, she would dream of those ghostly warriors. Dream she was riding before one of them on his horse, the taste of the salty marsh wind on her lips. His strong arm would be hard about her waist, unrelenting, and yet comforting in its claim on her. *Mine*, he would say in a voice without words. And then, in her dream, if she turned and looked up she would see the cold shape of her captor. Only he had no face; it was always veiled as if by a mist. She strained to see beyond it, but she could never make out his features. Whoever the warrior was, his identity was forever hidden from her.

Perhaps it was better so, she thought matter-of-factly. Perhaps in not knowing she was saved from disappointment.

And yet . . . Rose leaned perilously far from her window, gazing out into nothing. *And yet I long to see him, and I will never be happy until I know his face as if it were my own.*

Chapter 1

The small band of mercenaries rode out of the shadows of the forest and drew to a halt. Their leader, Gunnar Olafson, narrowed his blue eyes against the June sun. He looked across the meadows of ripening wheat to the dark rise of keep and ramparts, and beyond that to the vast expanse of the marshes.

This was Somerford Manor, and it was not as he had expected.

Gunnar had seen so much waste in his travels about England, good country lying fallow for want of enough men, or the will, to plant it. Though he was no farmer, it hurt Gunnar bitterly, in some fundamental way, to see the land so abused.

The coming of the Normans had meant more than a new system of government; in many cases it had meant an entirely new way of life. Such changes could not be wrought in a year, or even six. It would take a long time for prosperity to return to England.

Gunnar had been prepared for similar chaos here at Somerford. Instead he gazed on a golden harvest so abundant the grain was almost bursting from the fields, and the soil beneath appeared well cherished and rich. He could not help but wonder if this was the Lady Rose's doing.

He did not want to think so.

He did not want to think well of her.

Gunnar rarely associated with Norman ladies, and this particular Norman lady was already his enemy. Although he had never met Lady Rose, he was prepared to wish her ill.

"There are strong wooden ramparts around the bailey." Ivo, his second-in-command, leaned closer and gestured across the fields with his black-gloved hand. "And within the wall there is a stone keep—there are not many *stone* keeps built on manors as small as this. Aye, their defenses look good, Captain. They are prepared."

"But prepared for what?" Gunnar said in reply. "Are they hoping to keep out Lord Radulf's enemies? Or Lord Radulf himself?"

Somerford Manor straddled a corner of the great Lord Radulf's Crevitch estates, and shared boundaries with the lands of Lord Fitzmorton and Lord Wolfson. Gunnar knew that neither of these latter two barons was an ally of Lord Radulf, the legendary King's Sword, and both were wont to turn greedy eyes in his direction.

Lord Radulf had sent to Wales for Gunnar and his men because he had a bad feeling about Somerford Manor. *An itch*, he had told Gunnar in his low, husky voice. The itch had begun when he accidentally intercepted a sealed letter from Somerford to Lord Fitzmorton, asking for help in obtaining mercenaries. He wanted Gunnar to scratch it, while at the same time not upsetting his wife, the Lady Lily, who had made Lady Rose her protégée . . .

"You really believe this Lady Rose is in league with Lord Radulf's enemies?"

Gunnar shrugged off Ivo's question. "This is what we have come to find out."

"They will not suspect us?"

"They have sent for mercenaries and that is what we are. Why should they suspect us? They do not know it is Lord Radulf's orders we obey."

"And if the job is done well, then Radulf will see you have Somerford Manor as reward, Captain."

"Aye. But for those of you who want to stay here with me, there is a welcome place. For those who want to go, there will be recompense."

The others murmured their agreement, but Ivo shot his captain an uncertain look. "We have never dealt with a woman before, Gunnar."

Gunnar shrugged off Ivo's doubts. "A traitor is a traitor whether it be man, woman, or child. We will do our job, Ivo, as always. It may be our last."

Ivo nodded and scratched his chin. "Our last, aye. You know I am with you, Captain, as always."

Unsmiling, Gunnar turned to look at each of them, feeling the weight of their lives heavy in his hands, memorizing their faces. These five men had been with him for more years than he cared to remember: Ivo, Sweyn, Alfred, Reynard, and Ethelred. They trusted him, they relied on his steel strength and calm stillness, and they in turn gave him a reason to stay alive in a world he found increasingly lackluster.

Their fellowship was coming to an end.

"Follow me," he said quietly, and knew they would.

Gunnar led them from the shadowy forest and along the rough track in the direction of Somerford Keep. The meadows of wheat waved about them.

What would it be like to be master of all this? To be lord of Somerford Manor? Certainly he would have no trouble protecting and fighting for the land and the people; being a mercenary had taught him well when it came to warfare. But a man, even a lord, could not be always fighting. Mayhap he would marry as his mother was always telling him he should.

I am an old woman. I need grandchildren, my son. And you need a wife. If you remain alone you will grow bitter and nasty, and you do not want that, Gunnar, do you?

He smiled at the memory of her voice, her pale eyes all but closed and yet seeing so much. He had made her wait a long time, but maybe at last the moment had come. Soon, if his future turned out the way he hoped, he would need a wife. Not a Norman lady—they were for the wealthy or the ambitious, and being neither, he had no use for them. No, give him a good earthy peasant woman. Someone he could hold without fearing she might shatter, or kiss without going down on his knees for permission. A plain, good woman to keep him warm at night; that was what he needed to cure this melancholy that had lately afflicted him.

Aye, a woman in his bed and his own land beyond his door!

"The gate is open."

It was Ivo who spoke, drawing him back to the matter at hand. Gunnar frowned. The gate *was* open. Wide open. Such a lack of caution or care was not good. If they had been a band of outlaws, they could have ridden straight in. Five minutes, and all who lived would have been dead.

Had the Somerford garrison grown so careless that they had forgotten such simple precautions? Any lord or lady who neglected fundamental laws for the protection of people and property deserved nothing but contempt.

Gunnar and his men clattered across the narrow bridge, its sturdy legs straddling the deep ditch outside the wooden ramparts. The bridge was approximately the width of a cart, and they were forced to ride in double file, therefore exposed to the dangerous fire of arrows and slingshots from the walls above—if there had been men there to loose them. Gunnar noted that there was not even a single guard to give warning.

His face hardened.

The Lady of Somerford had much for which to answer.

"I will speak for us all," he reminded them, as they followed him into the bailey. "Take my lead. And remember, we are men who will do anything for money . . . even change our loyalties."

Ivo nodded, and Gunnar felt a surge of affection and gratitude for the dark brooding strength of his friend and second-in-command. Many times in the past Ivo had been at his back, and now it would be so again. One last time.

Inside the bailey there was plenty of activity, and for a moment no one seemed to notice them. A couple of oxen bellowed their resentment at being harnessed to a cart filled with wood. A smith was busy in his open forge, the smell of fire and metal so familiar to Gunnar that he breathed it in with pleasure. A trio of women were drawing water from a well, gossiping, laughing. One by one they stopped, gazing in alarm at the newcomers, though more particularly upon Gunnar himself—and now the women's eyes widened in admiration.

Gunnar didn't pay any attention to the staring women. They had turned to look all his life—ever since he was old enough to be called a man. Not that there hadn't been times when he enjoyed their bedazzlement to the full, but their admiration did not make him what he was.

Tall and broad-shouldered, Gunnar was aware that his chain mail tunic made him seem more so, and as he removed his helmet, his hair caught the sun like a fortune in copper coin.

Physically he was a big man, very much as he imagined his father Olaf the armorer must have been in his youth, his upper body grown muscular from wielding the swords and battle-axes made by his father, or working in the forge beside him when he was young. His dark red hair was worn long to his shoulders in the English fashion, and twisted into narrow braids either side of his face. His eyes were the dark blue of the oceans his ancestors had crossed so readily to raid unwary shores.

Slowly, all around them, the comfortable bustle of the bailey had fallen silent. Now, each and every one of Lady Rose's people was still and staring, totally focused on the new arrivals.

Gunnar was aware of the picture he and his men presented—hardened warriors in rough coverings of wool and hide and metal, armed for battle. Men for whom no crime was too great, or too unspeakable.

They were a pack of wolves set down in a dovecote.

"Ah," said Gunnar. "Now they are afraid. Now that it is too late."

"There are no guards," Ivo added, glancing about. "A few men, but they are either unshaven boys or ancients. Maybe the gate was open because it required too much strength to close it."

Sweyn chuckled, and then the smile slid from his face. "Someone comes, Captain."

Gunnar looked up, wiping all expression from his own face. The approaching figure was that of an older man with close-cropped dark hair streaked with gray. He wore a sword at his hip, and beneath his well-made brown tunic and breeches his body appeared sturdy and strong. Clearly a Norman knight—it was there in the arrogant way he walked, the hard look he gave them. Gunnar's information was that this man was probably Lady Rose's lover—and her coconspirator in treason.

"Sir Arno d'Alan," Gunnar observed softly to his companions.

Silently the band of mercenaries watched him approach. Gunnar's men were used to being insulted by such as Sir Arno d'Alan, and from the expression on the knight's face, today would be no exception.

"State your business," the Norman knight demanded, dark eyes narrowed as he peered at them against the bright sky, taking in their disreputable appearance and the casual way they sat their horses. In fact he was at a disadvantage on foot, but he acted as if he were not.

"I am Gunnar Olafson," Gunnar replied in a measured voice that conveyed his thoughts not at all. "Captain Olafson. And these are my men. We have come in answer to your need for fighting men."

"Olafson . . . ?" Sir Arno frowned, and then the lines on his brow cleared as he understood, his arrogant mask slipping into something more calculating. "The mercenaries. Ah, then, Captain, I am Sir Arno d'Alan, and this is Somerford Manor. I had heard that a troop of men was coming to our aid, but I did not expect anyone so soon."

"Your gate was open."

Gunnar stared down with expressionless blue eyes, one hand on the hilt of his sword. There was no criticism in his voice, but Sir Arno seemed to sense something. His lord-of-the-manor pose slipped.

"Open, you say?" Arno glanced across the bailey as if he hadn't noticed before. "Mayhap the Lady Rose gave the order. That need not concern you."

Gunnar considered whether to disabuse him of that fact, and decided against it. Arno would learn soon enough that any place where Gunnar Olafson was became his concern.

"You know why you are here?" Arno's voice was sharp, authorative, and all business. His eyes were sly, as watchful as a cornered fox.

"You are paying us."

It was the literal truth. "Yes," the Norman knight said slowly, "I am paying you. Therefore you will do exactly as I say."

Gunnar nodded, his blue eyes cold. "We will do most things for money, but if you want women and children killed you'll have to pay us extra."

Sir Arno was nonplussed. Gunnar could see the questions in the man's eyes: *Is he jesting? Should I fear him?* And then the mental shrugging of his shoulders, the reminding himself of his better blood and breeding, the unshakable confidence in his own authority.

"Good," said Sir Arno. "As long as you don't kill anyone without orders."

Ivo made a soft sound of disgust.

Gunnar's hand clenched more firmly on the hilt of his sword, but otherwise he made no movement. So far Sir Arno had done nothing wrong. Arrogance and cruelty coupled with complacency weren't treasonable offenses.

"Captain?"

Ivo's voice was not raised or markedly different, and yet there was something in it, a hint of surprise or perhaps warning. Gunnar looked up quickly.

And felt his wits dissolve in a hot shower of lust.

She was walking toward them.

Her madder-red gown was made of fine wool, and it molded to her tall, shapely body. A plaited gold girdle clung about her hips, a purse and various keys and gewgaws fastened to it. He could see the shape of her, the long length of thigh, the curve of full breast. Her face was a pale oval within the soft fluttering folds of her white veil. Dark eyes, lush mouth, skin like milk with the slightest hint of honey.

He had thought his body jaded—there were always women wherever he went, too many, and when he was hungry for them he supped. And yet now that same body reacted like that of an untried youth, startling him, jerking him from his complacency. He wanted to reach out and lift her across his saddle. He wanted to fasten his mouth to hers, taste her, drink of her lips.

For a man of such rigid calm, he felt raw and wild and out of control in a way he had not felt for years.

Maybe ever.

Great Odin, let her not be the Lady Rose! But even

as the prayer passed his lips, he knew Odin had denied him, for Sir Arno lifted his head and murmured, "'Tis Lady Rose. A word of warning, Captain. You will not mention who it was that sent you? The lady does not like to declare her business before strangers."

Gunnar barely acknowledged the caution. His eyes were fixed on the approaching woman.

It was the last thing he needed at this time and in this place, with so much at stake. Gunnar groaned softly to himself. Had he really believed his final undertaking would be easy?

The vision of sweet beauty approaching them was none other than the wanton and treacherous Lady Rose of Somerford Manor—the woman he had come to destroy.

Rose had not seen the mercenaries arrive.

She had been down to the storeroom, looking over a suspect barrel of salted meat. The meat smelled, but Rose had learned caution in her four years at Somerford Manor, one of them as sole ruler. It was prudent to keep everything, even smelly meat, until better could replace it. Besides, there were ways of making bad good again. Washing the meat thoroughly in vinegar, for instance, or burying it in the earth for a day or two. Still, they would not eat it, not yet, not unless they had no option. And even then—Rose wrinkled her nose—the situation would need to be desperate!

And then she reminded herself that it *was* desperate. They were undermanned and therefore vulnerable to attack from anyone who had the will to do so. And of late someone wanted very much to see the people of Somerford brought low.

Their troubles had begun with some pilfering in the village and escalated to a woodpile burned, a hoe stolen, a pig slaughtered and the choice bits taken off. And then last month some strangers had appeared in the village in the night and frightened the villagers badly by throwing stones upon their thatches, shouting and laughing all the while.

The villagers blamed the merefolk. Rose knew her people were superstitious, and since the troubles had begun they had grown worse. Sullen, afraid, angry. Like a bubbling cauldron filled with centuries of animosity, the situation had become too volatile. Rose had realized it was time to do something more than talk.

It was she who had put forward the suggestion of employing mercenaries, persuading Sir Arno they had no other choice.

"If we had some experienced men, Sir Arno, or at least men who *appear* to be experienced, I am sure that would settle the matter. These mischief makers, be they merefolk or whoever, would vanish back to where they came from and we would never be troubled again."

Arno looked pained. "I am training our men, my lady. They will be ready soon."

"Yes, but they are raw troops, Sir Arno! Boys, most of them. We have barely enough soldiers to guard our gates; how can we frighten off an attack, if one should come?"

Sir Arno d'Alan had shrugged, clearly wounded by her lack of faith in him. Rose bit her lip, wondering how she could win this argument without hurting her knight's feelings.

"It will be only for a short time. Until this problem is solved."

"And Lord Radulf? Have you mentioned your plans to him?"

Rose had pretended to examine her nails. "Not yet, no."

"My lady—"

Rose made an exasperated sound. "How can I tell Lord Radulf? He will think me incapable of managing Somerford. That I am too weak. A weak and feeble woman! You have warned me of that often enough, Sir Arno. He will take Somerford from me, and then what will become of me?"

She knew what would become of her. She would be thrown back into her father's care—a burden. An unwanted burden. It was not something she could think of for long before cold beads of perspiration dampened her skin.

Arno had looked sympathetic but there had been a gleam in his eyes. Almost as if he were enjoying her discomfiture, though surely that was impossible. "You think Lord Radulf is watching you, judging you?"

Rose was sure of it. She could almost feel Radulf's dark eyes fixed on her from five leagues away at Crevitch Castle. Although Radulf's wife, Lady Lily, had always supported her, she was presently occupied with her own troubles. And besides, Rose could not be always begging for her assistance. She must manage on her own. If she could just have the use of some mercenaries for a short time, she could sort out the problems at Somerford and everything would be well again. And best of all, Lord Radulf need never know.

"Mercenaries are not tame cats," Arno had warned her. "They will not purr and do as you bid if you stroke their fur."

Rose's eyes flashed. "No, but they will learn to jump for their supper or else they will not be fed! Don't worry, Sir Arno, I will manage the mercenaries, all you have to do is find me some."

And so he had—once Brother Mark had written the letter and Rose had sealed it, Arno had sent it off. And now word had come that the mercenaries were on their way. Although Rose had thought the offer of five marks excessive, Arno had assured her that was the standard fee in such cases. Still, she resented paying out such a sum when financially they were so stretched. Even though this summer's harvest looked to be a good one—the best in several years—and when the shearing was done there would be wool to sell, one never knew what might occur to upset one's plans. In the four years she had lived at Somerford, Rose had learned that much. You just never knew what new catastrophe was ahead. That money could be needed for medicines, for food, for warm clothing, and she resented using it to pay for men with swords.

With problems like hers, it was no wonder she sometimes woke full of anxiety in the darkest part of the night.

The smell of the bad meat was turning her stomach—that barrel was most definitely off.

Rose locked the storeroom door firmly behind her with one of the keys hanging from her gold plaited girdle, and climbed the narrow twisting stairs from the cellars to the kitchen.

It was warm there, the smells of bread still mouthwateringly in evidence. Rose noted that the gray kitchen cat had had her kittens and was ensconced in a cozy corner by the oven. Surely there was time to check on them? Just a moment. Kittens were always so tempting . . .

But that was when Constance found her.

"Lady!"

Rose jumped like a guilty child and looked up. "Constance? What is it?"

"Those men are come, Lady Rose. Sir Arno is speaking with them now. If you want to be certain they understand it is *you* who is the master here, you'd best get yourself down to the castle yard right smartly."

Frowning, Rose smoothed her red gown and settled her white veil so that it completely covered her dark hair. Constance, her wrinkled face and wizened body a disguise for her still sharp and youthful mind, shuffled closer and peered up at her. The old woman was tiny, but Rose was tall—it was a matter of wry amusement to her that her eyes were level with those of every one of the men on Somerford Manor.

"The mercenaries are here?" Rose repeated nervously.

Reading her perfectly, Constance touched her arm for courage.

"You are right," Rose murmured, stiffening her back. "I must go and meet them. Who knows what Arno is saying to them, offering them? He has no sense where money is concerned. If he believes it due to his self-importance to offer them double the marks we have agreed upon, then he will do so!"

It was Rose's aim to keep the mercenaries' promised wages as low as possible.

"Then go, lady, and don't dither," Constance chastised her. "You are master here, are you not?"

Rose raised her chin. "I am indeed, Constance."

And taking a deep breath, she hurried from the kitchen into the bailey.

It was very quiet.

Why was the bailey, usually a bustle of activity, so quiet? And yet it was not empty; people stood about. The silence was very odd. Her eyes flicked over the pale and frightened faces, seeking a reason, and were captured by a group of mounted men who were clearly the center of attention.

Tough and dangerous.

Those were the words that occurred to Rose as she looked at them. As if they were used to facing death every day. Which, of course, if they were mercenaries, Rose reminded herself impatiently, they were. Their clothes were chosen for warmth and protection rather than for appearance; the men wore chain mail or heavy leather tunics studded with rings. The big dark one had a thick cloak made of animal pelts—wolf, probably. And they were armed with a veritable bristle of weapons. Swords, shields, and axes. And their leader . . . but there Rose's thoughts lost all clear structure.

Her eyes widened in awe.

Their leader was like no man she had ever seen before. He was strange and exotic, and yet extraordinarily masculine. A dulled and shortened chain mail tunic covered his broad shoulders and chest; the metal was decorated with numerous dents as though he had lately fought hard for his life. A round shield hung across his back and one shoulder, the red background painted with the snarling form of a black wolf. His legs were encased in tight dark breeches, each powerful muscle of his thighs outlined as he gripped his big gray horse, forcing it to an unnatural stillness. Hair of dark copper fell long to his shoulders, two thin braids hanging either side of his face and giving him the look of a barbarian.

Or a Celtic warrior, or a . . . a . . .

"Viking."

Rose whispered the word, her breath squeezed in her throat. His appearance was barbaric and savage, but—and this was the most surprising thing of all—he was also the most handsome man she had ever seen. The strong set of his jaw, the sun brown of his skin, the unflinching blue of his eyes. It seemed inconceivable that a man such as this *should* be so handsome. He should be scarred and ugly, and that he wasn't must be a trick of nature, to dull the senses and bemuse the unwary, so that he could pounce. Or strike like a viper.

He is not like us.

Rose shivered. What had she been thinking to hire such men as this? To bring them onto her manor among the very people she was trying to protect!

Dear God, have I done the right thing?

"Sir Arno?" Her voice was breathless, possibly from her hurry across the bailey, but she did not think so. Fear and apprehension had tightened like bands about her chest.

Arno smiled his usual smile, and Rose felt suddenly wildly disoriented. Arno was the same and yet he seemed to pale into insignificance beside the mercenary. This was *Arno*, unswervingly loyal Arno, her husband Edric's friend, the man he had trusted completely—on his deathbed, and before witnesses, Edric had sought Arno's promise to obey and protect Rose.

Then why didn't Rose feel her usual confidence when she looked at him? Why did the familiar no longer seem so safe?

It was the fault of the mercenary leader.

He was so *un*familiar, this utterly foreign creature. He had turned her perceptions upside down, and, shockingly, his very strangeness drew her to him. It was an attraction against her will, but she knew it was there. Like, Rose told herself, a foolish fascination for an animal one knows is dangerous.

Rose took a long, slow breath, calming herself. *Stop this!* She was no silly wench thrown into a state by a handsome face; she never allowed men to rule her by her senses. She was Lady Rose of Somerford, a thoughtful woman, a practical woman, a woman of good sense. This nonsensical behavior had gone far enough.

After a brief pause, Rose felt collected enough to be able to meet the mercenary's blue eyes.

A mistake.

They were the blue of summer seas with the hint of an approaching storm. Piercing in his hard, handsome face, they delved into hers. Despite her preparation, Rose felt her stomach plummet. She was drowned in a hot wave of feeling that until now she had always believed . . . hoped to be foreign to her. Shocked, her thoughts spiraled, and she lost her emotional footing for the first time in her life. The whisper in her head was one of startled disbelief.

Is this . . . can this be desire*?*

Chapter 2

"My lady!"

Arno. Good, reliable Arno. With a dizzy sense of relief Rose broke eye contact with the mercenary and turned to her knight. She must have held out her hand, although she didn't remember it, for she felt his fingers on hers as he bent to press his lips to her skin. Struggling with the inappropriateness of her feelings, she forced herself to pay attention.

"Lady Rose, these are the mercenaries."

"So I see, Sir Arno. Are they . . . that is, do they speak—"

"Captain Olafson!" Arno was frowning up at the mercenary leader. "Dismount and show some respect. This is Lady Rose of Somerford!"

He spoke as if to a recalcitrant child who needed a lesson in manners. The hush, that had already fallen about them deepened markedly. Clearly everyone was wondering whether the handsome mercenary would respond to Arno's reprimand . . . or slit his throat.

Rose's own heart began a labored bumping, but from what cause she couldn't say for certain. It might have been Arno's tone, or it might have been the fact that she was once more staring up into those sea-blue eyes. Only this time she was aware, shockingly aware, that despite their pretty color they were the coldest, the most emotionless eyes she had ever encountered.

Captain Olafson clearly wasn't angered by Arno's words. They were nothing to him. With a shrug, he swung down from his gray horse—superbly graceful for a big, strong man—and stood before them.

Too close, she thought instantly, moving to step back. And catching herself in time. No, it would not be a good idea to show this man she was afraid of him. If he were even half as savage as he looked, he would enjoy her fear.

Even Arno appeared momentarily taken aback by the mercenary captain's size, and now the rest of them were dismounting with a muted rattling of harness and clink of wood and steel. They stood in the castle yard like a pack of wild and shaggy beasts. A child cried out, a woman hushed it. Rose realized that her people were afraid to make a sound in case it drew the mercenaries' attention to them, and their wrath down on them.

She also realized that, for the first time in a long time, she had to look *up* to see into men's faces.

Not an entirely comforting sensation.

Again she asked herself whether they would slaughter the occupants of Somerford while they slept. Would the promise of payment truly fix their loyalty? Indeed, were such men as these inclined to take orders from anyone, apart from whatever pagan gods they worshipped?

Rose drew a deep, sustaining breath. Well, it was up to her to see that they did! She was the lady of this manor, she had fought hard to retain her title, and while they were there they would listen to what she had to say.

She held her head high, cold dignity in place, and before she could think twice stretched out a hand that trembled only the merest hint. "I am Lady Rose," she informed them calmly. "Somerford Manor is mine, and while you are here I shall tell you what you can and can't do. Is that understood?"

Captain Olafson looked down at her hand as if he had never seen one before. Rose had a shocking thought that perhaps there was a reason that women did not trust him with their limbs, but before she could change her mind and withdraw the hand, he had swallowed it up in his own.

His fingers were startlingly warm.

Why had she thought they would be cold?

Again she would have pulled away, but by then it was too late and he held her fingers captive in his. He felt her slight tug—the knowledge registered in his eyes—but he did not release her; if anything his grip tightened. Apart from indulging in an undignified struggle, Rose could do nothing but stand and allow him his will.

The big, dark man behind him was smiling, though attempting to hide it. Did they find this amusing? Were good manners so foreign to them that they found them laughable?

Rose flushed angrily and tugged again, but it was too late. There was the sensation of firm, dry lips pressed to her fingertips, the soft brush of his long hair against her skin. Unwillingly she looked down as Captain Olafson unbent his big body, his narrow braids swinging back into place, the fair stubble on his jaw glinting in the sunlight, and his teeth white as he gave a satisfied smile.

"You are more than welcome to tell me what I can and can't do . . . my lady," he murmured in perfect French.

Anger shot through her, hot and satisfying. He had just humiliated her, made fun of her for his and his men's amusement, and she no longer cared whether he read the emotion in her eyes.

Sir Arno made a sound very like a growl. "Your manners, Captain!"

The mercenary barely glanced at him. Quite suddenly Rose's anger cooled. These men might kill her loyal Arno without a second thought, and she could not allow that. She placed her hand on the knight's sleeve, to press a warning. Captain Olafson's eyes followed the gesture and, if it was possible, hardened even more. As they slid to her face, she read the scorn in them.

Does he think less of Arno for taking his orders from me?

He had already turned away from her, back to Sir Arno, who was still glowering.

"You have the makings of a fine harvest," the mercenary said briskly, suddenly all business.

Rose noted Arno's confusion—what did the knight know of harvests?—but he bluffed his way through it, nodding importantly and agreeing that it was the best he had seen for many years.

"That is good," the mercenary went on, still ignoring Rose, "because the money you are offering is not enough."

"Not enough?" Arno repeated.

Captain Olafson nodded. "Ten marks or we leave. There is plenty of work to be had elsewhere."

"Ten marks!" Rose's anger left her before this new challenge. Ten marks was a fortune. "That is too much."

Captain Olafson's eyes flicked toward her but only briefly, and he did not turn and face her, keeping his attention on Arno, as if it were *his* decision that counted. Rose seethed.

"We are neither serfs nor slaves," he went on, his voice pleasantly deep but very chilly. "We do not have to agree to conditions that do not please us."

Arno released an impatient breath. Rose could see he did not like this any more than she, but she also knew he felt it beneath his dignity to haggle. "I am sure that we can come to some—" he began.

Rose stepped around him, planting herself squarely in Captain Olafson's line of sight. The blue eyes narrowed and there was actually a hint of some feeling in them—she didn't have time to try and read what it was. Certainly he was a fearsome sight in his tunic of chain mail, the pagan-looking shield at his back, a vicious sword strapped low on his hip, his Viking hair reaching past his shoulders. Rose was used to men who looked more civilized, but there was much at stake here and she dared not back down. Those five extra marks would ruin Somerford Manor.

"Sir Arno has already offered you payment for one month's work," she said in a brittle voice. "Five marks, with food and lodging. I thought the deal was struck. Are you going to go back on your word now, Captain?"

He stared down at her—yes, *down*. Rose tried not to show her unease. "I am not negotiating with you, my lady. I am telling you what I want. There was no deal struck."

He sounded cool and controlled, and completely inflexible. Rose narrowed her eyes, just as determined. "I do not like your answer, Captain. You have been offered a fair price. I will not be bullied into making you another."

The big, dark-haired man in the wolf-pelt cloak tapped him on the shoulder with a hand gloved in a black leather gauntlet. Without taking his eyes from hers, the mercenary captain listened to what his man murmured into his ear. Judging by the frown that creased his brow, he didn't appear to like it. Rose glared back, while her heart was threatening to batter its way out from inside her chest. Slowly his frown smoothed away and the emotion leached from his eyes, leaving them once more cold and dead.

He nodded sharply, once, and the other man stepped back.

"Very well. Six marks."

Rose would not have allowed even that concession, but before she could intervene Arno quickly said, "Done!" and then avoided her eyes. "It is a good bargain, lady," he added in a falsely jovial voice.

Rose bit her lip. Maybe it was a reasonable bargain in the circumstances. One they could afford, anyway, *if* the harvest was a good one. But that did not explain Arno's unusual forbearance—was he so desperate to have the mercenaries there? Was he more worried than he had allowed her to see? It seemed the only possibility.

The mercenary said nothing to her, treating the matter as concluded. Arrogant, Rose told herself, as he looked again to Arno. The sort of man who could take orders only from another man. But what could one expect from a Viking savage?

"How many men-at-arms do you keep here?" he was asking. "I saw one, maybe two. Are there others elsewhere?"

His questions were peremptory. Sir Arno shifted uneasily, not prepared to answer him. That was because he felt the answer reflected badly on him, thought Rose, but the mercenary had a right to know.

She swallowed her own indignation and, her cheeks burning but her voice strong, gave him his reply. "We have three men who belong to the keep and are able-bodied, but they are presently working in the fields."

"You set your soldiers to work in the fields, lady?" Astonishment shone clear in his eyes, before he quenched it.

"There are crops to be grown, Captain, or we will all starve. Soldiers have to eat, too. I myself helped during sowing time. Somerford Manor supports us all, so we must all work."

He nodded indifferently, conceding the point. "Where are the rest of your garrison, lady? Shearing the sheep?"

Rose felt her back stiffen in response to his cool sarcasm, but refused to rise to it. Instead she told him the bald truth. "The rest of our garrison went off to Lord Fitzmorton."

As she had expected, he wanted more—the lift of his eyebrow told her so.

"Lord Fitzmorton and Lord Wolfson are both powerful men, but they are always squabbling over who is the more powerful. At Christmas they clashed, and some of their men were killed. They were then both short of fighting men and sought to replace them. They do not care where they recruit . . . they turned their eyes in the direction of Somerford, and I could not pay as well as they. This is not the only manor to suffer—others also lost soldiers from their garrisons.

"However," she went on briskly, "we do have twenty villeins who perform two days' duty once a week." Honesty made her add, not so briskly, "Although most of them are either very old or very young, and one is crippled."

His mouth, already firm, tightened. "And why do you depend upon old and crippled villeins to guard Somerford Manor?" he asked in a deceptively calm voice. "Have your able-bodied villeins also gone to Fitzmorton?"

Rose was starting to feel like a child making feeble excuses to her guardian for some misdemeanor. *Ridiculous*, she told herself. *You are lady here, and he is nothing but a hired soldier. A peasant in chain mail. A Viking savage with neither manners nor courtesy.* Her voice lifted, growing in haughtiness as it always did when she was nervous, but in the circumstances this seemed no bad thing.

"Our able-bodied villeins are dead, Captain. Before I came to Somerford there was an English uprising against the king. My husband, Edric, stood with Lord Radulf against it, and many of our men went to fight. Lord Radulf won the day, but very few of Somerford Manor's men returned. He presented Edric with a gold goblet in remembrance of his loyalty and sacrifice." She remained emotionless for the mercenary's benefit, pretending indifference she didn't feel—death was always a waste. "Sir Arno has begun training some of the younger boys, though it will be some years yet before they are ready to fight. I have suggested to Sir Arno that the women might take up guard duty, until their sons are grown. Many of them are widows of the villeins who died in the uprising, and they are more than willing to take over their dead husbands' duties."

Eartha, the cook at Somerford Keep, had been particularly keen to don armor and stand guard, even to fight. Why could women not fight as well as men if the need was there? she had declared, and Rose had agreed there was no reason. Arno had thought differently.

"Sir Arno finds the idea of women garrisoning Somerford . . ." Unacceptable? Repugnant? Threatening? Rose wondered just how to put into words the expression on Arno's face at the time. In any case, she didn't have to find the right words because the mercenary cut her short.

"A garrison of women." He said it straight-faced, but with a twist to his voice that was almost a smile. His men laughed. "There are better things to do with women than kill them."

"Captain!" Rose's anger was near boiling point; in a moment she would say something to put them all in danger.

"Better to send the boys to fight."

Rose felt her anger fly out of her head. Briefly she struggled with his meaning, but there was really only one conclusion she could draw. Despite herself her reply was strained. "I don't care what you do where you come from, Captain, but at Somerford we do not send our children out to die."

The blue eyes narrowed, and then he shrugged as if such histrionics were of no interest to him. "You'd rather send out your women?" he asked with cool curiosity.

"If they want to go. It is for their homes and their children's lives that they would fight."

"Maybe that is so, lady." His agreement pleased her, but his next words froze any pleasure. "Sometimes it is necessary for women *and* children to fight. And to die."

There was something uncivilized in those eyes, thought Rose. Something wholly savage. Something soulless. Had she really felt desire for such a creature? Perhaps she had confused lust with fear.

He is not like us.

How could she think to control such a man? A man who would let children die in the wars of men? A shiver ran through her. Surely they would be better off facing their problems on their own, or begging Lord Radulf for help, whatever he might think of her for doing so? *Even if he takes Somerford from you and sends you back to your father?* Yes, even then! Rose looked toward Arno, sure that he, too, must have come to this conclusion, but to her consternation he refused to meet her glance.

"Women do not understand war," he said, but in such a fond, patronizing voice Rose longed to scream. As it was she gritted her teeth and turned back to the mercenary. With a curt gesture of her hand she drew his attention to their surroundings.

"Our defenses are strong—after the English uprising, Lord Radulf helped my husband to increase our strength. If there is an attack, everyone will come and shelter inside. If there is a siege, we have a deep well for water and, after the harvest, we will have food enough to keep us for many months. Although I have no doubt that long before we ran out Lord Radulf would have heard of our plight and sent us help."

"That may be so, Lady Rose, but—"

"Sir Arno should have explained to you that you are here for show, Captain Olafson. Nothing else. The people from the Mere have been stealing from the village, but they are more of a nuisance than a serious threat. At the moment they think us easy pickings, but when they have seen you and your men they will go elsewhere. That is all we require of you, Captain. To scare the merefolk away. And indeed, you are well qualified for that!"

He let that pass, replying dismissively, "If these merefolk are allowed to steal from your village then you have let your people grow fat and lazy."

Once again Rose felt the color come stinging into her cheeks. It was an insult. As if *he* could do better. Despite her resolution to be calm, her dark eyes flashed up at him. "Somerford has been at peace for four years, and if we have used that time to remember what it is like not to guard our backs at every waking moment, then I say that is a *good* thing."

"It is never a *good* thing to be unprepared. Death awaits at every man's shoulder."

"Mayhap death awaits at some shoulders more than others!" she retorted. "You have it wrong, Captain. You are mistaken. The merefolk are not vicious raiders. They have hurt no one"—well, apart from a pig—"and once they hear of your arrival, they will leave us be."

Captain Olafson smiled, but there was no warmth in it. "If they are clever they will leave, if they are not they will die."

A murmur of agreement rose from the creatures behind him. Like a pack of wolves barely held in check, they shuffled closer.

Rose wanted to tell them to leave; she wanted to declare that such men were not welcome at Somerford Manor. This was a peaceful place; there would be no fighting or slaughter. But they were here now, and however different she might wish things to be, in her heart she knew she needed them. So, instead of sending them on their way as she longed to do, Rose said quietly, "This is not war, Captain."

He looked thoughtful, his gaze fixed on some point far beyond her. "Your gate was open."

Frowning, Rose glanced to Arno and back again. "Open?" she repeated, puzzled. "But . . . the merefolk have been causing problems. It was necessary to leave the gate open in case the villagers needed to seek protection. There is no danger in it, surely?"

Arno had told her that and given the order, yet now, when she looked to him for confirmation, he carefully avoided her eye, uneasy again.

"If I am to stay here and protect you, lady, the gate will remain closed unless I give orders for it to be opened. Is that clear?"

"I don't see—"

"If we had been enemies of Somerford you would all be dead now. We would have ridden in at a gallop with no one to stop us, my men would have killed everyone here in the bailey, Ivo would have taken care of Sir Arno before he could draw his sword, and I would have come for you . . . lady. Now do you *see*?"

Arno was blustering, but no one paid him any heed. The Viking savage was staring at her fixedly now, and as if he had placed it there, Rose saw the scene he described in unrelenting detail. People running, screaming . . . She, alone in her solar, hearing his approach up the stone stairs, the door crashing open . . . He filled the doorway, dazzling her frightened eyes with the vivid colors of his hair and eyes. And then he strode forward toward her, drawing that wicked sword from its sheath . . .

Although—and now confusion replaced fear—the sword part didn't seem quite right. She could imagine him striding toward her, but after that it seemed much more natural that he should leave the sword where it was and pull her into his arms, claiming her mouth with his.

Rose found her head nodding of its own volition. She felt dizzy, every bit of her tingling . . . some bits more than others. *Stop this, stop it now!* She forced her voice out, forced it to obey her.

"Very well, Captain Olafson. The gate stays closed."

Her reply was his cue to turn his back on her.

Again.

At least, thought Gunnar, he had won *that* point, although it was clearly difficult for her to concede to him. She had nearly choked on the words, but the gate would remain safely shut from now on. There were other questions he needed to ask, other points to be made, but he decided it was better to leave it there, since he had the advantage.

Standing face-to-face with her, staring into her eyes, Gunnar had found himself imagining things that had more to do with satisfaction than safety. Even with his back turned, he could smell her sweet scent. Almost, he could taste her on his tongue. Quite suddenly he did not trust his normally reliable self-control.

"My men and their beasts have traveled far and need to rest. Show us where to stable our horses, Sir Arno," he said, forgetting in his haste to be away to make it sound more like a request and less like an order.

Arno's dark eyes narrowed, but thankfully he did not quibble.

Gunnar could feel *her* staring at his back as he walked away. Shivering like an angry kitten with needle claws. If she flew at him she would do about as much damage, but he did not think that would stop her from making the attempt. There had been passion in her dark eyes. Women like the Lady Rose were not easily subdued, and she alone had held the reins of Somerford Manor for over a year now. She would not give them up easily.

She was not what he had expected.

Gunnar had imagined the Lady Rose to be like other Norman ladies. In his experience they were either cold, haughty creatures, quivering with good breeding and reluctant to get too close to him in case they were soiled by his lowly presence, or else they were weak and clinging, unable to stand, it seemed, without the assistance of a stronger will. Get too close to *them* and they were liable to faint or swoon about his person.

In general, Norman ladies knew little to nothing of the practical details of guarding their property; they did not send their soldiers into the fields to work alongside the serfs and villeins, nor did *they* work alongside them; they did not dress their women up as men and order them to stand guard! In Gunnar's opinion, this Norman lady's ideas were quite remarkable, and although he did not agree with them, he found them . . . admirable? No. He did not want to admire her—that was not his mission.

His mission was to destroy her.

And yet from the first moment she walked—a simple word for such a heavenly movement—across the bailey toward him, he had sensed a serious breach in his defenses. An open gate in *his* wall. Maybe his men had sensed it, too, this ripple in his normally imperturbable calm, for he had felt them move instinctively closer, as if to cover his back.

She had been afraid of him—of them all, but of him in particular. Why else would she have stared at him when they first met as if she had been struck by a bolt loosed from a longbow? But fear had not stopped her from arguing over a few paltry marks. Why had he antagonized her? *So that she would know from the first you are not one of her serfs, or a tame Norman knight like Sir Arno d'Alan.*

And she had refused to pay—as if he were not worth the silver! He had felt his temper slip, surprising himself and Ivo—he *never* lost his temper. Ivo had had to remind him, quietly, the real reason they were there. Money was not the object—they would be well paid.

So you lost your temper over five marks?

No, not for that . . . Unwillingly, Gunnar recalled how she had grasped Arno's arm, the familiar intimacy of the gesture, and jealousy twisted in his gut. He, Gunnar Olafson, was jealous! He was *never* jealous; he had no reason to be. Women came to *him*; it was they who were jealous—of one another! But now he pictured dark eyes so large and beautiful, skin so fine and soft, a mouth so moist and ripe, and a firm, full body. The possibility of another man possessing all that . . . He clenched his jaw, hard. It was as if, he thought in disgust, he had never had a woman before.

In other circumstances he would have wooed her with his considerable charm, won her over, and taken her until he had rid himself of his need for her. But he was there for a reason other than to serve her, a secret reason, and rumor had it that she was sharing her favors with the knight.

So it is good that she is afraid of you? Did you enjoy persuading her you would allow children to be slaughtered in battle?

No, Gunnar told himself. *It was said for d'Alan's benefit, to further convince him of our brutality. If it drove the beautiful lady further from me, then that is good, too.* Except she hadn't fluttered her hands and turned faint. Oh, she had paled, but then she had argued the point with him.

Gunnar smiled wryly at the memory. This was no weak and feeble lady. Strong, yet—he remembered the nibbled nails on her slender hand—vulnerable. He found the combination very appealing.

And then his smile died. He had been thinking as if Lady Rose were an innocent party in all this. He knew better than that. If there *was* a plot at work at Somerford Manor, then Lady Rose must surely be in the thick of it. It was *she* who had asked for mercenaries; d'Alan was only the messenger. The letter intercepted by Radulf's men had definitely come from her, for it was *she* who had sealed the incriminating missive with the Somerford seal—no one but the lord or lady of the manor could use the seal. That letter was the reason Gunnar was there. No, Rose was no innocent victim, and next time he imagined bedding her he should remember that.

"One thing."

It was Arno speaking, and Gunnar turned his head to

look down at d'Alan's thinning pate, wondering what the knight wanted now.

"The Lady Rose," Arno said, as if he had read Gunnar's mind. "She is a sweet lady, but she has no head for . . . practical matters. She does not understand the ways of men and the world, so she leaves such things to me. It is I who give the orders, Captain Olafson, no matter what *she* believes. Is that clear?"

There was implacability in his stare, a cold belligerence beneath the gruff, knightly veneer. Gunnar stared back and knew Arno was lying. The woman he had just faced was unlikely to appreciate Arno's counter instructions one little bit. But if Arno was her lover, perhaps this was his way of concealing her treason? Protecting her?

Or himself.

"I understand you," Gunnar said quietly.

Arno moved closer, until Gunnar smelled the sharp, sour sweat beneath his fine clothes. The knight's voice was tinged with mockery. "Of course you do. We both seek the same end, after all."

Satisfied, Arno strode on ahead, leading the way. The mercenaries followed, playing the game, grinning at one another, pretending docility totally foreign to their natures. Sweyn said, loudly, "Women fighting wars? It will never happen."

Ivo stepped up beside Gunnar. "What did he mean?" he asked softly, dark eyes watchful. "Which 'end' does he speak of?"

Gunnar shook his head. They had gone from Radulf to Fitzmorton and there played their part well. Now Fitzmorton had sent them to Somerford. No one seemed to be making matters much clearer.

Ivo shifted restlessly. "Do you think there *is* a plot afoot here?"

Gunnar's voice remained calm. "Time will tell."

Behind them Sweyn told a joke, and the others laughed. Ivo leaned closer still. "How is your sword, Gunnar?"

Puzzled, Gunnar turned to his friend and saw the sparkle of wicked laughter in his eyes.

"Back there you were so hot for the lady, I thought it might have melted in its sheath. I have never seen you so struck by a woman—usually 'tis the other way around."

Gunnar's smile was grim—had it been so obvious? "I would that my sword *had* melted, Ivo. Then my problem would be solved."

Ivo snorted a laugh. "And disappoint so many wenches? Their wailing would be heard throughout the land." He gave Gunnar a considering look. "It would be amusing if this one did not fall into your hand as easily as all the others."

Amusing for you, thought Gunnar. "Women are a pleasant diversion. But I am working, Ivo; even if she is as sweet and innocent as the flower she is called after, I would have no time for the Lady Rose."

He spoke the words so confidently, even he believed them.

Chapter 3

Rose felt rattled; she needed time by herself. Captain Olafson had upset her in ways she did not understand—did not want to. He was a cold and dangerous savage, and on the outside she had responded to him warily. And yet, underneath, her senses were quivering like a harp's plucked strings. As if something unseen were happening between them, deep below the surface. As if, thought Rose shakily, the raw, sensual power of the mercenary had found a willing partner in her.

She was more than rattled; Rose was afraid.

Aye, she needed time alone.

Slowly, she began to climb the stone stairs to her own private chamber—her solar. The solar was a Norman lady's sanctuary, the place where she could be alone or with her ladies, where no one must disturb her without her permission. Edric had given her her solar.

When he and Lord Radulf had built Somerford

Keep, they had built it of stone. Stone keeps were still a rarity in England, especially on the smaller manors. But Somerford was unique, standing as it did on the very edge of the vast Crevitch estates, and abutting the lands of two other very powerful barons.

Lord Radulf had felt a stone keep was as necessary as a stout wall, and Edric had been eager to please his overlord, not least because he stood in awe of him. The cost of the building had been enormous, and Radulf had supplied the stone and workmen, and asked for additional costs to be sent to him. But Edric was an elderly Saxon husband with a young, noble wife, and he had wanted to indulge her. He had insisted she have a solar in the new keep, a private room for her own use. And he had insisted that he would pay the extra expense of it—and this had turned out to be more than he had ever imagined, but he had never blamed Rose.

Edric, in his sixtieth year when he died, had been a kind and courteous man. Rose knew she had been lucky in him, luckier than her own mother.

Rose paused halfway up the stairs, her hand on the cold wall.

From early childhood she had watched her mother's wild and destructive love for her father, watched him take pleasure in hurting her with his indifference, watched all that vitality slowly wither and die. When it came time to have a husband of her own, Rose had been terrified. Not for the usual reasons expressed by other young girls—that he might be cruel or he might be old or he might be mean. No, Rose's real fear was that she might fall in love with the man chosen for her. It was *love* that ruined lives, love that could ruin her life, just as her father had ruined her mother's life.

But Edric, a wily Saxon widower looking to please his new overlords by taking one of their own for wife, wasn't a man to inspire passionate love. He had never made her burn for him, not even a little. He had consummated their marriage matter-of-factly with only a slight discomfort, and for that Rose had been grateful, as she was grateful for his easy kindness and consideration, and the pleasure he found in her conversation and company.

A shy and gentle girl who had grown up in a frightening and violent household, Rose had entered into her marriage well trained as a housekeeper but with few other skills. It was Edric who gave her the confidence to grow into her position as the Lady of Somerford. And as time passed, she realized that despite what her father and mother and brother had told her, it *was* in her power to control her own destiny. When Edric died last year, Rose discovered the courage to rule alone.

Now, once more, she felt the old fear stirring.

Not just because of the problems they were having with the merefolk, although these were certainly troublesome. Not because of the lack of money, although this kept her awake at nights. Not because Lord Radulf, as her overlord, could take Somerford Manor from her, his vassal, if she displeased or failed him. Edric had sworn fealty to Radulf, as had Rose, but that did not make Somerford Manor entirely secure—she tried not to think of this. And not because the mercenaries she had hired to solve their problems with the merefolk were so much more . . . more *savage* than she had imagined—Arno had been right there, they were no tame cats to stroke and pet.

No, Rose was afraid of herself.

Afraid of what was lurking in her soul.

That in some secret chamber within, a hidden room of shadows, was a deep, dark, emotional well, just waiting to be tapped. And once broached, the black waters would rush out, unstoppable, drowning her, destroying her, just as her mother had been destroyed in the same flood. Breathless, she remembered again that dizzy, heady feeling she had experienced in the bailey when she first saw Captain Olafson. The thump of her heart, the tremble of her legs, the tightening in her belly . . .

Such a thing had never happened to her before, and she would *not* allow it now. Rose straightened her back, lifted her chin, and took a deep breath of the chilly, damp air in the stairwell. It cleared her head. Mayhap this had been a momentary thing? Some problem with the phase of the moon and her monthly cycles? For how could she even contemplate making wild, passionate love with a rude . . . heartless . . . conscienceless . . . Viking savage?

When Rose reached the solar she found it was not empty as she had hoped. Constance sat on a stool mending a well-worn linen chemise, diligently attempting to prolong its life. New clothing was becoming an urgent necessity, but Rose did not feel she could buy for her own back when her people went without. After the harvest, she hoped for the hundredth time, there would be coin and more for all that.

Constance was staring up at her, old eyes sharp with curiosity. "Have you spoken to the mercenaries?"

"I have." Rose wouldn't meet her gaze. "Sir Arno is taking them to stable their horses. They will probably eat their heads off."

Constance's lips twitched. "The horses, do you mean? Or the mercenaries?"

"Both!"

Rose gave the old woman a suspicious glance; Constance was showing uncustomary restraint.

"Mayhap you should go and show their captain his sleeping quarters. See to his bath," Constance went on, and now her voice trembled with the effort to keep it disinterested. "Do you think we have a tub big enough for him?"

"I doubt it," Rose replied dryly. "Have you had your fun now? I take it you saw him? Captain Olafson?"

All pretense vanished. Constance's eyes gleamed like pale jewels. "Indeed I did, lady! A Viking god."

Rose shook her head, wondering as she did so whether she was trying to convince Constance or herself. "The man may be a god, but he is also a savage. An unfeeling monster. He has no heart and no soul. If you think *he* is the new husband you are always seeking for me, old woman, then you are very, very wrong."

Constance had listened to the tremble in her lady's voice with growing trepidation. Something had upset her badly. She had not seen Rose so shaken since the day Edric had had to order the lopping off of one of his serf's hands for stealing, and that was after he had let him off with a reprimand two times.

"But he is so fine-looking!" she wailed, laying aside the once-fine linen chemise. "How can a man who looks like that be so black inside?"

"I don't know," Rose said grimly, "but believe me 'tis so. His soul is like a raven's wing, and as putrid as a midden. Content yourself with looking at his face, Constance, for that is the only pretty thing about this man."

Constance sighed and remained silent as Rose sat down.

"Six marks," her lady muttered darkly. "And food and lodging! Well, let us pray they are worth it. But I fear they will be nothing to me . . . *us* but trouble." Impatiently she reached up and removed the metal circlet that held her veil in place on her head, putting both aside. Her strong, dark hair was plaited into submission in one long, thick rope that tumbled down her back, while glossy raven tendrils curled about her flushed face. "I wish now I had never asked Arno to find me these mercenaries!"

"Where *did* he find them?"

"I know not—some knightly friend, he said. I left all such arrangements to him. Oh, I should have dealt with it myself!"

"You are in a fine temper," Constance said dryly.

"I am weary," Rose replied, and knew it was so. The Lady of Somerford must be hard, she must be tough. She must sit at the manor court and make judgment upon those who transgressed, who did not pay their rent or neglected their duties to the manor; she must order men to fight and mayhap die; she must rule in cases of stealing or assault or even murder. She must make the decision between life and death, and do that every day.

But Rose had been born with a gentle heart, and in such circumstances as these to have a gentle heart was the worst of all possible afflictions. And yet it was her gentle heart that had endeared her, a Norman lady, to her English people.

After Edric died, when it would have been so easy to give in and let Arno take over Somerford, when Rose teetered on the verge of saying aye, Constance had opened her eyes. Sir Arno did not love and care for the people as Rose did. He meant well, he was loyal, and he might be versed in the practical side of being lord of the manor, but he had no compassion for the English people. Would he set aside eggs for the smith's sick child, or remember old Edward's aching bones in the winter and order extra wood to be gathered for his fire?

Of course not! Arno would be more likely to consider a sick child a waste of eggs, and old Edward better off frozen.

Mayhap Arno was right and she was wrong, but Rose could not think so, and she could not live with her conscience if she allowed him to enforce such a regime here at Somerford. So she had gathered her courage about her and ignored the voice in her head—sounding remarkably like her father's—that told her she could not do it. She resisted the temptation to allow Arno to take the reins, and thereafter insisted all decisions that had formerly been made by Edric were now to be made by her and her alone. Somerford Manor was now hers, and as long as she was able she would hold it and its people safe.

"We are all weary," Constance answered, "but there will be time enough to sleep after death. If you want rid of this black-hearted mercenary, go to Lady Lily. She has always supported you. She likes you; she will listen."

"Lady Lily has troubles of her own, Constance. She is unwell with this second child she carries, and the first still so young."

"Radulf is a lusty husband."

Rose frowned. "Then she should have told him nay."

Constance smiled at her lady's naivete. "Is that what you did with Edric? And I'll be bound he meekly went and left you to your sleep. Oh, lady, you do not understand. If you were wed to a young, virile man whom you desired, you would not be able to say him nay, either!"

Rose shifted irritably. How dare Constance speak as though Rose were an ignorant virgin? As if she understood nothing of the relationship between a man and a woman? " 'Tis none of your concern, old woman."

"No. Right now this mending is my concern, so I will say no more, *my lady*."

That deserved a reprimand, and Rose opened her mouth to give it.

The shriek was so loud it made both women start.

Younger and spryer, Rose was first to the window. She leaned out just as the shriek came again. It tore through the bailey, which had just begun to resume some normality after the arrival of the mercenaries.

Constance, close behind her, clutched her arm. "What is it, lady? Is someone being killed?"

Rose had thought so, too, but though she scanned the yard frantically, she could see no blood. Then the shriek came again, and this time she spied the child. A young boy, he was swinging by his hands from the wooden gangway that had been built around the top of the ramparts. It was there the guard would stand to keep watch, and there, in times of attack or siege, that the people of Somerford would fire down on their enemies.

The boy was young, perhaps no more than three years old, and his feet dangled over the sizable gap to the ground beneath him. If he let go he would be hurt, mayhap even killed! And from the sounds he was making, Rose did not believe he could cling on much longer.

"Jesu, no," she breathed, one hand pressed hard to her quaking heart. Then, to the people standing about below, "Help him! Someone . . . please . . . help him!"

But before anyone could move, the mercenary Captain Olafson, with his men behind him, arrived in the bailey. Rose caught her breath with a squeak; behind her Constance choked audibly. He had removed his chain mail tunic, and his body was naked from the waist up. Hard muscle curved beneath bronzed skin, big powerful shoulders and arms; there was nothing soft about him. Despite the perilous situation, a memory of Edric flashed into Rose's mind—pale, skinny legged, his once-firm body stooped and sagging with age. The half-naked mercenary beneath her window was a revelation.

I wonder what it would feel like to touch him? Would he be as hard as he looks?

The thought had barely taken shape when Rose realized that, assuming the manor to be under attack, he had drawn his sword from the scabbard at his side, and was holding it before him. The blade was made of black metal and it shimmered darkly as he turned four feet of violent death expertly in his hands. He was very frightening. Terrifying in an elemental way. And the fascination she had felt upon first meeting him returned tenfold.

Dangerous he might be, but Rose wanted him with a deep hunger she hadn't known she possessed.

People were scattering out of his way. Geese ran honking, and a young goat skittered about on thin legs. A woman fainted, dropping her basket of eggs. They broke in a puddle about her feet, and one of the hounds gave up chasing the geese to lap greedily at the yolks.

Before Rose could do or say anything, the mercenary had grasped the situation and was again sheathing his weapon in the intricately carved scabbard at his side. The child screamed once more, stubby bare legs kicking wildly in the air. That was when, in a rush, Rose realized that everyone below her was either too afraid or too stunned by the sight of the mercenary captain to go to the little boy's aid. She opened her mouth to startle them into action.

He had anticipated her.

Captain Olafson was striding forward, looking so big and capable among the helpless onlookers. He reached up, just as the boy, with a last lusty cry, let go his hold. The child fell neatly into his arms and, with a rough gentleness that made Rose's skin prickle, the mercenary checked him for injuries. But the child yelled and began to struggle wildly. He was set down and, with a last wail, promptly took off as fast as he could manage, toward the keep.

"Probably more frightened of his rescuer than by any fall," Constance muttered, and shook her head. Her eyes were fastened on the man's bare chest as if she were a human leech. "Did you recognize the boy? I thought 'twas Eartha's son."

But Rose did not answer her. Her hands were gripping the windowsill and she was unable to move, for her gaze was also riveted on Captain Olafson. Her heart was thudding in her ears like a drum. *I know him. How can I know him?* And yet there was something suddenly so familiar about him, while at the same time he was utterly unlike any man she had ever seen before in her life. A familiar stranger? It made no sense.

Rose took a shaking breath. He hadn't moved. He stood in the place where the boy had left him when he ran, bare-chested, his copper hair gleaming in the sun, his long legs set apart in the dark breeches that clung like a second skin, one hand resting on the hilt of that terrifying sword. And then, with a movement that for some reason struck Rose as both eager and yet unwilling, the mercenary tilted his head and looked up. His blue eyes found her at her solar window as if he had known her position all along.

He looked straight at her.

It was as if their gazes were flint and tinder. They struck and sparked, setting fire to Rose's body and mind—a white hot blaze. It made her feel alive! She felt as if she had been asleep until now, a walking sleep, and then in a moment she was wide awake and eager to begin living . . .

Almost as quickly the impossibility of the situation—and her terrified recoil—sent Rose stumbling back, out of his sight. At the same time he spun on his heel and was walking away, brushing through his men in a manner designed to prevent comment and hurry them into following him.

Constance's breath spurted from her lips in silent laughter. "Is that your raven-black soul?" she asked innocently. "No, no, lady, you are mistaken. I believe you have hired yourself a hero. What think you of that?"

Rose found her voice, though it did not sound like hers. "I think any fool can save a child."

"Aye, but *would* he? 'Twas not the mercenary's place to take charge, and yet so he did. I did not see Sir Arno rushing to the boy's aid."

Arno would not do anything so undignified, Rose thought wildly. He was a knight; the child was a cook's son. There, for Arno, the matter ended.

She moved to warm her hands at the sulky fire. They were shaking worse now and she knew why, though she would never tell Constance. Captain Olafson was the cause. For some inexplicable reason, he had jolted her to the core. In the short time he had been at Somerford he had become the most important thing in it.

No! she thought angrily. *That isn't so. How could it be? He is a stranger, a creature beyond my experience, a man whose life can never really bisect mine . . .*

Why did he save the child?

The question cut through her. Was he really a hero, as Constance said? Then why had he told her that he believed children were expendable in men's wars? Why had he made her believe he had no heart? Such a man would not then turn around and save a child's life. A child who had no ties to him. There had to be a reason, one that made sense, not a fantastical explanation like Constance's.

If she could make sense of it, Rose could turn him back into the savage, soulless creature she believed him to be. And if she could do that, then mayhap all inside her would be calm again. Suddenly she craved normality.

"I had best get down to the kitchens," Rose said, as if her heart were not jumping about like a landed fish in her chest. "Eartha and the other women will need help. There will be much food to prepare—I imagine these mercenaries will eat more than all of us put together! I wonder if we should kill one of the pigs we have been saving for bacon?"

And she was gone before Constance could answer.

The old woman plumped down by the fire and stared into it. She did not need to be a seer to know that the big mercenary frightened Rose. Was it his strength she feared? His occupation? Or his maleness? Certainly Constance had never seen a man before with such a blatant attraction for women—witness him in the bailey just now! The air around him had actually sizzled with the promise of sexual fulfillment.

But was he capable of delivering on that promise?

Constance sat, thoughtful, as the fire spluttered and distant sounds drifted up through the open window. Whoever and whatever he was, if this man would save a child when no one else seemed capable of it, then it was plain he was a better man than Sir Arno. Surely that was all that really mattered in the struggle to come? And, aye, there would be a struggle. Constance might not be able to see into the future, but she knew that much.

There was trouble brewing, and whoever won the battle would take Somerford Manor.

And the Lady Rose.

Ivo downed his ale in one gulp, but his dark eyes were watchful over the rim. Gunnar sat on the bench in the corner while around him his men laughed and shoved and claimed their own sleeping spots. And yet he was very much alone.

Their captain had been much subdued of late. Not that he lacked as their leader—there was a solid core of steel strength inside Gunnar, a calm stillness. If Gunnar told them he would do something, then he would. He was utterly dependable.

Before Somerford, Gunnar and his men had been on the Welsh border, the Marches, where they had fought in the name of some chinless Norman baron. They had earned their money that time, Ivo thought grimly.

The Welsh had been hidden in the hills and the forests, waylaying the unwary, silent and deadly with their longbows and arrows. Gunnar's men had proved their worth again and again, but Ivo had sensed Gunnar's distraction.

The chinless baron was greedy, stealing land that was not his own.

"Why," Gunnar had said, "should we support a man such as this? Give our lives so that he can look out at the view from his window and say, 'This is all mine'?"

"It is our job," Ivo had retorted. "Do not think beyond the doing, Gunnar. It is dangerous for a mercenary to question too hard."

Aye, Wales had been a dangerous place. More than once Gunnar's warrior instincts had kept them from being skewered like pigs. And with each close call, Gunnar's melancholy had seemed to deepen. One night they had drunk deep, and it was as if the silent, calm Gunnar had sprung a leak.

"I do not want to end with an arrow bolt in my eye like Harold Godwineson," he'd said. "I don't want to die where no one knows me or cares."

"What other course is open to you?" Ivo had joked uneasily, hoping to jolly him up a bit. This was not the Gunnar he was used to. He, Ivo, was the emotional one; Gunnar was always so tranquil, so untouched by the turmoil about him. "Can you become a farmer with a plow? I do not see you rising, shivering in the dawn light, to plant barley and peas. Though I *can* see you cuddling against a plump lusty woman, plowing between her thighs."

But Gunnar didn't laugh.

"Maybe you could be a weapon maker like your sire," Ivo went on quickly, "forging great swords for great warriors and weaving chain mail for Lord Radulf."

Gunnar blinked like an owl.

"But the truth is, my friend," Ivo had told him softly,

encouragingly, "you are so good at being what you already are."

"Aye, you have the right of it, Ivo. I am no use for anything but fighting and killing. Where does a mercenary go in his old age? Better I die now, here, and get it over with." And then he had murmured beneath his breath, the slurred words meant for him alone. "Is there a place for such as me, where I can be valued, honored, and loved?"

Ivo had clapped him hard on the shoulder. "You're not old yet, Gunnar! Plenty of work and women left in you!" And eventually, after a few more drinks, Gunnar had agreed that he was right.

Now Ivo poured himself more ale, watching Gunnar pretending to listen to Sweyn's jokes, and remembering that drunken night. The next morning, as if wishing had made it truth, there had been a message from Radulf. They were needed at Crevitch—there was treachery afoot. Gunnar had been exhilarated ever since—or as exhilarated as a man like Gunnar could get.

Land. Somerford Manor. It was Gunnar's to take when he had accomplished Radulf's mission—proved the lady was in cohorts with his enemies as her letter suggested. Once that was accomplished the rest of them could stay on with Gunnar, or take their share in coin and move on.

From a distance it had sounded so simple.

But nothing was easy and despite his profession and his ability to lie seamlessly, Gunnar was a deeply honorable man.

Ivo said a silent prayer: *Let Lady Rose be an evil, treacherous bitch.* If that were only the case, then all would be well. Gunnar would take Somerford with a clear conscience and make his life there, live to a ripe old age a happy man. The warrior would have found the haven he had been secretly longing for.

But Ivo feared the lady was not quite as they had believed. She was beautiful for a start, although Gunnar had had beautiful women before. She was a Norman lady, but there had been a few well-bred ladies who couldn't keep their hands off Gunnar, and they had never slid under his guard. In fact, Ivo could not remember a single woman who had meant more to him than a warm body or a pleasant few hours.

Unwilling, he let the memories of the more recent past well up in his mind. The look on Gunnar's face as Lady Rose walked across the bailey toward them, as if he'd been struck by a bolt of lightning; how she had stepped around the Norman knight, placing herself directly in Gunnar's line of sight while Gunnar had been trying very hard not to look at her; and just now, when he looked up at her window—Ivo had felt the heat coming off him in waves.

Aye, Gunnar wanted her. 'Twas a pity she had come along at this time, when there was so much more at stake. Just when Gunnar was at his most vulnerable. When she could quite possibly destroy his whole happiness.

Chapter 4

At least the mercenaries did not eat like wild animals, Rose thought, watching them as she sat picking at her own food.

The main table stood upon a dais and ran sideways to the rest of the great hall, and from her place on it, Rose could see everyone. Below her, in the body of the hall, the mercenaries ate among the castle folk and yet in an island of their own. The Somerford people eyed their new guests with a mixture of suspicion and fascination, while the mercenaries spoke among themselves, often laughing loudly, clearly unfazed by their enforced isolation.

Mayhap they were used to it.

They still appeared very exotic to Rose, but she was becoming more used to the look of them. The big, dark-haired man with the single black glove had removed his fur cloak and now wore a plain tunic and breeches; now and again she would find him watching her, his gaze so fiercely intense it made her uncomfortable. The fair Dane with the lazy grin was telling a joke, while the other fair-haired man was laughing, in between yawns. The Englishman they called Alfred, with the ruined face, stared moodily at his meal, while a swarthy fellow named Reynard seemed content to listen. They were all big, strong men whose attributes Rose imagined would make them invaluable in their work.

It seemed more than likely the troublesome mere-folk would take one look at them and flee for their lives back into their watery marshes.

Furtively, unable to prevent herself, Rose glanced sideways. Of all his men, Captain Olafson was the only one seated at the main table. Sir Arno had invited him there. Such an action had seemed out of character, until Arno—seated on Rose's right—murmured to her that he would rather have the man where he could see him. Rose, who would rather have had Captain Olafson at the farthest end of the hall, reluctantly agreed.

Brother Mark sat on her left. A middle-aged, taciturn man who seemed to have his head closer to earth than heaven, Brother Mark had come from Wells six months ago at Arno's request, when the old priest had died. Brother Mark was not a warm man, and the people of Somerford did not like him; Rose did not like him much herself. Too often she found him gazing at the gold goblet Lord Radulf had given Edric, which held a position of pride on the shelf behind the main table. Sometimes she wondered if the glint in his eye was entirely appropriate for a spiritual man.

Constance, the steward's widow, sat beyond Brother Mark, at the end of the table. Her eyes were fixed on the mercenary captain, though not with the blank, dazed look that filled the eyes of most of the other women. Constance stared with bold curiosity, as if she were trying to see inside him.

But what is there to see within that pretty wrapping? Rose asked herself, glancing again in the mercenary's direction. *Are there any deeper levels or twists to his character? He is nothing more than a Viking savage, and that is the beginning and the end to it.*

But she was deluding herself, as that annoying voice in her head immediately reminded her.

What about saving the child? Why would a Viking savage play the hero?

Why indeed?

She ran her fingers restlessly along the arm of her chair. High-backed and sturdy, it had been Edric's and was now hers. Such an item of furniture was only to be used by the Lord or Lady of Somerford Manor—the rest of the folk in the hall sat upon stools or benches, or stood if there was nowhere to sit. The chair was a symbol of power.

There were carved panels on its back and sides, swirling tendrils of vines and plants, intermingled with strange beasts and serpents, all in a curling, writhing mass. The old priest had been prone to eyeing the chair uneasily and asking if it was pagan. Edric would laugh and tell him the chair had come from Wales in the possession of a distant ancestor. It had been a bride gift. Then some devilment would always make him add that there was a tale the chair had floated across the Bristol Channel by itself, fetching up on the shoreline to the north before continuing on its lonely travels across the Mere to Somerford.

Brother Mark was helping himself to a piece of succulent pork from a platter, and at the same time muttering Latin under his breath. He spoke Latin in a manner Rose had never heard before, but still, she was no scholar . . . Guiltily, she was aware that her dislike of him colored her feelings toward him.

Rose turned back to Sir Arno. He was speaking in his usual plausible and confident manner about Somerford's defenses; Arno always inspired confidence, even when sometimes he did not deserve to. But tonight he had been drinking before the meal arrived, and the wine was already affecting him. As she listened to their conversation, Rose realized that Arno was repeating her own earlier words: the mercenaries had been hired for show only.

"I believe the troublemakers are the folk from the marsh—the Mere, as they call it here," he said, his voice louder than normal. "They live hard lives, and if a chance came for them to make it easier, then I believe they would take it. I am sure that once they realize you and your men are here, captain, they will leave us in peace."

Arno sensed her attention and turned with an ingenuous smile. "Money well spent, do you not think so, Rose?"

Arno was normally a genial man, and it was a strong woman who resisted a smile like that. Rose had never had trouble resisting it, but she was annoyed by his familiarity in front of this stranger. She glanced warningly toward the mercenary and then frowned at Arno with a severity unusual for her. There was a brief flicker in the knight's eyes—annoyance, irritation, maybe both. His color heightened.

"Wine, girl!" he shouted, and held out his goblet to be refilled.

He *was* drinking more than normal. Perhaps Rose would not have noticed under other circumstances, or would not feel the need to reprove him for it. Tonight she did. It was the contrast, she realized, with surprise. For while Sir Arno drank steadily, with an almost careless disregard for his position and duties, Captain Olafson drank hardly at all.

He had barely sipped at his wine, although Rose knew it was good. Instead his serious gaze roamed over the hall, searching out its doors and dark corners, and resting often on the faces of its occupants, as if he wished to read their minds. He was watching, assessing, and yet if Rose had not in turn been watching him she would not have noticed the tension in him.

What did he presume would happen? Rose asked herself uneasily. The merefolk would burst in on them and steal their supper?

Captain Olafson appeared to be looking for treason at the very least, but if he thought to find it at Somerford he was sadly mistaken. It was too much . . . *he* was too much. Such a simple task required a simple solution—a couple of armed men would have done, not this battle-hardened crew and their barbarian of a leader. It would be like smashing an ant with an anvil.

Deep in her own thoughts, Rose nibbled on a pie, enjoying the rich and succulent taste. They had eaten sparingly for so long that tonight's supper had been an excuse to gorge. Tomorrow, she told herself firmly, they would resume their austere and sensible habits.

Rose let her gaze wander about her hall, automatically noting if anyone was lacking food or wine, and directing her servants in their direction. And then she saw Eartha and frowned. Eartha, as mistress of the kitchen, rarely showed her face in the great hall at mealtimes. That she should now be standing in the doorway with a jug of wine in her hands seemed strange . . . out of place.

As Rose watched, the woman began making her way through the great hall, dodging a groping hand here, a reaching arm there. Eartha's husband had died during the English uprising. An earthy, buxom woman with flaxen curls and angry blue eyes, Eartha was attractive; since her widowhood the men of Somerford had favored her and Eartha had not been reluctant to accept their offers. Although, to give her her due, Eartha was choosy, and she was a good mother to her little boy.

She was approaching the main table now, the wine jug clasped to her breast. 'Twas a wonder, Rose thought wryly, that with her eyes fixed unwaveringly on Captain Olafson she could find her way without stumbling.

But so were the eyes of all of the other women in her hall!

In fact, in Rose's opinion, they were behaving in a quite ridiculous manner. It wasn't just the serving women, either. Wives of many years' standing and girls hardly old enough to string two words together were all goggling at the mercenary captain. First one, then another, had made an excuse to approach the dais and perform some task or merely to linger there without reason, while others—including Constance—just sat and stared unashamedly in his direction.

Rose sighed, and supposed it was natural—Somerford Manor had been stripped of most of its marriageable-aged men. And Captain Olafson was an exceptional-looking man. But couldn't these foolish creatures see that the mercenary's beauty was but a disguise? A thin veneer for his savagery? He might sprawl, relaxed, on the bench, his chain mail replaced by a woad-blue tunic that clung to his broad shoulders and made his hair seem brighter and his eyes bluer, but he did not fool her!

Irritated and yet fascinated, Rose watched as Eartha arrived at a breathless halt before the mercenary. The wine slopped over the rim of the jug and stained her kersey gown, but she didn't seem to notice.

"Captain!" The word was a gasp.

The mercenary looked up, a question in his cool eyes.

Eartha continued in halting French. "I am called Eartha. I want to thank you for saving my son. He's a babe still, and if he had fallen . . ." Eartha shuddered dramatically and then edged closer, her eyes growing heavy. "If I can repay you in any way . . . ? Serve you in any way . . . ? I am willing."

Rose stiffened in her chair—she didn't need Arno's stifled guffaws to clarify Eartha's meaning for her. It might be that in this instance Eartha was offering to repay the mercenary's kind action in the only manner open to her—she had neither wealth nor power, only her looks and her body. Such exchanges were part of life, and Rose did not pretend they did not happen at Somerford.

Why then was there an uncomfortable tightness in her chest? A hot sensation in her throat?

"Well, Gunnar?" Arno was speaking with drunken familiarity. "What better way to warm your bed tonight than with a pretty wench? I say if she wants to show you her gratitude, let her!"

Rose frowned and wondered why no one else at the table appeared to find the comment objectionable—even Brother Mark was smirking. And yet Sir Arno did not normally speak so coarsely before her—he was most particular in his manners. What was the matter with him tonight? What was the matter with everyone?

Suddenly it was as if Rose were a stranger in her own hall.

The mercenary spoke quietly, and yet the noise about them ceased instantly. "Your thanks are unnecessary, Eartha."

Irritably, Rose noted the fascinated faces turned in his direction. Captain Olafson had sounded unmoved by the woman's offer, but Rose refused to believe that. Probably he was already plotting when and where he could claim his payment.

His answer had put Eartha at a loss—men rarely refused her favors—but then she appeared to remember her wine jug and quickly moved to fill his already full goblet. Of course the wine spilled. Realizing what she was doing, Eartha looked up at him and gave a nervous giggle. The interested watchers in the hall chuckled with her.

Gunnar Olafson smiled. A tug at the corners of his lips that broadened into something quite amazingly attractive. To Rose's disgust there came a collective sigh from the womenfolk in the hall. She could cheerfully have strangled them all for being so gullible. Indeed she was so *angry* . . .

Eartha, now refilling Rose's goblet, received a look

from her gentle lady that surprised her into a slack-jawed stare. Sensing that her offer might have been the cause of Rose's ill humor, she stammered in English, "Lady, I meant no harm. I . . . Forgive me. I did not know you wanted him for yourself."

The silence in the hall intensified. Constance, who spoke English, coughed and bowed her head to hide her gleeful expression. Rose felt her face burning as if she were too near the sun. It did not matter that most of the Normans there did not know what Eartha had said. The English did, and far worse, so did the mercenary.

"You forget yourself," Rose said in a frigid voice at odds with her fiery face.

Eartha bobbed a hasty curtsy. "Your pardon, lady," and scuttled away.

Gradually the quiet was filled by voices as conversation resumed, and soon it was as if nothing had happened. Constance made some comment to Brother Mark about the tastiness of the pork, and he replied at length. Normality returned.

Rose felt herself thaw a little. Beneath the table her hands were shaking. *Why does it matter?* she asked herself angrily. *Why should I care if he believes I want him, as Eartha said?*

Because it's true.

Her breath jammed in her throat. No, it wasn't true! How could it be? Rose cast a furtive glance in the direction of the mercenary.

He was staring down at the embroidered cloth that covered the trestle table, as if it fascinated him as much as he fascinated all of them. His thin copper braids had swung forward with his hair, shielding his face, and his big hand lay relaxed beside his goblet, a crisscross of white scars etched into the tanned flesh.

Gunnar. That was what Arno had called him. Rose spoke the name silently to herself, and was shocked by a prickle of awareness. A shiver traced her spine, curled low in her belly . . .

Stop it, stop it now!

Arno leaned toward the mercenary captain, his movements clumsy from the wine, and muttered some jest. He laughed loudly, not realizing at first that Captain Olafson had failed to join in. When he did realize, Rose saw the baffled anger in his expression: How dare this churl reject his offer of manly comradeship!

"Why *did* you save the brat?" Arno asked with a sneer. "Why bother if you don't want to bed the mother?"

Gunnar Olafson's scarred hand closed into a fist.

Rose held her breath, for this was the very question she wanted answered.

She was listening.

Gunnar could sense her interest, more than that—he could *feel* it. Like the wash of a warm ocean, it flowed over him; like the sting of salt, it alerted him. He had never before been so completely aware, to the exclusion of all else, of a woman.

They were a strange gathering. The priest too interested in his meal, the knight so arrogant and sure of himself that he drank too much; the sly-eyed old woman; and the beautiful, treacherous lady. Of them all, it was she who held the most danger for Gunnar.

He had heard the serving girl's words—*I did not*

know you wanted him for yourself. Gunnar did not know whether that was true, but he knew how *he* felt. His skin was raw and sensitive, the rod between his legs already half erect. He was still in control, but there was a recklessness burning inside him that had never been there before and his grip was at best tenuous.

He should not have looked up at her window, in the bailey, after he had rescued the child.

He hadn't wanted to look up; he just hadn't been able to stop himself. She had been leaning far from her window, the veil gone and her hair hanging forward over her shoulder in a thick, dark braid. He had imagined it loose, his mind instantly accommodating him with curling, ebony waves framing her beautiful face. Gunnar had actually felt his hands sliding through the silky, dark mass, holding her as he plundered her mouth with his, as he lifted himself and prepared to drive deep inside her body, again and again . . .

No! Gunnar pulled himself up, reminding himself of where he was, who he was, *why* he was there at Somerford Manor. The land was his if he completed this mission; a future of his own making. And for a mercenary, to own his own land was an unimaginable dream.

Somehow he would conquer this lust and send it fleeing like the enemy to his plans that it was. And now, just to be certain the lady never let him use his formidable charm on her, let him talk his way into her bed, Gunnar set out to make her *really* hate him.

"Why did I save the child?" he repeated Sir Arno's question calmly, unmoved as the drunken knight swayed in his seat. "Because such a death would have been bad luck. If I had let him die, then I would have had to make a sacrifice."

"Bad luck? Sacrifice?" Arno repeated stupidly, as if he doubted what he was hearing.

"Aye." Gunnar put his hand slowly and ostentatiously onto the hilt of his sword. "You see this?"

" 'Tis a sword." Arno blinked foolishly.

"Aye, but not just a sword. This is Fenrir. Fenrir, named after the savage Norse wolf. The black wolf. He demands blood, ever more blood, though he has drunk much in his time. If the boy had fallen and died, it would have brought us bad luck. Fenrir would have demanded blood, and I would have had to satisfy him."

Gunnar felt the shock shimmer about him, but did not lift his eyes from the bemusement in Arno's, as the knight's sodden mind sought to understand what Gunnar was saying. For some reason he did not want to see the expression on Lady Rose's beautiful face. If she had not thought him beyond redemption before, she would now. So be it. He was there at Somerford to fulfill his mission, and if that meant making a beautiful and traitorous Norman lady hate him, that was what he must do.

But once again Gunnar had underestimated her.

"Such pagan practices are frowned upon at Somerford, Captain." Her voice floated through the silence toward him, full of haughty command. "Brother Mark has set them to flight. You would do well not to mention Fenrir or your other nasty Norse creatures in this place."

She made his bloody threat sound like a mild infestation of ants!

His mouth twitched but he held it firm. He felt like

laughing aloud in delight, and something very much like admiration. "The Norse gods are not so easily ignored, lady," he said carefully, and slowly raised his eyes to hers. "Odin, Thor, Loki, Freyer . . . They are old and wily, and they demand that their desires be satisfied."

As I would like to satisfy mine.

She seemed fascinated by his mouth, as if she could see each word forming there, as if she expected him to say something remarkable. He wondered again what she would taste like. If he leaned forward and opened her lips with his . . . A jolt of desire made every muscle in his big body tense and go hard.

She was still looking at his mouth, her own lips slightly parted, her cheeks flushed. Her tone might be that of the unreachable lady of the manor, but her eyes said something else. With a shiver, he wondered if the woman Eartha had been right after all. Could the lady want him?

It didn't really matter.

She was not for him. This was the wrong place and the wrong time, and he dared not allow himself to be distracted.

Gunnar held on to that, steadying himself with an effort. "Lady?" he said sharply, and snapped whatever hot spell was between them.

With a blink her gaze returned to his. For a moment she seemed dazed, and then she woke up, lifting her head and straightening her shoulders. "As long as those desires are satisfied *elsewhere*, Captain."

Now he did smile.

Her eyes remained firmly on his, but they had a startled look, a frightened look. And Gunnar realized with a tingle of shock that her fear was not because of what he had said about Fenrir, but because of the attraction simmering between them.

"Well said, lady."

It was Brother Mark who spoke, his breath unpleasantly hot in her ear. Somehow Rose dragged her gaze away from that of the mercenary, turning her head and giving the priest her full attention.

"My lady," he went on earnestly, his rather blunt fingers clasped before him. Rose's dazed eyes noted the priest also had battle scars on his hands—unusual, surely, for a man of God? "We have spoken before of the need for a new church."

"I remember." They had indeed spoken of it, but there was no money for more building. Brother Mark seemed to believe that a new church should come before food and warmth and clothing. Rose, practical woman that she was, did not.

Brother Mark proceeded to tell her exactly what he wanted. It sounded like a smaller version of the cathedral at Wells—and not that much smaller. Rose nodded, pretending to listen, but in truth she was more interested in what was happening further down the table.

Jesu! She blinked. Here was yet another serving wench approaching them, and bearing yet another full jug of wine! Were they all completely empty-headed? Perhaps she should give an order that none should look at the man, for their own safety!

The girl drew closer. How would Gunnar Olafson react?

Before she could stop herself, Rose glanced again toward the mercenary. Yes, she noted, his goblet was still topped to the very brim with good red wine. What would most men do in such a situation? Rose had known only a small number of men really well—Edric, her father, her brother. Edric, kind though he was, would have laughed and made the wench feel foolish. Rose's father would have been angry, her brother, too, for they were not even-tempered men.

She paled. What if Gunnar Olafson were to draw that frightening sword of his and threaten the wench with it? Or cry out a pagan oath? Or maybe he would guzzle down what he already had, so that his goblet was empty? She tensed, waiting.

Arno was holding out his goblet to be filled—yet again. The knight, his voice noticeably slurred, was boasting about his powerful relatives in Normandy, and seemed hardly to notice the simpering girl. She moved on to Gunnar and waited expectantly, hopping from one foot to the other as if it were impossible for her to keep still in the presence of so impressive a man.

Rose held her breath, expecting the worst.

Gunnar Olafson gave the girl a calm smile and shook his head. It was done so unobtrusively that probably no one but Rose noticed. The girl blushed, smiled back, and retraced her steps.

Kindness, even disinterested kindness, was a rarity in the harsh world where Rose dwelt. To see it now, from a man she had wanted to believe incapable of any of the softer emotions, shook her to the core. Tears stung her eyes and she bowed her head, desperate to hide her own lack of control.

She was the Lady of Somerford Manor—she could not afford to be a woman, afflicted with womanly feelings.

Gunnar Olafson had explained to them why he had saved the boy's life—it was a pagan thing. Rose had been relieved to hear his reason was as unfeeling as she had told herself it must be. For Constance must be wrong; how could such a man as this be a hero? Heroes were not men with hair like fire and steely muscles and scarred hands. They did not own swords near to four feet long called Fenrir and wear shields painted with snarling wolves. And certainly they did not kill for coin!

And yet now, just when she was feeling justified in her initial judgment of him, he acted in a way that could only be called kind. Thoughtful. Even honorable.

What was happening?

Rose clutched the arms of her chair with the sensation that she, and it, were adrift on the sea. And then, thankfully, doubt and scorn came to her rescue, making her rethink her conclusions.

How could a Viking savage be kind? Sometimes her father and brother had been kind, but it was all a trick, a way to manipulate, to get their own way. That must be what Gunnar Olafson was doing. Storing up favors for weeks and weeks to come. A wench for every night!

For what woman would be able to resist him, Rose thought bleakly, if he were kind as well as handsome?

She lifted her goblet and gulped a mouthful of wine, promptly choking on it.

"Lady?" Brother Mark was eyeing her reddened face curiously.

"Rose?" On her other side, Arno dared give her a disapproving stare. In his inebriated state he had again forgotten the respect due her.

Despite streaming eyes, Rose reminded him. "It is *Lady* Rose, Sir Arno."

Arno d'Alan stiffened, his face pinched, brown eyes narrowed. He looked . . . not amused, not angry, not anything she recognized. Sullen, certainly, but something more that was unfamiliar. It disturbed her—a trickle of ice in her backbone—for the brief moment before she dismissed it. If she had hurt Arno's feelings, Rose told herself firmly, it was for the best—he seemed far too sure of himself these days, and she had allowed him to go on doing so without checking him.

"My apologies, *lady*," he said now, pretending contrition, but his voice was thick with drink and mockery.

"Do you always have such a serious effect upon womenfolk, Captain?"

The question came from Constance, and suddenly Rose had a new worry. Jesu, let the old woman not mention her hope of finding Rose a lusty man!

Gunnar Olafson had turned to Constance and was thus looking past Rose. His face was once more expressionless, as blank as if it had been carved from a block of wood, albeit an extremely handsome block of wood. Why, thought Rose, did she feel as if so much was going on behind it?

"There is something about me that women like—" He spoke the simple truth. "So I do not gainsay them the pleasure of looking."

Pleasure of looking! What arrogance, what conceit!

"And if they want to do more than look?" Constance asked boldly, in the evident belief that her advanced age allowed her to be nosy. "Do you give them that pleasure, too, Captain Olafson?"

Arno gave a snort of laughter, almost as if he were enjoying Rose's discomfort.

"Sometimes," Gunnar said quietly, his smile mischievous. "I would have thought you beyond the need for bed sport, lady?"

Constance crowed with laughter. "What were you before you become a soldier of fortune, Captain?" she continued to probe, eyes sparkling with curiosity.

He was taken by surprise—a shadow in his eyes.

"I was a soldier, lady."

"And did you fight at Hastings? What is it the English call it?"

"Senlac," he said, his voice grim.

"Aye, Senlac. Did you fight at Senlac, Captain Olafson?"

Rose waited, expecting him to disclaim the words, shrug them off, or retort that there were many men who fought at Hastings. He did none of those things. "Aye, I fought at Senlac. I fought with Harold Godwineson and the English. Now that you have unearthed one of my secrets, lady, be contented."

Constance smiled, showing many gaps in her teeth. "Oh, I'm content, Captain. For now."

"You fought with the English at Senlac?" Rose demanded, her voice far louder than she had meant.

A hush fell over the hall. She was aware of the other mercenaries suddenly focusing their full attention upon the conversation.

Gunnar Olafson sighed, and gave her a narrowed look that yet held a hint of humor.

"Aye, I did, lady," he answered her with a wry reluctance. "I thank you for spreading my fame far and wide."

Rose blushed vividly, refusing to acknowledge the goggling crowd. "I was surprised," she replied in a voice as unemotional as his. "I am sorry if you didn't want it known, though the people here at Somerford will like you for it. They remember the time before the Normans with longing. However, these days, not many men admit to fighting with the English. They are always on King William's side."

"Then many men are liars."

There was something about him, something in his hard honesty that appealed to her on a different level from his physical attractiveness.

Sir Arno laughed in drunken mockery. "They lie because they were on the losing side!" he bellowed. Constance shot him a glance full of dislike, while Brother Mark smirked into his wine.

"Aye, we did lose," Gunnar Olafson agreed, "but we fought bravely that day, and if we had not been so worn down from the march from Stamford Bridge, we would have won. And I killed many Normans; Fenrir ran red with their blood. He fed well at Senlac."

Arno's face was red, too, but with anger. "You forget yourself, Captain," he spluttered furiously. "Lady Rose lost her brother at Hastings. I myself lost many friends and comrades."

The rebuff was a just one. The mercenary's blue gaze shifted to Rose, but she would not look at him. Had he killed her brother with that sword of his? she wondered. And what would Arno think of her if she said that she didn't care? Her brother had treated her abominably, and when he had died she had been relieved—God forgive her, but it mattered not to her *who* had killed him.

"Lady!"

So intent upon her own thoughts was she that Rose had not noticed the stir in the room. One of the guards was moving toward her—old Edward, wearing his padded vest and an ancient helmet that looked as if it had done service in King Alfred's time. "Lady!" He came at a running shuffle, his eyes fixed on her, and in his haste he had forgotten to bow or lower his voice.

Sir Arno tried to rise from his seat, crying, "What is it?" but he was so unsteady that Rose reached out a hand to stop him. His muscles trembled under her fingers and he was breathing heavily. Another moment, she thought in despair, and he would be beyond speech.

"Edward?" she demanded. "What has happened?"

Edward was clearly agitated, his rheumy eyes wild, his gray-whiskered jaw trembling. "The villagers are shouting at the gate, lady! They say they're being attacked and their houses are burning. Please, lady, give me permission to open the gate and let them in!"

Chapter 5

Shock gripped Rose, but almost immediately she had regained her wits and risen to her feet. "Of course you must open the gate and let them in! At once!"

"And if it is a trick?" That deep, quiet voice was much closer than she had expected.

Gunnar Olafson was standing behind her.

Rose gave him an impatient glance, trying not to show how edgy his proximity made her. "Edward is not a fool, Captain. He knows his own friends and relatives. Let them in, Edward!" The old man scuttled away before anyone else could gainsay him. Rose turned to Arno, ignoring the mercenary captain. "We must send a troop of men to the village, Sir Arno. If the attackers are still there, then we will be able to capture them. If they are gone . . . well, we must help where we may."

Sir Arno stared at her glassy eyed. "Merefolk," he

muttered, and laughed. "Capture the merefolk? Ah, but *can* you, lady?"

The wine had clearly done its work, and he was incapable of making sense. She should be angry—she just felt bleak. Arno's drunkenness meant she would have to go herself.

Rose took a step forward, only to be halted again by a very strong, very warm hand clasping her shoulder. Startled, she turned and met Gunnar's calm blue eyes.

"Lady, is this not the reason *we* are here?"

She had forgotten. She had believed that, as usual, it was all up to her, that she must stiffen her shoulders and carry this burden as she had carried all the others. And now suddenly here was the enigmatic Captain Olafson, steadying her with his grip, offering to take this task upon himself.

She wanted to refuse him, and yet at the same time the thought of his help was an exquisite temptation. Rose found it curiously difficult to breathe.

Could she trust him? And did she want to?

Rose stepped back, away from the others, until the wall hangings brushed her sleeve. As if he read her mind, Gunnar followed, treading softly after her. He was so large that he blocked the hall from her sight, until all she saw was him, his chest and shoulders in woad blue, a pulse beating in his throat. His face was in shadow, his eyes dark hollows, only his hair caught the candlelight, an aura of molten fire.

She made herself look up at him and hoped her haughty exterior was firmly in place. A disguise for the tumult within.

"Captain, I will not have anyone harmed unless it is completely necessary, unless it is a matter of life or death, and even then I do not like it. Do you understand me?"

He stared back at her.

Can I trust him? Or is he, right now, just trying to think of a lie to tell me that will satisfy me? It was no easy thing for Rose to place the lives of her people in this man's hands. Why didn't he answer her? Mayhap it was just that she was a woman, and he did not take his orders from women. Best she disabuse him of that matter right now!

"You may think that Sir Arno rules Somerford Manor," she went on in her firmest tone, "but I am lady here, and I give the orders. If you cannot abide by that, Captain Olafson, then you had best step aside and let me go in your stead."

Something flared in his eyes. "I have no difficulty taking orders from a woman," he said softly. "I wondered whether you would trust me now that you know I fought against your brother."

Rose hesitated, carefully choosing her words. "That is not something that would cause me not to trust you, Captain. Many of the people at Somerford fought for Harold, any one of them may have faced my brother, perhaps even dealt him the deathblow. I do not hate them for that."

Still he stared and did not speak. As if she had said something remarkable.

"Well then . . . ?" she demanded impatiently. "Do we understand each other?"

"If I can find one of these outlaws I will bring him back to you, lady," he offered.

She tried to read his expression. The blankness had

gone; he looked curiously elated. "Why would you do that?"

"He will tell us his secrets."

"Why should he?" she replied.

He bent closer, crowding her. His body gave out heat and strength, his thigh brushed her gown. His breath against her skin was warm and faintly scented with cloves. "Because I am better even than the Lady Constance at making men give up their secrets. There are ways."

Of course there were, Rose thought, her skin prickling, and a man such as this would know them all. Savage tortures far beyond imagining. And yet what choice had she? What he suggested, capturing one of the merefolk, made perfect sense. She answered him carefully, her throat feeling constricted.

"Do not . . . do not do anything until I have seen and spoken to any man you capture. There must be no killing. Do you swear it, Captain? Do you swear to obey me?"

He held her gaze for a long moment. She sensed some struggle in him, though she could not read what it was in the vivid blue of his eyes. And then he sighed, a barely audible sound, and his voice came quiet and intense.

"Aye, lady, I swear it."

He didn't wait for more. Rose watched him turn and stride quickly through the hall, a brief nod sending his men hurrying to fall in behind him. And then they were gone and the keep seemed empty without them.

Rose felt shaky and hot, as though she had experienced something difficult and traumatic, and she knew it was not just that her village was on fire and her villagers crying out for help.

Gunnar Olafson was like no other man she had ever before encountered. He was not checked by the boundaries that confined other men. He had his own rules. He was a pagan, a savage, and a soldier who fought and killed because it was what he did best. And yet, despite all that—or maybe because of it—Rose trusted him.

She had asked for his word, his sworn promise, and he had given it to her.

He had given her his word, and she knew in some deep part of herself that he would not break it.

"Rose?"

Arno was watching her from the table, his brown eyes slightly more alert than they had been a moment before, and full of suspicion. Rose wondered if he had overheard her conversation with the mercenary and thought she had best soothe any hurt feelings. Arno might not be the most reliable of men, but he had been loyal to Edric and he was loyal to her.

"I have sent the mercenaries to the village, Sir Arno. It is why they are here, after all. But they will do as I tell them and nothing more. Our captain had best remember that, if he wants his six marks."

Arno gave a drunken smile at her dry tone. "So you do not approve of our handsome mercenary?"

Constance narrowed her eyes. "At least he can stand upright."

Arno glowered back at her. "Hold your tongue, old woman," he slurred, "or I'll cut it out with my dagger!"

"If you can hold your dagger steady enough."

Rose shrugged and left them to their pleasantries. Outside, the darkness had been made light with torches, and grooms were saddling horses for impatient men. As the gate creaked open, an unsteady mob hurried through. One woman sobbed hard, while a man was being supported by his companions. In the flare of the torches their faces were ghostly, pale and frightened. Voices babbled hysterically.

And then one deep voice cut through the noise.

"Ivo! Take Alfred and Reynard, and circle around to the far side of the village. The rest, with me. We have work to do. Edward, is it? Close the gate behind us!"

The troop of mercenaries set their mounts at the open gate and, horses' hooves thundering on the hard ground, quickly vanished into the night.

Rose stared after them as Edward—puffed up with his own importance—closed the gate behind them. The mild evening breeze that stirred her gown and her veil brought with it the smell of burning thatch. The scent of destruction. She allowed herself one brief image of Gunnar Olafson, riding into possible danger, and then she closed it off. There was too much else to be done.

Rose descended the stairs to offer her villagers what comfort she could.

Gunnar sat upon his gray horse while all about him the flames turned the village crimson and orange, and the smoke hung suffocatingly low. The heat seared his skin. Fire had caught in thatches and roared through the wooden-framed walls. Although the villagers and the men from the keep had worked desperately, the fire had gained too great a hold on some buildings. An irascible old serf called Hergat had died in one of them, too stubborn to come out to safety.

When Gunnar and his men had first arrived at the village, they had found the place in chaos and the attackers already fled. As no one seemed clear in which direction they had headed, there was little point in pursuing them into the darkness. "Better to wait for daylight," Gunnar had told them. "Whoever these people are, they will have left some trace." Then he instructed his men to help gather up the belongings of those among the villagers who wanted to make their way to the safety of the keep.

In fact, the arrival of the mercenaries had frightened the villagers almost as much as the attack on them, but once it was made clear Gunnar and his men were there to help, to be on their side, they were accepted . . . albeit warily.

Gunnar had himself helped beat out fires that were still capable of being snuffed—there were others beyond stopping, raging their way through cottages of timber and sod. In one instance he helped an old woman to corner and capture a small spotted piglet.

"The merefolk did this," the ancient crone had muttered darkly as she crammed the squealing animal into a willow basket and fastened the lid. "God curse 'em for it! 'Tis true they've always hated us and us them, but I never thought that one day they'd come and murder us in our beds!"

"You are safe now," Gunnar had assured her. "We will take you to Lady Rose's Keep."

Her wrinkle-wrapped eyes had peered up at him hopefully. "She be one of God's angels, our lady." The eyes blinked and widened. "You be a handsome one. I've never seen aught like you before in this manor."

"You will see me often from now on, old woman. I am here to drive the merefolk back where they belong."

She had given him a thorough and appraising look, ignoring the pig's shrieks. "Aye, I believe you could!"

Gunnar thought now of the marshy levels, the watery stretches, and their strange, dark islands. Was it really possible the merefolk had decided they no longer wanted to follow the old ways? Maybe the years of living beside Somerford Manor, watching the rich harvests come and go, had proved too tempting. Maybe the merefolk thought to drive off the villagers and make this land their own.

But what of Lady Rose and her secret need for mercenaries? Radulf believed she was quite probably a traitor, a vassal who was no longer loyal to him, and Gunnar trusted the King's Sword as he trusted few other Normans.

Gunnar shook his head; the whole matter smelled rank.

Impatient now, he urged his mount forward, unseeing as the bright flames around him turned to black smoke and crumbling ashes. A gaggle of geese ran past, squawking, into the darkness, their white feathers ghostly.

I gave her my word.

Gunnar's hand clenched upon Fenrir's hilt, the cold patterned metal warming to his touch. His word was precious to him, and once given he would hold to it, always.

He had given his word to Lady Rose of Somerford. The very woman he had come to spy on in the hope of exposing her treacherous, black heart. The very woman whose land he coveted.

Why had he given her his word?

Perhaps it was because of the way she had spoken to

him, so straightly, without guile—he had met few Norman ladies who did not use their looks or feminine weaknesses to gain advantages over the men around them. For a moment back there in Somerford's great hall he had thought she meant to take up a sword, don armor and ride out to protect the village all by herself!

She was brave and determined—he could admire that. But he did not trust her—he could not afford to trust her. If rumor was true, she already held Sir Arno in her toils, and Gunnar had himself seen evidence that there might be something between the lady and the knight . . .

They are lovers!

He wanted to deny the truth of it. The vision of Lady Rose flushed and tumbled from Arno's caresses made him angry in a way he could never remember being before.

He was jealous.

Odin help him if he should be caught up in her spell!

Gunnar shook his head. No, if there was a spell, then its name was *lust*. He was but a dog-wolf scenting the female of his kind. Lust could be dealt with, expunged. Radulf had said nothing about remaining celibate; if Gunnar had a chance to sample the Lady Rose, then maybe he should take it.

But could he have her once and walk away? Would his lust then be slaked, or would the churning inside him grow worse?

"Captain!"

Thankful to have his thoughts interrupted, Gunnar turned, and was instantly alert. Alfred was running swiftly toward him, dispelling the darkness with the fiery torch he carried in his hand.

The ruined side of his face showed up starkly—a maze of raised, white scars and puckered, pink flesh. The son of an English thane, a noble landowner, Alfred had been maimed in a skirmish against the Normans that had decimated his entire family. He had been a cheerful boy; he had become a sullen man—Alfred rarely smiled. Of all the men in his troop, Gunnar worried most for Alfred, and hoped the young man would remain with him at Somerford when this, their last mission, was done.

Gunnar's gray horse shifted nervously as it caught the acrid scent of Alfred's smoke-drenched clothing. "You have found something?"

Alfred glanced back over his shoulder, towards the mill that stood at the farther end of the village. There was a small cottage beside it, the blackened walls and glow of embers telling another tale of destruction. His voice was grim. "Aye, Captain, I've found a man. He's dead. Looks as if he was caught in the fire."

"Is he one of the villagers, like this Hergat?"

"No, Captain, I don't think so. Come and look."

Gunnar nodded and they moved off at a walk. He sensed there was more to this than Alfred was saying, but he would bide his time until he had seen for himself.

The miller's cottage was little more than a shell, although strangely the mill itself remained untouched. Maybe the attackers had been disturbed before they could set fire to the mill, or the miller had stopped them. As they drew closer, Gunnar could smell the river and hear the rush of its swift-moving water. Two figures were standing by the burned cottage, one a child and the other a young woman. The glow from the smoldering timbers showed the woman's face was smudged and her clothing dirty. At the sight of Gunnar on his horse she clasped the child hard against her, her expression at once afraid and defiant.

"The miller's children," Alfred murmured. "The miller himself has not yet been found."

Gunnar nodded at the woman—he saw now she was only a girl—and the child. "Where is this dead man?"

"Over here, Captain." And Alfred led the way around the cottage to the far side. He held the flaring torch over something on the ground, and Gunnar dismounted.

The body lay just outside the charred remains of what had once been the cottage wall, and although the face and upper torso had been burned away, the legs and feet were strangely whole and untouched. Obviously this had been a man, and an unusually large one.

Gunnar dropped to one knee, noting the finely wrought sword scabbard—the sword was missing—and the fine leather of the boots. There were no spurs, but there was a leather cord attached to the heel of one of the boots, as though a spur had once been attached there. The breeches were muddy, and there was a tear at the thigh where something sharp and deadly had been thrust through, into the flesh.

Alfred shuffled impatiently behind him.

Gunnar ignored him, leaning closer to examine the ragged hole in the man's thigh. A lance or spear wound maybe, which had crippled the dead man sufficiently to allow him to be bested. Who had attacked him and why? And who was he?

"Is this the miller?" he asked quietly, knowing it was not. The clothing told him little, but the sword scabbard was Norman. As far as Gunnar was aware, the miller was an Englishman.

Alfred released his breath. "No, Captain. No one I have asked in the village knows him, and yet there are none unaccounted for, apart from Harold the miller. I do not understand it."

"So he must be one of the attackers?"

"He is not from the Mere, Captain. His clothing is wrong, and besides, the merefolk are small. This man does not seem to belong to either side."

"I suppose if he *was* murdered, the villagers might be trying to hide it. His face and hands have been burned. Maybe he didn't fall into the fire accidentally; maybe he was thrown into it so that we would not know who he was."

As he spoke, Gunnar became aware of an inner ripple of unease. He had seen situations such as this before. In the England of William of Normandy, if a man was found dead, it was necessary for those in the vicinity to prove he was an Englishman. A dead Englishman was unimportant, and the villagers could deal with his death in their own way. But if the dead man should prove to be a Norman, then that was different. Then the truth must be ferreted out at all costs and the guilty one punished.

Normans *were* murdered by Englishmen, rightly or wrongly. If it was possible to disguise such a death, to make their overlords believe the body was in fact that of an Englishman, then it would be done. Gunnar had seen all manner of unpleasant acts performed to hide a clean-shaven Norman face or a short Norman haircut. Clothes were exchanged, boots were stolen, faces staved in . . . Sometimes the measures taken were successful, sometimes they were not, and then the Norman overlords would demand justice.

A life for a life.

If this man is not a villager and not from the Mere, then who is he? Why is his sword scabbard of Norman design, and why is it empty? And if he is a Norman soldier, what is he doing here on the very night of the merefolk's attack?

A vision of Lady Rose's luminous dark eyes blotted out the scene of fire and death before him. Was she behind this? Was this part of her plot? And if so, was she playing the game alone? And why, if that wasn't the case, did she need to pay for lowly mercenaries like Gunnar Olafson?

Suddenly the chilly night vanished, and Gunnar was once more fresh from Wales and seated before the roaring fire in the great hall at Crevitch Castle. Replete with good food and wine, and good company. Opposite him sat Lord Radulf, for whom Gunnar's father was armorer, and a man Gunnar knew and admired.

"I need a strong man at Somerford. A man I can trust."

"And you do not trust Sir Arno d'Alan?" Gunnar asked bluntly, without need for prevarication, for they had long been friends.

"He appears loyal, and yet . . . He is Lady Rose's man—he is loyal to her. I cannot believe he would act without her consent." Radulf moved restlessly in his chair, a favorite hound at his feet. "Why would they be looking to hire mercenaries? Men whose only allegiance is to the coin they are paid and without any scruples about what they will do for that coin? Do they plan to start a war? And why send the letter to my enemy Fitzmorton, why ask Fitzmorton for help in the matter? Why not me, when I am Somerford's overlord?"

"This letter that was intercepted on its way to Fitzmorton, was written for Lady Rose with d'Alan's full knowledge? It mentions him? And sealed with the Somerford seal? It would seem as if they are in this together then. Surely he would not turn traitor against you for the sake of his lady?" Gunnar found such a notion strange and incomprehensible—but he had not then met Lady Rose.

"There are rumors he is her leman, though Lily does not believe them. I have . . . wondered, I admit it. He is very attentive."

In Gunnar's opinion, Radulf seemed unusually loath to act in a matter that had a simple solution. "Then replace her, and him, now! "'Tis your right to do so. Why send my men and me to Somerford to catch them out in their plotting? We will arrest them and bring them back to you, and you can throw both the lady and her knight into your dungeons."

But Radulf fingered his clean-shaven jaw uneasily, the hawk ring on his finger flashing blood red. "'Tis not so simple, Gunnar. Lily has taken a liking to this Rose. She will hear naught against her, and now, when she is so near her time, I dare not upset her. I must satisfy my doubts cautiously."

The puzzlement cleared from Gunnar's face, and he grinned.

"I know, I know." Radulf's sigh was irritable. "You think me a fool. But if you had a wife, my Viking friend, you would not be so smug!"

Gunnar laughed, but he thought then—with surprise—that the King's Sword had changed. The bitterness that before he had always worn like a second skin had vanished, and in its place had grown contentment.

Although contentment brought its own burdens. Gunnar had noted the concern darting through Radulf's dark eyes.

Lord Radulf was worried for his wife, Lily, who was heavily pregnant with their second child. Here was a man, Gunnar thought in amazement, who had great estates, the king's friendship and wealth beyond imagining, and yet it was none of those things he feared losing.

No, he was worried about a woman!

Gunnar recalled the scene now, and his bewildered amusement at Radulf's predicament. His own way of life had never been suitable for a wife, or so he had always told himself. Would she traipse about the countryside with him while he hired himself out for war? Or would she wait at home for months at a time, never knowing whether he lived or died?

Land, my friend, Radulf had said. *Yours for the taking, if you can prove that Lady Rose of Somerford is plotting against me. There are reasons why it would please me to be rid of her, though I cannot yet share them with you. Aye, give me the lady, and I will give you her manor. 'Tis a fair exchange, Gunnar, and I will have a man there who I know I can trust.*

With the offer of land of his own, Gunnar's vision of his future had begun to change. Was it possible there was a woman for him who would be as Lily was to Radulf? Someone who would fuel his deepest desires physically, emotionally, and intellectually. Who would fit against him as if she had been born to be there . . .

"Captain?"

Alfred was looking at him strangely. Gunnar frowned, as if his abstraction was all to do with the present situation, and silently cursed himself for his lack of concentration. A dead man lay before him, and he was dreaming of taking a wife!

"Did the miller's family see this man before he died?"

While Gunnar had been occupied, the girl and the child had crept closer. Now Alfred beckoned them to join him, and Gunnar saw that the girl had long tangled hair and a slim body beneath her ruined clothes—the front of her gown was badly torn, and she held it in place with her hand. The child had the same tawny hair and eyes.

"These are the miller's children, Millisent and Will," Alfred said.

Gunnar nodded and rose to his full, formidable height. The miller's children stiffened, their eyes widening, but they did not back away, although they looked as if they wanted to. He noticed the girl's hands were blistered from her attempts to put out the fire, and there was a bloody scratch on her throat. In comparison the boy seemed unscathed.

"Where is your father?"

They glanced at each other and then the girl answered, her French awkward and interspersed with English. "He has gone. I don't know where. Maybe to Lady Rose's keep."

Gunnar had had plenty of experience with liars, and this girl was lying. Either she knew exactly where her father had gone, and why, or she knew something of the dead man.

"Your father would leave you alone here?"

"We were . . . parted. Perhaps he believed we had already gone."

"Perhaps."

Surprise flickered in her eyes that he should believe her so readily.

"Do you know this man?" He gestured to the body, keeping his eyes on her face.

She didn't look at the dead man, but instead turned away and shook her head. "No. He is a stranger here."

"You didn't see him when he was alive?"

Again the shake of the head, her mouth stubbornly firm, but tears shone in her eyes.

Obviously there was nothing to be gained from questions now, Gunnar decided, if he did not want a reputation as an ogre. If the dead man was a Norman, he would find out the truth tomorrow, or the day after.

"Alfred, we will take Millisent and her brother to the keep. They will be safe there. And send me Ivo."

He deliberately spoke in rapid French, and now the girl looked startled, turning to Alfred for an explanation. Alfred stepped closer, almost protectively. She eyed his scarred face curiously, but she seemed too dazed by what was happening to be repulsed. When Alfred shepherded her away, she came meekly, her brother's hand still gripped in hers.

Gunnar stayed, staring down at the body. A dead stranger in an English village, possibly a Norman stranger. Was it murder? This was a serious matter for all at Somerford Manor. Should he inform Radulf? The answer was clearly yes, and yet he was loath to do so. There was a puzzle here, and Gunnar was keen to solve it. Besides, if Radulf came now, the chance to gain Lady Rose's land would be lost to him. Lady Rose herself would be lost to him . . .

His body tightened at the thought of her.

He had not known himself capable of such heat.

The sound of Ivo's approach stilled his imaginings, and he waited while his second-in-command came to a halt.

"What is it?" Ivo asked, swiftly dismounting.

"A dead man no one wants to claim."

Ivo knelt down for his own inspection and, when he had finished, raised his brooding dark eyes to Gunnar's calm blue ones. "What will you do?"

"Stow his body safely for now. We need to find out who he was and who killed him. The miller has run away, I think. We will start there. In daylight."

Ivo nodded.

"Are we finished here?"

"The fires we could put out are out. The villagers who want to stay have found themselves somewhere to sleep; the rest are on their way to the keep for the night."

"Good. No sign of any merefolk?"

"Nothing. The attack was swift and silent, the damage was done before anyone knew what was happening, and by then it was too late. They all blame the people from the Mere but no one actually saw them."

They stood a moment together in thoughtful silence. Of all his men, Ivo was closest to Gunnar. A former Norman knight himself, though now disgraced and outcast, Ivo had found a haven in Gunnar's little mercenary band. In character he was Gunnar's direct opposite: passionate where Gunnar was calm, hasty to act where Gunnar was deliberate. And yet they were like brothers, and Gunnar had no doubt they were presently turning the very same thoughts over in their heads.

"What do you think it means?" Ivo could bear the silence no longer.

"I smell treachery, Ivo."

"Aye," said Ivo grimly, "so do I."

Rose had been unable to rest.

After she and her servants had settled the fleeing villagers in the great hall—tending to those with cuts or burns, feeding those who were hungry, and finding them comfortable places to sleep—she had sought the sanctuary of her solar. But she had been too restless to perform any of the tasks required of her, and instead paced back and forth before her unshuttered window, which afforded her a view of the smoky haze by the river Somer that had been her village.

Sleep was impossible, so Rose didn't even try. She decided she would await the return of the mercenaries and learn what she could of this latest attack by the merefolk. Sir Arno had already retired, too drunk to take charge of these matters for her, and Brother Mark had long since scuttled away to his own bed.

She was alone again.

Rose had never been one to fear solitude. To be alone in the crowded, tense home of her childhood, or the crowded, busy keep of her marriage, was a privilege indeed, and she had always looked forward to the few moments of solitude. But not tonight, not now. Suddenly Rose knew she would give much to have someone to turn to, to hold, to . . . love?

Rose shivered. Love destroyed! To wish for it was to invite her own downfall.

"You are cold?" Constance's voice came from the

doorway, its very familiarity comforting. "Close the shutters and go to bed."

Rose shook her head. "I cannot. They are not yet returned."

"Where is your knight—Arno? He should be down there now, ordering his garrison."

Rose wrapped her arms about herself and gave a wry smile. "Arno is presently beyond anything but snoring sleep. Do you know, Constance, I find myself wishing Edric were here. He would have known what to do in such a situation, and his people loved him, trusted him. Instead I must put my faith in a Viking savage who may very well have more in common with the attackers than with me and my people."

Not true! cried a voice in her head. *He gave you his word . . .*

"Your husband was a silly old fool," Constance said dryly. "If you need help, go to Lady Lily."

There was a fur-lined cloak laid over a chest by the wall, and Constance took it up and came to smooth it about Rose's shoulders.

Rose smiled her thanks, but her answer was firm. "You know I cannot. I will not run to Lord Radulf and Lady Lily whenever I have a problem. Sir Arno has the right of it there when he says they will think me weak and incapable of ruling Somer—"

Constance interrupted. "Sir Arno! That knight knows well how to play with you, child. Like a fish he tugs you in slowly, slowly. One day he will land you and that will be that."

Rose looked at her with genuine amusement. "Arno a fisherman? Whatever do you mean? I know you do not like him, Constance, but you are seeing that which is not there. Arno is loyal to *me*. If he is arrogant sometimes, well . . . he cannot help what he is."

Constance gave her a baleful glare. "I pray it is as you think, lady, but I fear one day you will discover your loyal knight is not quite so loyal. He lusts after you, do you know that?"

Startled, Rose turned to stare at the old woman. "He does not! And besides—"

"Besides, you are not interested," Constance finished for her. "Still, he looks at you with hot longing, lady, for all that you are untouchable to him. 'Tis not just me who has noted it."

Rose laughed nervously. "I think you are wandering in your wits."

"And I think you are lonely, my lady. Twenty-five years old and so fair." She clucked her tongue. "Lord Radulf should find you another husband, a proper one this time, a lusty one. 'Twas his headstrong wife stopped him. I warrant I know who wields the sword in that household!"

"Constance, hush! What are you saying? I do not want another husband. What if he should beat me? Or you?" she added, hiding a smile.

What if I should fall in love with him?

The smile trembled and died, and Rose wrapped her cloak more closely about herself, as if she really were cold.

"I doubt it would come to that," the old woman replied mildly.

Constance's thoughts were less ordered. What a shame that such loveliness should be wasted, or broken upon a weak and inflexible man like Arno. Constance sighed. She was old and could not live much longer. If only she could find a man—a strong and lusty man—a man who understood her lady and who saw her gentleness not as a weakness to be trampled upon, as did Arno, but as a strength. A gift. A strong man's love was what Rose needed. If Constance could find such a man, then she knew she would gladly entrust her lady to him.

"Mayhap you are right," Constance agreed at last. "You do not need another *husband*. A lover would do. Aye, a protector."

"Constance, I want no man—lover, husband, or anything else! I am content with my . . . with what I have." Rose turned again to her window. She had been about to say she was content with her dreams, but Constance did not know of them, nor would she. Her eyes strayed now, across the flat Levels, toward the dark bulk of Burrow Mump.

Marriage, she thought savagely. What was that? A contract for making money and gaining power, for making children to gain more money and more power. Lust? Why, any animal could feel lust. And love? Love was a dream, a fantasy . . . a ghostly warrior without a face.

And you are content with that?

Yes, Rose told herself desperately, I am.

The sound of men approaching the gate drew her back to more immediate matters. Big men on horseback, their chain mail gleaming in the torchlight, were clattering over the wooden bridge spanning the ditch. The mercenaries had returned. Rose pressed her hands against the cold stone sill, counting their heads. One, two, three, four!

Two were missing.

Her breath fluttered in her throat, but even as the unwanted fear gripped her, she heard *his* voice calling for the gate to be opened.

Gunnar Olafson had returned.

It was more difficult than it had ever been to turn herself into her depiction of the lady of the manor. To calmly turn and face Constance when her heart was pounding and her throat was dry. To say, in a voice that trembled only the slightest bit, "They are back. I will go down and meet them. It is time to learn the worst."

Chapter 6

She was standing on the keep steps with the torches flaring behind her. At first all Gunnar could see was her silhouette, the alluring shape of her body. His mind went blank; instinct took over. The hours spent in the devastation of the village, the dead man and the missing miller—all the important questions he could not answer were forgotten at the sight of her.

He wanted her.

It was as simple and as complicated as that.

He, a lowly mercenary, coveted a highborn lady. He might as well try and pull down the moon with his hand! She could have him whipped for his presumption, no matter that he was an honorable mercenary and she a treacherous lady . . .

Gunnar's innate arrogance reasserted itself. He was the son of Olaf the armorer, and in him ran the blood of Vikings and Norse kings—he had nothing about which to feel inferior. Let her try and put him in his place, he thought angrily, and he would show her where hers was. On her back in his bed!

The image was instant and vivid. Gunnar gave a silent groan as it filled his head . . . Her body naked among the bedding, her dark hair spilling over her gleaming shoulders and tangling in his hands as he pressed her down, his hardness against all that exquisite softness . . .

His rod was rock hard, painful in his tight breeches. As well the chain mail tunic was long enough to cover him—just. Gunnar's lips twitched and for a moment he was close to laughing at himself and the whole mess he found himself in. But there was more than his own future at stake here, and Gunnar was not a man to let others down. He allowed the humor to leach out of him, making himself cold, unfeeling. Less of a man and more of a weapon.

In control again, Gunnar dismounted. Behind him Alfred was lifting the girl, Millisent, down from his own horse. Her brother rode before Ivo, and Gunnar reached up for the boy, swinging him to the ground. The child scampered toward Rose, crying out, "Lady, lady, there was a fire!" in a high, excited voice.

"But you are safe, Will," she said gently, reaching out to touch his head.

The boy nodded seriously, glancing around at his sister. "Can we stay with you, lady?"

"Will—"

Rose smiled. " 'Tis all right, Millisent. You may stay as long as you like, Will, now hurry inside and see if Eartha's little boy is still awake."

Gunnar watched as the child received a nod from his sister and hastily vanished into the hall. Lady Rose had known his name, spoken to him as easily as if he had been her own brother or son—it was rare indeed for such a lady to forgo her dignity and the formality of her position to make a villein's child feel comfortable. Gunnar wished she had been sharp-tongued and uncaring. He did not want to admire her; he did not want to like her.

"Lady?" One of the villagers had come forward, wild-eyed, no doubt to ask for her favor. Rose leaned down to listen. She did not look like a treacherous woman. Her face was pale and tired within her veil, but still beautiful. Her fingers were laced together, twisting, so that she appeared anxious. Was that truth or pretense, or was her anxiety all for herself, and the possible exposure of her plot against Radulf?

And yet as he watched her reply sympathetically to the villager, Gunnar found it difficult to be objective. Suddenly he knew he needed to be alone; he would speak to her later, when his mind had regained mastery over his body. So thinking, he turned toward the stables and, with a sense of relief, began to put distance between them.

He should have known better.

"Captain Olafson?"

Her voice was breathless, as if she was running after him. Reluctantly, trying not to groan, Gunnar turned and found that she was.

"Please wait, Captain! I wish to speak with you."

She came quickly to where he waited, until she was so close that he felt his skin prickle with awareness of her. Why did she stand so near him? Surely, even if she could not see his arousal, she could sense the heat sizzling in the air about him? Sense the powerful grip he was having to exert to stop himself from simply reaching out, lifting her into his arms, and taking her to his bed.

But she didn't know. She was too full of her own concerns—although, perhaps, she felt there was *something* wrong. He was as tense as a drawn bow. He stood, arms crossed over his chest as if he could lock her out. Hesitantly she put out her hand and rested it lightly on his.

"Captain . . . are you unwell?"

Her hand was cold, with fine and delicate bones, the nails bitten down. His was large and callused, scarred from a life of fighting, and warm. Very, very warm.

Gunnar shivered, and found himself almost light-headed as he wondered what it would be like to have that slender hand between his thighs.

"No, I am not unwell," he said hoarsely. *I am being driven mad by my own lustful fantasies, may Odin help me!*

"Then tell me what happened at the village," she demanded.

He stared back at her as if he had lost the ability to speak. Her body was scented, and she was close enough so that he could smell her. Her eyes glinted in the torchlight, and her lips were lush and red against the pallor of her skin. He could lean down now and cover her mouth with his; he could lift her hand and suck each of her vulnerable fingers, one by one.

"What happened at the village, Captain?" There was an impatient authority to her voice. It cleared Gunnar's head. Somehow he assembled the necessary words, began sorting them into the correct order.

"Captain Olafson?" Very impatiently, and so close now that he was drowning in her sweet scent.

Gunnar cleared his throat. Tell her? Aye, he would tell her, and read the truth in her face turned up to his.

"Much of your village is destroyed, lady, and a serf called Hergat is dead."

Gunnar saw her flinch and knew he had been brutal, but he had what he wanted—a genuine reaction.

"I have left two of my men on guard with the villagers who wanted to stay behind. The rest of your people have sought the safety of your keep."

"Of course." She removed her cold hand, snuggling it back inside her cloak with the other one, and he felt the loss of it. Her eyes strayed past him, to a huddled group of sanctuary seekers. Her voice trembled. "And those who did this thing? Did you capture *them*?"

"No. They were already gone when we got there. Tomorrow we will begin our search, lady." His reply sounded like failure, but as always Gunnar oozed self-confidence. He stood before her, arms folded over his chest, legs apart, as if daring her to berate him. Gunnar almost wished she would, so that he could walk off and clear his mind of this sexual sizzle. How could he do the job required of him when all he wanted was to bury himself inside her?

But to his frustration she didn't argue, just nodded her head, quietly accepting his explanation, before turning away to give orders to her servants.

Gunnar stood, watching her, asking himself in bewilderment how his famous calm had so quickly and so easily deserted him. If the woman knew she was causing his usually solid world to crack and shiver, if she was using her wiles upon him intentionally, he might be able to resist her. If she was a practiced temptress, a woman who knew how to play the game, he would be able to counter her moves. He understood such women—they were the kind he was most familiar with.

Gunnar did not normally consort with highborn, high-strung Norman ladies. A mercenary found relief with whoever was available, and earthy women experienced in pleasure were his natural choice. And to make it worse, Rose didn't appear to realize the effect she was having on him—he'd swear it by all his father's Norse gods. How could he make his moves or protect himself in a game that she did not even know they were playing?

She was still giving orders.

As she spoke, she gathered the miller's daughter, who had been standing quietly beside her, within the safety of her arm. When she had finished allotting their tasks, Rose turned to the girl, taking in her dirty, ripped clothes and wild hair.

"Millisent, my poor child, where is your father?"

The kindness undid the girl. With a gasp, she crumpled against her shoulder, heaving sobs. Rose's arms closed about her in sympathy and alarm, and she turned back to look at Gunnar with big, startled eyes.

Reluctantly he came forward, until he could speak without being overheard by the villagers. She stood and waited, her eyes growing a little bigger as he loomed over her. "The miller is missing. He was not in the village, and Edward, there on the gate, has not seen him enter the keep." He hesitated, but she continued to watch him, sensing there was more bad news and trusting him to deliver it to her.

Her trust disturbed him; he made his voice cold, set up a barrier. "Lady, we found a dead man by the miller's cottage—a man who may be a Norman—and no one seems to have seen him before."

If she sensed his withdrawal, it didn't prevent her from moving even closer and gazing up at him, the girl still tucked in against her shoulder. "But . . . I don't understand. Is he from the Mere? One of those who caused the devastation?"

"Perhaps." Her face was lifted to his, guileless and open. Gunnar tried to read the lies in her, but all he saw was concern and bewilderment, and the same lonely melancholy of spirit he sometimes felt in himself.

"Perhaps? That is no answer, Captain." She moved yet closer, until the hem of her pale undergown brushed against his dusty boots.

Gunnar gritted his teeth and pretended he was made of iron. "We will know more tomorrow. For now we will consider him a stranger, because none of your villagers will *admit* to knowing him."

"You think they are lying," she stated softly, searching his face for clues.

"Mayhap," he murmured, giving her nothing more. But as he was beginning to learn, she didn't accept half answers.

"Mayhap? Either they are lying or they are telling the truth—how can it be both?"

He didn't answer, preserving his suspicions and his silence, but his gaze slid to the girl in her arms. A warning.

Finally she took the hint. "Then we will talk of this later," she answered him with quiet dignity and a stony glance from her dark eyes.

Gunnar nodded once in agreement and watched as she led Millisent gently into the great hall, where light and warmth gave an illusion of safety. And that was all Lady Rose was, Gunnar reminded himself grimly. Despite her delectable body and beautiful face, she was all illusion.

Alfred went to follow.

"Did the girl say anything?" Gunnar asked quietly, for Alfred's ears alone.

"No, Captain, but she is afraid. She is hiding something."

"Find out what it is, Alfred."

When he had gone, Gunnar stood a moment in the shadows, gazing at the woman in the light. It was madness. He knew it, and still was powerless to help himself. He wanted her. The need was primitive, irrational, but it was there. Maybe it only needed to be the once, he told himself feverishly. Just one time, and he could go back to being himself. And she would be out of his blood, forever.

It was late.

Rose stood at the inner entrance to the great hall, watching over the mounded shapes of sleeping bodies. The waning light from the fire picking out the pale curve of outflung arms or legs, and tousled heads peeping above the edges of warm cloaks or blankets. Gentle breathing, with an occasional snore, broke the heavy silence. Behind the dais, Millisent and Will, Harold the miller's two children, were safely cocooned in a curtained alcove with Eartha and her young son.

Rose had always had a soft spot for Millisent. Was it because the girl was motherless, and she saw in her something of her own childhood confusion and loneliness? Mayhap. The difference, however, was in their fathers, for whereas Millisent's father loved and cared for her a great deal, Rose's father had been cold and manipulative. Certainly he had never loved her, and as she grew she had learned not to long for his love or approval. Her father was skilled in turning such longings into weapons. Had she not seen enough of her mother's suffering to know that?

The lessons had been well learned. To be loved too little was to be constantly longing for more; to love too much was a fatal wound in the heart. It was much better not to love at all.

The hall smelled of stale woodsmoke; the villagers had brought the scent of the destruction of their homes with them in their hair and on their clothes. What had happened out there in the fiery night, during those first moments of terror? Almost, Rose could hear the screams and shouts, smell the burning, see . . . what? Merefolk intent on doing harm? Creeping out of the darkness and back into it again? Or had the attackers and their reasons for the attack been other than she believed?

And why had no one seen anything? she asked herself in frustration.

Why had Harold the miller run away into the darkness, leaving behind him a dead stranger? That did not sound like the man Rose knew. Harold was no fugitive, and neither was he a murderer. He was a stolid, kindly man who treated fairly all who brought their grain to his mill. A man who cared deeply for his family. Rose did not accept that he would abandon his children in such circumstances, unless it was for a good reason. But what was a good enough reason? Had he been taken against his will, dragged off by the merefolk to be held for ransom? But if that was so, why take Harold and no one else? And why do it so stealthily?

Rose sighed, feeling the burden of so many lives pressing down on her. She had too many questions and not enough answers; it was impossible to make sound judgments. She must wait until the morning, as Gunnar Olafson had said, except Rose knew that a dead stranger in an English village—particularly a dead *Norman* stranger—was more than just another paltry worry.

She had seen by the cautious expression in Gunnar's eyes that he understood that. Mayhap that was why he had seemed so reluctant to speak with her and answer her questions. He knew of the old ways, the old days, before King William came to stamp his mark on England. When Harold was king—and long before—murder had been a matter of wergild. Instead of declaring a blood feud, the relatives of the murdered man could be paid an agreed amount to compensate them for his death. This was the murderer's punishment—to pay for what he had done. Now such arcane laws meant nothing—Norman justice had come to replace them. King William decreed that the dead man must be proved to be English, or else he was assumed to be Norman. And, under William's law, a dead Norman meant that an Englishman must die.

A life for a life, that was the Norman way.

And if the dead man *was* Norman, it looked very much as if Harold the miller would be that Englishman.

Was that the reason Captain Olafson had looked so serious when he returned to the keep tonight? Rose knew she would have to question him again, but she was reluctant to do so. Whatever it was that had sparked between them during the meal in the great hall had seemed dead and cold by the time he returned from the village. It had been clear to her that, for whatever reason, he wished to escape her company as soon as possible. She had had to all but order him to wait! And he had been so emptied of emotion as he told her of what he had found, so icy—his men had shown more compassion and feeling than he! The one with the terrible scar upon his face, Alfred, had even helped her to make up beds and bathe cuts and burns, anointing the more serious ones with goose grease.

Alfred had told her that his mother used to do the same, the memory making him smile. "Where is your family now?" she had asked him, for he seemed too young to be a mercenary like Gunnar Olafson.

But his eyes had turned old and bleak. "The captain is my family now."

They were a strange bunch, these mercenaries. Rose's first impression of tough and dangerous still held, but she was beginning to realize there was a great deal more to them than blood and brutality. That did not mean she trusted them, but she was learning to read them better. Apart from their captain . . .

A step sounded behind her.

Rose stiffened. Constance? The old woman did not sleep as much as she used to. Eartha? Millisent, perhaps, unable to rest for worry of her father? Arno, guilty at his earlier drunkenness and seeing that all was in order?

But it was none of these.

She already knew who it was.

Mayhap it was the physical impression of size, of a big warm body close behind hers. Mayhap it was his musky male scent, tangled with that of leather and cloves. Mayhap she just *knew.*

And that frightened her, because it meant there was a link between them. She did not want that; it frightened her so much she could hardly breathe.

Slowly, unwillingly, Rose turned.

He was standing even closer than she had thought. A large and imposing Viking. His strong legs were encased in those tight dark breeches that clung to every line and muscle, while the blue tunic covered his wide shoulders and chest and the bulging muscles of his arms. The tunic was unlaced at his throat, and Rose could see a pulse beating in the shadowy hollow there. His copper hair was damp—perhaps he had poured water over it—and the rich color was muted further by the light of a failing torch on the wall close by. Broad forehead and wide jaw, high cheekbones and narrow nose; the masculine beauty of his face caused a hitch in her breathing.

His presence was overwhelming and Rose stepped back too hastily, stumbling and almost falling. Swiftly, instinctively, he steadied her. The grip of his fingers around her arm was firm and yet gentle, as if he were well aware of his greater strength and was taking care not to hurt her. "My lady?" he murmured softly, mindful of those about them sleeping.

Rose moved to shake off his hand with a curt thank you. Instead, as she looked up at him, she suddenly had a glimpse beyond the handsome looks that held all the women of Somerford in thrall. *He is weary!* she thought, stupidly surprised that a man like this could feel the same ups and downs as normal folk. There were dark shadows under his brilliant eyes, and the lines between his brows looked more marked. Red-gold stubble covered his lean cheeks and strong jaw, and he held his lips pressed hard together, thinning their normally firm shape.

Slowly, trancelike, Rose became aware that he was consuming her with his gaze, just as she was consuming him.

The strain on his face grew—did he struggle against some compelling emotion, some aching need? Struggled and lost.

He lifted his hand.

He is going to touch me.

No! Stop this, stop it now!

But Rose couldn't find the strength to stop it. She didn't want to.

He had long fingers with callused pads and scarred backs, and yet as he brushed them across her cheek his touch was so soft, so gentle, it was barely a touch at all.

Her flesh burned.

Rose heard her own gasp, felt the blood surge beneath her skin, heard her heart begin to beat faster. His closeness was making her dizzy—it was as if she were slowly spinning, around and around.

Frightened, looking for a diversion, Rose did the first thing she thought of—asked the question that had been occupying her before he came. "What happened to the man in the village?" Was that her voice, low and husky, so sensual?

Gunnar cupped her face, molding the delicate shape of cheek and jawline. He eased off the metal circlet that held her veil in place, and plucked the length of fine cloth from her hair.

For a moment he simply stared, and then he pulled undone the leather strip that fastened her braid, and thrust his hands into the thick mass of her hair, setting it free. It billowed like a dark cloud about her head and shoulders.

A faint, satisfied smile curled his mouth, his rigid control allowing for no more. That was what it was, Rose realized abruptly. Control. Gunnar Olafson reined in his emotions like a restive horse, forcing them to obey his will. He was a man of iron.

And yet he wanted her. It was there in the stark, tense lines of his face and body; it was burning bright and hard in his eyes.

The knowledge that she had shaken that control, that she had shaken *him*, pleased Rose in a completely feminine way. There was power here, the sort of power she had never experienced before. It felt exhilarating; it was a secret, voluptuous quivering, deep inside her.

Rose tilted her head back, keeping her eyes fixed on his, feeling his fingers tense against her skull. His answer came at last, a whisper.

"I don't know. That is something yet to be discovered."

Rose's voice trembled like winter reeds on the Mere. "Something you don't know, Captain? It surprises me to hear you admit it."

Again Gunnar gave her that faint smile, his eyes half hidden by his lashes. There was something so compelling about him, so irresistible. She wanted to touch him, to hold him, all of him. The need was swelling within her, building like a fire in dry tinder. She had always feared giving too much of herself to a man, but this feeling was so strong it was able to swallow up her aversion to intimacy.

He cupped her face with warm hands. His thumb

rubbed gently against her soft lips, testing the shape and texture of them. Rose parted them slightly, touching his flesh with the tip of her tongue. He shuddered, his iron control crumbling.

Her head was spinning faster. She knew she was going to kiss him, and knew she couldn't stop herself. Just once wouldn't hurt . . . would it? As Rose stretched up to his lips, Gunnar was leaning down. His mouth brushed softly against hers, and then he slanted his lips and opened them just a little bit, enough so that his tongue could taste her.

Rose lost all the strength in her legs. She sagged, leaning in against him, clinging to his shoulders. With a soft murmur she opened her mouth to him, and groaned as his tongue plundered within.

For a long moment he was her anchor, the calm center of her spiraling world. His hard, ungiving body was pressed to her soft curves. He was a creature made for war and fighting, a warrior. But he wanted her, and just now she held greater power over him than any armored opponent. Her trembling fingers slid into his hair, feeling the silky, damp fibers. Feverishly Rose knew she wanted to touch all of him, be free to allow her hands to roam where she willed. That was when the stark truth became clear to her.

Kissing wasn't enough.

Mayhap Gunnar felt the same, for suddenly he was moving, half carrying her. A few steps and they were beyond the reach of the betraying torch, hidden in the shadows by the wall. Rose knew she should protest, but his big hands had curved over her shoulders and around, stroking down the arch of her back, finding the dent of her waist and closing on the rounded flesh of her bottom. He pulled her closer and she felt the hard prod of his manhood against her belly.

His mouth savaged hers, almost brutal now in his need, but she did not pull away from him. Rose pressed closer, arms twined about his neck, her body melded to his. She was completely beyond the reach of the scolding voice in her head, everything forgotten but these new, wondrous sensations. Her breasts, flattened against that hard chest, felt painfully full, her nipples hard as pebbles. Could he feel them through his tunic? It seemed that he could, for he rubbed himself back and forth against her, at the same time using his grip on her bottom to lift her high onto her toes.

The soft mound between her thighs came to rest on the hard, solid ridge between his.

Rose gasped into his mouth, and at the same time Gunnar groaned. A shudder went through him, and he moved slowly against her, easing himself in yet closer. Pleasure sang through her, melting flesh and bone. For an endless moment Rose thought she would join him in the mindless dance that was their destination, and then his voice, harsh and low and barely recognizable, brought her thumping back to cold reality.

"I want you. Do not play with me, lady. I'm not one of your tame Normans."

Her chest was rising and falling violently. She felt heated and achy, her mouth swollen from his kisses, her breasts painful. Lower, between her legs, where Edric used to lie so ineffectually, there was a wild sensation that was unfamiliar and urgent. She wanted to ride upon his manhood. She felt wholly carnal, sensual . . . totally unlike herself.

Aye, there was power here, and much pleasure to be taken, but Rose was afraid. She stood on the brink of the precipice, and was frightened of what she would see in the chasm below.

That was when the voice in her head broke through.

What are you doing? Swooning in his arms like one of those silly serving wenches? He is a Viking savage, a mercenary, and you are the Lady of Somerford Manor!

Gunnar sighed, evidently reading the answer in her eyes. He stepped back, his blue eyes, turned almost black with arousal, fixed on her face. Slowly, reluctantly, he released her. She felt the chill of his leaving. Rose took a shaky backward step away, only this time he did not reach out to steady her. Instead, he stood watching her, silent and unmoving, as she took another step, and then another . . . And then she was turning and running in full flight toward the stairs that led to the floor above.

Gunnar stood listening to her retreat. He hadn't been able to sleep and had come to the hall to make sure all was well, or so he had persuaded himself. Instead he had found Lady Rose . . . He had lost his famous control—he didn't need the painful throb of his body to remind him of that. Lost it? Great Odin, it had shattered like thin ice when a fire is lit upon it! Yet he could not regret learning what she felt like under his hands, his mouth, his body. She was so sweet and so hot, and he wanted more.

Much, much more.

Rose was certain she would never sleep. Her mind was churning and her body still ached in a manner that embarrassed and shocked her. She tossed and turned, trying not to think of those brief, vivid moments with the mercenary captain. But the day had been a long one and dreams finally claimed her.

After wandering for a time in misty darkness, she found her dreaming self nearing Burrow Mump. As she approached, the earth suddenly opened into a cavernous hole, stretching back into nothingness. Out of the blackness sprang the ghostly warriors, their hair like smoke and the muscles of their chests and arms gleaming. Warhorses tossed long manes and snorted white breath, their hooves making no sound as they galloped through the air.

Terrified, Rose turned to run. Too late. She had hardly taken a step when she felt an iron arm close about her waist. Abruptly she was swept up, her feet dangling in nothingness, and drawn in against her captor.

All the strength seemed to drain from her then, as it was wont to do in dreams.

"Let me go!" she cried, but her voice had no substance. She turned, trying to see his face, but there was nothing there. Only the velvet night sky with stars blazing. As her eyes fluttered closed, something brushed against her cheek, and reaching up she felt a tendril of hair. *His* hair. Her fingers tangled in the long strands and found a narrow braid.

In the dream Rose opened her eyes. The braid lay threaded through her fingers, lustrous in the starlight.

It was the color of copper.

Chapter 7

Rose was pretending it hadn't happened.

The fact that she had allowed the Viking mercenary to kiss her was . . . well, impossible. Not to be borne. The feel of his mouth on hers—hot and urgent, making her head swim—had stayed long after he had released her. Indeed, was with her still. She had allowed Gunnar Olafson to kiss her, to fondle her—and she had kissed and fondled him back.

Heat crept into her face. Even now the sense of need pooled in her belly and quickened her heartbeat. Lust, that was what it was. What else could it be? She had known the man for a day.

Rose withdrew into her thoughts while she went about her tasks, hardly knowing what she did.

Her tasks were many.

The villagers had to be fed and cared for and comforted. Most of them were keen to return to their homes or to begin rebuilding, but there were others who had no wish to leave the safety of the keep. Places had to be found for them to sleep there in the great hall or in the bailey, and tasks had to be set them. Somerford Keep did not feed idle hands, could not afford to. It was summer, but the harvest would not begin until next month, and food was scarce. Ironically, it was during summer, while waiting for the harvest, when most of the peasants in England starved.

With such serious matters to consider, Rose knew she should not be remembering the feel of Gunnar Olafson's lips on hers.

She had spent a number of hours teaching Millisent the finer points of cleaning clothing. This, as she had explained to the girl with a smile, mainly involved hard work, but a paste of wood ash was useful when it came to whitening linen.

They were presently in the kitchen, engaged in the tedious business of making candles. Using a wooden board cut into regular holes, Rose had carefully fixed twisted linen threads through these holes. The threads were in fact wicks, and they would be dipped into a bowl of mutton fat again and again, until the candles had grown to the required thickness.

Millisent, at her side, watched closely and helped where she could. The girl had washed and changed into a plain, homespun gown supplied by the more buxom Eartha. The long sleeves hung over her hands and had to be folded up, while the hem swept the floor—it made her look younger and even more vulnerable.

While the servant women chattered around her, Rose dipped her candles once more into the congealing mutton fat, and knew with a sense of helpless dismay that she should be using this time to consider the measures needed to protect her people against their attackers. She should be deciding what to do about the dead stranger. She should be contemplating Harold the miller and his strange disappearance. And, apart from her current troubles, there would soon be crops to harvest—if they were not to starve.

Rose wiped a hand across her brow—it was very hot in the kitchen—and, catching Millisent's eye, smiled comfortingly. The girl was pale and worried, and it would do no good to add to her fears until they knew the truth. Will was playing in the corner with Eartha's child, the two of them giggling as if this were an ordinary day. Rose could not remember being so carefree when she was a child; she had too soon been burdened with adult cares. Serious and solemn, that was little Rose. Her mother had seemed always to be weeping and when she had deigned to notice Rose, she had tended to hug her too tightly, as if to make up for her previous neglect. Her love for Rose's father had been a terrible affliction to both her and her daughter.

Rose had never wanted love. She was no romantic. Few Norman girls dreamed of finding that sort of romantic love with their husbands—that was not what marriage was for—but Rose was even less romantic than most. Thankfully Edric had been kind and gentle; she had been grateful for that. There had been no passion between them, none of the aching intensity Rose had heard sung about in the sweet ballads. Such excess of emotion disturbed and frightened her, threatened her ordered existence. And yet, contrarily, most nights she did dream of it. Of *him*, her ghostly warrior.

And last night she had dreamed he wore his copper hair in narrow braids, like Gunnar Olafson.

Fear rose up in her, a thick black wave she could almost taste. The kitchen was too hot, too noisy. The intensity of her feelings—feelings she had always believed she could control—overset her outer calm, causing her hands to shake. Suddenly Rose had to escape. There must be somewhere quiet where she could think this thing through—reason with her mind instead of allowing her emotions to overcome good sense.

Rose turned to Millisent and said in a false, bright voice. "Here, now 'tis your turn." And she thrust the candleboard she had been working on into the girl's surprised hands.

"But lady—" Millisent blinked.

"Ask Eartha if you need help."

"Aye, I'll help you, Millisent." Eartha smiled kindly, glancing up from the table where she was rolling pastry for a fish pie. "There be nothing to it."

"There, you see?"

Millisent still looked as if she might object, but Rose gave her no choice. With another wooden smile, she turned and left them to it.

The stairs leading up from the kitchen were dim and deserted, and the air was cool and still. Rose stood a moment, taking deep breaths, grateful for the respite. Slowly her panic subsided, and order was restored to her erratically hammering pulses. She was able to consider her situation with some measure of tranquillity.

The dream had been only that—a dream. A fantasy fashioned by her overwrought mind. Her ghostly warrior was not Gunnar Olafson. He could *never* be Gunnar Olafson. It disturbed her that she could imagine, even for a moment, that he was. Her dream man had no face—he wasn't real—and thus it was safe to love him and to long for him. But Gunnar Olafson was very real indeed—an earthy, sensual warrior—and he was anything but safe.

Probably, Rose told herself, he was the sort of man who kissed every woman he came across. And she had not fought him, she had been more than willing, even encouraging. For a moment last night, as they stood locked together, she had believed herself capable of rattling the mercenary's control. She dismissed such imaginings now. Probably he had meant to seduce her from the beginning, and had gone about it in his cold, methodical manner. And she had been ripe for seduction.

Was Constance right; did she need a lover?

A vision came rushing over her—her bed filled with hard, powerful flesh and blazing blue eyes. Once again she felt swamped, breathless and shaking.

She had had enough of quiet.

Now she needed clamor!

With a gasp, Rose hurried up the stairs, trying to outrun her own thoughts, and burst into the great hall.

In contrast to the stairwell, it was awash with people and movement. The outside noise left no room for her own wayward thoughts. And at least the mercenaries weren't there, so she was spared the embarrassment of coming face-to-face with Gunnar Olafson. For now.

He was out hunting. Arno had told her so, and at first she had thought he meant for meat for the table—they were sorely in need of such with all the extra mouths to feed. Then she realized that of course Arno had meant "hunting" for whoever had attacked the village. She had an image of the mercenary troop pursuing the merefolk like a savage wolf pack chasing deer, and shivered.

Arno hadn't gone hunting, he had remained in the keep. "To protect you and your people," he had told Rose, shooting her a wary, sideways glance. As if, she thought, he had not drunk so deep last night that he could not lift his own sword. Perhaps he did not remember, or hoped she had not noticed it or was too polite to mention it? He had failed her last night, and today he was trying to make amends, but the fact remained.

Again her comparison of the behavior of the two men—Arno and Gunnar Olafson—made her uneasy. Surely it should have been Arno who remained sober and this morning took charge of the hunt, and the mercenary who stayed at home recovering from his drunken excess?

"God curse them, halffishes that they be. Aye, tails for legs!"

The imprecation brought Rose's head around. Faded blue eyes turned red from smoke and lack of sleep, set in a mass of wrinkles. The ancient creature was clasping a wooden cup full of milk in her crooked hands, and over the brim her gaze was fixed defiantly on Rose. As Rose was well aware, it was the general belief among her people that the merefolk were in fact halffish—grotesque creatures of skin and scale, designed for their watery home rather than dry land.

Rose bent down and tried a soothing tone. "Did you see the merefolk burning your house, grandmother?"

"Nay! They be too clever for that, lady. Hergat's dead, the old whip-tongue." Her eyes stared, unblinking, more surprised than sorrowful.

"I know. I'm sorry to hear it." Rose leaned closer, ignoring the snuffling of a small spotted piglet confined in a willow basket. "Grandmother, have you lately seen any Normans in the village?"

"Apart from yourself, lady, and Sir Arno? Not I."

"Did you see Harold the miller last night?"

"I heard his daughter scream," she said helpfully.

Rose nodded and touched the woman's bony shoulder. "Rest now. Drink your milk."

But the old woman hadn't finished. "He be a fine man, that Captain," she said, her pale eyes gleaming in a manner quite unbefitting her age and situation—almost lasciviously.

"Is he?" Rose replied, pretending disinterest. To her dismay she felt blood heat her cheeks.

"Oh, aye, lady!" she was assured. "Every woman in this keep would welcome him under her blankets! But maybe 'tis not the same for the nobility . . . ?" The old one bowed her head and coughed, disguising a chuckle.

Rose straightened, well aware of her flaming face and rigid bearing. Thankfully, before she had to think of a reply, one of her servants approached, eyes lowered respectfully. Or mayhap, Rose thought in mortification, she was chuckling, too!

"My lady, we are in sore need of more clothing."

Relieved at the chance to escape, Rose answered swiftly. "Constance will know what we can spare. I will go and ask her."

Once again Rose set off in search of the inner quiet she seemed to have lost since Gunnar Olafson came to Somerford. This time she climbed the stairs to the solar, where she knew Constance would be at this hour.

The ancient crone's insolence had been unbearable! And yet it was not normal for her to be so upset at what was only a bit of risqué joking. Life in the keep was close lived and there were few secrets between its walls. Men and women were attracted to one another, and were rarely coy about it or the subsequent couplings. Why had she not laughed back, made a jest about Gunnar's handsome looks? Joined in? It was true enough that all the Somerford women were enamored of the mercenary. Why could she not have pretended that she was, too?

Because for her it was no jest.

Slowly she continued up the stairs, wondering once again how she was going to face Gunnar Olafson. Perhaps she could hide herself away in her chamber? she thought feverishly. Pretend she was ill? But her people were depending on her in this time of hardship, and Rose had never been a coward.

Bleakly, she glanced from one of the arrow slits that had been built into the thick wall of the keep. The day beyond looked a fair one, and as expected, Arno's young recruits were training. The boys, stripped to their waists, thin chests shining with sweat, were practicing with wooden swords and shields. Arno was striding up and down, shouting instructions. By the gate, Edward stood on guard duty in his antiquated helmet and padded vest.

All was as normal; it was almost as if last night had never happened.

If only that were so, thought Rose with a sigh, and continued on her way.

It was near to darkness when the mercenaries finally rode back to Somerford Keep. As the gate was heaved open for them, the cry went up that they had a prisoner, and soon news spread from the bailey to Rose, sewing by the light of one of her own candles. She hurried out to see for herself.

The mercenaries' horses drew to a tired, clattering halt. The animals were dusty, their coats flecked with sweat; the mercenaries were not much better. Gunnar Olafson dismounted from his gray stallion, spoke briefly to Ivo, and then turned toward Rose. The dusk gave him an eerie look. With his pale face and dark eyes, he was a creature of dreams, not flesh and blood at all.

He stopped within two feet of her, so close she could *feel* him. Just as she had when he came upon her last night.

His gaze was like the thrust of a sword, intent and unswerving. Even had she wanted to avoid it, he would not have allowed her to.

At some point during the long day, Rose had finally managed to find peace. She had done it by convincing herself that the feelings she had experienced when he kissed her, looked at her, touched her, were naught but the fantasies of a weary and worried widow. He was very handsome, and such an attraction was to be expected. She had simply allowed her loneliness to turn that attraction into something that didn't really exist.

Like her dream warrior.

But now, one look from Gunnar and the harsh truth stripped bare every lie she had worked so hard to make herself believe. This was no fantasy, this was *real*. Rose wanted to close the small distance between them, to lean into him and feel the hard heat of his body against hers. To lift her face and close her eyes, and feel the eager press of his mouth on hers. Her breathing quickened, her skin felt as if it were too tight, her clothing abraded her breasts and thighs.

Pretense was pointless. Whether this feeling was lust or desire or simply bedazzlement, Rose wanted Gunnar Olafson.

Stop it, stop it now!

The voice came to her rescue again. Resolutely, Rose forced her eyes away from the mercenary, and instead turned to the figure that had been lifted down from one of the horses. Harold the miller, his clothing stained and dirty, had his head bowed in despair. He stood as if he were all alone and not at the center of such a noisy crowd. If he was not a guilty man, Rose thought in dismay, then he was certainly giving a good impression of one.

She approached, ignoring the warning murmur from Arno, who was following behind her. "Harold?" She spoke his name quietly, gently.

The miller did not move. Now that Rose was near, she could see that there were scrapes and cuts upon him, one across his cheek where the blood had dried. His boots were sodden and muddy, and his wrists were tied together, the skin raw and bleeding.

Nausea fluttered in her stomach, but she forced herself to be still and restrained and not cry out in her distress. Her voice was curt. "Untie him."

"Lady—" Ivo began the warning, but it was Gunnar who finished it.

"He may run if we untie him."

Rose flung him a furious look. "He is hurt. Untie him. I order it."

"Lady Rose, think what you are doing," hissed Arno,

but again she ignored him, her gaze clashing with that of the mercenary leader.

Gunnar lifted his brows quizzically, as if he questioned her good sense, but came without further argument and, raising Harold the miller's hands, slid his knife between them. The bindings fell away.

Arno drew his sword. There was an audible gasp from the crowd around them. But Harold did not try to run; he simply stood with his hands dangling limply at his sides. Gently, Rose placed her hand upon his arm. The cloth of his sleeve was cold and damp.

"Harold? You must tell us what happened."

He looked up at her then, his eyes huge in the torchlight, and she saw that his dirty face was streaked clean where the tears had run. His voice was a hoarse whisper she strained to catch. "I did not mean it, my lady. I did not mean to kill him . . . and yet I am glad I did."

There was an anguished cry. Rose felt her heart jump violently, and then Millisent brushed past her, running to her father. At the last moment Alfred caught her, holding her firmly as she struggled, his scarred face grim. Millisent pushed at his arms, squirming to be free, but Alfred bent his head, murmuring words too low for anyone else to hear, and after a moment the girl went limp. She hung in his arms as if all life had left her. Alfred did not let her go, instead he tightened his hold, turning her so that her face rested against his shoulder. Millisent lifted one pale hand and clung to his tunic.

"Are you saying you killed the man whose body was found beside your cottage?" Rose asked, keeping her voice steady with an effort.

But Harold wouldn't answer her, setting his mouth into a thin, stubborn line. Sick fear coiled in Rose's stomach.

"Harold?" she whispered. "You must talk to me of this. There may be a way around it, if you will give me a reason."

"There's no way around it, lady," he said bleakly, staring down at the ground. "I killed him. He had set the cottage alight and when Millisent ran out screaming, he grabbed her and pulled her to the ground. I stuck him in the leg before he could do more than rip her gown. I didn't know he was a Norman until he turned and drew his sword on me and shouted some French rubbish. I killed him then and took his sword and threw it into the Mere. We . . . *I* thought to burn the body, but God was against me and the fire went out before it could finish its work."

Pale but resolute, Harold looked up into her eyes. "It was me did it, lady. Me and only me. Millisent did nothing and Will is but a child. I killed the Norman and I will pay for it."

Millisent began to sob into Alfred's shoulder as if her heart was broken.

The girl must have helped her father drag the body into the fire, but what use was there in forcing her to admit it? Harold had protected his daughter; he would do so now.

And by Norman law he would die for it.

Slowly, unable to resist, Rose turned and met Gunnar's eyes. She had known he would be watching her, had felt it. He looked calm and still—a waveless sea while all about railed the storm. His solid tranquillity soothed her, and when she spoke it was in a surprisingly steady voice.

"Has he said more than this to you, captain?"

"No, lady. We came upon him in the woods. He said nothing to us, only turned and tried to run through a thicket. We caught him and bound him to stop him from hurting himself. He has said far more to you than he did to us."

"And you found no one else?"

"There were signs of a group of men entering the Mere. We followed their track a little way but they must have had a boat waiting—the water was soon too deep without one. It would seem that we must believe it was the merefolk who burned your village."

He put his answer in a way that puzzled her, but Rose did not have time now to solve puzzles. She turned again to the miller.

"Why was he burning your cottage? Are you sure he was a Norman? Did you see any of the merefolk with him?"

"A Norman burning a cottage?" Arno retorted indignantly. All this time he had stood near Rose, impatient and struggling to understand while Harold gave his explanation in English, and suspiciously watchful every time she turned to Gunnar. Now he was frowning and keen to take part. "No, lady! 'Tis clear to me that this lout killed the Norman in a rage and then ran off to hide his own guilt."

"I don't understand why a Norman would be present at the attack on the village, Sir Arno." Rose looked at Gunnar as she spoke.

Big and quiet, he stood with his arms folded over his

chest, his legs set apart, and his eyes on hers. At the back of her mind she could feel heat and passion, beating. Last night he had held her in his arms, anchoring her to solid ground as she soared and, almost, took flight to the stars.

I want you. I'm not one of your tame Normans.

No, Gunnar Olafson wasn't tame, despite his still, calm demeanor. Beneath that unruffled surface was more passion than she knew what to do with.

Arno stepped into her line of vision, shooting Gunnar a narrowed look. "Maybe this man, this Norman, was passing and saw that there was trouble afoot. He went to help and this fool, mistaking the matter, killed him. Probably the girl led him to believe she was willing, and when her father arrived she pretended otherwise. The English are well known to be deceitful and—"

Arno stopped abruptly, realizing he was standing in the midst of those same deceitful Englishmen. He cleared his throat and went on briskly. "I did not understand all this man said—as you know, Lady Rose, English is not my language." He made it sound as if this was a cause for celebration. "But I understand enough to have heard his confession. He killed the man and then tried to burn his body so no one would know. The law is clear."

Arno was right. And yet, in her heart, Rose did not want to pass judgment on Harold the miller. She believed him. He had been protecting Millisent. She understood why he had killed. In his position would not all of them do the same? Jesu, if only he could have captured the man rather than killed him. If only he had not made things worse by trying to hide the evidence. Yet, even so, there must be a way out of this mess without another needless death.

As if he had reached inside her mind, Gunnar said, "Whether it was an accident or not does not matter now. He has confessed. He must be brought before the manor court to tell his story there, and be judged upon the evidence."

Rose nodded unhappily. The cool night air felt very warm against her face, as if her flesh had lost all heat. Would she be able to sit in judgment on Harold? Give him over to the hangman? She swallowed—let it not come to that. He was defending himself; surely that allowed for leniency?

"Very well, Captain. See that Harold is locked up securely for tonight."

Millisent made a high keening sound, and Harold said in a gruff voice, "Never mind, daughter, never mind," as though he sought to comfort her.

Rose turned away before the tears in her eyes could fall, and began to walk quickly back to the keep. Behind her, a boy ran with a flaring torch, trying in vain to keep up. Rose ignored him, and ignored Constance hovering in the doorway. She wished herself suddenly far away. She knew that if Edric had still been alive he would have agreed with Arno, no matter that Harold had been justified in his actions, and that Edric was himself English—or maybe because of it. The law was the law, and Edric and Arno would have argued the miller's fate between them over a good red wine, but in the end they would have agreed that he would have to die. Now Rose was the lord here at Somerford, and it was unlikely Arno would discuss anything with her over a goblet of wine, or that she would wish him to. They would never agree. She did not believe in such harsh justice, such black and white judgments. Why could there not be shades of gray?

"Slow your steps, my lady!"

She was standing in the great hall, and Constance, breath wheezing, had followed her.

"I have nothing to say, old woman."

"Maybe not, but I do."

Irritably Rose halted. "Then say it and be done, for I am very weary."

Constance pressed a hand to her heart and gulped in air. "Let Arno sit in judgment on the miller."

Rose shook her head slowly. "It is not his place, Constance, you know that. I am lady here and I make all decisions, good or bad. I have to sit in judgment on my people if I am to retain my power and their respect."

"Lady," she whispered, "it will wound you grievously!"

"Nevertheless, I will sit in judgment on Harold the miller, and no one will say I have not done as I ought."

Constance muttered something under her breath about stubborn women, but Rose ignored her. "Send someone to the kitchens, Constance, and have food brought for the mercenaries. They will be hungry and it grows late."

When Constance went, Rose stayed a moment. She felt a little as the miller must have, standing in the bailey while the noise and movement of life went on around him, and yet alone. Soon she must sit in judgment on a man she liked and admired, who in her heart she believed had been forced to do wrong, who had been defending his beloved daughter. Aye, a brave man. And he did not deserve to die for that.

Turning about, she sought Millisent in the crowd, but the girl was not to be seen. Probably she had followed after her father to the cell where he would spend the night. Blindly her gaze slid over dozens of faces . . . and was caught and drawn into the very eyes she most wished to avoid.

It was full darkness now, and Gunnar Olafson stood in the doorway, silhouetted against the bailey, watching her. Alfred, his head close, was murmuring at his side. There was something almost furtive about them—what secret did they have that they had not shared with her? Her interest captured now, Rose watched as Gunnar made one last brief comment to his comrade, and then Alfred nodded and was gone back into the night.

Gunnar Olafson began to make his way across the great hall toward her.

Rose wanted to back away—she even flicked a brief glance behind her—but she was too close to the dais, and a retreat would mean climbing on it. Lady Rose did not run from anyone. She set her shoulders and lifted her chin and faced him, forcing her features into a replica of the calm mask that seemed to come so easily to him.

Gunnar came to a halt, too close as usual, and Rose was forced to look up. She felt at a disadvantage, and angry because of it. Those surging emotions were stirring again inside her, but she forced them down and hung on to her equilibrium.

"My lady." The dark blue gaze searched her own before sliding to her mouth and lingering there.

Rose took a shallow breath, refusing to let the memories of last night intrude. "What is it, Captain? I am occupied."

"Do you believe Harold the miller's story? Or do you prefer Sir Arno d'Alan's version?"

The mockery in his voice surprised her. He appeared so unruffled, and yet his voice was anything but.

"Why should it matter to you what I believe?" She spoke hastily, angry with him, herself, and Arno. But even as the words were spoken she was wondering if it *did* matter to him, if, like herself, Gunnar Olafson did not think Harold the miller should be hanged for what he had done. Curiously, she went on, "What is it that troubles you, Captain Olafson? Do *you* doubt what you have heard? Or is it just that you trust no one?"

Something gleamed in his eyes and was gone. He smiled coldly. "It is true I trust no one, lady."

"I can see that a man who takes coin to kill would find trust difficult."

She thought for a moment he might speak up for himself, tell her that she was wrong, but instead he shrugged in a manner designed to let her know her opinions were nothing to him.

"Do you know Lord Fitzmorton well, lady?"

He had surprised Rose. Did she know Lord Fitzmorton well? Now *there* was a question.

For a moment time slipped and she was a child again, gazing up, defiantly, into that brutal, handsome face.

Do as you are told, girl!

And then the stinging blow across her cheek, and her mother flying out of the shadows to her side. Angry, clutching arms, her face turned in quivering fury to the man.

Don't touch her! Don't you touch her, ever!

But he had.

Rose's gaze refocused, and somehow she managed an indifferent shrug to accompany the lie. "I do not know him well, Captain. Lord Radulf is my overlord, and Lord Fitzmorton is no friend of his."

Gunnar's face still showed nothing and yet she felt the full intensity of his interest. Had he read her secrets in her face?

"If Lord Radulf is your overlord, why did you not go to him when your village was first attacked? Why did you not ask *him* for extra men to help you guard your manor?"

Because Arno advised me not to! Because he said Radulf would consider me weak and incapable.

Rose would never tell him that. Why should she? He would probably agree with Radulf.

The color was hot now in her face but she refused to look away from those piercing blue eyes. Anger began to uncoil inside her. How dared he question her like this? As if *she* were *his* servant rather than the other way around.

"*That* is not your business."

He smiled, and the beauty of it quite simply took away her breath. Several women standing nearby gasped and stopped what they were doing, admiring him. Rose shot them a glare and they returned hastily to their business.

"I am being paid to protect you, lady," Gunnar said. "I was but trying to earn my money."

"You are being paid to do as you are told, Captain, and to keep your tongue still."

Arno would have stalked away if spoken to like that.

Edric would have shaken his head sadly at her lack of manners. Rose shuddered to think what her father or brother would have done.

Gunnar Olafson laughed.

Shocked, Rose stared as he threw back his head in genuine amusement, and then looked down at her with such blazing warmth in his eyes that it was difficult for her to breathe. There was silence in the hall, but Rose could not take her gaze from his.

"My tongue is a matter of interest to you, lady?" His murmur was soft, seductive.

"Of course not!" But she was breathless again, her cheeks hot, her hands trembling.

"No?" He gave her his smile, and now there was no doubting the predatory gleam in his eyes, the desire to have her. Rose felt the overwhelming urge to take that one step forward and press her body to his, lift her mouth to his. Give herself over completely to him.

Stop it! Stop it now!

"I . . . there are things I must do. I . . . forgive me, Captain, I . . ."

His mouth twitched as he bowed his head, but she spun around and was gone. Halfway up the stairs to the solar, she became aware of Constance tugging at her sleeve. The old woman was particularly persistent tonight.

"Have done, old woman," she begged. "What is it now?"

But Constance had no intention of "having done." "He is a fine man."

"Who is a fine man?" Rose retorted and kept climbing, hoping to outpace Constance. "Surely you have not followed me to tell me that!"

"The mercenary," Constance panted. "Captain Olafson. He is a fine man. He will make you a fine lover."

Rose blinked at her incredulously. "You speak of fine men and lovers at a time like this? He is a mercenary, a soulless creature who would kill for a coin. I have other worries—"

"Maybe, but that does not alter the fact that he is very handsome and you enjoy looking. I saw you just now, lady, *and* last night. He kissed you and you were not loath to kiss him back."

"You saw us?" Rose choked, and then slumped against the cold stone of the stairwell. "Of course you did! *You* would never miss such a thing."

Constance stopped in front of her, chest heaving, and her expression became sly. "Why do you not take him to your bed, Rose? Have him while he is here? Enjoy him and yourself. He is yours to command, and no one would blame you for commanding him into your bedchamber."

"You are wanting in your wits, old woman!" Rose cried, but to her horror her voice lacked conviction.

"If you do not take him then another will," Constance went on blithely.

"Then they are welcome to him."

"Huh! We shall see how you stare when Eartha is clinging to his arm, rubbing her big chest up against him. You will be cross then, lady, and I will know why. You should take him now. Why not? If you were a man, a lord, you would not hesitate to pick the best bedfellow for yourself. Why should a woman's lot be any different?"

"Because it is! Now go, Constance, and take your nonsense with you. I cannot listen to any more!"

Constance muttered her way slowly back down the stairs. Rose stared after her, breathing quickly. Harold the miller was to come before her manor court to be charged with the murder of a mystery Norman, and probably, to appease her Norman overlord and her king, she would have to sentence him to be hanged; the village was half destroyed and must be rebuilt before the harvest; the merefolk were on the rampage and might attack again at any time; and now Constance had run mad with lust.

And not even lust for herself, but proxy lust on Rose's behalf!

Why was it then that a tiny voice at the back of her mind was whispering to her that Constance was right?

What the old woman had said was in part truth. If Rose were a man she would be free to take any woman she desired and no one would say her nay, or even raise an eyebrow. It was accepted that that was the way of things. Gunnar Olafson desired her. She saw it in his eyes. Felt it in his kisses. If she commanded him, it would not be as if she were forcing him to do something he did not wish to do. And God help her but she was in desperate need of a pair of strong, warm arms about her in these troubled times! Perhaps for one night, just one, and then all would return to normal?

"And mayhap I have run mad, too!" Rose gasped, shaking her head, and turning wearily to climb the remaining stairs.

The solar was warm and she was past tired. Swiftly Rose undressed and climbed into her bed, drawing the curtains to shield her from drafts and—she hoped—bad dreams. In another moment she was asleep.

The dream started as usual, with her approach on

foot to Burrow Mump and then the warriors springing forth from the earth. Only this time, as she turned to run, she realized that one of the horses was known to her. A gray stallion, fine and strong. With a cry she tried to lengthen her strides, her heart pounding, but it was already too late. A muscular arm folded about her waist and lifted her up. Hard flesh, surrounding her, safe and yet very dangerous.

"Mine." His whisper brushed her cheek, warm and scented with cloves.

Chapter 8

Rose awoke, bleary-eyed, to begin her day. As she dressed and allowed Constance to brush the tangles from her hair, she listed in her mind the many duties she had to perform. It was something she did every morning, and yet today, with every task she listed, her spirits sank a little lower. She glanced toward the shuttered window, where the sun was leaking through the gaps. It seemed to beckon to her.

"Where are the mercenaries, Constance?"

The old woman didn't pause. "They have ridden out, lady. I know not where."

So Gunnar Olafson was hunting again.

"I shall go to the village this morning," Rose announced, and braced herself.

As expected, Constance began to splutter like an overfull pot. "But lady, it is not safe! You cannot go into danger!"

"I am not going 'into danger.' I want to see the damage that has been done in my village. If I were Edric you would not be making feeble excuses to prevent me from going."

"You are not Edric."

"Well then! Send an order to have my mare saddled. I will set out immediately." Her voice was firm and authorative—her lady-of-the-manor voice.

Constance knew better than to argue with her when she was in this autocratic mood. But she didn't have to like it.

"Aye, my lady-stubborn," the old woman muttered, and stomped off unwillingly to do her bidding.

Rose settled her veil firmly on her hair, straightening the metal circlet that held it in place. She was looking forward to escaping the confines of the keep. Of course, her work was important, but what was the point of making candles and sorting through their limited stock of food when a man's life rested in her hands? Harold the miller was locked up for killing a man, and if she did not find a way to save him, he would be hanged.

How could Gunnar Olafson care about a man he did not know? And Arno would not show sympathy for an Englishman accused of murdering a Norman. Who else was there to do it but Rose? She wanted to see the setting of Harold's crime with her own eyes.

Aye, thought Rose smugly, she would cast her eye over the scene, and offer her people what consolation she could on the destruction of their village, and be back in the keep by midday.

It was not that simple.

Arno was horrified by the very idea. "My lady, you cannot go to the village! You will be placing yourself in danger."

Rose stood her ground. "I have made up my mind, Sir Arno. I will ride this morning."

He narrowed his eyes at her, but Arno, like Constance, had learned when she could be turned from her course and when she could not. "Very well, lady," he said through thinned lips. "But I will accompany you."

Rose opened her mouth.

"Whether you wish it or not!"

Rose sighed and managed a resigned smile. "Then I wish it, Sir Arno, and thank you."

They set out, clattering across the bridge. Rose lifted her face to the sun and wished her journey was one of pleasure. It seemed a very long time since she had done *anything* for pleasure. Beside her, Arno was looking from side to side, his hand firm on the hilt of his sword, obviously ready to do battle for her if the need arose. Here was loyalty, whatever Constance might say and think.

Rose recalled the scene at Edric's deathbed a year past. Edric had been determined to speak to Arno, no matter his own weakness. When Arno had come to his bedside, Edric had grasped his hand, pulling him nearer as his eyesight failed. The old man had seemed shrunken with illness, diminished, yet oddly determined.

In contrast, Arno had appeared reluctant, uneasy, as if he would rather have been anywhere other than by Edric's deathbed.

"Swear your allegiance to my wife, Sir Arno," Edric had croaked insistently. And, when Arno was still hesitant, perhaps unbelieving that Edric was really dying: "On your knees, sir, and swear!"

Arno had dropped down immediately, and his voice

had shaken with emotion as he had sworn his allegiance to Rose. When it was done, Edric had fallen back, satisfied, and slept. He had never awakened.

Remembering the moment now, Rose was certain Arno would never betray her. He might have his faults, but he was loyal. Rose refused to believe otherwise.

The burned village was a grim place beneath the blue summer sky. Rose rode slowly through stark reminders of the tragedy. Despite their predicament, her people gave her a ragged cheer, followed by respectful bows or curtsies. So much lost, she thought hollowly.

"What will we do, Sir Arno?" She spoke without really expecting an answer. "How will we rebuild all this before the harvest is due to be brought in?"

"It is time to look to your friends for help, lady," he said soberly, an unfamiliar gleam in his eye.

"I don't know if I would call Lord Radulf my friend," she replied slowly. "Lady Lily has always been my patron, but she is unwell, Sir Arno, and I cannot turn to her. And you know I don't want Lord Radulf to believe I am weak. He will take Somerford from me."

Arno pulled a face, his fingers clenching and unclenching his reins in an oddly nervous manner. "Maybe there are others who would listen more favorably to your cry for help, Rose. Lord Radulf is not the only powerful man here in the southwest of England."

Surprised, Rose turned in her saddle to face him. "Arno? Are you counseling me to treason?" She managed a shaken laugh. "You are jesting me! We will manage somehow."

Arno looked away from her searching gaze, his hands suddenly still, and then, as if coming to a decision, nodded to himself. "Lady, you and I have been together much this past year, since Edric died. I have been patient. But now, I want you to consider—"

A commotion at the farther end of the village brought Rose's head around, and she stopped listening. A big man on a gray horse was galloping swiftly toward them. Rose felt her surroundings tilt momentarily as her dream world and the real world collided, and then she tightened her grip on herself.

Beside her, Arno swore under his breath. " 'Tis our brave mercenary captain," he said, with such bitterness that Rose recoiled.

She had no time to reply; Gunnar Olafson was already upon them. He drew up, charred earth scattering, his horse tossing its head as he restrained it. The round shield hung in its customary place over his shoulder. He was wearing his helmet, and now he took it off, tucking it under his arm. His face was streaked with sweat, his copper hair hanging in long damp tendrils. His eyes were sharp as blue spears, and Rose read his anger before he said a word.

"Lady, you should not be here."

Rose pushed her intense reaction to him from her mind, noting instead the hard set of his jaw, the grim line of his mouth. Gunnar was seriously displeased with her, but she refused to allow that to intimidate her. "These are my people and this is my village, Captain," she said evenly.

" 'Tis not safe," he growled.

For once, Rose thought in surprise, *she* was the calm one.

"You forget, Captain, Sir Arno is with me."

Gunnar gave the knight a cursory glance, insulting in

its brevity. Arno hissed in a breath, his hand going once more to his sword.

"And *you* are here, Captain Olafson," Rose added, as if she had not noticed what had passed between the two men. "*You* will protect me, won't you?"

His wide chest heaved as he drew a deep breath, held it, and let it go. "Aye, lady, I will."

She leaned toward him, dizzy suddenly with her own power. "And you will obey me, Captain? You swore to do that, too."

Gunnar Olafson had been very angry with her, but now as he stared into her eyes, the anger seemed to peel from him, leaving his face as still as a mere pond. "I did swear that, Lady Rose, and I do not make such promises lightly."

What did he mean? There was a message there in his eyes. A glow. It spread through her body, rippling across her own calm and threatening a serious disturbance. He saw it; his mouth quirked. He leaned back in his saddle, and his anger was gone.

"Have you seen what you came to see, lady?" he inquired.

Rose nodded, and with an effort said, "And now I wish to see where it was that the merefolk escaped into the Mere, after they attacked my village."

Arno made a further protest, but Rose did not take her eyes from the mercenary. *He* was the real power here, not the knight. It was Gunnar who would make any decisions concerning her movements and her safety. Rose understood that now for the first time, and she was all the more determined to have her way. To assert her rightful authority.

Abruptly Gunnar nodded his head. Calling out to two of his men—the two fairheads—who had been sitting upon their horses at a distance, waiting, he wheeled about and led the way.

"Come." Rose glanced to Arno, and only then saw how flushed and angry he appeared. His own authority had been usurped, she realized with an inner sigh. Later on she would have to soothe Arno's ruffled feathers—she had always done so before, and she was confident she could do it now.

They rode by the ruins of the miller's cottage and the mill, empty and silent but thankfully untouched. Once the harvest was in they would need Harold to grind the grain. Where would they find another like him, so particular in his work and yet so reliable? What a waste it would be, if he were to die.

The woods covered the slopes to the west, but to the north the land fell away, flattening into meadows of green grass and yellow cowslips, and then sinking into the wetlands. Reeds and saltgrass poked from the mud and water, and wild duck and snipe hunted in the deeper pools.

"There, where the land dips low." Gunnar Olafson had drawn up his gray horse and, lifting his arm, pointed out across the Mere. "We followed their footprints as far as that low island and then the water grew too deep. They must have had a boat."

Rose scanned the horizon, frowning against the hazy glare of sun and sky. The wetlands, the Levels seemed to go on forever—flat, marshy, endless. The islands rose up out of them, the knoll of the dark and mysterious Burrow Mump looming like an ill omen against the summer sky. The home of her ghostly warrior. Her gaze skittered away before the doubts and fears could return to plague her. Instead she turned her mind to the attack of two nights ago, those shadowy, faceless men who had run from the burning village. Anger shook her.

"Will they come again?" she wondered aloud.

Gunnar glanced sideways, and Rose could feel him reading her. The temptation to meet his eyes was great, but she held back.

"Maybe we have frightened them away," he said, with nothing in his voice to tell her whether he believed his own words.

It was then she heard it, the thud of many horses approaching.

Gunnar turned first, his hand going to his sword. It slid silently from its scabbard, the lethal black metal gleaming like ebony. Arno tugged at his own sword and forced his horse around, cursing and digging in his spurs when it refused him. Several horsemen came up over the rise. They were strangers, grim-faced, armored. Rose was instantly aware that this was no friendly visit.

"Ride back to the keep, Rose!" Arno commanded, finally managing to turn his horse and place it between her and the approaching men.

Rose threw off her numb shock, gathering herself to obey, when suddenly Gunnar Olafson's powerful arm curved around her waist and she was lifted onto his horse.

"No!" It was a gasp. Whether she was rejecting his presumption, or the sensation of hard male flesh all about her, Rose wasn't sure. She began to struggle.

Gunnar had no time for doubts. "Keep still, lady," he ordered through gritted teeth, and tightened his arm. "They are Fitzmorton's men."

Rose froze, her eyes widening. He was right! The flapping banner was blue and yellow—Fitzmorton's colors. A cold, numbing fear spread through her. Why would Fitzmorton send his men here, now?

Mayhap he had found a use for her at last?

Fitzmorton hated Radulf, and she was Radulf's vassal. Was she now to be the pawn in this game between two powerful men? No, Rose determined, she would fight to the death before being taken captive by Fitzmorton . . . and besides, Gunnar Olafson would protect her.

In that moment, and for no reason she could properly understand, Rose was certain of it.

"Fitzmorton?" Arno had repeated, frowning. Then, his brow clearing: "Aye, Fitzmorton's men. But what do they want here, now?"

Gunnar had been looking at him curiously, as if something in Arno's manner struck him as odd. Now he turned back to the approaching riders, and his blue eyes narrowed. "They are on your manor, Lady Rose. Did you invite them here?

He looked dangerous, she decided, peering up at him. She was breathless as she sat, pressed against his hard chest, her thighs resting upon his, his powerful arm squeezing her, and realized she had not been this close to any man, apart from Edric, in her whole life. And Edric had never felt like this.

"No, of course I did not invite them here!" she gasped, and brushed aside a swathe of dark hair. She had lost her veil and her braid was coming undone. She tried to straighten, to edge away from this unbearable closeness. "Please put me back on my horse, Captain! There is no need—"

To her dismay, but not her surprise, he ignored her. The troop with the blue and yellow banner came to a halt before them. Their leader urged his mount forward a little, and to Rose's consternation she saw amusement in his gray eyes as they took in her rigid demeanor, and the muscular arm wrapped possessively about her middle. His thin, rather austere face relaxed, he was even handsome in a priestly sort of way, but he was not a man Rose would ever trust. Even as the thought occurred to her, the man's gaze slid from her dishevelment to Gunnar behind her, and his face went blank with surprise.

Gunnar stiffened, his body going solid as stone. He even seemed to have stopped breathing. It was then that Rose understood: they knew each other.

"Gunnar Olafson." There was no denying the recognition in the man's voice, or the dislike. "What misfortune brings you here to Somerford Manor?"

Gunnar's shock was already fading as he looked ahead to this new challenge. *Miles!* The last person he hoped to see, though in hindsight he should not have been surprised. It was natural that Miles should have aligned himself with someone like Fitzmorton. Gunnar was just grateful that Ivo wasn't there—his friend had returned to the place in the woods where they had found the miller, hoping to find something, anything, to help solve the mystery of the attack on the village.

"Miles." Gunnar sounded as if they were meeting in perfectly normal circumstances. "You are with Fitzmorton, then. Why am I not surprised?"

Miles snorted a laugh. "God rot you, Gunnar, I hoped you were dead."

In his arms, Rose had been rigid with fear and with an equal determination not to show it. Now she went pliant, as if she might be about to faint. Or maybe his grip around her was too tight? Gunnar loosened his hold, and felt the soft weight of her breasts upon his arm. A sweet scent rose from her uncovered hair and her warm body; it filled his nostrils, threatening to divert his mind from their very real danger. Gunnar forced himself to coldness—more of a weapon and less of a man—concentrating on the enemy before him.

"Why are you here anyway?" Miles demanded, glancing suspiciously at Arno and then away again. "I had heard you were in Wales."

"I was."

"I have been to the north, seeing to Lord Fitzmorton's lands there," Miles's gaze traveled over Rose as he spoke, taking in her dark hair and beautiful face and lush shape. He nodded at her breasts. "You always did take the most desirable wenches for yourself, Gunnar."

Gunnar would have enjoyed striking the smirk from his mouth and watching him bleed. He held in the violence and gave a cold smile. "This is Lady Rose of Somerford, Miles." His voice was as icy as Norse snow. "You are standing on her land."

The smirk vanished. Miles glared a moment at Gunnar and then bowed his head to Rose in a manner far too brisk and soldierlike to be apologetic. "Lady, I am sorry."

Gunnar had decided there was little point in making an issue of his rudeness. Matters were tense enough. But he wasn't sure how Rose would react. Most of the

Norman ladies he had known would take serious offense at Miles's remarks . . .

Rose wasn't most ladies.

She nodded coolly, accepting Miles's apology as if it were her due. Gunnar admired her for that, although her next words startled him. "You are known to Captain Olafson, sir?"

Miles's gray eyes flicked to Gunnar and away again. "Aye. We fought together . . . long ago. I am Sir Miles de Vessey."

"And why are you here at Somerford, Sir Miles de Vessey?" she asked him in that soft, authoritative voice that could have extracted obedience from the lowest serf to the highest baron in the land.

But Miles was as cunning and slippery as the eels that lived in the Mere. "When I returned from the north it was to learn that one of Fitzmorton's men had gone astray, lady. He was traveling across Somerford Manor with messages to Lord Radulf at Crevitch Castle, and didn't return when he was meant to. I have come to find him."

Gunnar had been content to allow Rose to ask the questions, but now he felt her tense. A missing messenger from Fitzmorton and a dead Norman. He did not need her warm fingers, slipping into his to press a warning—he had already drawn the same conclusions. Still, he could not help but wonder at her bored tone when again she spoke. "Then you are on your way to Crevitch Castle?"

"Aye, lady."

"Then we will not delay you—"

"Hell and damnation!" It was Arno's muttered imprecation that brought Miles de Vessey's head around.

Rose sighed, and Gunnar squeezed her fingers in comfort or warning, he didn't know which. "Will no one tell him?" Arno growled, turning from one to the other. "We have a dead Norman and Sir Miles is missing a man—does that not strike anyone as odd?"

Gunnar watched Rose widen her eyes in assumed surprise. "But why would one of Lord Fitzmorton's men set fire to the miller's cottage and assault his daughter?" Her even voice was designed to dampen Arno's certainty.

"If he did," Arno retorted in disgust, not in the least dampened. "We have only the miller's word for that, lady."

"And that of Millisent, his daughter."

"Exactly," Arno said, as if she had been feeding his argument rather than her own.

"What is this?" Miles's gray eyes were turning from Gunnar to Rose, and there was distrust in every line of him.

Arno did likewise, and when he saw the reluctance evident on both their faces, he scowled. "Come with me," he spoke grimly to Miles de Vessey. "There is a body lying unburied in the village. You can judge for yourself whether it is your missing man."

Arno rode away, and Miles, with another soldierlike bow to Rose, followed with his men. Gunnar nodded for Sweyn and Ethelred to accompany them. Sweyn grimaced, eyes on Miles. "Did you know *he*'d be here, captain?"

"No." Briefly Gunnar wondered how he was going to extract them all from an increasingly complicated situation, and then he dismissed what-might-bes and concentrated on here and now.

"If Miles questions you, say nothing," he commanded his men. "We have been instructed to protect Somerford Manor and its lady. The money is good. That is all you know."

Sweyn grinned and rode off, with Ethelred following.

Rose had turned her head to look up at him, so that she could see his face properly. The turn of events had made her pale and anxious. "Why will Sir Miles ask questions?"

Gunnar hoped his eyes were blank. "It is in his nature."

"Why should your men tell him anything but the truth; what else is there to tell?"

She was suspicious and he didn't blame her. Did that mean she was entirely innocent of any involvement with Fitzmorton, or was she simply leading him in the direction she wanted him to go? Gunnar wished he knew.

"If the dead man is Lord Fitzmorton's messenger . . . ?" she murmured uncertainly.

"Do you want the sour truth, lady, or honey-coated lies?"

Rose frowned, shifting in his lap, her soft bottom pressing against his thighs. Gunnar winced. "I want the truth."

"Then I will give it to you. The more powerful the man, the harsher the punishment. If the body in the village is Fitzmorton's messenger, then there will be no reprieve for your miller."

Her lips parted on a little sigh but she didn't look away. Suddenly he wished both the foolish miller and Miles de Vessey to hell. He was holding Rose in his arms and there were more pleasurable things to do.

* * *

Rose could see a pulse beating smoothly in Gunnar's throat. The tanned texture of his skin was broken by gold-red stubble on his cheeks and along his jaw—he hadn't had time to shave that morning. His own gaze was roaming over her face, probing, searching, and she wondered what he could see. All her fears about Fitzmorton and the miller and the dead Norman laid out like counters for his perusal? Or her growing awareness that they were now even closer than they had been the night before last, when he had kissed her.

While Miles de Vessey and Arno had been there, Rose had maintained her calm authority—her lady-of-the-manor face. But now they were gone and suddenly she was very close to tears. Was it safe for Gunnar Olafson to know that? Women in her position should hide their weakness—she had learned *that* on her mother's knee. And still, when Miles had spoken of the dead Norman and she had realized the implications, she had voluntarily placed her hand in Gunnar Olafson's, and felt his strong, scarred fingers close firmly on hers. As if it were the most natural thing in the world.

"Miles de Vessey is not to be trusted," he said, after what seemed an age. His voice was husky.

Still, Rose stared back into his eyes, seeking . . . what? She only knew that they were as blue as the ocean, that they evinced everything she pretended to be but was not, and that they soothed her like a balm.

She looked away, before he could draw out her very soul, and took a deep breath for courage. He was still holding her, his body against hers, and it felt so good. Better than anything had felt for a very long time. She did not want to move, and yet in a moment he would lift her back onto her horse and she must straighten her shoulders and resume her lady-of-the-manor face and pretend she felt nothing for the mercenary captain.

"So Miles de Vessey is known to you, Captain," she said quietly, and it was not a question.

"Aye, lady. Whatever he tells you . . . promises you, do not believe him."

"I have never seen him before; why should he promise me anything?"

"Sir Arno d'Alan knows him."

That brought her head up and around. She had planned to deny it, but as her lips opened to spill forth the words Rose realized he had spoken the truth. Arno *did* know him. Remembering now, Rose was suddenly conscious of the fact that Arno had not been surprised to see Miles, or if he was, it was only that he should appear abruptly over the rise like that. Aye, they were known to each other; Miles had not even asked for Arno's name!

The realization made her very uncomfortable, and she swiftly sought an acceptable, comfortable explanation. "Mayhap Arno knows Miles from the days when my husband was alive," she said in a stiff little voice. "There was a time when we had negotiations with Lord Fitzmorton, after he stole most of our garrison."

Fitzmorton had found their attempts at negotiation amusing, Arno had told her.

If anything, her explanation caused the probe of his gaze to grow more intense. Rose knew then she had changed her mind. She wanted very much to be returned to her mare, she needed to escape the hold of this man who seemed to have such power over her, emotionally and physically.

"Your loyalty is misguided, Rose," he said quietly. "Or is it more than loyalty?"

His familiarity with her name was not to be borne. Rose opened her mouth to tell him so, and instead was surprised to hear herself saying, "Arno has stood by me during hard times, Captain. You have been here but a short while—you do not know—"

The glint in his eyes startled her to a halt. He cupped her chin with his hand, lifting her face even closer to his, and his mouth swooped down until his lips brushed hers. "Ah, but I *would* know you, Rose. I would know every inch of you. I want to put my hands on your body, my mouth on your mouth. I want to be inside you."

Her blood was drumming in her head. The taste of him, the feel of him, the nudge of his manhood against her hip . . . It was as if he had put a spell upon her, tamed her to his hand. Rose sat, frozen, knowing if she made the slightest move to acquiesce she would be lost. And this would be a very bad moment to give her senses over to desire.

She pulled away from the grip of his hand on her chin. She straightened her back and froze her expression into one of haughty indifference. "Please return me to my mount, Captain," she commanded him coldly. She seemed to wait a long time for his response, so long that she began to be afraid he might not do as she asked, that he might run his hand over her breasts and kiss her, and then what would she do? Her breath grew ragged.

Abruptly, and with little tenderness, he gripped her about the waist and deposited her back onto her saddle. "Oh!" Her gown was twisted about her legs, exposing her stockings and the flesh of one thigh, her hair covered her eyes and hampered her movements. Flushed and cross, Rose adjusted her skirts more modestly, and then tossed her long dark hair over her shoulder. She shot him a glare. "I will not thank you, Captain."

He glared back at her, and then, as before, the storm cleared from his features as he regained his phenomenal control. "I do not want your thanks, lady," he replied evenly. "You know what it is I want."

Rose pretended not to hear him. Gunnar might have regained his control, but just now, as she gazed into his handsome face, she had felt as if she were close to losing hers. And although she was afraid of the consequences, aye, terribly afraid, she did not think that would be enough to stop.

Chapter 9

Miles de Vessey had finished viewing the body by the time Rose arrived, the mercenary captain close behind her. The only glimpse she had of it was of a tightly wrapped bundle. As she drew up her mare, Arno was already striding to her side. His face was grim and serious, but his eyes shifted from hers. "Lady . . . 'tis as I feared. The dead man was Lord Fitzmorton's messenger."

"Are you certain?" Even as she asked the question, Rose knew it was a forlorn hope.

Arno nodded. "Sir Miles recognized his sword scabbard." He glanced past her, and his expression hardened still more. "You'd do better to listen to me, lady, than the Viking. He is here for his six marks, he cannot advise you on what is best for you and Somerford Manor."

"No, Arno, he cannot," Rose retorted coldly. "That is something I must decide on my own, without interference from him or you!"

He took a step forward, and he looked so angry, for a moment she thought he would drag her from the horse. Arno! He had never looked at her like that before. Shocked, Rose lifted her hand as if to fend him off. At the same moment Gunnar spurred his horse forward, forcing it between Rose and Arno, placing himself as her shield.

Rose gasped, and as she was struggling to bring her frightened mare back under control, she heard Gunnar's two men draw their swords on her other side. Arno stumbled back, shock and anger fighting for supremacy on his face.

Miles de Vessey laughed. "Brawling over a woman, Gunnar?" he jeered softly.

Gunnar did not take his eyes from Arno. "Take care, d'Alan." His voice was as cold as it was deadly. "You forget yourself."

Arno's face was red with his fury, and he spluttered for words to express it. Evidently he could find none, for he shook his head and stomped away to a safer distance, presenting them with his back.

Rose took a shaken breath, lifting her chin a little more. "Thank you, Captain, but I can manage now."

Gunnar raised an eyebrow as if he doubted it, but nevertheless he moved back behind her, allowing her to resume command. The fact that he had done so was surprising in itself—Rose had found most men less than amenable when it came to being ordered about by a woman. But then Gunnar Olafson was *not* most men.

Miles de Vessey was still watching the exchange with interest, but now he seemed to tire of it. His voice came brisk and businesslike. "I want to take Gilbert's body back to Lord Fitzmorton, lady. He has a wife who cherished him and will wish him buried close to her."

Pity filled Rose for the woman. Thus far she had thought only of Harold and Millisent and Will—she had forgotten that the dead man, too, must have those who mourned him. He might have been willing to attack a young girl, but would his wife know that? Just as Rose's mother had been willfully blind to her father's twisted ways, so might this woman have closed her eyes to her man's dark core.

"Of course, Sir Miles," she said quietly. "Take his body with you, and tell her . . . I am sorry."

Miles bowed his thanks, though he looked a little surprised by the promptness of her reply. Perhaps, Rose thought, he was not used to having his requests granted so easily—Lord Fitzmorton, she had heard, was a hard master. Miles turned to give his orders, and the men from his troop set about preparing for the journey.

"Sir Arno?"

Her knight still stood some feet away, sulking. At her call he stiffened his shoulders, and Rose thought he might ignore her. But Arno was too loyal for that. With obvious unwillingness he turned, eyeing her under lowered brows, his arms folded. "Aye, lady?" he asked gruffly.

"Will you stay and see these men on their way?"

He nodded, his mouth twisted in what might have been a smile. The bitterness she had noticed before still clung to him, and there was a look in his brown eyes that spoke of self-contempt. Puzzled, Rose wondered why, and tried to recall what they had been speaking of before they were interrupted. Arno had mentioned seeking help from Radulf or . . . Fitzmorton? He had spoken strangely, though she had been too occupied with her own troubles to pay him much mind. But now she recalled how he had mentioned their time together in this year since Edric had died, and how Arno thought they might . . .

Her eyes widened.

Jesu, he was going to ask to marry me!

Arno was still watching her, and she wondered uncomfortably whether he was able to read her mind. If he could he showed no sign, simply nodding and murmuring in reply to her request, "Aye, lady, I will."

"Thank you, Sir Arno." Her voice sounded husky and unsteady. To her dismay, Rose realized she felt sorry for him, and it was more than likely he had seen the pity in her eyes. How an earth was this to be mended?

"Lord Fitzmorton will want to see justice done."

It was Miles de Vessey's clipped tones that had interrupted her confused thoughts. Slowly, Rose turned back to him, and found that he was watching her closely, his gray eyes without emotion. Was he merely stating a fact or, as sounded far more likely, issuing a thinly veiled threat? This man was more dangerous than Arno could ever be. Best she keep her wits about her and not be distracted by other matters.

"We all want to see justice done," she replied gently, and tried to ignore the fact she was so disheveled, her hair loose all about her like a serf's, that it must be difficult to believe she was a lady at all. She lifted her chin another notch.

"Sir Arno tells me you have captured the man who murdered poor Gilbert?"

Poor Gilbert! She hoped her face did not betray her thoughts. "It is not yet proven."

"He has confessed," Arno cut in swiftly, evidently

keen to impart the good news. His sideways glance to Rose told her that he was also keen to repay her for her treatment of him.

"Lord Fitzmorton will want to oversee the punishment himself," Miles announced in a commanding voice. "I will take the prisoner with me."

"No!" Rose heard her own fear, and hoped they would think it anger. She waited a moment to regain some measure of control over herself before she continued. "No, Sir Miles. This is my manor, and I will oversee any punishments meted out to my people. Reassure Lord Fitzmorton that justice under Norman law will be done."

"As you say, lady," Miles murmured with another bow, but he didn't appear to be pleased. Rose very much feared she had not seen or heard the last of Miles de Vessey.

She turned away, urging her mare back through the village, in the direction of the keep. She felt weary and sad and a little frightened, but she did not allow her back to slump or her head to bow. They—Arno and Miles de Vessey and his men—would be onto her like crows on carrion if she showed the slightest weakness.

Since Edric had died, she had fought hard to maintain her rightful position—and all the myriad difficulties that went with it—and she had fought to hold on to her power just now, when Miles and Arno would have stripped it from her as easily as a rabbit's skin. Aye, she had won this battle, but the victory was not so sweet—it was her right to preside over her manor court; just now Rose wondered if such a right were really worth fighting over. She was to sit in judgment on a good man like Harold the miller, and punish him for protecting what was his from someone who had meant him harm.

And there were still so many questions!

Why had the Norman, Gilbert, been in such a place at such a time? Had Harold mistaken the matter after all; had Gilbert been there to help? But Harold was no fool, and Millisent would not lie about such a thing. Mayhap the Norman had come upon the merefolk attacking the village and thought in the melee to take something that was not his? An opportunity gone very wrong.

Miles de Vessey or Arno could bully her all they liked, but Rose knew she could not judge Harold until she had the whole tale.

Gunnar was watching her profile as they rode. He had been watching her for some time, but she was oblivious to him, too caught up in her own thoughts. He was a man used to reading what went on in his opponents' minds, and he had no difficulty seeing the anxiety in the pallor of her skin, or the tension in the vertical lines between her brows.

He had done as she asked of him. He had sat behind her, waiting, listening as she fought for, and held, her ground against the likes of Miles and d'Alan. Refusing to let them bully her, answering their bluster with cool authority, and receiving their agreement as if it were her due.

She was an admirable woman, the sort of woman any warrior would be proud to have at his side. 'Twas unfortunate Gunnar was here to take her land from her and catch her out in treason.

If there is any treason.

The voice in his head did not surprise him. Gunnar

knew he had been doubting that she was a traitor since the first moment he saw her. As for Arno, aye, he was the kind of man to excuse himself any sort of evil, and then to be quick to blame others for his own weakness. But this woman . . . no, she was loved by her people and she loved them. Why would she give them up to Fitzmorton, knowing what would happen to them? She could not even bear to give up the wretched Harold!

He noticed that the lines between her brows had grown more pronounced—he wanted to smooth them away with his finger . . . or his tongue. Her hair, so thick and glossy dark, was long enough to curl against the saddle as she rode, covering her back and hips in a shining cloak. It looked heavy. He wanted to lift it off her neck with his hands, blow softly against the sweet flesh at her nape, press his lips to the tender places there.

Gunnar did not need to look down to know he was near to fully aroused, just from watching her, thinking about her, imagining what he would do to her if he had the chance. And the chance was coming. There was a heat between them that could not be doused by other than a passionate mating. She must know that as well as he.

"Lady Rose."

She started as if she had forgotten he was there. Slowly, reluctantly, she turned her head. Gunnar waited until their eyes had locked. Instantly she was aware of him—a flush rose under her skin, her breasts lifted and fell more quickly, her lips parted. Desire, need . . . she felt it, too. Gunnar wondered what she would do . . .

say, if he lifted her from her mare and lay down with her in the sweet summer grass. Would she protest? Or would she welcome the diversion, the chance to soothe the ache in her body? Would she open her arms and her legs, and take them both to Valhalla?

Maybe she could read his thoughts in his gaze, for she said, her voice low and husky, "There is no need for you to be here, Captain. Go back to Sir Arno and the others. I will ride on alone."

"You are paying me for protection and I will give it."

She waved a hand dismissively at his calm reply, as if she didn't care one way or another.

"You do not trust me, lady?"

Her gaze sharpened, she licked her lips. He watched the movement, could not help it. He wanted her to lick *his* lips. In a moment he would be beyond control—there was a fine sheen of sweat on his skin beneath his chain mail, and it wasn't because of the warmth of the sun.

The lady seemed to have been considering her words, for now she spoke in a blunt manner that signified absolute honesty. "Aye, Captain, I trust you. I think I must. I think I have no choice."

He searched her eyes. He had drawn his own answers from the morning's events, and added them to the various things he had seen and heard since he arrived at Somerford. There was a tale of deceit and treachery to be told there, and Gunnar was almost ready to tell it. Maybe Rose had found answers of her own, but were they the same as his? It was time, Gunnar decided, to find out.

"Sir Arno knows Fitzmorton," he said carefully. "He has had dealings with him. He knew Miles de Vessey just now—that he hadn't even bothered to ask his name was a careless mistake, but Miles is always arrogant."

Rose turned her face away, her hair falling over her cheek and shielding her from his gaze.

"Fitzmorton's man, Gilbert, was in the village the night of the attack," Gunnar continued. "I think it is Fitzmorton who is behind the attacks, not the merefolk. It has been made to look like it was the merefolk, but no one has ever seen them. Your villagers are already so full of suspicion that they just assumed. Sir Arno and Fitzmorton are in league. They thought to frighten you so much that you would be easily persuaded to hand over Somerford Manor to Arno, and then Arno would allow Fitzmorton to step in. He covets Lord Radulf's Crevitch estates, and if he had Somerford, he would have an advantage when it came to making war on Radulf."

"You are stabbing in the dark," she said weakly, and pushed her hair irritably back from her face. She looked flushed, angry, but her eyes slid nervously from his. "You don't know whether any of this is truth, Captain. You are spinning a tale."

Gunnar ignored her protests, she would naturally be angry and resentful to discover she had been duped. "When your husband died, you were expected to rely more heavily upon your knight—to give up your power to Arno, lady. Instead you held on to it. All this time he has waited and you have remained strong, and now he has given up trying to persuade you with words. Now he has begun to take action."

She was watching him like a rabbit watched a wolf, as if she expected him to draw his sword and strike her. He understood. He had just torn down her safe little world and left her bewildered and bereft. She must be feeling as if *he* were her destroyer, not Arno.

"Arno wouldn't hurt me," she insisted, her voice soft and breathless, her dark eyes wide. "I know he wouldn't hurt me."

He narrowed his gaze. "Why? Because he lusts after you? Have you given him what he wants, lady?"

Angry color flared in her pale cheeks, fire burned in her eyes. "You forget yourself, Captain," she said.

Jubilation swelled inside him. She and Arno were not lovers; they never had been. She was an innocent when it came to need, to desire, to the hot ache that drew men and women together. The widow of an old man, she had much to learn, and Gunnar exulted that he alone would teach her.

But now he smiled without any trace of humor, his feelings hidden. "If you have denied him in the bedchamber, too, then he will have grown to hate you. The black and bitter hatred men ache with when they want a woman who does not want them. Has he asked to wed you?"

She glared back at him, but unlike Arno or Miles he was unmoved. Abruptly Rose lost the will to fight him. Was he right? She was heartsick at the thought of it. He had been there for such a short time and already he was turning her safe, comfortable world upside down.

But Arno was Edric's trusted friend!

"Lady, does he want to wed you?"

She couldn't meet his eyes. "He may have done. He has been . . . strange. I think, just now in the village, before you came, he meant to do so. That was why he was so angry when you interrupted him. I fear he thinks you . . . he believes you . . . I . . ."

She did not want to finish the words, but after all it was not necessary. He understood, she realized, casting him a quick glance. He was grinning at her in a way that set her heart bumping about in her chest like a landed fish. How was it possible for a man to be so mesmerizingly handsome? Aye, his mouth was curved up at the corners, his blue eyes gleamed, but it was just a *smile*. Jesu, just a smile! Was she as weak and foolish as her mother, to allow herself to be so affected by a man's smile?

"Please yourself, Captain," Rose said petulantly, tossing her head, disguising her reaction as best she could. "Come with me or stay here, but I am returning to Somerford Keep." And she turned her horse and galloped off, as if she were intent on outrunning him. Did she hope he'd stay or follow? Rose didn't know, but she needed the sanctuary of her keep and the mindless familiarity of the tasks that awaited her.

Gunnar grinned and kicked his gray horse into pursuit, being sure to remain just behind her. Now was not the time for pressure or argument. She was suffering, and she was afraid. She had no one to trust but him, and he was a stranger, a mercenary who did as he was paid. He could not blame her for being suspicious. So he rode behind her all the way to the keep, watching her straight back and the sway of her hips beneath all that dark hair, and pretending not to mind what her innocence of treason would mean to him.

He would lose the chance to have Somerford Manor.

Gunnar looked about him, at the countryside he had

begun to consider his own. The golden harvest was ripening swiftly now, almost bursting from the fields, and the soil was well cherished and rich. This was Lady Rose's doing, he knew that now. She was one of those rare women who understood the earth. Who was willing to be still and silent long enough to hear its soft murmur. She grasped the importance of allowing her people enough time to tend their own crops and beasts, instead of working them to death in the service of her own wealth and glory. And they loved her for it.

She even worked alongside them, when it was necessary.

He pictured her, dark hair bound up on her head, her hem kilted about her smooth legs, bending her straight back as she tilled the soil. A smile tugged at his stern mouth, but he held it back. If he was master here, she would not need to do the work of a peasant. He would do it for her, gladly.

The amusement died, and now he had no urge to smile. Aye, he would be willing to work like a beast in the fields for her, if she would take him to her bed for a single night.

May all his father's pagan gods help him.

Alfred stood in the alcove near the fireplace. He knew he should be elsewhere—there was work to be done—but he could not seem to pull himself away from her. Millisent. Her red-brown hair was plaited and hung in a long rope over her shoulder, while her too-large gown of homespun was girdled in bulky folds about her small waist. She looked younger, alone and woebegone, as she sat on one of the stools, a length of cloth in her hand. Supposedly she was mending a rent in the castle bed linen, but in fact she did nothing but sit and stare. At nothing.

An old woman sat beside her, crooning to a spotted piglet in a willow basket, but the girl took no notice of her. She was too deep in her own thoughts.

Alfred wondered if it were possible to fall in love in a single instant. A single breath. For that was all it had taken. The swing of a sword, the blink of an eye. He had seen the girl, hurt and afraid, by the burned cottage, and suddenly the urge to comfort had overwhelmed him—the need to help another, which he had thought vanished from his heart. For too long he had felt sorry for himself—there had been the losing of his family, and then the ruin of his face, bad enough *now* with its puckered scar, but before . . . Children had run screaming from him, and grown men had held up their hands to shield their eyes.

And now here was someone who needed *him*, who had turned to *him* without a second thought. He had felt his own pain melt like frost in the sun.

There was more to it than that, of course. The burnished color of her hair in the firelight, the soft feel of her skin against his hand, the soothing murmur of her voice, her courage in the face of such adversity. All these things combined to make his heart sing whenever he saw her, and for a moment he would forget what he looked like. He was able to pretend he was just the same as everyone else.

Alfred stood in the alcove by the fireplace and watched Millisent, knowing she was presently unaware of him, too caught up in her own travails to recognize his feelings for her. Or to want them. But he was ready;

the next time she wanted him he would be there. And as long as she needed his strength he would give it. Soon, he knew, she would blink and wake up, and see him as he really was.

Alfred did not expect forever; he was grateful for just one more day.

Rose tried to close her eyes, but the darkness was not soothing to her. The stillness of the solar was not a balm. Instead of gentle, rocking sleep, she saw again Millisent's face, when she had told the young girl what Miles de Vessey had said. Pain had etched lines about a mouth still soft and young, and Millisent had cried out in her agony.

"Oh please, please, do not punish my father! He meant only to save me! You cannot punish him for that?"

Rose had felt the tears in her eyes. "If 'tis so, Millisent, he must plead mercy. I will listen. The law will not punish an innocent man . . ."

"The Norman law?" the girl had retorted, forgetting herself in her despair. "My father has killed a Norman; how can any Norman justice be fair?"

Rose tossed and turned in her bed, the girl's desperate voice ringing in her head. Millisent had been right; what could Rose reply that was not a platitude or a lie? Harold had killed a Norman, and Lord Fitzmorton would not believe—did not care—that Gilbert had been involved in something reprehensible. He believed the murderer must be punished, or else chaos would reign in the land.

Mayhap it amused him to cause Rose as much trouble as he could. For old time's sake.

She felt so alone! And now she could not even trust Arno, because she had begun to wonder whether he was in league with Lord Fitzmorton—unthinkable, and yet the seed of doubt that Gunnar had planted was growing. If she told Arno she had no intention of ordering Harold to be hanged, what would he do? Tell Fitzmorton's man, Miles de Vessey? And then Miles would come to Somerford and enforce Fitzmorton's kind of justice. She dared not give them cause to do that. Rose knew she must now tread very carefully indeed.

Distraught as she was, Millisent must have seen in her lady's eyes that Rose was as helpless as Millisent herself when it came to the question of Harold's punishment. The girl had turned and run sobbing from the hall. Rose had felt so wretched, she had even contemplated turning to Brother Mark for advice. But one glance into his cold eyes, and she had thought better of it. Brother Mark would tell her she must listen to the advice of the men about her—Arno in particular—to bow to their will. Men, he would tell her, were rational creatures, whereas women were irrational and emotional beings and required a steady male hand.

Even Constance was not available to listen to her fears, and inform her, "I told you 'twas so," in a gloating voice. Constance was too busy with the villagers, and had nodded off to sleep over her meal in the great hall. Rose had put aside her own urgent need to talk, and had ordered the old woman to bed.

The night felt airless, so still. Heavy cloud covered the stars, trapping warmth close to the earth, bringing the humid promise of rain. Her edginess increased. Much had happened today, most of it bad. And yet . . . she remembered the look in Gunnar Olafson's eyes with a tightening low in her belly. He wanted her. She could not mistake such a thing, surely? Or was it a trick he played on all women, making them think he desired them? How could she trust him, believe him?

Restlessly, Rose turned again, gazing at the narrow dark shape of her window. She had opened the shutters earlier, hoping for a breath of air. Now lightning flickered, startling her into sitting up. Wearily, she climbed out of her bed, pulling a robe about her naked shoulders, tossing back the long braid of her hair as she leaned on the sill.

The air beyond the window seemed cooler, but not much. A light breeze teased her hot skin and molded the thin cloth of her robe against her body. She felt a stirring inside her, a tremor that increased her unease. Lightning came again, illuminating the Mere and its islands. Burrow Mump loomed up in silent reminder of all she longed for and could not have. Rose knew she should be worried for the harvest—storms could flatten the crops—but what could she do? Order Gunnar Olafson to ride out there with his men, and shield the wheat with their outstretched arms?

Rose smiled as she imagined them standing in the fields like big, nightmarish scarecrows. Then memories of the day returned to haunt her, and her smile faded. It was true she could do little about dead Gilbert and the threat of Lord Fitzmorton's justice, or about the coming storm. But she *could* offer some comfort to Millisent. Mayhap the girl was still awake, mayhap they could talk . . .

Rose knew then that she would never allow Harold to hang. The solution was simple after all. She would go to Lord Radulf and lay all before him. He would probably remove her from Somerford Manor forthwith—send her back to her father and all that that meant—but at least she would have saved Harold's life, for Rose was certain Radulf would not hang Harold for what he had done. Not when he learned that Fitzmorton was involved.

Aye, tomorrow she would send word to Lord Radulf, throw herself upon his mercy, and pray that Lady Lily eased his anger.

Silently, Rose slipped from her solar and began her journey down the stairs, determined to offer this comfort to Millisent. One of the torches on the wall flared up against the darkness, making the shadows jump and jiggle. She pressed her hand to the cold, familiar stones as she made her way carefully downward to the great hall, where Millisent slept behind a curtain with Will and Eartha and her little son.

So intent was Rose upon the curving, uneven steps, she did not see him until she was almost upon him.

He was standing directly before her. A huge dark shape that came up out of the blackness so suddenly her heart leaped in her breast. She opened her mouth to cry out in fear and surprise. No sound came forth, frightening her even more. She turned to flee, her thin robe tangling about her legs. But he caught her easily, gripping her arm and swinging her in a dizzying arc. Rose collided with an extremely large and hard chest, and then a pair of big, muscular arms closed about her. It was like being in a warm, dark cave of male flesh.

Rose opened her mouth, drawing in breath.

"Do not scream, lady." Gunnar Olafson's warning voice was soft and deep, part of the warm night.

Rose doubted whether she could have screamed, for

he was holding her so tight. Her heart was knocking inside her, fast and shallow, while, against her cheek, his heartbeat was solid and sure. *I should be afraid. He is a stranger, a violent man who hires out death for coin. I should be frightened of him.*

But she was not.

This trembling in her body was not fear. This softening of breasts and thighs was not fright. Her fingers, trapped against his chest, crept upward, testing the soft linen cloth of his shirt, feeling their way over the hard muscles beneath. She turned her head a little, and found her nose pressed to bare flesh, where the laces at his throat were untied. Briefly, she felt giddy, like a child playing a spinning game, and then she pressed her palms to that solid wall of muscle and gave a sharp push.

"Release me, Captain."

Not surprisingly, he didn't move an inch. " 'Tis not safe to be outside your chamber at night, lady."

"This is my keep!" she retorted, pushing again without success. "My home. I am safe here."

He drew her even closer, stilling her struggling with ease. His mocking breath stirred her hair, whispering in her ear. "Are you?"

Was she? Now that she no longer knew whether Arno was friend or foe, was she really safe? And what of the mercenaries? They had sworn to protect her, and she had believed it . . . until now.

"What do *you* here?" she asked sharply, leaning her head back to try and see him in the darkness. The torch farther up the stairs flared in the draft from her open solar door, and the flame seemed to catch in his eyes. He was smiling, but it was not the sort of smile to relieve her anxiety.

"I do not sleep well."

"If your bed is uncomfortable, Captain, you should ask for another," she replied with studied coolness. "Unless it is your conscience that keeps you from sleep." A man like this must have many heavy matters on his conscience, death and blood and betrayal.

He laughed softly, untouched by her gibe. " 'Tis not my conscience keeps me from sleep, my lady. Will I show you what keeps me from my bed?"

She opened her mouth to demand a proper answer, and realized his hands were moving down her back, deftly following her soft curves. With a gasp Rose pressed closer, trying to escape him, but the movement only melded her body more firmly against his. Whichever way she turned, there was no escape. He was everywhere.

Briefly he paused, spanning her narrow waist, and then his chest expanded on a deep, silent breath as if he had come to some decision, and he cupped her buttocks in his big hands, and drew her up firmly against him. The hard, unyielding ridge of his manhood answered her question.

" 'Tis you," he murmured, his lips hot against her temple and traveling down. "I want you."

"No." She sounded weak, a feeble thing. Her voice, her muscles, her will . . . all seemed to have been suddenly sapped of their strength.

He nuzzled at her cheek, tasting her, his unshaven jaw abrading her, his narrow braids tickling her skin. Inside, her heart began thudding anew, while outside her skin grew hot, burning wherever he touched her. His mouth had reached hers, almost but not quite meeting, so close that she could feel him, all but taste him.

Gunnar leaned down and oh-so-gently, sucked on her lower lip.

She melted.

"No?" he mocked, his breath hot in her mouth. His hand was sliding up between their bodies, searching for the opening in her robe. His fingers delved and found, slipping inside the thin cloth. The callused tips felt rough against her soft flesh, and so warm. His palm was hard from many years of fighting others' battles, but she could not think of that. Not now, not now . . . His hand closed over her breast and she knew she must have found heaven.

"Lady, this doesn't feel like 'no.' "

Like the traitor it was, her body responded. Her nipple beaded into his palm, her flesh aching and swelling. He began to rub gently, back and forth, and she gave a soft groan. Rose felt him smile against her lips.

And then, abruptly, he spun her around, making her cry out in surprise. The outer stone wall of the stairwell was against her back, cold against her heat. He placed himself a step below her, his body leaning heavily into hers. The glow of the torch reached them more easily now, like fire in his hair, although with his head bowed his face was in shadow. But he could see her, and he looked long, perusing the dazed glow in her eyes, the pink flush in her cheeks, the tremble of desire in her lips.

"I think you want to say aye, lady. Your body tells me aye."

He bent and took her mouth with a savage, controlled thoroughness, stealing from her any last chance she had of denying him the truth. She did want him, oh so much, so much. It was as if all her life had been building up to this moment, with Gunnar Olafson, on the cold, dark stairs in Somerford Keep.

Her arms came up, her hands clinging to his shoulders. He brought his thigh up between hers, pressing inexorably against her soft, swollen female flesh. The pleasure was undeniable, and nearly unbearable. Rose went rigid. He lifted his mouth from hers and smiled into her eyes, his handsome face hard with his own desire.

"Tell me you want me," he said, an order, as if she were one of his mercenary troop.

But Rose shook her head in denial, as if she weren't all but lying in his arms, her robe open to the touch of his hands, her mouth swollen from his kisses.

He laughed, as well he might. He lowered his head and began to suck on her breasts, finding the nipples, his tongue doing things she had never even dreamed of. The sensation was exquisite. Quite unable to prevent herself, Rose arched against him, catching at his hair, tangling her fingers in the smooth strands. Her legs trembled so much she rested her weight on his intruding thigh. A dark, voluptuous rapture spiraled through her as her most sensitive flesh rubbed on hard muscle. She moved a little against him, to ease the unbearable ache between her thighs. And made it worse.

"Gunnar, please," she managed, her throat dry and tight, her body trembling as though she were chilled and not burning hot.

When he removed his thigh she made an instinctive sound of protest, but he was only shifting her, lifting her, his hand opening her robe until she was bare to his touch from neck to toes. His fingers drifted down over her belly, combing through the dark hair at the juncture of her thighs, and slid into the hot moist core of her.

Shocked, startled, Rose pushed against him, just as he rubbed his thumb against that swollen, wanton part of her. A blazing jolt of excitement rippled through her. She groaned and felt his fingers work their magic again, opening her still further to his touch. No man had ever looked upon her like this before; no man had held her captive with the power in his hand.

"I can give you pleasure, lady," her Viking savage whispered teasingly in her ear. "Let me show you."

"Gunnar, I don't . . ."

"You do, Rose, you do."

"But this is not . . ."

He rested his brow against hers and sighed. He was shaking, she realized suddenly. And he was burning up. It wasn't just she who was affected by this violent storm of desire. He, too, was as caught up in its toils. Somehow, knowing that made her feel less his slave and more his equal. Made everything all right.

"You will feel better . . . after," he promised her. "You will be able to sleep."

"And will you, too, be able to sleep?" Her voice was breathless, husky, sensual.

He laughed as if he were in pain. "Don't think about me, my Rose. This is for you. All for you."

"To sleep would be nice," she began cautiously. "But do you not think Constance's mulled wine would do just as well?"

His thumb moved again, gently, subtly, teasing her aching flesh. Despite herself, Rose moaned deep in her throat, following his movements, allowing him freedoms such as she would never have believed herself capable of an hour ago.

"No," Gunnar told her with clear certainty, "I don't."

Again that subtle shifting, and the throbbing between her legs was raised to a new level. One finger, two, slid inside her, stretching her, making her long to clench her body about him, hold him close, while his thumb did such things . . .

Could this be right? Rose asked herself feverishly. Was it possible to feel like this? Her legs were trembling so badly she was resting entirely on his hand, while her arms clung about his neck, afraid if she let go she would fall down. His mouth was on hers again, his tongue tasting her, thrusting into her, tangling with hers. She was moving of her own accord now, rubbing herself against him, unable to help herself, unable to stop herself.

Never before, never before, the voice whispered in her head.

Never before had it been like this.

Outside the keep, thunder rolled, the humidity increasing, but the storm just seemed part of the waking dream Rose now found herself in. And then it happened, a wild uncontrollable clashing of her senses, a tempest inside her as well as out. Rose cried out, a hoarse gasping cry, feeling her body turn as warm and liquid as Constance's mulled wine. As she fell, he caught her in his arms, holding her hard against him, covering her mouth in a kiss to muffle the sound, and then smoothing the loose wisps of hair back from her face with a tenderness she was too dazed to recognize.

Just for a moment he was her dream, her ghostly warrior, who had finally found her and made her his.

And then he laughed, and spoiled it all.

Rose felt a chill. Had he laughed because he was pleased? Because he had made her into nothing more than another lustful woman, unable to resist his handsome face and hard kisses? Fodder for Gunnar Olafson, and his own high opinion of himself! Aye, she thought blankly, that must be it.

She should be angry. Mayhap in the morning she would be, but suddenly Rose just felt very tired. He was right in that, at least—she wanted only to sleep, and this time she knew she would.

"Let me go," she whispered, a catch in her voice, and pressed her palms once more against his chest.

Gunnar went very still; he must have sensed the change in her. He searched her face in the dim torchlight as if he were trying to see inside her. "I did not hurt you?" he asked sharply, and she realized with surprise that the thought that he might have caused her pain worried him.

Confused, Rose shook her head, and embarrassment came to join the maelstrom of emotions already battering her. To be speaking to a man she hardly knew about matters so personal, so private, was beyond awkward.

"I gave you pleasure?"

For such a confident man, he sounded oddly uncertain, even vulnerable. Surprised, Rose forgot her raw feelings as she met his gaze. There was a hot glitter in his blue eyes; aye, she did not need the bulge in his breeches to tell her he was still very much aroused. He had given her pleasure, but he had taken none for himself.

"Aye," she said, "you did."

He smiled, that dazzlingly beautiful smile. She almost reached out and touched him then. Until she realized that if she did, he would follow her up the stairs to her chamber.

Was she ready for what would happen after that?

Rose had hesitated too long, and doubts swooped in. He was a stranger, a paid mercenary. Aye, he was handsome and she had found ecstasy in his arms just now, but it was not safe to allow a man to take control of you in such a way. 'Twas true this was only lust, but it seemed that even lust had its dangers.

He knew. His face was shuttered, his desire under control again. "Go back to your bed, Rose," he told her softly. "I will be here. I swore to protect you, and so I shall."

Rose licked suddenly dry lips. His control slipped, and he watched the movement with such avidness it frightened her, and yet thrilled her, too. On one level she might have submitted to him, allowed him to teach her some of the pleasures a man could give to a woman, but she had lost nothing by it. Mayhap she had even gained.

She wanted him, but he wanted her, too. And because he was Gunnar Olafson he had given her the power to say him aye or nay, and that was a mighty power indeed.

Catching up her robe, feeling like dancing, Rose fled back up the stairs to safety. And sleep without dreams.

Chapter 10

The warmth of dawn was softening the harsh lines of Somerford Keep and raising white mist upon the surface of the Mere, when Gunnar Olafson found his bed at last.

He lay down and closed his eyes, trying to sleep, but she was still there, as she had been since last night when he held her in his arms. Rose, stepping down the stairs with the torchlight behind her, her pale, glorious body clearly visible through the thin stuff of her robe, her eyes dark and secret. Rose, flushed and feverish, wild with the pleasure he was giving her. *Gunnar, please* . . . Why was it, when he remembered those words, he felt an ache in his chest that was every bit equal to that between his thighs?

He groaned and turned on his side. He had been hard for so long he'd forgotten what it was like to have release. Maybe he was damaged in some way . . . It didn't matter. He wanted her, more than he had ever wanted any woman before, and last night had been worth the pain he was suffering now.

"Gunnar?"

This voice was deep and gruff, as different from Rose's as it could be. Gunnar kept his eyes closed. He felt Ivo lean over him, and then a sharp blow to his shoulder with a fist. Gunnar's eyes opened unwillingly, and he squinted up at his friend.

Ivo looked as if he had been running his hands through his black hair. It was in wild disarray. His eyes were just as black and wild in a face ravaged by emotion.

"You have heard about Miles, then," said Gunnar warily.

"Sweyn told me. It would have been better if I had heard it from you, *Captain*."

Gunnar sat up and faced his angry friend as calmly as he could manage with his body aching from very little sleep. He had known Ivo too long to believe he would really throttle him, despite the barely controlled savagery that seemed to envelop him. Ivo might be fierce and intemperate, but he would never murder a friend.

"Miles is Fitzmorton's man. He came seeking the dead Norman, and has now given him a name—Gilbert. Lady Rose sent him off with the body, but I fear he will be back. Fitzmorton wants Somerford, Ivo, that is what this is all about, and Miles will get it for him."

Gunnar remembered Fitzmorton's handsome face, lined with discontent, the hour he had spent in his company. Gunnar had been playing a part, on Radulf's say so, but Fitzmorton didn't know that.

"You are good at obeying orders, Viking?"

"If the rewards are adequate, my lord."

"Oh they will be, they will be. I have had a request from Somerford Manor for mercenaries." He held up the letter Radulf had allowed to be delivered. "They are having problems. Do you think you are the man to solve them?"

"A sword will solve most problems, my lord. But I thought Somerford Manor belonged to Lord Radulf."

Fitzmorton had laughed. "Did you? Radulf might have might and the king's ear on his side, but I have blood, Captain Olafson. My own flesh and blood."

Ivo was staring at him, his face contorted. And then he rubbed his hands roughly across his skin—the dark stubble grated. When Gunnar had first come across Ivo, he had had a black beard as wild as his hair. A truly frightening and fearsome sight. Now he was just fearsome.

"He was in the north. Why has he come here now?"

"I don't know, Ivo."

"Will he turn Fitzmorton against us?"

"He will try."

"And d'Alan?"

Gunnar rubbed his shoulder, still aching from Ivo's blow. "Arno d'Alan spoke to me tonight after the meal. Miles had told him not to trust me so I told him it was Miles who was not to be trusted."

Ivo grunted. "So we keep on with our mission?"

"Aye, for now. Just stay out of Miles's way."

"Why does he always reappear like this, just when I think I am free of him?" There was true anguish in Ivo's voice, a depth of despair almost beyond Gunnar's understanding. Gunnar had lost friends in battle, he had seen things that would make other men curl up and ask to die, but he had not watched a beloved sister destroyed in the hands of evil. Such a memory was Ivo's burden—his sister's death at the hands of Sir Miles, his half-brother.

"Maybe," he suggested softly, "you will never be free of him, until you finish with him."

Ivo's dark eyes were reddened with lack of sleep, and maybe more than that. He held up his gloved hand—the deformity was not evident through the leather, but Gunnar had seen the missing fingers. "Until I kill him, do you mean? I tried once, remember? Miles is my brother, my own flesh and blood! I hate him, Gunnar, but he is my brother."

Lord Fitzmorton had said that—*flesh and blood.* It had not made sense; it still did not.

Gunnar had never had a brother, but he understood the ties and bonds of family. Even hate could be a bond.

Ivo looked away, his mouth a thin, tight line.

Gunnar pretended to stretch and yawn. "Miles might not come back. Fitzmorton might send him north again." He shrugged, "I am not always right, my friend."

Ivo managed a faint smile. "Neither are you always so modest." His eyes narrowed, as if something had suddenly occurred to him. "Where were you? I waited for hours. Have you found a woman? Of course." He shook his head in resignation, his wild hair dancing about it like a black halo. "Gunnar Olafson always has a woman in his bed, wherever he goes. If you were in hell, my friend, an angel or two would follow you down."

Gunnar managed a laugh. "Not this time. I was keeping watch on Lady Rose. She is in danger, Ivo. Her knight is untrustworthy, and now she knows it."

"But are they not lovers?"

Gunnar kept his face smooth and expressionless, but there must have been something in his eyes to give him away. As Ivo's pale face broadened into a wide smile, transforming his fierce features, Gunnar cursed himself for a fool.

"You *do* want her for yourself. And you are jealous of every other man on Somerford Manor. Ah, Gunnar, take her body if you must, but do not seek to own her every word, her every look. You will go mad."

Gunnar lay back down and closed his eyes. "You do not understand," he said coldly. "She is not what you think. She is an honest woman caught in an intolerable situation. I must save her, Ivo."

Ivo took a moment to think this over. "I do not doubt you will save her, Gunnar—if anyone can, it is you. But if you rescue the lady, you will lose the land."

"Why would I want land?" he mumbled, closing his eyes again. "We still have the whole of Wales to subdue, my friend . . ."

Ivo laughed softly, and then his voice grew serious again. "Be careful. Men have been blinded before when it comes to the woman they lust after. Is she really what you think her, Gunnar, or has your desire turned you into a fool?"

But Gunnar kept his eyes closed, pretending to be asleep. After a pause Ivo returned to his own bed, settling noisily for a few moments of rest before they were all due to rise.

Gunnar knew well enough he would lose the land,

but then it had never truly been his. It had always belonged to Rose, and now that he knew what she was, he could not see himself stealing it from her and being able to live with himself.

When she had asked him last night whether his conscience kept him awake at night, he had not told her the truth. It did. Not because of the men he had killed and the blood he had spilled, but because he knew in despair that he could not have what he dearly wanted. A haven, land for himself and his men, a chance to put his skills to a use other than killing for coin. He would have been a good lord, but now he could not take Somerford without losing his honor. And what would he be without that? He would be like Miles de Vessey and Lord Fitzmorton—men without souls.

Honor is all very well, Gunnar, but can you touch honor? Can you eat it and drink it? Can you ease yourself upon it at night?

The voice was his mother's, but it was gentle, understanding, accepting. Gudren knew her only son too well.

"I am an old woman," she had informed him, her pale eyes all but closed in the smoky room at Crevitch. "I have had five children, but only one lived beyond the birthing. You are all I have, Gunnar. I need grandchildren, my son. And you need a wife. You will grow bitter and nasty, like Forkbeard. You do not want that, Gunnar, do you?"

As Forkbeard was his mother's worst-tempered billy goat, Gunnar had assured her that he did not. "But wives do not like their husbands going away to fight and not coming home for months, sometimes years," he had reminded her. "What wife would put up with that, my mother?"

"Have you tried asking?" she had retorted, half smiling.

"I know the answer already."

"Then if you have not tried, you have not met the woman you want to ask."

"You are a maze, Mother, and I cannot find my way to the point you make."

Gudren had laughed and hugged her big son, and pride and love, mingled with exasperation, shone in her eyes.

Gunnar wondered what she would think of him now, if she knew that he hungered after a Norman lady. A lady whom Radulf believed treacherous, a lady whose land he could be master of, if he proved her so. And then he wondered what Rose would do, if he asked her to wait for him while he went off fighting—for weeks, months, and maybe even years. Would she laugh in disbelief, or turn her back on him in disgust?

Gunnar rolled over again on his thin mattress, and knew Ivo was right. He was a fool.

Rose squeezed her fingers hard against the carvings on the armrest of her chair. The lord's chair, the Somerford chair. The serpents and twining vines, the little mocking faces and strange animals, they seemed to grow warm and come to life beneath her touch. Her head ached but she did not believe that anyone watching her would know that. She had on her cold and regal face, as she sat on the dais in the great hall, sat on the chair that had resided there at Somerford in stone keep and timber hall, and long before anyone could remember.

The meal was not sumptuous. Food stocks were low. If it were not that one of the mercenaries—Ivo, the big, dark one with the gauntlet—had had a successful hunting foray into the woods, they would have been dining tonight on salted fish. However, the lack did not appear to upset Brother Mark, who tucked into his meal, grease to his elbows, making noises Rose thought were made only by pigs.

"I did not think priests ate like beasts," she said, and delicately sipped at her wine.

He looked up at her warily, dislike in his eyes. "I see no harm in enjoying my food," he announced, licking his fingers.

"No, Brother, and nor is there," called Arno from Rose's other side. "Lady Rose is out of sorts and vents her spleen on others."

"Shall I pray for you, lady?" Brother Mark asked slyly.

Rose forced back her anger. "I thank you, Brother Mark, but there are others more in need of your prayers, I am sure."

Arno snorted laughter in a way designed to hurt her, while Brother Mark smirked and fell silent. Rose sipped her wine and ignored them both. Since yesterday, in the village, Arno's friendship and loyalty had turned to hate—or at least, that was how it felt. It was as if he wanted to make her miserable, mayhap as miserable as himself.

Rose wished now that she had sent a messenger to Lord Radulf, as she had planned to last night. But somehow, this morning, everything had appeared brighter and she had reestablished her confidence in her own ability to unravel this mess. No, no, she had thought, she would not throw herself upon Radulf's mercy. That way lay the repossession of her lands. Instead she would hold her manor court and clear Harold of blame, and then if Lord Fitzmorton's man dared question her judgment, she would send him off with a pithy but ladylike speech about honor and decency.

She must have been light-headed. She knew now that it was madness to believe she could drive off a man like Miles de Vessey with a few well chosen words. And what of Fitzmorton himself? She shivered. He was not some beardless boy who would simply stand and allow her to castigate him. He was a vicious and warlike baron, and one who was more likely to slam his fist into her face than listen to her carefully prepared speech.

Surely she knew that better than anybody?

It was all the fault of the mercenary, of Gunnar Olafson. He had made her as dizzy as a summer bee. He had made her believe the impossible was possible.

Rose was very aware of him, seated beyond Arno. Not once had she looked directly at him, and yet she knew that he wore a brown tunic over a white linen shirt, washed thin with age, and that both fit him very well. She had not looked at him, because she did not think she could meet his eyes without her face catching fire. The memory of last night had burned into her like a brand; she had been reliving those hot, sweet moments over and over again throughout the long day.

And he would know it if he gazed into her eyes.

Rose sipped her wine again, watching as her people ate. The women were as fascinated as ever with Gunnar Olafson. Eartha had already been to fill his goblet, and several of the other serving girls had arrived to make certain only the finest morsels were on his plate. As if he couldn't do such things very well for himself!

Mayhap, incredible as it seemed, she was jealous.

She wanted Gunnar Olafson for herself.

And the awful thing was, how did she know for certain that he had not done the same to any one of them as he had done to her? She would be foolish indeed to think she was different in his eyes from any of the other women in this hall. The men Rose had known best, her father and brother, would not let the fact that she was a Norman lady bother them, or influence their actions. A woman was a woman, and a man did not care what was in her head or in her heart, only what was between her legs.

Her mother had come to believe that, just before she died. She had warned Rose again and again, full of remorse for her own blind actions, hoping her daughter could steer a safer course. Those had been days of bittersweet reconciliation between mother and daughter, and her death had been all the more unbearable because of it.

Remembering now those terrible times, Rose asked herself how she could be such a simpleton as to believe a word Gunnar told her. With such a warning as her mother's misery before her, why had she allowed him to hold her in his arms like a lit candle in the darkness of the stairwell? And why had she been remembering it ever since?

"Lady?" Arno was staring at her curiously. Rose realized he had spoken to her several times and she had not heard him once. Now that he had her attention, Arno nodded into the body of the hall.

Following his direction, Rose saw that Edward was walking toward her, his old face beaming. People moved aside to allow him passage, their voices drifting to an uneasy silence. Behind Edward was another, younger man, and he was wearing Lord Radulf's colors.

Dizziness swept over her, dimming her vision, making her skin prickle.

Lord Radulf has come to take Somerford from me.

And then, far worse, *Lord Radulf has sent word that the Lady Lily is dead.*

But, if that were so, why was Edward smiling as if King Alfred had returned from the Mere to lead the English once more to victory?

"Lady Rose, it be good news!" Edward cried, and then flushed at the loudness of his own voice in the hush. He turned to the other man, jabbing at him with his bony elbow. "Tell them then, Steven, tell them!"

The man—he was only just old enough to be graced with that title—stepped forward with a smile as broad as Edward's. He was dust-stained from travel, and his brown hair was darkened with sweat. He had ridden swiftly to Somerford, and it was clear he bore only *good* tidings.

"Lady Rose, I have come bearing news of Lady Lily. She has been delivered of a fine son, an heir for Lord Radulf!"

The hall resounded to loud cheers, mingled with the drumming of heels on the floor and the slamming of palms on the trestle tables. Not everyone at Somerford was particularly fond of Lord Radulf, but they all admired his lady—besides, good news had been sparse of late.

Rose patiently allowed her people to show their pleasure, before holding up a slender hand to quiet them. The noise dropped away, and all was hushed once more. "This is wonderful!" she told Steven, her voice ringing with genuine relief and pleasure. "We will all give thanks that Lady Lily has been safely delivered of a son and heir. Lord Radulf must be mightily relieved."

"Aye, lady, so he is." Steven grimaced. "And so are we all at Crevitch, for he has been raging about for weeks, consumed with worry."

Rose smiled. "Then I am doubly glad for your sake, Steven."

Whatever she feared for herself from that mighty baron, she knew full well that he loved his wife, and treasured her beyond all else. Such marriages were rare and precious in King William's England. An uncharacteristic spike of jealousy tore at her, and Rose was ashamed of herself. From what she knew of Lily, that lady richly deserved her good fortune. Had Rose really expected to find similar happiness to that of Lily and Radulf? She had never sought it, preferring to keep such dangerous emotion at a distance. Love was like the toss of a dice, too unpredictable to take a wager on.

"Lord Radulf commands all of his vassals, and all of their people, to give thanks and celebrate his good fortune."

"There is no need to command," Rose declared, raising her goblet. "To Lord Radulf and Lady Lily, and the heir to Crevitch!"

The toast was repeated throughout the great hall, and drinks were duly raised and drunk.

'Twas a relief to hear good news among all the bad, thought Rose once more. She glanced about her, and noticed that Arno was staring sullenly into his goblet. Her elation evaporated—it must be true, then. Arno was Fitzmorton's man, and Fitzmorton coveted Somerford Manor. It appeared she now had no choice. Her situation was dangerous indeed. Before Steven left she would write him a message to take back with him to

Crevitch. A request for help, and a plea for understanding. Perhaps, in his moment of great joy, Radulf would see fit to forgive her her lack of honesty and come to her aid. Mayhap he would not take Somerford from her, a weak woman, and hand it over to one of the strong and violent men who held difficult stretches of this country. Someone who would keep Fitzmorton on his side of the border, and treat her people abominably . . .

The messenger, Steven, was still standing before her, a goblet in his hand, but he was looking further along the table. With a jolt Rose wondered whether he might have taken note of Arno's less than exuberant face and be preparing to report it back to his lord. But it wasn't Arno he was staring at. It was Gunnar Olafson.

Even as Rose turned in his direction, they were breaking eye contact, pretending their attention was elsewhere. But not before she had seen Gunnar nod his head, just the barest of movements, and noted Steven's half grimace in reply. It happened so swiftly she might have imagined it . . . but she hadn't.

They knew each other.

She dared not begin to consider what that might mean. There were too many other problems consuming her. Later, she would think of it later, when she was alone in her solar.

"You must eat and drink, too, Steven." Constance's voice, full of innuendo, broke in on Rose's silence. "I do not think this will be our last celebration—Lord Radulf is a virile man. His lady will have many children."

"Is that a prediction, old witch?" Arno sneered. He was drunk, but not so drunk as the night of the attack, and his mood this time was corrosive. Rose wished he would drink enough so that he passed out under the table, and then they could all be more comfortable.

"I am not a witch." Constance gave him a scornful look. "Anyone with the eyes to see knows it will be so. Lord Radulf is happy with what he has . . . he does not hunger for what he has not."

Arno's face flushed an unpleasant red. "Aye, well, old woman, we all hunger sometimes. Even you." And he laughed as if he had made a joke, and elbowed Brother Mark into joining in. The priest smiled reluctantly, eyes flicking uneasily around the table.

Beyond Arno, Gunnar Olafson's eyes met Rose's. She found herself caught and held by their calm, still blue. All around them people shouted and celebrated, Arno and Constance argued, Brother Mark gorged, and the serving women ogled. None of it mattered. Rose felt that she and Gunnar had their own special silence, and they existed only within it.

And then Steven raised his goblet and spoke in a clear voice. "To my lord and lady. Long may they live."

The special moment was broken.

As Rose turned away, Gunnar leaned back, feeling light-headed, his tired eyes stinging from the smoke that swirled about the hall. He was tired, aye, but not tired enough evidently. His body hardened, desire singing through him. She only had to look at him with those deep, dark eyes and he wanted her. And she wasn't even aware of it.

One of the Somerford hounds slunk under a table, scrounging for scraps. It reminded him of Sir Arno—sly-eyed, groveling to the powerful, but always willing to turn on anything weaker. Like Arno, the creature would find little joy—food stocks at Somerford were low until the harvest was in and the animals that had been fattened over the summer could be killed in the autumn. Ivo would have to go out hunting again tomorrow.

His gaze followed the prettiest of the Somerford wenches, the cook, Eartha, as she made her way to Rose. Just now the woman's ready smile was missing, as she bent and began murmuring in her lady's ear with an intensity that spiked Gunnar's interest.

The atmosphere in the hall had been merry verging on hysterical ever since Steven had come to share the good news. And it *was* good news. Gunnar was very glad to hear that Lily was well, and that Radulf and his wife now had a son to add to their little daughter. He had been puzzled at first as to why Radulf had sent Steven, his favorite young knight-in-training, but Steven's steady gaze in his direction had made it clear enough. He was to let Steven know what was happening so that he could report back to Radulf. Even at such a moment as this, the King's Sword was watching his enemies—maybe Lily's safe delivery of an heir made him even more determined to keep the peace at Crevitch. Men like Fitzmorton and Miles de Vessey did not understand that—they lived for war.

And just as well, Gunnar told himself bracingly. If there were no wars and no squabbles between the great of this land, he would be without a job. And it seemed as if he would be needing work now that his dream of owning his own land was receding. Maybe Radulf could keep him permanently at Crevitch? Then he would be close by Somerford, if—Gunnar cut the thought off there. No, to stay would remind him of all he might have had. It would be better to get as far away from Somerford as possible, into the north, and forget he had ever seen the Lady Rose.

Eartha was still whispering. Rose nodded, head bent, her grave, beautiful face in shadow. Gunnar could not help but examine the graceful curve of her neck, the hollow near her jaw where he had kissed her last night—one of the many places he had kissed her last night. Was there a faint blue bruise against the pale honey of her skin? Had anyone else noticed? He would have to be more careful next time . . .

Gunnar almost groaned aloud. *Next time!* She had not spoken a word to him, and tried her best not to look at him, and he still believed there would be a next time. Was she ashamed of what they had done, or just ashamed that she had done it with him? Was he a complete fool, as Ivo had warned him, and was she playing a double game with him? Could she be planning to rid herself of Arno by using Gunnar? Was she that devious?

He did not think so—and he was usually a good judge of character—but he supposed it was possible. Anything was possible. And he was certainly not as clear-headed as he would have liked.

Gunnar could not hear what they were saying, but Eartha's whispering went on and now the lady's back had stiffened, her fingers turning white as she gripped her chair arm. Eartha stepped back and, with a sketchy curtsy, went on her way. Rose did not move, continuing to stare down at her plate, deep in thought. Now her fingers were tracing the carvings on the arm of her chair, and it was more like a caress than an idle touch.

Gunnar hid a smile. He had examined the chair himself the day after his arrival. It was Norse, he had no doubts about it, and very old. Maybe some enterprising Englishman had stolen it from a Viking invader, or one of those invaders had thought to set up his own little kingdom, and had this throne carved for himself. Whoever and wherever it had come from, it was not the sort of chair he would have expected the Lady Rose to be seated upon. Had she ever truly examined the carvings on it? Maybe he should enlighten her . . .

Abruptly she rose to her feet. Her smile was vague and strained—she was pretending all was well, but she didn't fool him as she stepped down from the dais, saying, "Please, do not stop the celebration. I will be but a moment."

Arno did not need any encouragement, it was debatable whether he even heard her. Brother Mark continued to stuff himself in a most ungodly manner, but Gunnar was not surprised, he had already concluded the good brother was no more a priest than he was. Only the old woman, Constance, was observing her lady. Here, at least, was someone with her wits about her. As Gunnar watched, Constance gathered together her wily strength, preparing to rise and follow Rose.

"Lady Constance." Her head swung around at the sound of her name in his quiet voice. "Do not disturb yourself. Ivo will see that no harm comes to her." Even as he spoke, the big man was rising from one of the tables below and ambling after Rose on her journey across the crowded room.

The woman Eartha was waiting by the door that led

from the great hall into the bailey, and when Rose reached her they went out together. In a moment, Ivo had followed with a deceptively leisurely grace.

Constance looked at Gunnar and smiled, but her eyes were sharp. "I will keep her safe," Gunnar heard himself saying, and the words made him go still with surprised dismay.

Did it matter so much to him that she was safe? His body was aching from last night, the memory of it like a whip to his flesh. He needed release, and he was well aware that he had only to glance about this hall and he could find it a dozen times over. But not from *her*, the one woman he really wanted. The ache in his body was for the Lady Rose, and no one else would do.

And what does that mean?

It means I lust after her, nothing more, he told himself reasonably. Gunnar knew he was very good at being reasonable.

Lust? Are these tender feelings for her really lust?

Desire, lust, it means the same. What do *you* call it?

The voice sniggered, and held its tongue.

Gunnar allowed that to go unanswered. What he felt, he told himself, was unimportant. What *was* important was that Lord Radulf be made aware of the situation here at Somerford Manor, before Lord Fitzmorton arrived and it was too late. What would having the land matter to him if the blood of the Somerford people was soaking into it, and the beautiful Lady of Somerford was dead or forcibly wed to a man like Miles de Vessey? Gunnar knew well enough what happened to women when Miles was weary of them.

Constance was smiling and nodding at him, as if he had spoken aloud. A burst of noise from down in the hall blotted out her words, but Gunnar saw her lips move. He thought she said, "You are the one," but that made no sense. Aye, he must have been mistaken, decided Gunnar, and returned to his silent brooding.

Chapter 11

"Harold?"

A large hand clenched about the bars on the window in the door of the cell. A torch flickered in the draft, deepening the shadows. Harold the miller, pale and woebegone, peered out at them.

"Lady?" whispered Harold, seeing Rose. "You have come to free me?"

The hopeful spark in his eyes was tentative at best, and when she didn't answer it died into dull acceptance. Harold had prepared himself for death. Rose knew then that Eartha had been right in insisting that she come to see the miller.

"Aye, how can you?" he was answering his own question. "I killed a Norman and I must hang. 'Tis the law."

"Norman law!" spat Eartha, and gave Rose a half-frightened, half-defiant look.

"You forget yourself, Eartha," reproved Harold.

"Lady Rose is our lady. Norman or English, she has always taken care of us, watched over us. It is not her fault that I killed a man."

"Yes, but it is why you killed him!" Eartha declared. "Should you die for saving your daughter, sweet Millisent?"

Rose came closer, meeting his gaze through the cell bars. "Eartha has spoken to me about letting you go free, Harold. She says that you promise, if I do, I will never see you again. Is that what you want? To run and hide for the rest of your life? Never to see your children again?"

Harold glanced into her eyes, and then sighed and shook his head. His own eyes filled with tears. "No, lady, it isn't what I really want. But neither do I want my children to see their father hanged. To run and hide seemed to be best of a bad lot."

Eartha shook her head. She had spoken long and eloquently in the great hall, asking Rose to set Harold free. He would vanish, she had said, he would hide. They could pretend he had escaped and no one need ever know, and no one would ever find him.

Rose knew of other escapees from Norman justice. Freedom might be a much lauded thing, but where was the freedom in hiding in caves and forests, forever fearing that the next person you met could be there to drag you back to face your Norman masters?

She could not see Harold—thoughtful, careful Harold, who loved his children—living such a life. She could not reduce a decent, honest man to such a fate. But neither could she see him hanged.

Suddenly it seemed a simple matter to obey her heart and ignore the warnings her mind was screaming at her.

Rose reached up to the bars, and her voice was firm and authorative, as if she really was in control of the situation. "I will not allow you to die for a man like Gilbert, Harold. You were justified in what you did, and so I will tell Lord Fitzmorton. But . . ." She took a deep breath. "If he is not to take matters into his own hands, we must win Lord Radulf to our side. I will send word back to him with his messenger. At such a time as this, he will be in a mood to grant favors."

Harold looked away, but she had already seen the grave doubts in his eyes. "There is danger for you in that, lady," he murmured uneasily. "Are you sure—"

"Aye! She must send word to Lord Radulf!" Eartha was breathless with her enthusiasm, her pretty face aglow. "He is a man, and only men have power over life and death.

"Women, too," said Rose. "Remember, tonight we celebrate the birth of Lady Lily's son."

But Eartha seemed incapable of making the connection, far too single-minded. She came forward to the little barred window. "I will tell Millisent. Fear not, Harold, I will care for her and Will. You were always kind to me and my little boy, and now I will repay that kindness."

Watching them, Rose felt hollow. Lord Radulf might well grant her her wish, but he would no longer see her as a safe vassal to hold Somerford. He would speedily replace her, and how could she blame him? She would save Harold's life, but at the expense of saving herself.

Rose stumbled as she climbed the last step from the cell, her legs heavy, her heart heavier. Would Radulf return her to her father or would he marry her to another of his vassals? Whatever fate he decided for her, it amounted to the same. She would be given away like a counter in a game. A game she had tried so hard to play to the advantage of her people, and had now lost.

She remembered again her father's face, half illuminated by the candles upon the table.

"You will marry this Edric, although he is not worthy of you. Radulf and I have agreed upon it."

"And you swear to leave me be, Father? You swear you will not use me in your games?"

"Games?" he mocked. "War is no game!"

"I want to live my life quietly. I want to pretend I am no longer your daughter."

He laughed harshly, and she might have thought she had hurt his feelings.

If he had a heart.

"Lady?"

Rose started. Turning swiftly, she found one of the mercenaries standing behind her, a shadow in the shadows. *Gunnar?* The longing in the thought shocked her, and she tensed defensively, drawing herself up to play the part of indifference. But it was not Gunnar who came toward her with intent dark eyes.

"Ivo? What do you here?"

"I am obeying Captain Olafson's orders, my lady."

Rose frowned, trying to ignore the manner in which he towered over her—why did all these mercenaries have to be so tall! "And what orders are they, Ivo?"

"I am to keep you safe, lady."

Something trickled through her, something warm

and comforting and completely unfamiliar. Gunnar Olafson wanted her safe.

Of course he does! Fool. You are paying him to keep you safe!

The mocking voice brought her feet back to the bailey with a jolt. Ivo was watching her with a carefully blank look in his eyes that made her wonder whether she had just given herself away.

"I doubt I will be carried off in the midst of my own keep," she said coolly. "Your captain would do better trying to catch the attackers than watching me." And she set off briskly back toward the great hall.

But Ivo simply ambled along beside her. "He has his reasons, lady, and I would trust him above all other men. He is good at what he does."

Rose glanced at him curiously. There had been a great deal of admiration in Ivo's voice but, more than that, there had been affection. The question was out before she could stop it. "You have known him for a long time, Ivo?"

He smiled—he had a nice smile. It completely transformed the fierce angles of his face. "He saved my life, lady. I would be dead now if it were not for Gunnar. The others will say the same, Alfred and Sweyn, Ethelred and Reynard. He has saved all our lives, in different ways. We would give those lives back, if it meant saving his."

He was completely serious, thought Rose with wonder. What sort of man was this, to inspire such complete and total loyalty?

"You were in Wales before you came here." It was not really a question.

Ivo nodded. "Wild country and wild people. Somerford is better, even if my brother *is* here." He stopped, as if he had said more than he wanted.

"Your brother? Who is your brother?"

Ivo took a deep breath. For such a fearsome-looking man, he had very soulful eyes. "Miles de Vessey, lady. He is my brother, although I wish it were not so. He is not to be trusted, ever."

"Oh? Is he so bad, Ivo?"

Ivo held up his hand, the one he wore the glove or gauntlet upon. "Lady, Miles did this when we were boys. He thought to cripple me so that never again would I best him at swordplay."

Rose's throat felt dry. "And did you?"

A smile glinted in Ivo's dark eyes. "Aye."

They had reached the hall and Ivo was bowing as she moved on past him, into the smoky, noisy warmth.

Rose was relieved to see that Arno had moved to one of the tables in the body of the hall, and was playing a drunken game of dice with the two fair-headed mercenaries, Sweyn and Ethelred. Brother Mark had gone and Constance, too, had retired for the night. Gunnar Olafson and Steven were standing together, heads close. The expressions on their faces belied any pretense at polite conversation. Gunnar made an angry gesture and Steven nodded, his brown hair flopping forward over his eyes.

In a moment Rose knew she would be near enough to hear what they were saying. She quickened her step.

As if sensing her presence, Gunnar glanced up. His expression changed, the calm mask slipping over the anger, his eyes growing cool and watchful. At the same time, Steven bowed and backed away, merging into the shadows by the dais, and leaving them as private as they could be in the crowded hall.

"What were you speaking of?" Rose said sharply, close enough now that they could not be overheard.

"Of Wales, lady. Steven's family hold lands on the Marches."

He was lying and she knew it, but what could she do? If she accused him he would laugh in her face. Too late she remembered last night in the stairwell and felt a low, deep ache in her belly. Why had she not walked straight through the hall and taken herself to the safety of her chamber?

"There is no need to set your men to watch me, Captain," she said grumpily.

He raised his eyebrows. "I seek to protect you, lady."

"It feels like watching." Her voice was icy polite, although her cheeks felt over-hot. She was disturbed, agitated by his presence. The memories of last night had risen up between them, and Rose was finding it difficult to breathe.

And he was aware of it. He must be. How could he not be? There he was, standing before her, broad-shouldered, legs set firmly, his mouth saying one thing while his eyes said another. And Rose understood with a growing sense of despair that last night in the stairwell hadn't been enough. She wanted him again. Tonight.

Time for them was running out. When she did as she had promised Harold, and sent word to Radulf . . .

Gunnar smiled, a tug at the corners of his lips. He was beyond handsome, and she had to stop herself from swaying toward him. Without taking his eyes from hers, Gunnar indicated the chair upon the dais. "Tell me about this chair, Lady Rose."

The change of subject confused her, but she was happy to follow it. Her chair seemed a far safer direction for the conversation to take than the images swirling through her head.

"If you like, Captain. This is the Somerford chair, and it is very old. An ancestor of my husband's brought it here, and it has been treasured ever since. There is a legend . . ."

"Tell it to me."

That sounded more like a command than a request, but Rose let it pass. She was happy to talk about the chair if it would take her mind off her fears for her future, and the hot, passionate memories probing at the edges of her mind.

"It is said the chair came to Somerford by itself, floating across the Mere and washing up on the shore. Before that . . . 'tis a mystery."

He nodded, but his eyes were aglow. As if he were aware of a secret, as if she amused him. Defensively Rose crossed her arms and frowned.

Again Gunnar smiled, that breathtaking smile. "Let me show you something," he said, and he held out his hand.

She did not want to take it, truly she did not, but somehow she already had. His fingers closed over hers, large and warm and strong, and he led her up onto the dais and around the table, to her chair. Bemused, Rose stood and watched as he crouched down on his haunches, closely examining one of the side panels. Her eyes flicked over the muscles of his thighs, the way the stuff of his breeches strained over all that hard flesh, the way his hair fell forward as he leaned toward the carvings, gleaming with a mixture of bronze and gold and chestnut.

Touch him. See if he feels as good as he looks. As good as you remember.

This time the whispering voice in her head bore a remarkable resemblance to Constance's. Rose swallowed and managed to ignore it.

"Look," he said softly, forcing her to lean closer to hear him. She followed the movement of his finger as he swept it across a swirl of tendrils and vines, and rested it lightly, almost affectionately, on one of the cleverly wrought little creatures.

" 'Tis a face," Rose said matter-of-factly, trying to break the sense of intimacy he had created.

"That is the hero Sigurd. He learned to speak to the birds. See, they are all about him." He smiled at her surprise.

"I see them." Had she noticed the myriad of winged creatures hiding among the foliage before? Probably, but she had not known their significance until now, until Gunnar Olafson explained it to her.

He pointed again, his finger steady, his touch on the wood gentle despite the many scars upon his hand. How could a man who lived such a brutal life be so gentle? And was he scarred all over? The picture rose in her mind, taking what little composure she had managed to gain. Gunnar, his body bronzed and gleaming, wearing only a smile. She had only ever seen Edric naked, but then she had not allowed her eyes to linger, had no wish to. She had seen enough of Gunnar that day in the bailey to know he would be different, young and handsome. A man like no other.

Rose held herself stiff and still; she prayed for the strength to be indifferent.

"And there is Idun, with her apple tree," he said, his voice warm with humor, evidently oblivious to Rose's difficulties. "If you eat the apples, so say my Viking ancestors, you can never grow old."

Idun had long tresses of hair, they twisted about the trunk of the apple tree and through the branches as if she were a part of it. There was something wanton in her smile, as she held out her apple and offered eternal life.

Touch him. Go on. Take his hand and lead him up the stairs to your solar. To your bed. Make him yours before someone else does. Before you are forced to leave Somerford and wed another. You may never have another chance. Is that what you want? To forever dream of what might have been? Is Gunnar Olafson to become another of your ghostly warriors, no more than a wisp of smoke in your arms? This man here is warm and real—a real *warrior. Take the chance!*

The voice had filled her head so loudly, Rose was certain Gunnar must have heard it. But no, he was pointing to the back of the chair now, saying, "And look, this is Yggdrasil, the largest of all trees. Its branches reach the heavens, and they are heavy with the dead."

The dead? Blinking in shocked surprise, Rose moved even nearer to him, looking where he indicated. 'Twas true. The leaves and branches had been carved beautifully, and yet among them were the unmistakable shapes of hanged men.

She shivered. "Why have I never noticed this before? I do not understand. This chair is from Wales! Are the Welsh legends not different from the Vikings?"

"This is no Welsh chair, lady. These are Norse gods. I know them well." His eyes were warm and intimate, as if they were much more than lady and mercenary. He was so close, his breath touched her, she felt the heat of his body. Shakily, Rose reached out a hand to grasp the back of the chair, her legs on the verge of crumpling.

"Oh," was all she managed in reply.

He moved closer again, and now his shoulder brushed against her. The tingle ran down her arm into her fingers. Was that intentional? Was he seducing her? And yet he didn't appear to notice.

"See here? This is Freyja, the goddess of love. Of lust. Of desire." He was looking directly at her now—she could feel his gaze on her cheek as if he were touching her skin. Rose dared not turn her head, afraid he would see what she knew was in her eyes. "Do you see there? She is with one of her lovers." His voice was a warm murmur, the sound rippling through her like a warm ocean, and just the timbre of it made her breasts ache.

God help her, she wanted his mouth on them. She wanted his hands holding her, stroking her, setting her free like one of Sigurd's birds, high above Yggdrasil and the clouds. Far away from all that kept her weighed down here, at Somerford Manor.

She didn't want to look where his finger was touching, but she couldn't seem to help it. Rose turned and stared at the little carving. Legs and arms intertwined, the rounded curve of a plump breast, a smooth thigh, long snakelike hair whipping about bare torsos. It was simply done, and yet incredibly erotic.

Rose took a small sharp breath and wondered if her face was as heated as it felt. She folded her hands tightly together in case she was tempted to reach out and touch Freyja and her fortunate mate.

"And there, lady," that wicked voice continued, "is the goddess Freyja's mortal lover, Ottar, before she turned him into a bull."

This time Rose stared without blinking, shocked into silence. It was as if she were seeing the carvings for the first time, and in a way she was. She had always thought them strange and wondrous, but now she realized they were also extremely sensual. Pagan. No wonder the old Somerford priest had looked at them askance.

Her eyes focused on Ottar, where Gunnar pointed now, and she understood clearly why it was Freyja had favored him. He was carved in profile, tall and strong, his hair long at his back, and between his legs . . . Rose doubted that was a spear he was holding in his hand.

"Jesu!" she gasped, and squeezed her eyes tight shut.

Gunnar laughed, as if he were genuinely amused and delighted with her. He rose to his feet and stood half behind her, blocking any chance of escape. Rose felt flushed and crowded—she desperately needed to move away from him, and yet she was unable to move without touching him. And she was afraid that if she accidentally brushed against him she would fling herself into his arms and beg him to . . .

Take this chance, it may be your last!

Her heart was thundering in her breast. Last night he

had held her in his arms and she had reveled in what he did to her. Rose could not deny those brief moments were filled with an intensity she had never experienced before. But it had not been enough—she could admit it now. She wanted him to take her as a man took a woman, to lie with her as Freyja was lying with her Ottar. And the voice was right. This might be her last opportunity to be with a man she found attractive.

Who knew what corner of hell the future might find her in?

Gunnar had moved in, bending over her, and now his breath stirred against her throat, the sensitive flesh reacting, prickling, making her shudder. Rose had to grip the chair back with both hands.

"You seem likely to fly to pieces, lady." His voice was as soft as a caress. "Do I frighten you so much? Or is it yourself you are afraid of?"

She was no weakling. It would never do for Gunnar Olafson to believe the way to power lay through sharing her bed. Until Radulf removed her, she was lady there, and any order she gave he must obey. Somehow Rose forced her chin up, turning stiffly to face him despite his proximity. "You are mistaken," she managed, although her voice shook. "I am not afraid of you."

He was looking down at her, his eyes so blue and vibrant. The heat in them burned her skin.

"I am not afraid of you," she repeated, more to convince herself. "I am the Lady of Somerford, and you are a mercenary. I give the orders. Do not forget it, Captain."

He didn't seem angered by what she had said; his smile grew broader. "Then order me to show you what the mercenary can do for the lady."

There was no doubting his meaning, it was there in the glitter of his eyes, the curl of his hips. He wanted her. He was offering to give her as much pleasure as he had last night. More. And she had only to ask . . . Well, wasn't that exactly what she wanted?

"Have you shown many ladies what you can do, Captain?" she asked.

Some other emotion flickered in his confident blue eyes. Surprise? Confusion? Annoyance? The timbre of his voice cooled. "Are you interested in my fidelity, lady? Or my prowess? I can give you my body, I can give you the pleasure you crave, but be warned . . . my heart is my own."

"I'm not interested in your heart," Rose said, and was sure she meant it. She needed him as a lover, and he was offering himself to her. Some devilment made her ask, "This was not in our original agreement. How many extra marks would you charge me, Captain, for this service?"

"No extra, lady. It would be entirely my pleasure."

Briefly, Rose wondered if she had lost her mind entirely, and then she didn't care. There were probably far worse things to come. Just for now, let pleasure reign.

"Very well, Captain, we have a bargain. Come to me . . . later, when everyone is abed."

He bowed as if he were her obedient servant, when Rose knew very well that he was not. She had not promised, she told herself, as she whirled away. She could always change her mind and not let him in. But she knew, deep in her heart, that it was too late to go back.

Too late, because she did not want to.

* * *

The air was still and sweet with summer. Rose stood a moment, staring into the night. Across the Mere, Burrow Mump rose against the star-filled sky. Tonight the island seemed a long way away. Tonight she had put aside dreams and ghosts. Soon they might be all she had to comfort her, but for now there was a flesh and blood man to be enjoyed.

You want him. Constance's voice sounded in her head. *And yet you are afraid of him.*

I am afraid of how he makes me feel.

Like a woman? scoffed Constance gently. *You should not be afraid of that. Every woman should feel such pleasure at least once in her life. Some feel it not at all. I was lucky with my husband. Now is your chance, Rose. Do not allow it to slip by.*

And if he has changed his mind?

He won't. I have seen the way he looks at you.

Rose felt the color in her cheeks and turned again to the window, her dark hair smooth as a velvet cloak around her. She had combed it and left it unbraided, wrapping her thin robe about her nakedness. There was only one small candle flickering by the door. She sat in darkness by the window, knowing that when he came she would see him first.

Rose had few advantages where Gunnar Olafson was concerned, but that was one.

She did not feel like herself. Just now her body might be cooled by the evening air, her heartbeat even, her thoughts measured, but as soon as he touched her all that would change. She would lose her equilibrium. She would become nothing more than another willing woman in his arms. So any advantage was worth pursuing. Aye, she would sit in the shadows and watch him in the candlelight, and pretend she was in charge of the situation.

Rose's mind drifted back to the moments by the Somerford chair, and the Norse carvings whose meaning he had explained to her. Gunnar was like those carvings—in some ways he was brutal, in others he was beautiful, and always intensely seductive . . .

The knock on her door was soft, but still Rose jumped. Her breath sounded very loud in the silence, and she pulled her robe closer about her, suddenly wishing she had not undressed. And yet how foolish to think another layer of cloth could protect her from Gunnar Olafson!

"Lady?" His voice was muffled. He knocked again.

Rose did not expect him to wait indefinitely. He would think she had changed her mind, or he would feel foolish and leave. No man liked to feel foolish. Mayhap it would be best if she did not . . .

The door opened wide.

He stood on the threshold, the candlelight catching in his hair and eyes, playing shadowy games with his handsome face and impressive body. His hand was on the hilt of his sword, and he had it half out of its sheath, ready. He was frowning into the chamber, trying to pierce the shadows.

"Captain Olafson."

His gaze moved swiftly to the window. Slowly, he returned his sword to its scabbard, and came further into the room, closing the door behind him and dropping the bar in place. The candle flame wavered, darting crazily on the walls and ceiling beams. He did not seem to care that she could see him and he could not see her.

When he spoke at last his tone was ironic. "Were you sleeping that you did not hear my knock, lady?"

"Did you think I had gone back on my word, Captain?"

"I wondered." He stepped further into the room—he was so big, he crowded her despite his distance. "You called me Gunnar last night . . . lady."

Rose had set out her words in her head, but he was making it difficult for her to remember them. She licked her lips and tried to regain her composure.

He took yet another step, looking directly at her, one hand still resting on his sword hilt, the other loose at his side. Was he stalking her? A wolf edging closer to its prey? Rose rushed into her speech before her courage could fail her entirely, but her voice was hurried and breathless.

"A man like you, Captain, must be well versed in what women like most. That is why I have chosen you—I require the best."

His face was beyond the soft light of the candle now, but she thought he smiled, as if the shambles of her carefully prepared speech had amused him.

"I have been a wife, so do not think I am innocent of the ways of men," she went on with grim determination. "I want a bedmate, nothing more. Do not think to win me to your ambitions, whatever they be. I will not give you gifts, Captain, nor will I promise to further your career or sing your praises to those high in the land. This is a private matter, between us, and whether it lasts for one night or . . . or more, we will not speak of it beyond these walls. Do I have your word on that?"

He was silent now, watching her, the secrets hiding in his face. What was he thinking? Rose wondered, her body tense as she perched stiffly upon the window seat. Was he going to refuse her? Laugh at her? She remembered that he had taken a long time to consider her last request for a promise, in the hall the night Edward came begging for permission to open the gate. Maybe he was simply weighing the benefits to himself in this new arrangement.

"You have my word, lady."

He came at her again, and now he was nothing but a dark shape against the pitiful candle. A huge dark shape. Rose looked up, trying to see his face. He stretched out a hand and she felt his fingers brush against her hair, lingering, so gentle for such a big, powerful man. Would he be as gentle when he laid her upon the bed and took her as a man takes a woman?

Startled and made breathless by the thought, Rose jumped to her feet and slid out of his reach. He did not move, watching her, waiting. His stillness was intimidating, as if he was gathering his strength for the next assault on her senses. She wanted him—her body was warm, so warm. Her hands shook, her legs trembled. She could smell her own desire, the musky scent of a woman who wanted a man. And still she pretended she was in control of the situation.

"I command you to take off your clothes, Captain," Rose said, her voice brave.

He did not move. Mayhap, she thought shakily, he would refuse? March angrily from the room? She almost hoped he would, for then she would be able to breathe normally again. Be herself again.

Be alone again . . .

"Your command is my wish," he said, his voice soft and deep, like a hot brand too close to her skin. And—

Jesu!—he was unbuckling his sword belt, slowly, purposefully. It came free, and he glanced about him, and then decided to place it carefully upon the window seat where Rose had lately been seated. Next came his brown tunic, and he lifted this over his head, dropping it carelessly on the floor at his feet.

Now he wore only his breeches, leather boots, and a white linen shirt. The shirt was worn so thin that his skin shone golden through it, and the laces were untied to halfway down his chest. Rose caught glimpses of the hard, curving muscles that covered that wide, wonderful chest.

She folded her arms hard about herself, tugging the robe around her as if it were chain mail and would somehow protect her from him. The truth was she had only her position as protection, but as long as she kept her head he would not know how weak and feeble she was before him.

Do not let yourself love. It was her mother's voice. Brown eyes, so much like Rose's, were hollow with pain as she gave her daughter the only advice she had to give. *Do not let yourself want. And if you do . . . don't let him know it. Remember, 'tis men who have all the power in this world.*

Gunnar lifted his white shirt over his head and tossed it onto the floor at her feet. Rose forgot her mother's warning as all thought was wiped from her mind.

He was built like a god.

All hard muscle and golden skin. He was so strong, his shoulders broad, his arms powerful, his chest a hard wall, narrowing down to his waist and stomach, to where the breeches covered him like a second skin. Rose wanted to groan aloud. She wanted to touch him, to run her hands over all that magnificence, she wanted to lean into him and kiss his mouth.

He was untying the laces on his breeches, his blue eyes fixed on her. Rose caught her breath as the waist loosened, and for a moment he let them fall as far as they could. A line of darker hair ran from his stomach down into the shadows of his groin. Was he teasing her? But even as the doubts threatened to bring her back from the brink, he was peeling the breeches slowly down over his hips and thighs.

He was already aroused. His manhood jutted toward her, so big . . . No wonder he had laughed when she trembled before the carving of Ottar. Surely Edric had never been so big? How would she manage? Rose lifted a trembling hand to her mouth and began to chew on one of her already ragged nails.

Gunnar finished tugging his breeches down over his powerful thighs, pushing the cloth past his knees, and then quickly pulling off his boots and completing what she had commanded him to do. When he straightened he was completely naked, and Rose was sure that her heart stopped in her breast.

He was beautiful, with the sort of masculine perfection she had not believed possible until now. He was the sort of man that women were drawn to despite themselves—no wonder they had gazed, bedazzled, at him in the hall. Rose could not despise them now, for she was just as smitten by him as all her womenfolk.

But Gunnar Olafson was not just beautiful, he had a magic ingredient that enslaved her senses. She didn't just want to touch him, she wanted to possess him. And that made her present position dangerous, much more dangerous than she had imagined.

"I do not think," she managed, her voice trembling violently. "I fear that I cannot—"

Suddenly he was there, although she did not remember him moving. His body was so close now she felt his heat, smelled his male scent; his copper braids swung forward as he bent his head and searched her face with his bright, brilliant gaze. His voice was implacable. "Yes, lady, you can. And you will."

Rose's heart jolted. He took her mouth with his before she could reply. He had kissed her before, but not like this. He was forcing her mouth to cling to his, his tongue searching, overcoming her fears with the sheer strength of his passion. Rose swayed and leaned against him, afraid she might otherwise crumple at his feet. Her hands reached out and found nothing but warm flesh and ungiving muscle. He found her breast, cupped it through her robe, fingers rolling the hard jut of her nipple, and Rose moaned deep in her throat as her body arched involuntarily toward him.

He lowered his head, his mouth open and hot against her rounded flesh, suckling on her through the thin cloth, while his hands drew her in closer against him, until their lower bodies felt joined together from the hip down. Rose swayed back, his arm about her waist holding her safe from falling, and Gunnar obeyed the unspoken invitation she was offering. He kissed her throat, and then ran his tongue down into the opening of her robe, finding her naked skin.

The room was spinning. The ache between her thighs was reaching a dangerous level, making her reckless. Rose forgot her determination to remain in control, she forgot who was commanding whom. Forgot everything but her own urgent needs. His manhood was rigid against her belly and she reached down, and found him. Her touch was light, a mere brush of her fingers, and yet he seemed to throb against them. She heard his gasp against her breast.

Curiosity briefly overcame caution—she brushed him again, her fingers lingering, encircling the hard, satin rod. He moaned, his body going even harder, his muscles rigid with tension. Astonished, Rose froze and then heard him give a shaken laugh. "What do you command now?" he asked her in a hoarse, rough voice. He lifted his head, and his handsome face was as tense as his body, his eyes almost pleading. "Tell me quickly, Rose, because I am fast losing what control I have left."

Stunned, she gazed up at him. Gunnar Olafson losing his control, just because of a little touch like that? But how could that be? He was *always* in control. That was one of the reasons she was so afraid to give herself completely over to their passion.

Tentatively, very carefully, as if she were handling a dangerous object, Rose wrapped her hand more firmly about him. He closed his eyes and shuddered. Rose ran her fingers up and down the long, thick length of him, gaining confidence, no longer afraid, sensing that whatever she was doing, he was enjoying it. He didn't want her to stop. Amazingly, astoundingly, Gunnar Olafson, that male god, was now in *her* sway. And Rose liked that very much.

He groaned again as her hand tightened, and rested his brow on the crown of her head. His breath was hot, his arms were trembling. "I want . . ." He swallowed and tried again. "I want to be inside you, lady. Command that."

Rose stroked him once again, smoothing her fingertips over the broad head of his manhood, where it wept desire. He moved in her hand. She wanted to smile, she wanted to laugh, she felt as if she had been given a secret spell. This was power she had never known she had, power she had never had the opportunity to explore. And now, for some reason of his own, Gunnar was allowing her to do so.

So absorbed was she, she did not notice that her robe had fallen completely open. Not until his hands slid inside, eagerly exploring the fullness of her breasts with their dark pink nipples, running over the gentle curve of her belly and down, through the curls of dark hair to the moist, hot core of her.

Rose gasped and momentarily stopped her own explorations, pressing against his hand. He was watching her in a hungry, intent way. As if he wanted to remember her like this forever. But that made no sense, thought Rose dazedly, and then he moved his thumb against her, and she forgot to think.

"I command you to take me as a man takes a woman," she whispered in a ragged voice, reaching for him again. "I command you, Gunnar."

She expected . . . Rose didn't know what she expected. Maybe for him to lay her gently on the bed and climb atop her. Instead he moved so swiftly she cried out. He reached down, gripping her firmly about the waist, and lifted her into the air until their faces were level. Her eyes opened wide in shocked surprise.

"Put your arms around my neck," he said with quiet intensity, "and your legs around my waist."

Rose slipped her arms about his neck, fingers twining in his hair, and then more slowly, uncertainly, she curled her legs about his big, muscular body. In such a position, she could not help but press herself intimately to him.

Blue eyes glittered into brown, and then his palms followed her curves down, closing on the soft flesh of her bottom. He shifted her, correcting her position, and just like that his manhood was prodding at her sheath, easing toward the slippery heat at her center.

She gasped, pushing at his shoulders, feeling herself trying to stretch to his size, her body stiffening in rejection. He hardly seemed to notice. Sweat was sheening his face, and his breath was shallow. The muscles in his arms tensed and hardened—he was holding her entire weight—and he lowered her a little more, filling her.

The sensation was beyond her experience, beyond anything she had dreamed of. Gunnar was making her his, and Rose had the feeling that she would never be the same afterward.

He moved again, easing her down on him, and she clung, moaning. His mouth covered hers, his tongue sought hers. And still he held her against him, her entire weight taken by his arms and hips and legs. Surely in another moment he would put her on the bed? Edric had never done such a thing as this—not that he would ever have been capable of holding her in such a way. In Rose's experience men and women mated in bed in the darkness, beneath the covers, and they were quick and silent about it. They did not stand in the center of a room, naked, blatant, consumed by their passion.

Gunnar eased her up, until he had withdrawn almost completely, and then lowered her again. Deeper now, taking his time, accustoming her body to his. Rose let her head fall back, her hair a heavy tangle. Every thought was concentrated on the place between her thighs, where he was joined to her. He took the opportunity to bend his head and suckle at her breasts, his tongue deliberately circling each nipple and sending shivers of unbearable excitement rippling across her skin.

Rose felt her body clench about him, desperately trying to keep him inside her as he withdrew again. She tried to push herself down more quickly, leaning forward to kiss his throat, her mouth open and wet and wanton. Their bodies were damp now, slipping against each other, and she was tugging at his hair, pulling his head down, his mouth. He kissed her, and it was beyond pleasure.

He moved her upon him, harder now, still deeper, and sensation began to hum through her bones. "Gunnar," she managed, "please. Please . . ." And as if he had been waiting for just that, Gunnar tilted her hips closer toward him, moving her in some way so that when he entered her the next time he brushed against that swollen nub within her dark curls.

Rose cried out, arching and twisting in his hands, shaken with the tremendous force of the release he had given her. He lifted and lowered her again, once, twice, until he was so deep within her she felt him touch her womb. His seed spilled out into her as her sheath squeezed and clenched violently, and at the same time he threw back his head with a hoarse shout so loud Rose feared the whole of Somerford must have heard.

And yet, as she slumped against him, wet and gasping and shuddering, wondering if she had the strength to ever stand on her own again, Rose knew she did not care.

Chapter 12

Someone was nuzzling against her nape, breathing in her scent, sprinkling light kisses across her sensitive skin.

Rose opened her eyes.

The candle by the door had burned down to a flickering stub of yellow grease, and the room was full of shadows. She was on the bed—he had carried her there afterward, laying her down as if she were the most precious of creatures, before stretching out beside her and pulling the covers over them both. For a time he had seemed content to just lie there, his arm heavy about her waist, his thighs tucked warmly in behind hers, his breath soft against her hair.

They had stayed like that, as comfortable as if they had known each other all their lives. They hadn't spoken. There didn't seem to be anything to say. Rose was replete, limp, unable to dredge up a single worry or care, and Gunnar was content to let her rest. She had even dozed, dreaming of nothing but warm darkness, cradling her, rocking her.

But now he was moving again.

As well as his mouth on her skin, his hand had shifted to close on her breast, exploring the full firm flesh, teasing her nipple into a peak. And lower down, where the hairs on his thighs tickled the tender flesh of her bottom, his manhood had begun to grow thick and hard.

Despite herself, Rose thought again of the carving he had shown her. Ottar, standing with his rod in his hand, waiting to service his goddess. She giggled, thinking of Gunnar standing like that by the side of her bed, waiting for her command.

"You think this is funny?" His warm voice was a husky murmur in her ear.

He reached down, slipping his hand between her thighs, lifting her upper leg so that he could push his fingers into her slippery heat. Rose stiffened and arched back against him. Suddenly her breathing was unsteady, and satiety gave way to doubt.

" 'Tis too soon!" she gasped.

He stopped. "Are you sore?" he asked her, the question far more personal than any she was used to hearing.

"No," she said sharply, and then wished she hadn't.

He chuckled softly, his breath tickling her, and heaved himself up so that he could look at her properly. Rose gazed up into his handsome face, her senses spinning out of control from such foolish things as the shape of his jaw, rough with golden stubble, and the way his copper hair hung in a tousled frame around his face. There was a little curve at the corners of his mouth—that half smile he gave her when he meant to prove a point—and his eyes, so blue, the gleam in them hot and hard, melted her resistance.

Between her legs, something much bigger than a finger sought and found her entrance. He thrust his hips, driving deeper, his smile growing as he watched the pretended indifference on her face dissolve into blind passion, and a need so desperate she could not contain it.

"There is nothing wrong in wanting a man," he said, his voice only slightly strained. "It does not lessen you, Rose."

Her breasts were aching and he plucked at the nipples, sending tremors of pure pleasure through her belly, to the place where they were joined. He pushed in still deeper, easing the last bit, until he was filling her completely.

"I want you," he murmured, and buried his face in her hair, breathing in her scent. "I admit it. Desire does not lessen me, it makes me more of a man."

She cried out as he quickened his pace, driving into her with strength and purpose. His fingers slipped from her breasts, moving unerringly down to where the throbbing ache was growing. At his touch, Rose cried out breathlessly, arching back against him, opening her legs. She felt herself to be on the edge of that wild place he had taken her to before, but this time he seemed intent on keeping her from it. His fingers teased and then moved away, bringing her to the brink but never quite over.

Frustrated, Rose tried to follow his hand, tried to grab it with her own. He caught her wrists, holding her prisoner, his smiling mouth against her temple. He was all around her, engulfing her, and yet he was not in the place she wanted him the most.

"Gunnar!" she moaned. "I command you."

He laughed again, holding himself inside her, feeling her body contracting about him. She felt so good. Better than any other woman, and there had been many. He already knew tonight wouldn't be enough. He needed her every night, and more often if he could get her to accommodate him. Would she let him lead her from the hall at breakfast and take her behind the dais? Would she let him lift her from her horse in the woods and take her in the buttercups? Would she come to his narrow bed and climb atop him in the night, making him weep with his yearning for her?

"Ouch!" Gunnar jerked from the sting across his buttocks. Her smile was wickedly pleased as she met his surprised stare. She had managed to free her hand and had reached around and raked her nails over him. So much for taking the time to daydream. Gunnar brought his thoughts firmly back to the present moment, capturing her hand in a relentless but careful grip.

"No," she said, struggling against him. Gunnar settled the matter by resting his fingers lightly against her swollen nub. She went still, breathing quickly. He eased his rod into her again, enjoying the tight, hot feel of her. She was making little gasping noises now, and when he rubbed her more firmly she cried out, forgetting everything in her pursuit of pleasure.

Gunnar had known she was passionate, had sensed it long before their moments in the stairwell, but she had surprised even him with her raw, earthy need of him. She tried to control it, tried to rein it in, but he already knew her too well. She was his match in bed and out, the perfect mate for a warrior.

'Twas a pity it could not be.

"Gunnar," she whispered, and her hands were free again, but now they held his forearm, gripping it hard as the spasms took her. He felt the beginning of the end as her sheath tightened about his rod, and with a moan he let himself go with her, cresting the wave with Rose in his arms.

Rose was running from the warriors from Burrow Mump, her feet flying over marsh and earth. She veered to the side, toward the woods, but one of them followed. The warrior on the gray horse. She cried out just as he swooped down on her, catching her up. Her hair was unbound and now it tumbled across her face, blinding her so that she could not see him properly. Except, just before he tucked her before him on his saddle, she had a glimpse of his eyes.

They were blue. Blue as a northern ocean. Blue as Gunnar Olafson's.

Gunnar stared into the darkness, listening to the woman's soft breathing. It was very late—the night had almost given way to morning. Soon the birds would begin their calling and the keep would begin to stir to the new day. The night would be over, forgotten. Except that Gunnar knew he would never forget.

He had wanted her since the moment he saw her. He might have mistrusted her, disliked her, planned to take what was hers, but there was no denying he had lusted after her as hotly as any he-wolf on the scent of a bitch in heat.

Maybe that was all it was. Maybe, after a few more times in her bed, he would have rid himself of the need for her . . .

She stirred, sighing in her sleep, turning into his arms. Without thinking, he smoothed a strand of hair from her face, watching as her dark lashes fluttered against her pale cheeks. Her red lips were slightly parted, her stubborn chin softened by sweet dreams. He thought her the most beautiful woman he had ever known, and yet he knew she was not. It was just that, for him, she was perfect.

Was she really as beautiful on the inside? What if she was using him to further her own plans? He had seen for himself her ability to play a part, to pretend at being what she was not. She wasn't as good as Gunnar, but she was good.

Abruptly, he bent his head and kissed her, thinking, *If she is false she will not be able to hide it in the moment of waking. If she is false I will read it in her now.*

Her mouth softened, clung, and she moved languidly to slide her arms around his neck. Her fingers twined in his hair.

"Gunnar," she murmured, as if she knew it was he before she opened her eyes.

She looked so sweet and wanton—he wanted to ride her until they were both breathless. And then, as if she had only just heard her own voice saying his name, her eyes opened wide. He watched the emotions pass through them—shock, and then wariness, and then caution. She did not trust him, and Gunnar could not blame her for that.

He did not really trust her.

"Lady," he said, as cool as if they were not lying naked in her bed. "Do you have any more orders for me? It is almost dawn and my men will be up soon, and I need to be there to lead them."

He had surprised her, but she pretended it was not so. She opened her mouth, just as he moved against her, making her aware of his arousal. "Oh," she managed, but he knew then she had no intention of sending him away . . . yet. He lifted himself over her, positioning himself on his elbows so that his weight was barely upon her. One hard thigh slipped between hers. She was warm and soft, and he ached with need.

"Lady?" he whispered, rocking against her, keeping his face calm and remote. A soldier taking his orders; that was what she wanted, wasn't it? To pretend there was nothing in this but animal lust? Well, he could do that, he, too, was good at playing a part—his mother had once called him Loki, the god of lies and deceit. She had said it with a smile, as if she knew better, but he had wondered if one day the smiling liar would overtake the honorable man in him.

Another reason he had wanted to turn his back on his present life forever.

"I . . ." She cleared her throat, hesitated, and then her hands came to rest lightly on his upper arms. "Captain, as you are already so well prepared, you could . . . I mean, once more before you go would be . . . Unless three times is too many?"

She was a complete innocent, despite being the old

married woman she had proclaimed herself last night. He had not been misled by her game then, and he was not now.

Gunnar slid smoothly into her and she was wet and ready. He almost smiled. "You doubt my strength?"

"Oh." she caught her breath. "I . . . I only feared . . . That is, Edric could barely manage once every change of the season and—"

His mouth twitched but he still did not smile. "I am not Edric," he said and, reaching down, lifted her thighs to open her wide to his ministrations.

To his amusement, she tried desperately not to show how much it affected her, but a flush colored her honey skin, and her dark eyes grew blurred. She turned her face away.

"No," he said harshly. "I want to see you this time. I want to read it in your eyes, the moment when you leave your body behind."

Slowly Rose changed position again. Last night had been raw enough, but meeting his eyes like this seemed particularly decadent. Why then did she feel a tremor of excitement? Why did his watching her as she reached her peak make her tremble and sigh against him? She might as well admit it to herself. Nothing mattered now but having Gunnar Olafson between her thighs and in her bed.

The movement of his body upon hers was bringing its own pleasure—before she had needed his hand, but now it seemed as if she could find paradise without his aid. Rose gazed into his eyes and read in them the hot rise of desire, and more than that. Satisfaction, maybe, and a glow that frightened her with its intensity.

"Let yourself go, Rose," he murmured intently. "Now, now . . ."

One more thrust, and Rose was arching upward with a low trembling cry. She slipped away, beyond the familiar chamber, out into the summer dawn, to dance on the cool breeze. With a low groan, Gunnar followed after her.

When he moved off her, swinging his legs onto the floor, Rose was surprised enough to open her eyes. He had said he would go, but somehow she had still thought he would stay.

Fool! Did you imagine he would remain here all day? What would your people think of that? What would Arno and Lord Radulf think? You cannot just forget your troubles because of the mercenary's handsome face.

Gunnar Olafson was tugging on his breeches, tying them about his waist. The light was creeping across the land, and now shone weakly through her open window. She could see his back, the muscles rippling and tightening as he bent to pull on his boots. His skin was golden smooth apart from a collection of white scars. The scars had been invisible last night, but now she saw where a sword had struck him a glancing blow, and a knife had slid across his shoulder blade . . . Each scar must have a tale to tell, and each scar could have meant his death.

Rose shivered.

Gunnar lifted his sword from its place on the window seat, buckling it about his hips. If she had forgotten what he was, then she was reminded now.

A mercenary.

A man who fought and killed for coin. A Viking savage. And yet he had shown her things last night that Rose had never seen or felt before, and she knew deep in her heart that he had changed her forever by simply being with her. How could she ever be the same again?

Her body ached with unfamiliar use, but it was a pleasant ache. Aye, her body was well used and content, but inside Rose felt like weeping. The day was coming upon her so quickly, and bringing with it all the temporarily forgotten problems. And questions. All the decisions still to be made. She faced the fact that she would have liked this moment to go on forever. Jesu, why could they not have lost themselves in each other for a little longer?

He was drawing his worn linen shirt over his head. There was a mend beneath one sleeve. Mayhap, Rose told herself, she could find him a new one. Sew him a new one. And then she stopped the thought cold, remembering what she had said at the beginning. *I will give you no gifts.* If she went back on her words he would think her weak. Aye, a weak, easily swayed woman—a woman sick with love for him.

You can have my body, but my heart is my own.

He had said that to her last night when she had asked about other women. He had warned her then—Gunnar Olafson was no lovesick ninny. He had given her what she commanded and no more, and now he was leaving.

He was dressed.

He turned to face her, and now he was again that calm, distant man she had grown to know . . . and God help her, to trust.

"Sleep, lady," he said. " 'Tis early yet, and you are weary."

Before she could answer he strode to the door, lifting

the bar and opening it a crack to look out. Evidently there was no one about, for he slipped quietly through and closed it behind him without a backward glance. There was silence, but a silence more complete than any Rose had ever experienced.

He was gone.

Rose closed her eyes, stubbornly vowing not to think of him. Today she must write a message to give to Steven, a call for help to Lord Radulf. She must sign over her own fate for the good of her people and Harold's life. Today she must put aside her own happiness for the sake of others.

But at least, Rose told herself, she had had last night. The wild pleasure that Gunnar had given her in the hot darkness was more than she could ever have imagined. It would live with her forever, no matter what became of her. A talisman against the frightening days ahead.

And then she gave a bitter laugh, for despite her vow she had thought of him after all.

"I saw them over there, Captain. Three full days before the village was burned. Half a dozen men, maybe more. I didn't think to mention it until now . . . there was so much talk of merefolk, and these men weren't."

Edward pointed with a steady finger, his stumpy legs planted on the firm ground at the Mere's edge. Gunnar narrowed his eyes. Water and mud and islands, nothing more. If the men Edward had said he saw came from out there then they were long gone.

"What were these men doing, Edward?"

The old man answered readily enough. "They met with someone, Captain. They all stood about a moment and argued and waved their arms, and then the men got back in their boats and paddled away. The someone they met with walked off toward the keep."

"And you did not recognize who this was?"

"Whoever it was was cloaked from head to toe, Captain, but 'twasn't a big figure. Shortish for a man, or . . . mayhap even a woman."

Rose.

The name came to him instantly, and all his old mistrust rose up. At the same time pain curled deep in his belly, as if he had eaten something rotten. Could Rose have been meeting with these men, plotting with them to burn down her own village?

"I'm near enough to certain the men with the boats weren't merefolk," said Edward.

"What did they look like?"

"It was dark." Edward was cautious.

Gunnar turned and fixed his calm gaze on the old man. "Were they Normans?"

Edward was no match for Gunnar Olafson. "They looked like soldiers, sir."

Probably Lord Fitzmorton's men, hiding out in the Mere, ready to attack. Rose had met with them, and they had planned the details of the assault, and then she had gone home.

It did not ring true.

Gunnar looked out again, across the watery levels toward one particular island of dark, brooding appearance. He was weary from last night. His body was finally relaxed after days of rigid tension and he wanted nothing more than to sleep, but there was to be no sleep for him yet. He had questions to answer, and Somerford to take care of.

If not Rose, then who could it have been that night?

Not Arno—to put himself in a position of possible capture or disclosure was not in his nature. Nay, more like he would send a note. Or a messenger. Would Arno have sent someone in his stead, someone he trusted, who was party to his treason against Somerford and Lord Radulf? Did Arno have such an ally at Somerford Manor?

"Could it have been Brother Mark?" Gunnar asked quietly, and watched Edward's wrinkled face.

The old man thought hard, and then nodded uncertainly. "Aye, 'tis possible, Captain. Brother Mark be shortish, and he wears a cloak. Aye, mayhap 'twere Brother Mark."

Gunnar nodded with a sense of satisfaction. Another mystery solved. Arno and Mark were friends, and they were both in the plot with Fitzmorton to take Somerford. Probably Arno had only brought Mark there for that reason—the man was certainly no priest. He bore the scars of battle upon his hands and his knowledge of priestly matters was abysmal. Not that that prevented him from being a priest, for Gunnar had met some poor excuses for priests, but there was something cunning about the man, something base that gave the lie to his claims of piety.

"Thank you, Edward," Gunnar said at last, and smiled. "You have helped me much and I will not forget it when the time comes."

Edward glanced up at him sharply, perhaps hearing some note in his voice he did not like. "You do be on the Lady Rose's side in this matter, Captain? We Somerford folk do love our lady. Don't be thinking otherwise. 'Tis Sir Arno we don't like. He shows us one face but he has another he keeps well hid. Ever since he came here, he's been watching her, hoping for more than he has a right to. Lady Rose trusts him because her heart is good; she doesn't believe he'd betray her."

"She is fond of him, then?" The words were careless, as if it mattered to him not at all. Gunnar was surprised how difficult it suddenly was for him to assume such a pretense.

Edward snorted. "You think they be lovers, Captain? Nay, they're not lovers! Lady Rose is too good for Arno, Captain. He was Lord Edric's friend, and so she trusts him for that reason. Do you know he swore allegiance to her over Edric's deathbed?" The old man raised a cynical eyebrow. "Edric made him do it."

"And you think . . . ?"

"I think Lord Edric knew very well what Arno was about. I think he made him swear his allegiance to Lady Rose to keep him true to her. Mayhap he hoped Lady Rose would marry again, to a man strong enough to deal with the Norman. He didn't realize our lady would see that Arno did not love her people as she did, and so for our sake she would stand alone. Lady Lily helped her in that—Lady Lily be a strong woman herself."

As Gunnar returned to the keep he felt almost lightheaded with relief. It must be so. Edward was right. Rose was no treacherous lady. No, *he* was the treacherous one. He quickened his pace, full of a dark, unfamiliar anger. *He* was here as Rose's man but he was actually Lord Radulf's spy. Worse than that, for he was seeking to steal what was hers. And when Rose learned of it she would feel betrayed.

She would probably never forgive him.

* * *

Constance had been watching Rose since she entered the bedchamber that morning to help her dress. The old woman had a gleam in her eye, but as yet, to Rose's relief, she had said nothing. With luck she would believe the signs of exhaustion on Rose's face were due to no more than a restless night—Jesu, it wasn't as if she didn't have plenty of troubles to keep her awake! She didn't want to speak of Gunnar yet. She felt too unsettled to consider what would happen now, and Constance would force her to think hard.

"Lady? The red gown today with the blue undergown?"

Rose nodded, allowing Constance to choose, standing docile while Constance tugged the cloth over her head and settled it into place. Constance's gaze fixed on the bed and instantly Rose tensed. Although she was sure she had smoothed away all evidence of Gunnar's occupation, he was such an overwhelming presence, it was as if some sign of him remained. Would Constance sense that he had been there?

Thus far the old woman had not said a word.

"The plaited gold girdle, lady? And the red calfskin shoes?"

"Aye, Constance, thank you."

Constance finished with the girdle and shoes and set to brushing her lady's hair, strong strokes through the curling, midnight thickness. Rose sighed for the dozenth time, wondering how she would look at Gunnar today—yesterday had been bad enough, but now there was much more between them.

She closed her eyes, remembering despite herself. It had not been at all as she imagined. She had thought he would lie with her once and leave, mayhap even use her like a . . . a camp follower. Instead he had taken her with relish, lavishing his body upon her. She had feared from the first moment she saw him that he would enthrall her senses, and so he had, but in return he had given her a new sense of her own power over him.

She had not expected that.

Rose had learned last night that Gunnar Olafson was not the invulnerable warrior she had thought him. She could make him sweat, she could make him shudder, she could make him groan for release. He was a man, capable of feeling pain and pleasure, hurt and joy. And knowing that had changed everything.

Constance had begun to braid her hair, standing close behind Rose, her fingers still quick and sure for all her years.

"Sometimes," she said quietly, "the character of a man is more important that his bloodline." She nodded to herself, twisting the dark strands into one thick rope. "A man with honor, a strong man who can see right from wrong, aye, he would be a far better option than a man with powerful friends who whores and swears and cares not at all for his wife and family."

Rose had stiffened, staring straight ahead as if Constance held a dagger at her back. So much for thinking she had escaped Constance's eagle eyes, she thought despairingly.

"I have heard tell that the Vikings are near enough to kings, in their own country."

"They are savages and murderers in ours," Rose retorted in a small, hard voice.

"Lady, your own father is no shining example. Old Edric was frightened of him, but he still married you, and not only because Radulf, his overlord, told him to.

He did it because you were beautiful and sweet, and the old man lost his heart to you. Maybe he even felt sorry for you, when he met your father and saw what he was. One day you will have to wed again, and your second husband may not be as easy to manage as your first."

Rose shook her head; of all her people, Constance was the only one who knew of her past. "Constance, this is not helping . . ."

"To marry beneath your family and position may not be 'beneath' you in other ways, that is all I mean to say." Constance finished with a rush, determined to complete her speech.

Rose took a deep, slow breath. "I see that you have guessed what happened between Captain Olafson and myself. It was lust, Constance, nothing more. You said yourself I needed a lover, and last night I took one. That is all. Please don't think it more than that."

Constance finished the braid and let it fall gently against Rose's straight back. "Do you truly believe that? I have seen the look in your eyes . . . in his eyes, and I know there is more to this than lust."

"No." Rose pulled away and stood up. Her heart was pounding, her eyes wide, her hands shaking. "Please, let me hear no more of it, Constance. I will hear no more!"

And she was gone, all but running down the stairs. Constance stared after her with a humorless smile. "Aye, my lady, you may run this time, but there will come a time when you can run no more. And then you will see that this old woman was right."

Chapter 13

"Steven?"

He looked up at her warily. The youthful face had a greenish tinge, and brown hair hung into red-rimmed, hazel eyes. Rose bit her lip to prevent a smile. Radulf's messenger had overindulged last night and was now paying the price. Belatedly he struggled to stand, but Rose put a gentle hand on his shoulder to prevent him.

"No, Steven, rest your legs."

"My thanks, lady." He sounded as if his throat had formed a crust.

"You have been with Lord Radulf long?"

He managed a wan smile. "Aye, lady."

"And you revere him? Aye, I see you do. You must be more than thankful his lady is delivered safely and he has his heir."

The smile was broader now. "I am thankful for both. Lord Radulf is . . . is very fond of his lady."

"Besotted, in fact?" teased Rose, who had seen the couple at first hand. "They are very lucky, Steven, you do not know how rare 'tis for such a union in these times."

The boy nodded seriously, but his eyes held a puzzled look as he watched her, wondering what she wanted from him.

Rose got to the point. "I wish you to give a message from me to Lord Radulf and Lady Lily." She held the parchment in her hand, the wax stamped with Edric's seal, a large fish swallowing a smaller fish.

Steven cleared his throat. "Aye, lady, I will deliver your message safely."

She smiled without humor. "It says that the people of Somerford Manor celebrate the birth of a son for Crevitch, and that one day he will be our lord."

"Aye, lady."

"There is more." Rose met his eyes and noticed the glazed look clearing from them as Steven sensed her anxiety. Carefully, she placed the parchment on the table before him. For a moment she was tempted to speak the words aloud: *I am asking Lord Radulf for his support—one of Lord Fitzmorton's men has died in Somerford village and my miller has admitted to the crime. But there were circumstances . . .* But she shook her head impatiently; better if Radulf read them himself. "Tell him that he must come as soon as may be," she said hastily, and even then wondered if she had said too much.

"Aye, Lady Rose, I will tell him that. He must come to Somerford." He hesitated uncertainly, and then rose to his feet, tucking the parchment inside his tunic. He was as tall as she—not a boy then, despite his youthful face. "Do not worry, lady, whatever is wrong Lord Radulf will put it to rights."

Wryly, Rose smiled her thanks, and went on her way.

In truth she felt numbed. It was done and soon Steven would be gone, taking the fateful message to Radulf at Crevitch castle, some five leagues to the west. Lord Radulf would understand the danger and send his men, if he did not come himself. Somerford Manor would be safe from Fitzmorton, and Harold would live on to be an old man. Aye, all would be well.

Except for Rose.

She would lose Somerford Manor. No longer to be the lady here, no longer to be loved and respected, no longer to sit in her hall and feel she belonged.

No longer to lie awake at night worrying for the welfare of your people. No longer making decisions that give and take life. No longer butting your head against the stubborn, brutal stupidity of men like Miles de Vessey . . .

There was that. But, as Rose was aware, such decisions were all part of being the Lady of Somerford. And would the new lord be as fair, as mindful of the people as Rose had been? Mayhap it would be someone like Arno, selfish and uncaring, looking upon his English people as mere cattle.

But at least it will not be Lord Fitzmorton.

No, at least *they* would be spared that awful fate.

Rose glanced at Brother Mark as she left the great hall. He was watching her, and bowed his head slightly in response. He had written her the message that morning, copying as she dictated, his pen scratching busily upon the parchment. When the letter was sealed, she had sworn him to silence, and he had given his word.

As he was the only person at Somerford who could read and write, Rose had had no choice but to trust him with this important task.

Millisent had glanced up as Alfred came into the hall, but now she looked quickly away again. No one would have guessed by her action that she had been waiting for him.

Alfred himself certainly did not.

He hesitated a moment, on the verge of approaching her, but she was busy with some needlework. Instead he turned abruptly toward his companions, where they sat huddled together over a game of dice.

Millisent stared down at her stitching, not seeing the uneven work. Since her father had been arrested she had thought only of him, of how she could help him. Then last night Eartha had whispered to her that all would be well, that Lady Rose had promised. Millisent trusted Lady Rose. If her lady said she would make all well, then so it would be.

With the burden of her father removed from her, Millisent was free to think of other things. And, oddly, she had found her thoughts centering on the mercenary, Alfred. Before, blinded by her fear and her grief, she had not thought to question his constant presence, or his kindness and support when she most needed both. Now she wondered, and was a little embarrassed to recall how she had wept on his shoulder and clung to him that night in the bailey, when her father had been captured.

Alfred's face was scarred. It had been burned when the Normans killed his family, so the one called Ivo had told her. Previously Millisent had been so caught up in her own concerns she had not noticed it—well, except in a vague sort of way. But now she looked at him more carefully, and was . . . surprised. Not frightened, and not repelled, no, not that. Just a little surprised that she had not noticed before.

Some of the other women shuddered and said the sight of him made them queasy. Millisent did not find that. She thought he must have been handsome once—the other side of his face was nice to look at. And even the scarred side wasn't so bad, when you were used to it. Besides, it was his eyes she looked into most of the time, and they were brown, their expression sympathetic.

It was his eyes she remembered when she lay in her narrow bed, tucked away in the curtained space that belonged to Eartha and her young son, and now must also accommodate Millisent and Will. His eyes, and his arms so firm and comforting about her as she had wept. For a man who had suffered much, he was generous in the giving of himself to others.

Millisent had learned it was not always so. Some men grew harder, crueler, as if their suffering had eaten away what kindness once existed in them. Alfred was not like that. He watched over her—or had done until recently—and if she or Will needed him, then he was there. Except that Millisent had not really appreciated how much she had come to rely on him, until now.

And that was her current dilemma. Now that she had finally noticed Alfred's interest in her, he had withdrawn it.

Did he think she didn't need him anymore? Or had he become bored with her self-pity? She wanted to thank him, to express her earnest appreciation, but she felt suddenly too timid to approach him. A mercenary, a man who had traveled and seen much, would find tedious a girl who had never stepped outside Somerford Manor in all her life. He probably had a wife somewhere else.

Millisent was surprised how much that thought upset her.

The group of mercenaries were making loud conversation, absorbed in their game. Their captain had left abruptly after old Edward had come to speak with him, and they were awaiting his return. The messenger with the wary eyes, Steven, had gone back to Crevitch. He had given Millisent more than one passing look, but she had not returned them. He was just a boy—Alfred, he was a man.

"Sweyn has won again!" Ivo bellowed it out as if he couldn't believe it. He glanced at Alfred in disgust. "Keep your money safe in your belt, Alfred, if you wish to keep it. The Dane has the devil's luck."

Blond, handsome Sweyn grinned and ignored him, warming the dice in his hand before throwing them again. A terrible groan went up from Reynard, his luckless opponent.

Alfred smiled and glanced over his shoulder, to where Millisent sat. She was watching him, but she looked away again quickly. That was the second time she had done that, as if she didn't want him to know she was looking. But now there was a flush in her cheeks and her movements seemed too studied to be natural.

Apart from the faint color, she looked pale with the strain of the past days. Fragile. An unexpected tenderness filled him. Was he losing his mind to feel this way, and to allow it to take hold of him like this? She was a pretty girl, aye, but it was more than that. There was something about her that made him want to watch over her, protect her . . . love her. Idiotic, when he thought about it.

What would Millisent, the pretty daughter of a prosperous miller, want with an English mercenary without a face? And why was she staring at him? A wave of misery darkened his mood.

Of course, *his face*.

Few women had ever been able to look at him without commenting upon it, and then either shrinking away from him in horror or else draping themselves over him in sickly sympathy. He didn't want pity. He wanted to be treated just like anyone else. The Normans might have marked him—he could survive that—but it was the pity of so-called friends that threatened to destroy him utterly.

He remembered, the night of the village fire, Lady Rose had treated him as if she had not even noticed there was anything wrong with him. She had not spoken to him as if he were simple, just because his face was marked. She had appreciated his help and told him so, and even laughed when he told her a humorous tale from his boyhood. 'Twas no wonder Gunnar Olafson couldn't keep his eyes off her . . .

Millisent was staring again, her amber eyes big in her small face, her unruly chestnut hair fanning out in wisps about her head. This time she didn't turn away immediately, and . . . Alfred blinked. She was smiling. A shy glance upwards and with it a very definite smile.

Bemused, Alfred murmured some excuse to his companions and stumbled over to her on legs that didn't feel as if they belonged to him.

She was sewing again, but from the trembling of her

hands he didn't think she would get very far with it. Did he frighten her?

The dark misery washed over him again. Aye, probably he did frighten her. He should walk right past her, forget her, pretend she had not stirred something in him that had been deep-buried ever since the Normans came and took away everything that mattered to him. He had never thought to make a life of his own—his life had seemed over, but now he found himself thinking of beginning something new, something fresh.

There it was! That smile again, a little uncertain now, beckoning him closer, like a rush-dip in a dark cellar. Alfred stood a yard or so from her, hesitating. She was stitching furiously now, and just as he had decided he was mistaken again, and half turned to go, she gasped and dropped the needle. A bead of scarlet blood was bright against her fingertip, and as she stared down in dismay a droplet fell onto the clean linen and soaked in.

Millisent lifted wide eyes to him. "It will stain," she whispered, sounding as if she had just committed a crime every bit as heinous as her father's.

Alfred tried not to smile, but she must have seen the laughter glint in his eyes, because she frowned and turned her face away. Suddenly he was beside her, without remembering closing the distance. He squatted down by the stool where she sat, and reached out to take her wounded hand in his.

Millisent stiffened, her face still hidden, but she did not try to snatch her hand back. Alfred thought that was a good sign. Slowly, carefully watching for any hint that he might repulse her, Alfred lifted her finger and touched it gently to his tongue.

The blood was salty.

Her hand trembled, and then abruptly relaxed into his. She turned to gaze at him, her lips parting, soft color staining her pale face.

Emboldened, Alfred drew her fingertip into his mouth, sucking gently. Her eyes grew wider, and they were full of wonder. And that was when he knew. She did not mind his ruined face, when she looked at him she did not see the scars as something apart from him. She saw *him*, and she liked what she saw.

Alfred held the hurt finger in his, examining it closely. The bleeding had stopped, not that it had ever been very great. He was almost sorry—he had enjoyed the feel of her in his mouth.

"You have made it better," she whispered, and tears filled her beautiful eyes. "Thank you, Alfred."

Alfred had a feeling she was thanking him for more than this, but he did not ask. He did not want to break the spell. Instead he smiled and gently released her, rising to his full height.

"Will you walk with me in the kitchen garden?" he asked her quietly. And instantly he wanted to draw the words back, afraid she would say no.

Millisent hesitated, glancing down at her stitching, and he was certain then she was going to refuse. Her laugh tingled over his skin. She laid the linen aside, and held out her hand toward him. "Aye, I will," she said, and Alfred grew dizzy with the promises he saw dancing in her eyes.

Rose had been watching the door for hours. Or so it seemed.

The mercenaries had spent the afternoon helping rebuild the village. Rose knew they had little time left before the harvest would have to begin, for then they would need every available hand to work from dawn till dusk in the fields.

Now the evening meal was ready to be served and most of the household had already assembled in the great hall. A couple of hounds tussled together by the fireplace, until the foot of a passing servant separated them.

Millisent had been following on her heels like a shadow all afternoon, and although the girl had been too dreamy to be of much use, Rose had not had the heart to send her away. Harold still resided in his cell, and there he would stay until Radulf came. Rose had made certain he was cared for, and repeated her promise to Eartha that all would be well . . . but in her heart she was sick. And yet how could she watch Harold die, or stand by while Fitzmorton tore Somerford to pieces? No, this was the only way.

The meal could not wait any longer.

Rose moved to the table on the dais, and glanced over at the hovering serving wenches. Reading her correctly, they clattered out to fetch the meal.

Brother Mark was approaching, rubbing his hands together in anticipation—Rose had never met such a greedy man. "The boy . . . the messenger went off safely?" he asked her, leaning close so that no one else could hear.

"Aye, he did," Rose said, trying to ignore the crawling-flesh feeling that being close to Brother Mark always gave her.

"Good, good." He laughed, and then, sensing her surprise, subdued himself and looked away.

Sir Arno wasn't there yet. He had been delayed by some unspecified matter, and had sent word for Rose not to wait. What matter could keep Arno from his meat and his wine? Rose wondered, for he was nearly as greedy as Brother Mark.

She had not spoken to him, not properly, since the incident in the village. Rose knew it would need to be done soon, but she shied away from it. Soft-hearted as she was, Rose did not like to hurt people, and she feared that in Arno she had handled matters very ill. If she had only known of his love for her, she might have tread more carefully, refused him in a way he could accept without losing face. Now he was angry and his feelings wounded.

Now he was dangerous.

She glanced up at the door again, and promptly forgot Arno and Brother Mark and everyone else.

Gunnar had come at last.

He approached down the length of the great hall with his confident, ringing stride, and simply everyone turned to look at him. As he passed his mercenary band, he paused long enough to murmur something in Ivo's ear. The big dark man nodded seriously, and then Gunnar had passed on, climbing the dais to Rose's table.

Without Arno there, there was no bolster between them. When he sat down he was looking directly at her, and Rose felt her insides curl. This was the man who last night had held her in his arms, covered her mouth with his, and taken her body with his in a way that she feared had spoiled her for all others.

"My apologies, lady," he was saying with his lips. "I had a matter to attend to." His eyes were saying something else altogether.

"Everyone has matters to attend this evening, so it seems." Rose's voice was chilly with nerves.

Gunnar gave her a questioning smile.

"Sir Arno is also late," she explained, gesturing to the space.

He looked startled, as if he had only just realized Arno wasn't there. His narrowed blue gaze flicked about the hall, taking swift note of everything and everyone. Rose waited until he had turned that piercing look back onto her. "Is there something wrong, Captain?" she asked him softly.

She had leaned closer, and he too bent toward her, so that their faces were almost touching. "I am hungry, lady, that is all," his murmur was deep and soft. His gaze slid lower, brushing her mouth, her smooth throat, the curve of her breasts beneath her red gown.

Rose tried to catch her breath. Suddenly her mind was again filled with memories of hot kisses and gasping cries, and his hard body moving inside hers. Jesu, what was wrong with her? Why could she not restrain herself as she used to? It was as if a riverbank had burst within her, and now it was impossible to hold back the tumbling water.

"I am sure the meal will arrive soon, Captain," she managed, glancing rather desperately at the door to the kitchen.

Gunnar shook his head. Beneath the table his hand brushed hers. "But later . . . when I hunger in the night, lady? Will there be aught for me then?"

"Do you often hunger in the night?" she asked him, her voice strange, her flesh tingling.

"That depends." He was stroking her palm with his finger. Rose shivered—how could a touch so simple feel so exquisite?

"Upon what?"

"On the repast available."

The laughter bubbled up inside her. Rose bit her lip on the image of herself naked upon a silver platter, but her eyes danced. He was *teasing* her, stirring to life her waking desire in a manner no man had ever done before. When she had thought of men and women mating it had never seemed to her a matter for lightheartedness, for laughter and joy. It was a task, just like any other, part of the bargain that was made between them when they wed, or the way to make children.

Now Gunnar had shown her another side to it, and Rose was delighted, despite feeling uncomfortably hot all over. Was this a preliminary to later, to tonight? When he came to her? Aye, there were promises now in his eyes, and her fingers had turned over and were clinging to his.

"I want . . ." she began, her voice a shaken whisper.

"Forgive me, lady!" Arno had arrived, shouldering between them, his face flushed and his eyes bright.

Rose pulled herself back, physically and mentally. Had Arno heard? Seen? He did not seem to have, although then again he was not quite his usual self . . . She eyed him curiously. Arno was excited. Something had happened. She opened her mouth to ask for an explanation, too late. The servants had arrived with the food, and the chance was lost in the familiar business of serving and eating.

Rose took a dainty bite of the fish pie, washing down Eartha's fine pastry with a sip of her wine. Constance slipped hastily into her own seat, with an apologetic glance at Rose. "I was taking Harold's meal to him," she explained.

"Why bother?" Arno had heard her.

Rose turned to look at him questioningly, though she feared she already knew what he would say.

"Why bother wasting good food on a dying man?" Arno did not surprise her, but she was dismayed at the loud heartiness of his voice.

Quickly she looked down into the body of the hall, hoping no one else had heard. Several unsmiling faces were turned in their direction, and one of them was Millisent's. The girl had lost the blush that had looked so pretty on her cheeks earlier, and her eyes were wide and afraid. As Rose, dismayed by Arno's brutality, wondered how she could undo his damage, Alfred rose from his place with the other mercenaries and set himself down beside Millisent.

The girl turned towards him, and something in her expression, something in the tilt of her head, told Rose all she needed to know. They were in love. It surprised her, and yet . . . it was not such a surprise, surely? They had been thrown much together since the night of the fire, and Rose had discovered for herself how kind and sensible was Alfred. A reliable man, yet one who had also suffered, the sort of man who would greatly appeal to a girl who, in an instant, finds her safe world turned upside down.

As Rose watched, Millisent reached out her hand and touched Alfred's mouth, a light brush of her fingers, but it was obvious she would have liked to kiss him instead. And by the look in his eyes Alfred was more than willing to reciprocate.

Suddenly Rose felt like an interloper, and turned back to her fish pie. Was that how *she* looked, when she watched Gunnar? Were her own feelings as easy to read as those of Millisent? Jesu, she prayed not! The thought made her cringe. How could she keep the respect and obedience of her people, if she showed no more sense than to become besotted by a handsome-faced mercenary?

They would laugh at her! And Rose would not blame them.

She did not look in Gunnar's direction again. The sight of Millisent and Alfred had sobered her, frightened her, and woken her out of her silly dream. Instead she thought of Lord Radulf in his stout castle at Crevitch, receiving the message from Steven and then calling for his men and setting out for Somerford to make all right. Of course, then he would discover that, far from being the strong and sensible woman she had thought herself, Rose had been far too interested in enjoying Gunnar Olafson to see disaster approaching.

Constance drew the brush through her lady's hair, candlelight gleaming on the dark, glossy strands. It tumbled about her, feeling heavy on her back and shoulders, pulling at her slender neck as she sat on the stool wearing her thin robe. The weight of her lady's hair seemed symbolic to Constance, and she wished there was some way of lightening her mood.

Tonight Rose was subdued, lost deep in her thoughts. Not a good sign, as Constance knew from past experience. 'Twas better if Rose did not think too hard when it came to her own happiness; she was constantly finding excuses not to do those things that pleased her most. It was almost as if she did not believe she deserved pleasure, did not deserve happiness, when everyone at Somerford—from the oldest to the youngest—wished her all the happiness in the world.

Constance wielded the brush again. "Gunnar Olafson is a fine man," she said, treading carefully.

Rose frowned.

Inside Constance sighed, but she refused to be daunted. "He has much to offer."

"He is certainly handsome," Rose replied bitterly. "I am shallow enough to notice that, Constance. Perhaps that is all that matters to me, his beauty. I thought I was better than the other women, but in truth I fear I am no different."

Constance assumed a somber look, her eyes lowered. "Are you certain, lady? Is *he* not different from other men? I ask this because, although Gunnar Olafson might be handsome, and all the women may stare, he has not used the situation to his advantage, has he? He has not gone from one bed to another, has he? It is *you* he favors above all others, and only you."

Rose rubbed her temples as if they ached. "I offered him money to come to my bed," she admitted, and there was shame in her voice.

Constance almost groaned out loud.

"He did not take it," Rose went on miserably. "He said it was . . . it was all part of his service. And he . . . he did it three times, Constance." Her eyes were dark and enormous, as she met the old woman's startled gaze. "I thought he would only do it but once, and then he woke me and did it again, and then come dawn he did it again. And each time was just as wonderful as the first . . . I did not know until then, I did not understand what you meant when you said it would be different with a young and lusty man. A man I wanted."

Constance choked back laughter as she listened to her lady's artless confessions, but her voice trembled only slightly when she replied. "It sounds to me, lady, as if Gunnar Olafson came to you because it pleased him to do so, and not because you coerced him into it. A man, being what he is, may take a woman once, even if he does not like her particularly, but *three* times." She shook her head with certainty. "Nay, lady, that could only be for his own pleasure, because he craved her as a thirsty man craves water."

The rigidity went out of Rose's shoulders, hope filled her unhappy eyes. "Do you think so, Constance?"

"I do, lady."

As if on cue, there was a knock on the door. Rose jumped as though it were the devil calling, but Constance did not hesitate. She went swiftly to open it.

"Constance!" her lady gasped behind her, starting to her feet, but it was too late. The door had been swung open and Gunnar Olafson was in the room. His gaze met hers above Constance's head, and then took in her loose hair and thin robe. When his eyes returned to hers, the blue was afire with passion.

The old woman reached out to touch his arm, gently, speaking in a voice too soft for Rose to hear, and then she slipped out behind him and closed the door. They were alone, and the chamber was suddenly much smaller and more airless than Rose had imagined.

"I don't—" she began.

"I find I am hungry, lady," he said.

"Oh." Rose hesitated, her thoughts skittering all over the place. "Are you . . . are you very hungry, Captain?" Why did she always sound so breathless when she wished to sound sensible?

"Aye, very hungry," he mocked. One step and he had her in his arms, his mouth covering hers as if he really were ravenous for her. His hands tangled in her long dark hair, twisting through the silken strands, gently pulling her closer against him.

Her breasts were aching, her nipples were tight and hard, and she wondered if he could feel them against his chest. Probably. Her legs trembled, her head spun, and that treacherous warmth was building between her thighs. Wanting him, willing to do anything to have him again.

His thick arousal dug into her belly, and she remembered what Constance had said. A man must desire a woman to take her as many times as he had taken Rose last night. Gunnar Olafson desired her, at least there was no doubting that.

She touched him, rubbing the hard shape of him through his breeches. Gunnar groaned, arching against her hand, and then kissing her again as if he were drowning in her. Rose stretched up on her toes, trying to get closer, and he reached down and lifted her, giving her the contact she craved.

Pleasure speared through her, making her twist and gasp. But it wasn't enough. After last night simply touching would never be enough again. She wanted him inside her and she knew—he had raised his head, those so-blue eyes gazing deep into hers—that he wanted that, too.

Gunnar carried her toward the bed and laid her down upon the soft covers. Her robe slipped across her skin, opening enough to show one dark pink nipple, the curve of her stomach, the long length of one thigh, and the shadow at the apex of her legs. He was watching her, his face hard and tense, as he began to untie the laces of his breeches.

Rose held her breath, wanting him so much, and yet spellbound by the picture he made. Gunnar was a beautiful man, and yet there was something savage about him, something untamed. Surely no woman could hold him for long. Certainly Rose did not expect to. Her warrior, her man, her lover.

The laces came undone, and he pushed his breeches down over his hips and thighs. His manhood sprang forth, big and bold. Rose started to sit up, needing to touch him, to kiss him, but he was already on top of her. One hard leg pushing hers apart, his hands thrusting aside her robe, and his mouth hot on her breasts. His hair was tickling her skin, and she slid her hands through it, anchoring him there as he tasted her, drew her into his mouth. Rose moved her hips, pressing to the hard muscle of his thigh, enjoying the friction.

Still it wasn't enough.

"Gunnar," she whispered, "please," reaching down, closing her fingers around him.

He groaned a laugh. "I cannot think, lady, when you do that."

"You do not need to think."

He moved so that he was poised above her and, when he had her full attention, began to slide into her, slowly, oh so slowly. Rose could not take her eyes away, shocked and fascinated by the sight of all that rigid flesh joining with hers.

"It doesn't seem possible," she breathed, growing tense.

But he pushed in a little further, stopping only to allow her to adjust to his size. " 'Twas possible last night," he reminded her in a strained voice. He clasped her bottom and tilted her hips, so that she was even more open to him, and began the same slow, inexorable entry.

Rose grasped his forearms tightly, the simmer inside her growing to a burn. She wanted him, and suddenly his consideration was driving her wild. Rose took matters into her own hands. Her hips moved against him, thrusting up, taking all of him inside her. And he was right, she could do it, and the sensation was beyond pleasure.

Gunnar caught and held his breath, trying to recapture his prized control. Watching him through her lashes, Rose moved again, pushing herself onto him as he tried to withdraw, silently urging him to hurry. His big body shuddered, and he began to thrust in earnest.

Already the first tremors were rippling through her, her gasps turning to soft moans. He drove hard, cupping her bottom, rising above her like some pagan god. Rose knew herself to be beyond thought, beyond caring, knowing only that here, now, with him, she was complete.

Gunnar reached down between their bodies, finding that throbbing bud, and Rose surged up against him, crying out, dissolving around him. With an answering shout, Gunnar too was lost.

For a long time Gunnar did not move, simply allowing his breath to return to normal, his heart to slow, just enjoying lying against her. If this was lust . . . *if?* He searched his mind uneasily. What else could it be? Rose was the widow of an old husband, and suddenly she had discovered desire. He just happened to be the man in the right place at the right time. She might want him now, and he was pleased to oblige her for his own reasons, but that was all.

Your own reasons being?

A need that was consuming him. So that when he was away from her, all he thought of was getting back to her. And when he was with her, all he wanted to do was stay right there.

His rod was still inside her; he felt it growing and hardening again, filling her. She was still swollen from his rough lovemaking of moments ago—he had tried to be gentle, but she had driven him mad and he had lost control . . . Great Odin, he *never* lost control. At least, he never had until he laid eyes on Lady Rose of Somerford Manor.

She moved beneath him, drawing in a shaky breath, and he realized with surprise that she was laughing. Her dark lashes lifted, and she stared up at him with teasing dark eyes.

"Are you hungry again, Gunnar?"

There was a new certainty about her, a new confidence. Had he done that? He couldn't help it, he smiled back, and felt as if his heart were dissolving in his chest. "Aye, lady," he breathed. "Starving."

She stretched her arms above her head, and then reached up to encircle them about his neck. Her body was pressed to his, soft and warm, and oh so willing. "Then if you are hungry you must sup," she told him with that wanton tremble in her voice. "I insist."

"Then, lady, if you insist . . ."

Gunnar did as she bade him.

Chapter 14

"Lady?"

Constance stood before her. Rose looked up from her seat in the great hall, eyes wide and blurred with her own thoughts. She had been remembering the expression in Gunnar's eyes when he joined his body to hers, hot and yet determined, as if he were marking her in some way. Making her his. And she had wanted him to, more than anything. Wanted to be his . . .

Rose blinked, glancing about her and then back to Constance.

"Lady?" the old woman repeated patiently, a humorous gleam in her own eyes. "You remember Olwan the peddler? He is come."

Olwan? wondered Rose. And then, abruptly, memory returned. Olwan the peddler. Of course. Edric had been fond of the little man and made certain to ply him with food and drink whenever he came to Somerford. His visit occurred once a year, when Olwan would trade with the Somerford people during the late summertime, the prosperous time. Although—Rose blinked herself further awake—it was usually much later, after the harvest, when money was more abundant.

This year the harvest was yet to be brought in, and there was little to barter or spend. Still, even if she couldn't buy, Rose thought, it would be pleasant to cast her eye over Olwan's wares. A distraction for them all.

The peddler soon had his trinkets spread upon a trestle table, and the women were gathered about, enjoying themselves immensely.

"I have a brooch, and I have been saving it for you, lady," Olwan said in his Welsh lilt, his dark eyes full of a sincerity Rose did not believe for a moment.

But it was all part of the pull and tug between buyer and seller, and Rose smiled, saying, "I doubt I can afford it, Olwan," as she bent to examine the treasure.

The brooch looked old. It was made of bone, and the markings on it were a little like the carvings on the Somerford chair. Rapacious vines and tendrils mingled with the curling tresses of a woman's hair. She was shown in profile, and was holding up an apple with one hand. Surprised, Rose recognized Idun. Was this a coincidence, or were Gunnar's savage gods giving her their blessing? Mayhap they were handing her the apple to eternal life . . . or love.

Love?

The soft word acted on her like the most violent of curses. Rose's throat closed up and her hands began to shake. The brooch almost slipped from her grip and shattered on the floor.

"Lady?"

Olwan's voice was soft and very near her ear. Rose

started and drew back, suddenly conscious of the sour, unwashed smell of the peddler's body. It was a moment before she heard what he was saying.

"Lady, I have come here as quickly as I could from Lord Fitzmorton's lands, and I have news you need to hear."

Rose frowned, both the brooch and the peddler's reek forgotten. "What is this news, Olwan? Why do I need to hear it?"

"There is a knight called Miles de Vessey. Do you know him?"

Her dreaminess vanished. "To my cost, aye, I know him."

"Then you will not be pleased to hear he is on his way here, to Somerford, to keep watch when you sit in judgment at the manor court upon one of your people."

No, Rose wasn't pleased. The chatter of the women around her faded, and she felt queasy with a combination of fear and anger. Miles de Vessey was returning to Somerford. Had Fitzmorton sent him? But why did he come so soon? Whatever the reasons, he would be unlikely to stand silently by while she freed Harold for murdering Gilbert the Norman. Could she order her gates closed and hold Miles and his men out? Even with the addition of the mercenaries, the Somerford garrison was weak. Would Radulf get there first? He must have her message now—why had he not come?

"Is he far behind you?" she asked Olwan in a calm voice that did not show the hurried thudding of her heart.

"If he has rested, then a day or two, no more. I came as quickly as I could."

Rose met the dark eyes of the peddler—Edric had always trusted him, and she had no reason not to. "Thank you, Olwan. I will not forget this. When you are finished here, be certain you eat and drink your fill. We are most grateful."

Olwan bowed deeply, but still he hesitated. "Lady." He sighed. "There is more. Miles de Vessey spoke of you in my hearing. He was not . . . respectful. He means to hurt you, though it will be pleasure for him."

He looked afraid and worried, and Rose did not need to ask what Miles had said. Somehow she managed to maintain her composure, but her thoughts were running wild. What had Ivo said in the bailey, *Do not trust him, ever*? She remembered Miles's cold gray eyes the day by the Mere with an involuntary shudder.

Olwan was still watching her.

"My gratitude, Olwan. I am well warned, thanks to you."

Olwan bowed again. "Keep the brooch, lady, in remembrance of your husband, who was always kind to a poor peddler. Besides, it is said to be good luck, and you need it more than me, I think." He smiled regretfully, and this time left her to her thoughts.

Rose closed her fingers on the bone brooch and felt it mark her flesh. Where was Radulf? she asked herself again. Had he received her message? Mayhap the babe had delayed him, but he should be here soon, striding about, glowering at her, demanding to know exactly what was happening. If Miles came first he would insist on the judgment being made at once. He would want to see Harold hanged as soon as possible, and when Rose set him free . . . Miles would hurt her, and without Arno's support she would be powerless to stop him.

No!

Rose took a breath. Her mind collected itself and centered.

One word.

Gunnar.

It was like a balm, smoothing her jagged edges. What good luck had been smiling on her the day she decided she needed mercenaries at Somerford Manor? What happy coincidence had chosen *these* mercenaries over all those who might have come to her aid? Aye, Gunnar. He would know what to do; he would help her to decide on her course of action. She desperately needed his calm good sense, his unshakable strength.

Gunnar was more than a match for Miles de Vessey.

Rose hurried out of the hall, leaving behind her the women and Olwan's patter. Any gladness she had felt only moments before at this unexpected treat had drained from her now, leaving her feeling alone and frightened. The blue sky and warm sun in the bailey seemed incongruous. Danger was everywhere—she could smell the scent of it on the breeze, as foul as the peddler's unwashed body.

Old Edward, standing proudly on guard at the gate in his ancient tunic and helmet, had seen Gunnar Olafson go to the stable.

"Now there be a man who can take care of himself! He won't let anything happen to Somerford Manor, lady. We should all feel safer now Captain Olafson be here."

"I agree with you wholeheartedly, Edward," Rose said, and knew it for the truth.

The stable was on the far side of the bailey. To get to it she must pass the exercise yard, where Arno was busy training the young boys of Somerford Manor. She would have preferred not to encounter Arno just now. Mayhap, she thought hopefully, he would not be in a talkative mood. Mayhap he was still sullen from their encounter at the village.

As she drew closer, Rose glanced surreptitiously at her knight, noting that his fleshy face was puffy from drink and his eyes were circled. Her steps slowed. His body looked lax and portly, no longer fit and hard for battle, as he had boasted to her so often. Arno had been overindulging lately, and the excesses were beginning to stamp their mark on him.

Arno overindulged when he had a guilty conscience. But what could Arno feel guilty about? What had he done?

And suddenly the pieces fit together, and Rose thought she knew.

Lord Fitzmorton was sending Miles de Vessey to Somerford because Arno had betrayed her. He had sent to warn them that she meant to free Harold. Aye, Arno had betrayed her. Again! Gunnar had been right, as she had feared. Arno was in league with Fitzmorton.

Anger began to burn slowly through her, and she no longer wanted to avoid Arno. He looked up as she approached, and to her surprise his expression was dejected and miserable. Did his conscience trouble him? Did he dream of Edric's accusing finger pointing at him from the grave? If his perfidy gave him no joy, Rose thought coldly, she would not pity him. Suddenly it seemed important to let Arno know she was not the soft and gullible fool he had constantly thought her.

"I have heard word that Miles de Vessey will be present at the miller's trial," she said in her most authoritative voice. "What say you to that, Sir Arno?"

To her surprise, Arno did not demur. Instead he nodded, and his misery gave way to a weak sort of bluff self-assurance. "Aye, that's so, lady. It was I who suggested he come."

Her voice shook with fright and anger. "Arno, do you know what you have done?"

He looked away, his mouth hard. "I have saved you from destroying yourself for the sake of an English murderer, Rose, that is what I have done."

She shook her head at this self-justification.

"I wanted to marry you," he went on, and his sideways glance was sly. "I've wanted that ever since Edric died."

Here then was the truth at last. Rose tried not to look shocked. She had known something like this was afoot, and yet to hear him say it aloud . . . "And it was *me* you wanted, Arno, not Somerford Manor?" she asked him dryly.

Arno shifted uneasily. The sweat from his exertions with the boys trickled down his face. "Aye, well, there was that, too. I will not lie to you, Rose. Edric promised me Somerford years ago, before I came here as his knight—he could not pay me, and in lieu of money, when he died the manor was meant to be mine. But then, when he was dying, suddenly he changed his mind and forced me to swear allegiance to *you*. If you had wed me, Rose, then all would have been well! I tried to woo you, but you would not listen to me. You could not see my true feelings for you, or maybe you just did not want to."

He looked sullen, his lip protruding like that of a small child who has been denied what it wants the most.

Should she feel guilty because she could not love Arno? Because, not being of a grasping and treacherous disposition herself, she had failed to recognize it in him?

"And so you have betrayed me by turning to Lord Fitzmorton. Betrayed Lord Radulf, too."

"Radulf!" scoffed Arno. "He does not deserve to have so much!" Then, cautious again, he went on, "Lord Fitzmorton wants justice for his dead soldier, that is all. Justice is his right, and Miles de Vessey will see that he gets it."

Rose shook her head, ignoring Arno's further efforts to justify his actions. "I have sent word to Lord Radulf, Arno. Ask Brother Mark. He wrote my message. Radulf will be here very soon, and God help you then."

Arno smiled, and then tried to hide it.

Shocked, Rose stared back at him, not understanding and yet beginning to be terribly afraid.

"Oh Rose," he murmured softly, his brown eyes glittering with a combination of mockery and satisfaction, "do you not realize yet that our good Brother Mark is no ordained priest? He is a friend I thought might be useful to me, so when the old priest died I sent for him. He lived in a monastery once, long ago, so he knows enough to pass as a priest if you do not look too closely. And, fortunately for us, lady, he can read and write."

The truth stunned her. Rose tried to find words to voice her question, but she already knew the answer.

"Then the message I sent with Steven to Lord Radulf?"

"Spoke only of your joy at the birth of his heir."

"I see."

"Nay, you do not see at all!" He smiled at his own cleverness. "Brother Mark saw you speaking to the boy when you gave him the message. We could not risk him reaching Radulf too soon, even with Brother Mark's harmless message."

Rose stared. "What have you done to him?"

Arno shrugged. "He is unharmed. I will release him when Miles comes."

Would he? Rose didn't like the way he was avoiding her eyes.

"You mean to give me up to Fitzmorton then," she whispered. "Oh Arno, you don't understand what that means!"

She stepped around him and set out across the bailey, toward the stable. He followed after her.

"One baron is much the same as another, what does it matter if it be Fitzmorton or Radulf? Rose? Where are you going?"

"I am going to find Captain Olafson," she said, her voice rallying. "He will not let you hold Radulf's boy hostage, and he will not let a man like Miles de Vessey set one foot onto my manor!"

Arno snorted in disbelief. "Do you think the mercenary will care? He will go with whoever pays the most. Fitzmorton is his master, too, Rose. He has been all along."

"I do not believe it!" Rose cried, hurrying into a run.

"Ask him then, lady! Ask him!"

Rose picked up her skirts, careless of her people turning to gape at her in amazement. Arno had struck her to the heart with his confession, and now, to say that Gunnar, too, would betray her . . . After the moments they had shared in her chamber? No, she would not believe it! Suddenly she could not bear to.

After the sunny bailey the stable was dusty and dark,

and Rose stopped abruptly, blinking, searching the shadows. Her breath was heaving in her chest, as if she couldn't quite take in enough of the musty air, and she felt light-headed.

"Lady?"

His voice. She heard his step as he came from one of the stalls, and then she could see him. He looked weary and worried, and a tremendous tenderness filled her. She wanted to touch his face, smooth the lines from about his mouth, the dark shadows from beneath his eyes. Rose clenched her hands into tight fists at her sides, stilling the urge.

"I have had bad news," she said in a rush.

He narrowed his blue eyes. Did she imagine the watchful look that crept into them? "Wait," he said harshly and, jerking his head at a boy who had been shoveling straw, waited until he had gone. "Now, lady, what is this bad news?"

"Miles de Vessey is coming to oversee the trial of Harold the miller. To see that *justice* is done," she added bitterly. "Arno told me that he has told Miles that if Lord Fitzmorton is not represented I will set Harold free."

Gunnar moved closer, reaching out. Rose stepped back, away from him, knowing if he touched her she would not be able to say what needed to be said.

"And I *was* going to set him free, of course I was! I do not think he is guilty. I even sent word to Lord Radulf, with Steven. I asked Brother Mark to write a message for me, and now Arno tells me that Brother Mark did not write it—instead Arno sent his own message to Miles. And they have hidden Steven away somewhere, taken him prisoner! They mean to take Somerford for Fitzmorton between them!"

Gunnar stiffened, as if her words startled him in some way, but his steady gaze did not leave her face. She sensed movement behind all that cold calm, a shiver in the surface, as though something powerful were happening beneath.

Doubt grew inside her, but she held it back, denying it.

"Now Arno tells me that this is all my fault, because I would not let him subdue me. My fault!" Tears stung her eyes, but she wouldn't let them fall. "Captain Olafson . . . Gunnar, I ask you now, remembering the promise that you gave to obey me. I ask you to prevent this terrible thing from occurring. Save Somerford from Fitzmorton, for he is behind all this, I know it! Save my people from Miles de Vessey and Arno. Save *me*."

This time he clasped her shoulders, his big hands warm and firm. The dust motes danced about his copper hair. "Trust me, Rose," he said, his soft urgency slicing through her agitation. "I will do what I must."

It was not what she had hoped he would say.

Rose tried to read the answer she wanted in his eyes, but they were hot with the same need that had been in them last night, confusing her. He bent his head, slanting his mouth to cover hers, and her resistance melted.

With a soft groan she pressed into him, all that hard flesh and muscle. Her warrior, her man. Even in such a moment as this she could give herself completely over to wanting him. Rose knew to her dismay that if he had lifted her now and carried her into one of the stalls she would have gone willingly.

A hard, bitter laugh sounded from the doorway. Arno had followed her after all. Rose felt Gunnar still, and then he pulled back from her, giving her space. His eyes were fixed on hers.

"I knew it. You are the same as all the rest of them, Rose. Panting over a handsome face," Arno sneered, and there was hurt and jealousy in his voice, mingling with the fury. "I hoped you were better than Eartha and the other kitchen sluts, but you are worse. They must rely upon their smiles and their pretty faces, they have no real power. But you can order him to your bed, and so you have."

Rose blanched.

"And all along he fooled you," Arno went on with a sort of perverse satisfaction. "He is Fitzmorton's man. He is worse than I, because it is whoever pays the most who secures his loyalty. You have given yourself to a soulless monster, Rose." He turned and cocked his head at Gunnar. "Do I lie, *Captain*?"

Gunnar's face had gone grim. He looked at her a moment more, as if he were trying to tell her something with his eyes. Whatever it was she could not read it, felt incapable of reading it. Her mind and body were numb, as if she had suffered a tremendous shock. At any moment she knew it would wear off and the pain would come. Even now it was hurtling toward her like a black wall . . .

Gunnar offered Arno a shrug. "Aye, you're right, 'tis payment that seals my loyalty. I am a mercenary, Sir Arno, I do not ply my trade for the love of it."

Gunnar heard her gasp, as if he had slid his sword beneath her ribs, but he did not look at her. He dared not. He had already seen the expression on her pale face and it would haunt him forever. But he had a part to play if they were to come out of this alive. Aye, he was playing his part, and at the same time he was watching Arno, testing him, judging him . . . hating him.

Arno nodded as if the answer was what he had expected. "Sir Miles does not trust you, Captain. He has said so to me and his master. Lord Fitzmorton has reserved his judgment—he will trust you until he sees no more use in you. But I believe Miles is wrong. You see, I can read you, Gunnar Olafson. You are a simple man, and you are no longer young. Time has worked on you. There is a point when a man wants to stop fighting and settle. Is that not so?"

Gunnar wondered if his genuine shock was clear on his face.

"'Tis the land you want," Arno went on, enjoying himself. His eyes slid to Rose, soaking up her pain as if it gave him great satisfaction. "He, too, wants Somerford, lady," he explained in a gleeful voice. "Isn't that so, Captain?"

His throat felt dry but he knew what he had to do. If she was to survive, then so must he, and with Miles only a short ride from the gates, Arno must believe him to be as evil as the rest of them. He made himself cold, killed all feeling. Gunnar turned and let his eyes run over her, much as Miles had done when he came upon them at the Mere's edge. Her beautiful face colorless with betrayal, her dark eyes wide and teary, her stubborn chin held tight to stop the trembling of her mouth. The madder-red gown, the same one she had worn when he first saw her, clung to body, and even now he wanted her.

Would she remember his words? *Trust me, Rose. I will do what I must.*

Gunnar looked at Rose and deliberately destroyed any lingering belief in him she might have had. And felt as if he destroyed himself at the same time.

"Aye, I want the land," he agreed. "I am tired of this roving life. 'Tis time I settled, took a woman, and stayed in one place long enough to see her swell with my seed. Somerford is as good a place as any, and I have already plowed the lady."

"Oh very good, Gunnar, very good. I will enjoy watching you die when Lord Fitzmorton no longer needs you."

The hatred in Arno's voice was a palpable thing, but Gunnar did not hear it. Rose had tears on her cheeks, and they burned him. She had forgotten trust, if she had ever felt it for him. She truly believed he meant what he said—Gunnar cursed his ability to lie so well.

But he could not let his emotion show through the cold, hard shell he had drawn about himself. Arno was looking between them, his jealousy feeding on Rose's misery and Gunnar's brutishness. Well, let him! There would be time for Arno later, and Gunnar would relish his vengeance.

"No one will leave Somerford until Miles de Vessey is come," Arno said now, his voice gaining an authority that had been missing for a time but was now back tenfold. "Follow my orders, Captain, if you want to stay alive."

Arno was suspicious.

Gunnar widened his eyes in surprise. "Why shouldn't I follow them?"

"You saved Eartha's son—there are times when you seem altogether too tender for what you claim."

"Tender?" he repeated coldly, and his laugh was pure disdain. "If I am tender then Miles is a saint, d'Alan, and we both know that is not the case." He leaned closer. "Beware your friend de Vessey, he will kill you if he can."

Arno gave him an unblinking stare.

Gunnar allowed himself a small smile before he walked away, out of the stable and into the bailey. "No one leaves the keep today, Edward!" his shout drifted back to them. "Bar the gate and do not open it until I say you so!"

In the cool shadows of the stable, Arno turned to Rose. She was clinging to the rough wood of one of the stalls, and wondering if she was about to faint. She stared back at him, numb and shaken, and thought he should have felt satisfaction to have hurt her so. But there must have been some trace of his love for her left, for his eyes were not gloating, only pitying. As Rose watched, trembling against the stall, passion rose up in him, the hopeless desire she had scorned all this time, and he seemed helpless to stop it.

"Fear not, Rose," he said in a gruff voice. "I will not let the mercenary touch you again, him or Miles. You are mine, and soon you will know it!"

She thought then he would come and take her in his arms. The idea of him touching her threatened her stomach. Taking a deep breath, Rose pushed away from the stall. Ignoring him as if he weren't there, she stumbled outside like one who had drunk too much wine.

Reeling a little. Uncertain of her step. Arno watched her go, not stopping her, maybe seeing that she was beyond words.

She had been betrayed. She who had sworn never to be betrayed!

Arno who said he loved her and yet would give her to Fitzmorton. The thought of Fitzmorton was like a dark, deep pit, and she didn't want to go there.

Gunnar.

Rose clenched her hands and kept walking. She had thought herself so careful, so wary, and all the time he had been using her, laughing at her. She had run to him for help, and he had given her betrayal.

Never again.

"I cannot believe it!"

Constance stood, white-faced, before her lady. Frantic, Rose had dragged her by sheer physical force up to the solar, and there they were now.

"You had best believe it because 'tis truth. They are in league with Lord Fitzmorton, and his . . . his creature, Miles de Vessey. Miles is on his way here now. He is supposedly coming to hear my judgment on Harold, but really they mean to take Somerford Manor for Fitzmorton. Then it will be between the three of them who will hold my land and me!"

Stubbornly, Constance shook her head at the wild look on her lady's face, her eyes black pools. "But Gunnar Olafson is a hero, Rose! Remember?"

"He said he belonged to the highest bidder, Constance," whispered Rose, and tears seeped through her lashes and began to run down her cheeks. "And he said it as if there were nothing wrong in it!"

Constance went even whiter, swaying as if she might faint. Reaching out blindly she clung to Rose, pressing her shaking lady hard against her own body. "Then I curse him," she said in a high, furious voice. "I curse him, Rose!"

After a time, Rose's sobs quieted and she straightened, wiping her face, gathering her strength about her once more. Her mind seemed to be stirring again, rising to the occasion, and she began to plot and plan. It did no good to think any more of the man who had held her in his arms and loved her . . .

Love?

Nay, Gunnar Olafson would not know the meaning of that! It was lust he had felt. Jesu, how could she have been so wrong about him? She had thought him to be one man and all the time he had been another. Rose felt seared and wounded, like her mother. Betrayed beyond healing. Never again, never ever again, would she give a man any sort of power over her. She had been warned since childhood and yet she had forgotten all that. Aye, but now she had learned her lesson well and truly.

"Constance," she said, calmly enough for a woman whose heart had just been torn into rough pieces. "Go down to the kitchen and send Eartha to Harold the miller. He must be gotten out of the keep. Tell her to take the keys and set him free—Edward will have them."

Constance nodded jerkily and turned to the door, but glanced back before she reached it. "You will be all right, lady?"

Rose nodded. "I *am* all right." Her delicate features grew hard. "Do not think I am beaten yet, Constance. There are things I can do before Miles comes and I am stopped."

Constance nodded grimly, and left Rose to her silence. She was soon back, wide-eyed and shaking. "Lady, he is gone! Harold is gone! And so are Millisent and Will! I do not understand it . . ." She was wringing her hands, all but hopping up and down in her agitation.

Rose caught Constance's hands, drawing her to a stool and pressing her down. "Constance, they are not—" she began, thinking the worst.

Constance shook her head violently. "No, no, lady, they are not killed! Eartha said that Alfred, the mercenary with the ruined face, came to fetch Millisent and Will a short time ago. And now they are gone. I went to Edward, but he was not on the gate. One of the other mercenaries was there—the Dane. He would tell me nothing, not even when I cursed him. He . . . he laughed! He said they were safe, but I have looked everywhere I can think of, and I cannot find them." She was wringing her hands again, and Rose covered them to still her.

Her mind had become very clear.

Gunnar Olafson had done this.

He had guessed what measures Rose meant to take, and he had acted first—that he should know her mind so well worried her, but she could not think of that now. Harold and his children had gone with Alfred. Rose shivered to think what fate awaited them.

"Where is he?" she whispered. "I must speak with him."

"Alfred?" Constance was staring up at her, shrunken by this new turn in events. She looked like a small, wizened child.

Rose knelt down before her, making her voice firm. Never had it been so important for her to play the part of the lady of this manor. Somerford needed her now more than it had ever done.

"No, Constance, not Alfred. I must speak with Captain Olafson. He has done this, he can undo it. Mayhap I can appeal to him . . . somehow."

Constance blinked at her as if her eyesight were failing. "No, lady," she gasped harshly. "Do not give yourself to that man again! I was wrong, oh so wrong, I thought . . . Do not sacrifice your sweet self to such a one."

Rose's smile was grim. "You forget, old woman, I have already made the sacrifice . . . several times, in fact. It will be no different, and if it means I can help my friends, then I must at least make the offer."

She meant it. Constance shook her head, but Rose continued to persuade her, and eventually the old woman gave in and went off to do her bidding.

Rose sank down on the stool. She was shaken and wounded, but not mortally. There was a new resolve growing within her. She would not be beaten by men like Fitzmorton and Miles de Vessey and Arno d'Alan. They were brutal and ignorant, and they did not understand the strengths a woman could garner. But she would show them now.

And Gunnar Olafson?

Anguish filled her. The pressure in her chest and throat was unbearable, so that she longed to scream and rend something.

I will give you my body, but my heart is my own.

Aye, because he had no heart! He was made of cold Norse ice. Rose remembered now all the times he had spoken of death and killing and money, as if only the last mattered to him. *My sword is called Fenrir and he feeds on blood.* How could she have forgotten that! And yet while she had been in his arms, she had forgotten all the distasteful things, pushed them from her mind. Now they were rushing back, those blood-soaked words.

If Fitzmorton and the rest of them were monsters, then Gunnar Olafson was an abomination. A creature without compassion, who knew not the meaning of kindness or love. How could she think to win him over to her side, to help her save the lives of the miller and his family? Jesu, how he must have laughed to himself when she asked for his promise to obey her! And how he must have laughed when she commanded him to her bedchamber . . .

Rose stilled.

Or maybe not.

Although Rose knew she had willingly allowed herself to be deceived in the mercenary's character, she was not so certain she had been deceived in his desire for her. True, she was naive when it came to matters between men and women—one elderly husband did not make her an experienced lover. But Gunnar *wanted* her. She had not imagined the look in his eyes, the way he had arched against her hands, so eager to touch him, to worship him. Oh aye, he had enjoyed her worship!

Command me to be inside you, lady.

Rose hid her heated face in her hands. She had wanted him, too, but she told herself now that his deceit had killed forever her own lust. But what of him? Why should a Viking savage want her any less now than he had before? For him nothing had changed. Mayhap her hatred of him would even increase his pleasure in taking her.

Earlier, she had sat in the great hall and dwelt on last

night spent in Gunnar's arms. Remembered the expression in his eyes when he joined his body to hers, hot and yet determined, as if he were marking her in some way. Marking her as his.

Aye, that was exactly what he had been doing.

'Tis time I settled, took a woman, and stayed in one place long enough to see her swell with my seed. Somerford is as good a place as any, and I have already plowed the lady.

Despite the crudity of his words, he had meant what he said in the stables just now.

He wanted Somerford Manor, and he wanted her.

Aye, this was something Rose could work with, use on him. If Gunnar Olafson still wanted her, then she could turn his desire around and destroy him with it.

Chapter 15

Constance found Gunnar Olafson in the great hall. He was speaking with Ivo, his second in command. The two big men looked serious, and although their voices were too low for anyone else to hear, it was obvious to Constance things had not gone according to plan. Ivo appeared even wilder than usual, his hair windblown and tangled, his dark eyes blazing. In contrast, Gunnar was still and calm. He radiated confidence and reliability—leadership. Aye, he was a born leader, 'twas a shame his heart was as black and rotten as Rose had said it was that day in the solar.

Constance hovered at the edges of their conversation, awaiting an opportunity to intervene. Even now, looking at the mercenary captain, knowing what she did, she could not believe him to be an evil monster. So handsome! The air about him hummed with sensuality. Constance sighed. It didn't seem fair. She had wanted Gunnar Olafson for her lady, she had believed that here was the man she had been waiting for, who would stand by Rose and love her. She had been so certain he was that one that she had even told him so to his face.

And now all appeared lost.

Ivo hurried off, intent on carrying out whatever orders he had been given. Constance turned her face away as he passed, so that she would not have to meet that fearsome black gaze. There was something even more frightening than usual about Ivo, he fairly shimmered with rage. In contrast, Gunnar had coolly lifted a mug of ale to his lips and was swallowing it down, his throat working. It was only when he had drained it to the very dregs and replaced his mug on the table that he noticed Constance, waiting. Cautiously, before he could send her away, she crept forward, keeping her eyes on the ground.

"Captain, I . . . my lady wishes to speak with you." Constance was relieved her voice did not shake too much.

He did not move, though a quick glance upward showed a tightening of the muscles in his arms, the clenching of the hand resting upon the hilt of his sword.

"Can she not come herself?" he asked, but it was softly said, not the roar of a monster.

Constance shook her head.

And then she heard him sigh—there was a world of sadness in that sigh, a world of regret. It was the sigh of a man who has lost all hope.

Constance was thrown instantly into doubt and confusion.

Surely an evil monster would not sigh like that? And had she not seen him save a child from a possibly fatal fall when no one else would move to help? And had she not seen him show kindness to the silly wenches who gazed slack-jawed at him during mealtimes? And what of the manner in which he looked at the Lady Rose, as if she were all he had ever wanted in a woman and more?

Nay, this man was not evil! She had been right from the first. Constance dared a look up into a pair of wary blue eyes.

"Does she hate me as much as I think she does?" Gunnar asked her, and there was a wry twist to his lips Constance had never seen there before. As if he mocked himself for caring.

"Aye, at least that much."

"I told her to trust me."

"My lady does not trust men easily. Her experiences with them have not always been . . . agreeable."

But still he was wounded by her mistrust—Constance sensed it. He had wanted Rose to cast all else aside on the promise of his word—barter with the lives of her people, her lands, her own life. And she had not known him above a week!

Gunnar must have read the amazed amusement in her face. He folded his arms, the muscles bulging, and gave her a frown.

"Lady Constance, do you recall what you said to me last night, when I came to her room?"

Constance thought back to the moment when she had opened the door—the look in the mercenary's eyes as they met Rose's, that blind blaze of emotion she recognized so well. They had already forgotten she was there, and Constance had slipped past Gunnar to the door, saying . . .

"I said, 'Open your heart to her.' " Constance shifted uneasily before the intensity of his gaze. "My lady is tender-hearted, Captain," she explained, choosing her words carefully. "I saw in that moment that you could hurt her badly. I wanted you to be honest with her, show her she had nothing to fear if she did the same."

Again that wry smile. " 'Tis not easy to open your heart when to do so could cost lives."

"I understand that, Captain. I am not a fool. You have your work to do—whatever *that* may be. But my lady will not easily come to trust you again, not fully, maybe not ever. She is gentle-hearted, but she is also strong and stubborn."

He smiled.

Constance's voice softened, and she returned his smile. "Aye, like the flower she is named after, my Rose has thorns."

Gunnar glanced past her, and his gaze sharpened. Constance turned to look back, and saw Arno farther down the hall, partaking of his own ale.

"Can you look as if you're afraid of me?" Gunnar Olafson asked her quietly, frowning all the time as if he meant to strike her dead on the spot.

Constance nodded jerkily.

"Then do it. Now." He leaned into her face, glaring. His voice rose to a shout. "Get out of my way, you old witch!" And he brushed rudely past her, out of the great hall and toward the stairs. Constance cringed, pressing herself to the side of the hearth. The hand she clutched to her fluttering heart shook convincingly.

Arno guffawed, enjoying seeing the old woman bested, and poured himself another ale.

* * *

Rose was prepared. She was, so she told herself, tranquil in mind and body. This was simply something else that must be done for the sake of others, and Rose was always prepared to make such sacrifices. She would bargain with him just as she had done before. She *knew* he wanted her. She did not believe he could pretend such a thing, not so many times as he had taken her. No, he wanted her, and that could only work in her favor.

The knock on the door was loud, peremptory. His call of "Lady Rose!" was a demand for entry.

With trembling hands, Rose lifted the bar, and then he was pushing open the door and striding in. As if he already owned Somerford Manor, she thought angrily, and the anger helped to steady her. Rose turned to face him.

Jesu, he was big!

He made the solar seem tiny. Her composure wavered but she held on to it with both hands.

Forget what has happened between us thus far. Forget how he made me feel when he held me in his arms. That is over and done.

This was the real Gunnar Olafson before her now, his face impassive, his eyes empty of any feeling. This was the man who had kissed her in the stable and a moment later looked at her as if she were no more than a tasty hunk of meat on a hook, who spoke of taking Somerford, and her, for his own, as if it mattered not that they were not his to take.

I have already plowed the lady . . .

When he said it, the image had been so sharp, Rose had not known whether to weep for what might have been, or to scream her outrage. He wanted *her* to swell with his seed. It had been there in his eyes, in the way they shone so hot. He wanted to take Somerford from her, but he wanted her as well. Like the ghostly warrior of her dreams, he would snatch her up and carry her away as his prisoner.

Only this time she would not be able to wake up.

"Captain," Rose said, and was glad to hear her own voice so unwaveringly authoritative—the voice she had learned to assume in moments of trouble. This was not a time for begging or pleading, as her mother would have done. It had not worked on Rose's father and it would not move a man like Gunnar Olafson. How could it? This creature would not be shamed into penitence by a few tears.

"Aye, lady? I am waiting to hear what you have to say."

He was impatient to be gone, pacing across to the window and back. His hand was closing and unclosing on his sword hilt, as if he might draw it out at any moment. His glance flicked to her and away again. Such restlessness was unusual for Gunnar—even in the short time Rose had known him, he had seemed amazingly unruffled. The still center of a storm. And yet here he was, behaving more like Ivo. Aye, clearly he was a man with much on his mind. Mayhap that, too, would work in Rose's favor.

"I have heard that you have moved Harold the miller."

He stopped. "So?"

"I do not want him hurt. Him or his children. I know Lord Fitzmorton wants justice for his man Gilbert, but killing Harold in cold blood is not justice."

He was watching her. "Do you think I will hurt him?"

She searched his handsome face, but where was the

point in trying to find feelings where there were none? It was easy to pretend to herself that there was a hint of hurt in his blue eyes or a touch of self-mockery in the curl of his firm lips. But Rose had discovered she was adept at attributing emotions to Gunnar that were not real. He was a cold-blooded monster that she had endowed with all the virtues she so longed to see in a man, and she had been silly enough to think him real.

"Please do not hurt Harold and his children," she said quietly.

He frowned and opened his mouth to reply. Thinking he meant to tell her bad news, Rose went on hastily, frankly.

"I am willing to bargain for their lives."

"Bargain?" He eyed her warily—they were on opposing sides, after all. "What do you have that I could want, lady?"

But he knew. She read it in the sudden blaze of his eyes, saw it in the abrupt tightening of his mouth. Mayhap he wouldn't make her say it aloud.

He wanted her, he had wanted her since the first moment their eyes met in the bailey. Just as she had then, Rose sensed desire's heady presence in the room, and—God help her!—felt her body begin to soften and ache. Rose turned away, so that he could not see her humiliation.

He was going to make her say it after all.

"There is me, Captain," Rose informed him in a cold little voice.

He said nothing for a long time, but she could not turn and face him. She did not dare. Not because she was afraid of him, but because something had happened to her. For although she knew full well what he was and what he had done, her body didn't care. His mere presence was enough, just being *close* to him. Was this what her mother had fought against? Rose asked herself. The bitter realization that, no matter what promises she made to herself, they would inevitably be broken?

His step was soft behind her. He was so close now that she could feel the heat of his body. His arms came around her, forcing her back against him, so that she had the urge to gasp for breath. Then she felt him, already fully aroused, hard against her. She realized then that this was a test. He had done this on purpose. He wanted to know whether she was really willing.

Gunnar's hands slid up her body, cupping her breasts impertinently through her gown, pressing her soft flesh into his callused palms. Rose stood rigid, refusing to weaken against his touch. Her mind was stronger than her body, she told herself. She could overcome the weakness. She could!

He found her nipples, hard as buds. His fingers were delicate as he caressed them, sending arrows of sheer pleasure into her treacherous body. Rose heard herself gasp, and wanted to scream in despair as her resolve began to crumble.

He did not laugh, as she had thought he might. Instead he bent his head, his mouth hot against her neck, sending more shivers of want through her. Rose's head fell back against his shoulder, and she closed her eyes. One of his hands slid down over her belly, seeking the hot core of her, his fingers sliding into the apex of her thighs. Even through the stuff of her clothing, she sensed the pleasure to be gained, longed to give herself over to it. Want pooled between her legs, and she trembled with the effort of not pressing against him. In another moment Rose knew she would be totally lost.

Violently, she pulled away, taking a couple of desperate, shaking steps before she turned to face him. Her chest was heaving, her hands clenched at her sides. She must have looked like a madwoman. She took in a gulp of air.

"You have not agreed to your part of the bargain," she reminded him, and was not surprised by the hoarseness of her voice.

He looked as if their impassioned embrace had disturbed him not at all. If it had not been for the faint flush on his tanned cheeks, the glitter in his eyes, Rose would have believed him untouched by their encounter.

"Do you remember what I said in the stable?" He surprised her with the question.

Rose glared at him, her weakness receding as she regained some control over her senses. This was better; she was *really* angry now. "What you said? Do you mean the part where you were willing to betray me to Fitzmorton for a few more marks? Or, Captain, do you mean the part where you admitted to wanting my lands and getting a child on me?"

He shook his head at her in mocking disapproval. "None of that, lady. I mean the part when I told you to trust me."

Rose stared at him a moment more. She felt confused, but didn't want him to see it. Surely he did not think she could trust him now? Did he think her a fool, to believe any man just because he asked her to do so?

"I trust no man," she said coldly.

And Gunnar believed it.

She *had* trusted him, for a time. He remembered her asking for his word the first night there, and then by the

Mere when Miles had come, her fingers resting so trustingly in his. Aye, she could deny it all she wanted, but Gunnar knew she *had* trusted him and, by Odin, she would trust him again.

But, for now, Gunnar knew he had no option but to secure her obedience in any way he could. Her life depended on it. And if that meant using fear and threats, then so be it.

He smiled a cold-blooded smile and fingered the hilt of his sword, as if his breeches were not stretched tight over the evidence of his lust. It amused him that she was having difficulty keeping her eyes away from that most eager part of him. She might no longer trust him, but she still desired him.

"Listen to me now, lady. You have a choice to make. Both Miles de Vessey and Arno want you—which do you prefer?"

She stared back at him defiantly, but she couldn't hide the flicker of fear in her eyes.

He let his smile grow. "Aye, I thought not. Then listen to me, Rose, and listen well. I have sent Harold and his children with Alfred to safety—"

"I don't believe you."

He laughed harshly in surprise, quelled it. "Constance believes me."

Rose's lip curled. "Constance is half in love with you, Captain. You could be cutting her throat, and she would believe you meant her no harm."

Now *he* was angry. She had finally gotten him angry. He saw her stiffen as she read it in his eyes, saw the doubt, but she did not step back, did not retreat, although she must be longing to. Aye, by Odin she was brave! A beautiful, courageous woman. Was Rose his fate—assuming he could save both their lives?

"Believe me," he said quietly. "The miller and his children are safe, for now. I have hidden them away from Arno and his friends. I thought I might have a use for them later, when Fitzmorton comes. He will pay well for them."

The lie was more successful than his attempt at the truth had been.

Her face went white. "You monster, have you—"

"I agree," he said abruptly.

She stopped, confused, her chest heaving. "You . . . agree?"

"I agree to your bargain," he explained. "Fitzmorton would pay me with coin, but I prefer flesh. You were right, Rose, when you thought to tempt me with your body. I could take you now, but you would fight me, and I want you willing. I want you as you were before."

She had nothing to say.

"I'll be back tonight, lady," and he came right up to her, looming over her. She flinched but stood her ground. He put his lips against her ear. "Be sure to let me in," he whispered.

She nodded.

"But for now, give me a token of your honesty. Show me you mean what you say."

"I . . ." Her eyes widened, glinted with anger.

"Quickly, or I may change my mind."

She bit back the words she really wanted to say. Trembling, her hands clutching onto his tunic, Rose stretched up on her toes and fastened her mouth to his. He did not move, and with a frustrated groan, she began to kiss him, her lips soft and warm. It was enough.

More than enough. Gunnar was suddenly kissing her back, hard and unstoppable, passion flaring like a lit torch inside him.

And then he was gone, the door slamming after him.

Rose staggered, hand to her bruised mouth, breath sobbing. How would she manage tonight? she asked herself, on the edge of hysteria. How would she play at lust, when she knew, to her despair, that she would not be pretending at all?

"Ethelred is here."

Ivo's voice was quiet beside him, but Gunnar hadn't been sleeping. He sat up on his bed, and saw Reynard do the same. "And?"

"They are just beyond the woods. Miles and about twenty men. They are moving slowly, but even so we don't have long, Gunnar."

Not long, but long enough. Gunnar met his friend's eyes and leaned closer. "Listen to me, Ivo. This is what we must do . . ."

He hadn't come.

Rose had waited for hours, at first pacing in agitation, and then lying stiffly in her bed, eyes fastened on the door. Time after time she had imagined she heard him, her heart surging. But each time the door had stayed closed. He had not come, and now it was so late Rose doubted he would.

What did that mean?

Had he decided he did not want her after all? That Fitzmorton's coins were more tempting than a woman he could take anyway? Had she not convinced him enough with her kiss? He had told her he wanted her willing, had she not been willing enough? Or had he sensed her true feelings?

And what are they?

That I loathe him!

Aye, that is obvious. Loathe him so much you can't take your eyes off him. You want him, lady, don't deny it. You want to reach out and undo the laces on his breeches and take his—

"No!"

Rose did not realize she had cried out aloud until the sound of her own voice echoed back to her. She swallowed hard, reining in her wild emotions. No. It would not do to think such things, even if she feared they might be true. Strange as it was, she had thrown in her lot once more with the mercenary. He might be a monster, but Rose knew deep in her secret heart she would rather bargain with him than either Miles de Vessey or Arno.

Was she mad to do so?

"Lady?"

Rose sat up, staring wide-eyed, her dark hair falling loose about her, the covers clutched to her chest.

"Lady? Open your door."

There was a command in his voice—he was a man used to obedience. Rose was tempted to refuse or pretend she was still asleep, but what would be the point in that? He would probably smash down the door and then he would be angry with her. She had made a bargain with him, and if she went back on it then she would be compromising her own integrity, not his.

Rose climbed out of her bed, pulling her robe about her, and with her toes curling on the cold floor, walked to the door. He was a large shadow just outside it. The torch that usually burned on the wall had been doused—the smoke stung her nostrils. As she stood, confused, every sense suddenly alerted, another shadow joined Gunnar's, and then another. Rose began to quickly close the door.

He caught it in his hand. Slowly, inexorably, he forced it back until, with a cry, Rose stumbled backwards into her chamber. Gunnar followed her and she squeaked, thinking he would strike her or—as she had once seen her father do to her mother—pick her up and shake her. He did neither. He walked right past her, to the window. The shutters creaked as he flung them open and peered out into the night.

Rose held her breath, watching him warily. Torches burned and flared by the gate, and in their light she could see Arno and Sweyn on guard duty. The Norman was strutting backward and forward, waving his arms and talking in an agitated manner. The Dane was standing with arms crossed over his chest, watching him steadily.

In the darkness of her chamber, Ivo had come up softly beside his captain. Behind them stood the one they called Reynard, with the swarthy good looks.

"What now?" Ivo's voice was a deep hum.

"When Miles comes, you go down and play the part we agreed on."

Ivo shifted as if he wasn't happy.

Gunnar reached out and grasped his arm. " 'Tis what Arno is expecting. I know you want to fight, Ivo. I know how you feel, for I feel it too, but remember there are more lives at risk here than yours and mine. If there is no fighting then no one will be hurt. These are innocents, Ivo, just as was your sister."

Ivo nodded brusquely, but Rose could almost hear him grinding his teeth. "And you?" he asked Gunnar.

"I will take the lady."

"They will want to see her—Miles is probably already dreaming about what he will do to her."

Rose tried not to move, but the pictures they were conjuring were making her legs tremble. She grasped the curtained pole at the base of the bed.

"Find Constance, the old woman, and tell her to hold them off. Her lady is too frightened to speak or some such nonsense. And if they ask for me, then I am abed with some wench and you're not brave enough to disturb me until I'm done."

Ivo snorted a laugh. "It will be as you say, Gunnar."

And he was gone.

Reynard handed something to Gunnar—a piece of clothing?—before he too turned and vanished into the darkness, leaving Gunnar and Rose alone. He was watching her, silhouetted against the faint light from the window. Rose had heard what they said, but she did not understand it.

I will take the lady.

Take her where? And why? Miles was coming—that was why Arno was waiting down there—and when he arrived all would be at an end. They would no longer pretend he was coming to oversee Norman justice. Fitzmorton wanted Somerford and Miles would take it for him.

The time for pretending was over.

"Do you think to gain ransom from my family for me?" she asked, and was pleased with the firmness of her voice. "There is only my father, and I fear he will think it a waste of good money. He was relieved to be rid of me to Edric, he will not want me back again, especially if he must pay for the privilege."

He was silent. Rose did not like the silence, and she filled it, her voice not quite so steady this time.

"Do you mean to sell me to Lord Fitzmorton? What use will he have for me, when he has stolen my manor? Unless he wants to marry me to one of his men, so that he can tell the king the manor came into his hands justly. Is that it, Captain, is that what you mean to do?"

There were tears in her eyes but she would not let them fall. Her breathing sounded harsh in the darkness.

"Lady, we must go."

Rose clenched her fists and only just prevented herself from stamping her bare feet. "Answer me!"

"There is no time for answers. Your keep is about to be overrun by Fitzmorton's men. You are not safe here. We must escape."

Escape? Rose felt even more confused, but she put that aside and fastened onto another, more important matter. "I will not leave my people."

"Your people will be safe enough if there is no fighting, and I have given those orders. It is *you* who are in danger, not your people. Get dressed now, lady. We have no time—"

"I will face them, not run," she declared.

But he caught her arm and swung her around against him, her bare skin, only just covered by her thin robe, abraded by the coarse stuff of his breeches and tunic. His sword belt dug into her—she could feel every metal stud that decorated the leather.

"Miles de Vessey wants you," Gunnar said with soft menace. "He will not wed you first, lady. And he is not like me—he will hurt you. And if you do not leave now, if you stay to face him, he will consider it an invitation to do as he likes with you. Ask Ivo. Ask him what Miles is capable of!"

He was angry. It took her by surprise. She wondered for the briefest of moments what it was Miles had done that was so shocking. And then the voice in her head was shrieking, drowning out all other thoughts.

Don't believe what he says! Don't trust him!

The truth was, she had no choice.

If she stayed she would surely die—or wish she had. If she left now with Gunnar Olafson she had a chance of escaping, even mayhap of finding her way to Lord Radulf. Saving Somerford and her people. Whatever the mercenary's true plans for her, she might be able to outwit him, elude him, or, if worse came to worst, lull him with her body into believing she was no threat.

It came down to a simple choice. Leave now and take a chance. Stay and surely die.

"Very well," she whispered, harsh pride overcoming her need to cry. "I will agree to come with you. Let me dress."

He hesitated, as if he was not sure whether to believe her, and then with a brisk nod he released her. Rose hurried to her chest, taking out the first garments she touched and pulling them on. Her fingers trembled and fumbled with the ties, with the stockings. She moved to snatch up her hairbrush.

"Leave it," he said sharply. "There is no time for more." Beyond him, toward the woods, Rose could see movement. Shadows shifting beneath the starlight. Miles and his men.

She turned and would have swung her cloak about

her shoulders, but he pushed the garment he already held in his hands toward her. "Put this on."

Puzzled, Rose shook it out. It was a cloak, but older than her own, the cloth was thick and . . . She wrinkled her nose. There was an odor clinging to it that was familiar—grease, rancid meat, and incense? What did that remind her of?

"Put it on," he said again, growing impatient.

Rose bit back her questions and slipped the cloak about her, trying not to shrink from its contact. At least it was thick and warm. Hastily she tucked her long hair inside as she pulled the hood lower over her face. She had barely finished when there was a soft tap on the door and Constance called for entry.

Gunnar went to let her in. When Rose turned, the old woman was behind her.

"Lady," whispered Constance, her cold hand finding Rose's. "They say Fitzmorton's men are at the gate. You must flee."

This was Constance, who sometimes annoyed her but more often had loved her throughout her years at Somerford. It occurred afresh to Rose just how dear the old woman was, and she returned the pressure of her clasp. "What if they hurt you? If my going will bring down their anger on you, Constance, I—"

Constance snorted with derision, as though her eyes were not shining with tears. "I am not afeared of *them*, lady! I have lived through some terrible times. Besides, I am old and can be stupid if 'tis necessary. I will make them think me half-witted, so they will let me be. Now hurry, go with the captain before 'tis too late."

Gunnar's hand pressed against her back. Rose found herself moving forward onto the darkened stairs. She glanced behind her, but Constance had already closed the door, and she heard the sound of the bar falling. Gunnar's breath was warm against her ear. "Whatever happens, keep your head down, and say nothing."

They started down the stairs.

Rose stumbled once, but he pulled her in against his body, holding her firm when she would have tried to wriggle out of his grip. His step was swift and sure, and they were soon at the entrance to the great hall. But they didn't go that way, instead Gunnar turned down again, toward the kitchen.

The low room was dark and empty, apart from the gray kitchen cat and her kittens, curled by the oven. Gunnar moved silently through the room, to the door that led into the small garden. He unbarred and opened it and, after a brief glance outside, drew Rose after him.

Her head was immediately filled with the sweet and spicy scents of fresh herbs, and the earthy reek from the midden. Her cloak brushed against a rosemary bush, and then Gunnar was leading her onward again. They were close to the wall of the keep, moving in the direction of the bailey.

Beyond the gate, horses were clattering across the bridge. Miles and his men had made good time. "Open up!" The shout rang in the silence. "Open up in the name of Fitzmorton!"

"You, there! Help me!" Arno was beckoning to old Edward, who appeared too shocked to move. "Do as you are told, you dolt!"

Sweyn stepped forward, brushing by Edward and murmuring something to him at the same time. The old man stared at him a moment, and then slowly, sullenly, came to help unlatch and pull open the heavy wooden gate.

Rose turned to look up at Gunnar. His eyes were fastened on the stable, judging the distance, judging the chances of them reaching it unseen. And then what? How could they possibly ride out of Somerford Keep without being stopped?

"What will we do?" She was shivering. With cold or fear? Rose wasn't certain.

Gunnar said nothing, but his arm tightened about her, drawing her in closer to his warmth.

Fitzmorton's men hadn't waited for the gate to be opened fully. They were already galloping in, the distinctive blue and yellow banner flapping at their head. Rose recognized Miles's voice, carried eerily on the night air.

"Where is the lady?"

"She is in her chamber," Arno replied promptly, destroying any hopes Rose might have had that he would stand up for her. "I have just now set a guard on her door."

A guard at her door?

Rose shut her eyes with a dizzy wave of relief. She had escaped just in time.

"Good, good." When she looked again, Miles had swung around and had begun shouting orders to his men. They were dismounting, some heading off across the bailey, others towards the keep. Edward and Sweyn remained side-by-side by the partly open gate, the old Englishman and the sturdy Dane.

Gunnar's voice was so soft, it was like a thought against her ear. "Wait and watch. When you see me point to the gate, walk quickly toward it. Once you are outside it, run. I will catch you up."

She stared at the shape of him, the glitter of his eyes. "They will know me!"

"But you are Brother Mark," he said. "You are wearing his cloak. Keep your head down and walk as he does, and no one will ask you to stop. Why should they? Lady Rose is in her chamber with a guard at the door."

Brother Mark! That explained the cloak—no wonder the smell had been familiar. "And if the real Brother Mark should come?"

"He won't." Gunnar's voice didn't change, but there was a coldness in it.

Rose opened her mouth to ask about Brother Mark, and then changed her mind. She didn't want to know after all, she thought, hugging her arms about herself.

Gunnar stared down at her another moment, and then, seemingly satisfied that she would do as he had told her, he stepped away. But at the last moment she caught his arm.

"What of you?" she whispered anxiously.

Something like triumph flared in his eyes, and Rose could have cut out her tongue. He thought she was concerned for his welfare! Worried for *him*! Even if that were so—which it was not—she would never have let him know it.

"If you are killed I will soon be recaptured," she explained in a furious murmur. "So, Captain, answer me now. What of you?"

He smiled, that familiar tug at the corners of his mouth. "We need a horse," he said patiently, and with that he was gone.

Chapter 16

She was alone.

Rose huddled back against the wall. The lack of his warm arm about her, his large comforting presence, left her empty. Jesu, what now? A sense of aloneness swept over her, and she realized with a sudden, deep sadness that she had always been alone. Her position and her past made it so.

Did it always have to be? There had been a moment, when Gunnar had held her in his arms. When Rose had almost believed she might have found someone who would stand by her. More than a dream, a real flesh-and-blood man.

She had learned her mistake, and it hurt.

Stop it, stop it at once! This is no time for self-pity, Rose!

The familiar scolding voice in her head was almost a relief. This was no time to lose what composure she had left. If there was ever a time for Rose to be the lady of her manor, it was now. She took a deep breath, and then another. Her body stopped shaking and her head cleared. After a moment she was able to lean forward and peep carefully around the corner of the garden wall.

Gunnar was walking across the bailey. The flaring torches turned his copper hair to gold and glowed on his tan tunic and black breeches. He moved as if he had all the time in the world, and nothing concerned him. How could he appear so? Rose asked herself. Why was he not as weak and terrified as any normal person would be in such a situation? Despite all that had happened, Rose could not help but feel admiration for him.

"Olafson!" Arno had seen him approaching. "Where in the devil's name have you been? What have you been doing?"

"There was a woman." Gunnar shrugged, and a smile warmed his voice. "As for what we were doing . . ."

"I thought you were too *honorable* for such things," Arno sneered.

"I am tired of being honorable." The humor vanished. "You were right when you said I am getting old and tired, Arno. 'Tis time to try my hand at corruption."

"Captain!" Ivo came running toward him out of the shadows.

Gunnar turned to face him—he appeared to brace himself. "What is it, Ivo?"

"They are taking the manor. We must stop—"

He got no further. Gunnar drew his sword from its sheath and took one step forward, burying the blade deep in Ivo's side.

Rose felt her nails break on the stone wall, and yet there was no pain. Only a sort of light-headedness, as if she were watching a play. She could not seem to look away. As she watched, Ivo's legs buckled and Gunnar caught him in his arms, as if he were embracing him, and then he simply let him fall. A dark stain spread and grew on Ivo's white linen shirt. The big man gave a shudder and lay still.

Arno was staring at Gunnar as if he doubted his own eyes. He sidled uneasily around him as if he might bite, and dropped to his knees by Ivo's side.

"He breathes," he said, his voice devoid of expression, but in the torchlight his face was pale. "Just. You have sliced him through, Olafson. No one can live long after that."

Gunnar glanced down at his former friend impatiently. "He wanted to fight Miles de Vessey—they are not the best of friends. I thought it best if I put him out of the way." He caught the eye of Reynard, who was lounging nearby, as if he saw Gunnar kill one of his men every day. "Here, take this man away and find him somewhere to die!"

Rose watched as Reynard and another man came and lifted Ivo between them, awkwardly carrying him away. Gunnar did not even watch them go.

The sense of watching a play continued. She shook her head in disbelief, swallowing the queasy feeling clenching in her stomach. She should turn and run, back into the keep, find somewhere to hide. But where could she conceal herself so well that Miles and Arno would not find her? And besides . . . she doubted she could walk very far without collapsing on the ground. Her cheek was pressed so hard to the stones, the tender skin felt raw.

Rose took a shallow breath, blinking back tears.

Why would Gunnar kill Ivo? Why do that, when he was in the process of rescuing her? It made no sense, nothing made sense . . . Gunnar and Arno were still in conversation. When the buzzing in her head had faded, Rose was able to listen again.

"We are taking Somerford for Lord Fitzmorton." Arno seemed to have forgotten Ivo already. "No point in waiting any longer, now Lady Rose knows the truth."

"I see that."

Arno shifted uncomfortably, as if he noticed something in the other man's eyes. Or perhaps he just needed to justify himself. "It was always mine! Edric swore an oath it would be mine when he brought me here—he owed me a debt he could not pay. But then when he died he made me swear allegiance to his wife, made me swear another oath before them all! Where is the honor in that? Edric deserved to lose Somerford, but I waited, I hoped I could win it through fair means. Well, I am tired of waiting! Somerford *is* mine, and Fitzmorton is eager to help me claim it."

"Or claim it for himself," said Gunnar softly.

Arno frowned. "Why so? I am his man, and I will serve him well. He knows when to value loyalty. I will rule Somerford, and he will be a step closer to taking Crevitch."

"Where is Miles now?"

"I have sent him to fetch Lady Rose."

"*Sent* him? I'll wager he volunteered."

"Sir Arno!" The shout came from the keep. One of the original Somerford garrison was peering toward them, looking shocked and uncertain. "The lady has barricaded herself inside her chamber and refuses to let us in. Sir Miles is going to break down the door."

Arno swore and started toward him, pausing only to call over his shoulder, "Close the gate and set a guard on it!"

Gunnar turned and stabbed a finger at the gate. "Close that gate!" he shouted. "Brother Mark? Come here and help them!"

Now was the moment. Now was when she must step out and make her escape. *I cannot do it, I cannot do it . . .*

"Brother Mark!" he roared.

Rose pushed herself away from the wall and walked on wobbling legs into deadly danger.

Gunnar saw "Brother Mark" appear from the shadows and more or less glide across the bailey. The figure passed by several of Fitzmorton's men. None of them looked up. Arno half turned again, no doubt puzzled by his friend's sudden appearance, but then a loud crash and a scream from inside the keep claimed his attention once more.

Gunnar shouted again, urging the men at the gate to hurry, and quickened his own stride. One of the soldiers' horses was tied loosely to the handle of a cart, as if the rider could not be bothered to see the animal properly stabled. Gunnar grabbed the reins and tugged it after him; it was done so smoothly his action appeared perfectly normal.

Ahead of him he could see that Edward had stopped trying to close the unusually stubborn gate and was gaping at the approaching "Brother Mark." Sweyn, who had been using his own strength against Edward's to hold the gate open, was trying to hide a smile. As the brother reached them, they closed around him, their bodies sheltering him from anyone watching. All three began to tug at the gate, and then suddenly there were only two. Brother Mark had slipped around the gate and vanished into the night.

In a moment Gunnar, too, had reached them. With perfect timing he swung himself up onto the horse and, with a telling glance at Sweyn, was also gone into the darkness. The gate closed with a dull thud behind him. He was safe . . . for the moment, but Gunnar did not pretend to himself that he had very long.

Rose had already reached the far end of the bridge, running, her skirts kilted up to her knees. Her pale undergown shone like moth's wings in the darkness—he should have told her to wear dark colors. Gunnar didn't even slow his pace a fraction, he simply reached down with one arm and snatched her up. She cried out and clung, and then he had her tucked safely before him.

Her hands, clutching at his forearm where it was wrapped about her, were icy. Her cloak hood had fallen back, and her dark hair blew into his face in a sweet scented cloud. "Did they see?" she gasped, when she was able to speak.

"Aye, but they don't believe it. Yet."

Gunnar turned the stolen horse off the village road, heading across the pale fields toward the darker woods, and at the same time realized what he should have known before. The horse was lame. That was why its master had left it unattended—the animal was useless. It would not get them far.

Urgently he scanned the dark trees before them. It was possible they could hide out there for a time, but Miles would eventually find them with his hounds and his men. He looked toward the village, but there would be no help there, and the villagers could be killed simply for sheltering them. Crevitch was safe, and Radulf was probably even now waiting for word from him, but it was too far on foot with Miles snapping at their backs.

That left the Mere.

Why hadn't he noticed that the horse was lame? Why hadn't he noticed that Rose's undergown was white? Why hadn't he realized what Arno was up to and gotten her to safety long before now? Once such details would never have slipped by him. Since he had come to Somerford it was as if his mind had lost something of its alertness, its capacity for anticipating his enemies, its ability to think clearly.

Wryly, Gunnar admitted why that might be: he was more concerned with getting between the Lady Rose's thighs than carrying out his mission.

There had been women before, plenty of them, but none had wound him up in a spell like this one. Suddenly he understood what his mother, Gudren, had meant when she said that he had not asked any woman to wait for him because he had not yet found the right one. There was something different about Rose, something unique and special. When he held her in his arms she just felt right.

He cursed silently, she had turned him into a lust-crazed fool! They were running for their lives, and here he was dreaming of a pretty future. And it was but a dream—it could never be real.

Gunnar came up over a rise and turned the laboring horse northward, heading for the place where the attackers had made their escape across the marshes.

* * *

The change in direction seemed to bring Rose out of her abstraction. She lifted her head, the scent of the salty Levels awakening her from her bad dream. "Where are we going?" she asked, and her voice was sharp, more alert than it had been. Good, that was good.

"The horse is lame." Gunnar said it so matter-of-factly, she was momentarily deceived into thinking it was unimportant.

"Lame?"

He hesitated. "We have a chance on foot if we go into the Mere."

She knew then the scope of the problem they faced. The lame horse was disastrous, but to escape on foot through the Mere!

Rose gazed out across the silvery marshes. On a clear night like this she could easily see the sparkle of water, the jagged rise and fall of reeds, and the lumpy shadows of the islands. But setting off into the Mere on foot? It was like another country, one unknown to her and therefore all the more frightening.

They would probably die.

As if reading her doubts, Gunnar said with his usual quiet confidence, "You will be safe with me, Rose."

So easy to believe him, as she had believed him before. Well, she would not be fooled again. Rose gave a strained little laugh. "Will I? Will I be *safe* with you, Gunnar?"

"Aye, lady." He sounded surprised by her doubt. Oh, he was clever, so clever . . .

Rose turned her head and looked up, meeting his calm gaze, seeing the shape of his head against the starry night, the breadth of his shoulders. He was so strong—he exuded strength! And she so *wanted* to feel safe with him. But how could she? How could she ever feel safe with him again?

"You killed Ivo." The words were stark and unadorned.

His pale eyes gleamed silver, but she couldn't read them. "Aye, so it appeared. Arno believes it, and so will Miles. They think him dead, or at least dying. Miles hates his brother—if Ivo had been alive, Miles would have killed him as soon as he knew I had escaped with you, lady. Maybe before."

"So you killed him first?" she choked.

"I pretended to kill him. There was a bladder of pig's blood under his shirt, strapped about his waist. I punctured it. Ivo did the rest. 'Tis an old trick, simple but effective. Reynard will see Ivo is placed somewhere out of the way, and then it is up to Ivo to make his own escape out of Somerford to safety. Probably while they are hunting us," he added grimly.

Rose wondered if she were going mad. Was what he said now the truth? Ivo's death had looked very real to her, but it could have been as he said . . . She remembered again the strange sense she had had that the scene she was witnessing was a play. And yet he had lied to her before.

Was there really a single word this man uttered that she could believe? She should insist he set her down. Now! She should insist on finding somewhere else to hide. Now! No one went into the Mere by choice—not unless they were merefolk—and even then it was generally believed they would rather be on safe dry land.

But Rose knew she had come too far to turn back. Even if she had a choice, even if he would have let her go. At Somerford Keep, Miles de Vessey was casting his greedy eyes on all that had been hers, and Arno, who had pretended to be her loyal knight, would be willing to tear her apart to get his share. And behind them all stood Fitzmorton, Radulf's deadly enemy.

Fitzmorton, whom she hated most of all.

What was the point in struggling? She had no choice but to place her fate in Gunnar Olafson's big scarred hands.

For now.

The ground sucked at Rose's shoe, as if it had an insatiable hunger for calfskin. She tugged it out and took another step forward, lifting her skirts as high as she could, though they were already dripping and muddy at the hem, her stockings filthy to the knee. The air reeked with the smell of rotten vegetation and still water. In front of her Gunnar Olafson was a dark shape against a star-filled sky.

Rose followed him as if she had done so all her life.

Far ahead and to their left rose the sinister bulk of Burrow Mump. Although there was no moon tonight, the stars were very bright. Would the ghostly warriors rise from the earth? Or would they remain safe in their underworld home?

A loud splash and a curse interrupted her thoughts. Rose watched as Gunnar appeared to do a laborious dance on the quaking surface of the Mere, before he stumbled backward and sat down hard.

"Are you all right?" She stepped closer, feeling her shoe sink again.

"I can't find the path."

Until this moment there had been a path, of sorts. A narrow strip of solid ground that snaked its way through the unstable mud and water. Gunnar had followed it carefully, deep into the Mere. Far behind them was the distant shape of Somerford Keep and its encircling hills, but that was all.

Rose sat down, too, no longer caring about her skirts, suddenly just too weary to be standing.

"They won't find us now, will they?"

"We need to get to one of those islands," he replied. "Find somewhere to hide. When the sun rises they'll see us out here, and they'll get to us. Miles won't let me have you if he can help it."

She thought about that. "So this is a game between the two of you? Like tug-of-war? And I am the prize."

"Maybe. But be sure of one thing, lady. I do not mean to give you up." He was staring at her earnestly in the starlight, but Rose refused to believe in him.

She made her voice chilly—why not, it matched her poor frozen toes. "You and Miles know each other well, don't you?"

He straightened up, wiping his dirty hands across his tunic. "We have fought together from time to time, but his way of fighting was never mine. He has no honor."

Honor. Aye, it was something Gunnar Olafson appeared to set great store by. But as Rose had learned to her cost, appearances could be deceptive. He was a liar and a brute, and yet still he spoke of honor. Well, why not put his honor to the test?

"Will you take me to Crevitch, to Lord Radulf?"

He seemed to be observing her in the darkness. Was he waiting for an explanation?

Rose turned her face away, staring at nothing, her voice struggling to be as emotionless as she wanted it. "I know Lord Radulf sees me as a weak counter in his game, something to be used and then discarded when it has lost its importance. But I must think of Somerford now, and he is the only one who can right the wrong. He has the men to fight Fitzmorton; I do not."

"Radulf will listen to you, lady."

Surprised, Rose turned again to face him. "You sound as if you know him." Her face was open, puzzled. She waited.

Gunnar was tempted to tell her the truth. Would she believe it? Earlier, in her chamber, she had preferred to believe him a murdering monster, and he had played along with her, making their bargain of the flesh. Now he wanted her to look through the pretense and see *him*. Even though it was probably already too late.

He took a chance.

"My father, Olaf, is Radulf's armorer, my mother, Gudren, is midwife to Lady Lily." He spoke softly, in the matter-of-fact way that robbed the words of their power to surprise. "They are loyal to him and have been for many years. I have made my own way in the world, but Radulf is a good man, strong and true. When he asked me to come to Somerford in answer to your request for mercenaries, to play at being Fitzmorton's man, I agreed. I was in Wales when his message came and I was glad to leave. I was tired of petty squabbles between barons who wanted more than they deserved, and this seemed like a chance to do something important, something that needed doing. Radulf was very . . . concerned."

She was no fool. She understood what part of the tale he was leaving out. "You mean he didn't trust me. Aye, well, 'tis to be expected. A woman, alone. The Normans think women are useful for breeding and no more." She flashed him a glittering look, and Gunnar knew she was remembering what he had said in the stable at Somerford.

The words had been for Arno's benefit, but he chose to let it pass. Instead he laughed and said, "If Radulf was ever a typical Norman, then Lily has put him right! He sent me because he dared not upset her so near her time by coming down on you himself and demanding an explanation! Aye, it was underhand perhaps, but—"

"If all this is true, what did he offer you in return?" Her quiet voice stopped him dead.

How did she know? Gunnar wondered. Again she had cut through his clever words and found the truth. Was she a witch? She looked mysterious and secretive in the night shadows, her face a pale oval, her eyes large dark hollows, her hair a black cloud brushed by starlight. And yet if he touched her skin, Gunnar knew she would be soft and warm, if he kissed her mouth she would be hot and needy.

She already suspected the truth, and it was a time to be honest, so he told it to her.

"He offered me Somerford Manor."

She was silent a moment. "Ah," she said.

Nothing more. No screams of hurt and anger, no agonized weeping, no recriminations. Gunnar would have known how to deal with all of those. But that soft "ah" as if she had known all along that he was only after her land. He could say more, try and make her understand . . . There was no time.

First he must save her life. Then he could think about winning back her trust.

Gunnar stood up. Grimly, he looked about him. "I

think I see where I went wrong," he said confidently. "Come. It will be dawn soon, and we have far to go."

He reached down to help her to her feet.

Rose gave him her hand, but removed it as soon as she was up. He sensed her cool withdrawal and could not blame her for it. Gunnar sighed, and concentrated on the here and now. He moved forward again, finding solid ground, cautiously pressing on into the Mere. Ahead of them lay one of the many islands, this one a low, flat-topped mound silhouetted against the stars. If they could reach it before the sun rose, they might be safe for a little while.

Gunnar wondered if Ivo had escaped by now, following after Alfred and the miller's family, to Crevitch. Had he found the messenger, Steven? Sweyn, Reynard, and Ethelred could take care of themselves. They would know how to read the situation and what action to take when and if it became necessary. Ivo had been the one he had been most worried about, Ivo whom Miles hated and would have killed for the flimsiest of reasons. 'Twas a shame Ivo had not dealt with his elder brother years ago, but to Ivo blood-family was sacred. In essence, Gunnar supposed, that was the difference between Ivo and Miles.

The island seemed to be getting bigger, which meant they must be getting closer. The solid path had given way to reeds, the land had given way to watery marsh. Gunnar searched along the bank, sloshing through the cold saltwater that reached up to his thighs, but there was no alternative. They would have to cross the pond—a width of about twenty feet—to the island. Maybe they would be lucky and the water would not be too deep.

Rose was watching him, and again he had the odd impression she was reading his mind. Odd, because no woman apart from his mother had ever been able to do that.

"Can you swim, Rose?"

She shook her head. He saw the movement clearly enough, and realized the darkness was lightening. Soon it would be dawn.

"Take off your cloak."

She cocked her head to the side, uncertain, but he gave her a tired smile meant to reassure her.

"I am going to throw your cloak over onto the island, so that you will have something dry to put on when we get there."

Slowly she drew open the ties at her throat, slipping the cloak from her shoulders and handing it to him. Gunnar unsheathed his sword, ignoring the way she stiffened at the sight of the dark, deadly blade. He bound the wool about the sword's hilt and blade as best he could, then he stepped back, hefted the weapon in his hand like a spear, and threw it with all his might. The throw was good, and it reached dry land with plenty to spare. Gunnar turned back to Rose.

"When I am in the water, I want you to put your arms around my neck and hold on to me. I can swim with you upon me. You will be safe."

She looked as if she would like to dispute that, but whatever words were clamoring behind her lips, she held them back. Gunnar stepped down into the water, sinking up to his chest in reeds. He felt her behind him, and then her arms wound about him, fingers clutching his shoulders, careful not to strangle him with her grip. She was trembling, and he felt the tremors in her body as it pressed to his. Was she cold? Or, more likely, was she afraid of him?

Gunnar waded out into the dark pool, deeper. The surface rippled, blurring the reflection of the stars. He heard her gasp as her feet lost purchase, her arms clung closer. At first she floated behind him, her gown holding the air and rising up about her in the dark water like angels' wings. And then, as the wool grew soaked, her clothing sank, dragging her down. The weighty pressure on Gunnar grew. He had walked as far as he could across the pond, but in the middle the bottom quickly dropped away, and he had no choice but to swim.

He was a reasonable swimmer—he had learned early. But he did not often swim with another person clinging to his back. The weight of her clothing was drawing them both down, and he struggled to keep his even breathing from turning into gasps. She had linked her hands about his neck, and he felt choked. He reached back with one arm, and tried to shift her further up onto his shoulders, adjusting her weight more comfortably.

"Do not let me go."

Her voice was a frightened whisper through chattering teeth.

"I won't let you go," he said quietly, as calmly as he could. And then his feet touched the muddy bottom, and he was walking, throwing himself forward with every ounce of his great strength, dragging them both through the tall fringe of reeds to the relative safety of the low island.

Rose's clothing wrapped about her legs, hampering her when she tried to walk. She fell to her knees, bedraggled and exhausted. Gunnar left her a moment, circling the small island, ignoring the tremor in his own legs and the aching weariness in his head.

When was the last time he slept well? First his lust had kept him wakeful, and then he had plundered his strength in the heady joy of Rose's bed.

As he had thought, the island was small and had little enough to offer them. Except—Gunnar smiled with satisfaction—on the far side and hidden from the distant shore was an obviously manmade structure of close-packed sods and turf. A shelter of sorts. A stunted tree grew over it.

He went back to fetch Rose. She was huddled over his sword, her cloak still twisted around it. As he approached he saw her struggling desperately to lift it, murmuring what could only be curses under her breath.

"Rose?"

He'd startled her. With a gasp, she dropped the weapon back onto the ground and turned to stare at him. In the pearly dawn light her face was near gray with exhaustion. Her gown clung to every curve, molding over full breasts and rounded hips, following the long line of her legs to where her muddy, stockinged toes peeped out beneath the hem. Her hair was like black waterweed, sticking to her white face and arms and back, furthering his impression of a drowned woman.

"If you want to slay me with my own sword," he informed her gently, "you will have to learn to lift it." And with a negligence that caused her to clench her jaw in fury or misery, he bent and lifted the sword with one arm, carefully untangling the cloak from the blade. He tossed Rose the dry garment, and slid Fenrir safely back into its scabbard.

"There is a shelter on the far side of the island," he said. "Go and take off your wet clothing and put on the cloak. You will be able to sleep more comfortably then."

She gave him a long, cool look—difficult, Gunnar thought with some amusement, when she was shaking and shivering like that. He stared back at her. She was no match for him, and eventually she turned and stalked off in the direction he had indicated, fighting to keep herself upright and her legs from buckling.

Gunnar gave her a few minutes.

When he went to join her, Rose had done as he said. Her wet clothing was tossed on the stunted tree to dry, and she was curled up inside the sod shelter, the dry cloak wrapped tightly about her. Her eyes were closed, but he could see from the way she was still shivering that she wasn't asleep.

Slowly, Gunnar unlaced his tunic, slipping it over his head, following it with his thin linen shirt. Next he removed his boots and his sword belt—this latter he set close to hand—then his breeches. Naked, he half crawled, half walked into the shelter. Clearly the place had been built for men much smaller than he.

Rose hadn't opened her eyes, but he knew by the tight look around her mouth that she had been listening to the sounds he made and knew he was undressing. Gunnar smiled to himself. It was flattering, but if she expected him to take her after what they had been through that night, then she was mistaken.

"I am cold, too," he said matter-of-factly. "It is warmer for two together than one alone."

She opened one eye and stared at him balefully. He took that as an aye, or near enough to one, and tugging the cloak out from under her, lay down beside her, lifting her head onto his shoulder and wrapping an arm about her waist. Carefully, he spread the cloak over them both, tucking it in about them. It was only just big enough, but the heat of his body was better than any cloak.

She shivered a little longer. Her skin was cold and damp, and although it appeared as if she had wrung out her long hair and twisted it loosely into one long rope, it was still sticky with saltwater. Slowly, as his heat enveloped her, Rose's body began to relax. Instead of holding herself stiff and aloof, she snuggled closer in against him, her breasts squashed up against his chest. When he lifted his thigh over hers, drawing her in even further, she groaned softly.

Maybe he wasn't so tired after all, Gunnar thought, as he felt himself become half aroused. But there was no urgency. It was a good feeling, a comfortable feeling, and he didn't need to do anything about it. Oddly, there was comfort in simply lying with her in his arms.

Gunnar lay watching the dawn break through the low doorway of the shelter, watching the rising sun cast long shadows over the Mere. In front of them was more of the same—water and islands, stretching on and on. But there was also something else, something well worth seeing. A boat, a small narrow craft, lay half hidden in the reeds on this side of the island. At least from now on they would not have to get their feet wet.

Gunnar smiled with satisfaction as he closed his eyes at last.

Chapter 17

Daylight brought birds. A great cloud of them wheeled up over the Mere, crying out raucously. They splashed and dived into the glistening water, hunting out their first meal of the day. Fish jumped or darted silver in the dark water, and the insects fluttered and buzzed, intent on making the most of their short, busy lives.

There was such abundance here—Rose had not expected it to be like this. Looking from her keep window she had seen the mystery of the Mere at night, the flat stretches of mud and water channels during the day. Her people caught fish and eels at its edges and made salt by evaporating away the water in shallow troughs. But here, in the midst of it all, Rose experienced a sense of wonder.

Gunnar had left her to dress in her still-damp clothing, and when she had finished she went in search of him. He was standing in the reeds with a boat. It was narrow and made of timber, and he seemed to be inspecting it for any rotten patches or holes. Sensing her presence, he glanced up at her with a grin.

Like a boy who has surprised even himself with his cleverness.

Rose felt her stomach lodge in her shoes. Desperately she tried not to stare as his wrinkled, salt-stained clothing clung to his muscular body. His copper hair was stiff and tangled into ringlets from his swim in the pool, and golden stubble softened the strong line of his jaw. Only moments before she had been lying in his arms, completely enclosed within his hard strength, soaking in his body heat to the marrow of her bones.

Her feelings confused her.

And frightened her.

When he had killed Ivo, she had hated him, although she was tied to him by their escape. And then—and she still wasn't certain of the truth of this—he had told her Ivo's death was a trick, and he was not Fitzmorton's man after all, but Radulf's man. He was a spy for Lord Radulf, and his reward for rooting out Arno's plot was Somerford itself. Her lands, her manor, her people.

She should hate him for that.

Why couldn't it be that simple?

The boat must have been in good order. Gunnar was holding out his hand toward her. "Come, lady. We must go now. Miles is probably fast closing in."

Miles de Vessey was the demon that was driving them farther into the Mere, and farther away from her home. If she should hate anyone, then it was Miles de Vessey.

Rose gave Gunnar her hand. He helped her over the tangle of reeds and into the narrow boat. Then, when she was settled, hands clinging to the sides, he climbed in himself. The boat was very small, and their combined weight made it low in the water. Gunnar had no oar, but he used his sword, using the broad blade to propel them across the next wide stretch of water.

The waterways of the Mere were interconnecting. Small channels ran through reed beds and more solid looking marsh, and they followed these, sometimes needing to backtrack, on and on toward the farther islands. Rose grew used to the ever present screech and squabble of birds, and the creatures themselves seemed hardly to notice them, apart from dodging cannily out of their path. As their boat slid along, a mother duck paddled furiously away from them, its half-grown ducklings following in an erratic line.

Rose smiled in delight at the picture they made, and before she remembered, had glanced at Gunnar to share her pleasure.

He was watching her.

Her smile faded and she turned back hastily to her previous occupation of staring straight ahead and trying not to notice the movement of the muscles in his arms as he piloted the boat, or the way he narrowed his blue eyes against the brilliance of the day. He truly looked the part of a Viking now. One of those raiders who sailed over the seas intent on carnage, Rose told herself angrily. A thief and a murderer and a liar, that was Gunnar Olafson.

Then why did her heart feel sore in her breast? Why did she long for things to go back to what they had been before, when he held her in his arms? When he looked at her with heat and longing in his face?

Before she learned the truth. Whatever *that* was!

"See over there?"

Rose looked up. He was pointing to a larger island; it appeared green, almost lush. There were even trees growing in a copse at one end, and wisps of dirty mist rose from the middle. Or was that smoke? Rose sat up straighter. Smoke meant people, a village. Smoke meant food, and Rose realized suddenly that she was very, very hungry.

"I think there are buildings." Gunnar spoke her thoughts aloud. "We need food and shelter, Rose."

"Merefolk?" Her voice was uneasy, and she clutched the sides of their fragile craft and ignored the rumbling in her stomach. "But will they harm us?"

"I'll protect you."

She looked at him with angry eyes. "Why do I find it so hard to believe you when you say that?"

Aye, she was angry! And the feeling was growing nicely as she fed it with images of his perfidy. He was like Arno, only worse. Even Edric, kind gentle Edric, had lied to her. He had promised Somerford to Arno and then perjured himself in Rose's favor. What had he thought would happen? Rose supposed he had expected her to wed again, to someone strong enough to hold tight to her manor. He would have believed her too timid to stand alone.

But she had. She had kept Somerford safe . . . until now. Now, when Gunnar, who should have been the answer to her prayers, had instead become her nightmare.

He had betrayed her. Like all men, he was not to be trusted and certainly never, ever to be loved.

Love no man, for he will surely destroy you if you do.

And now what would become of her? Even if she could reach Radulf and save Somerford, her own life stretched before her, an exile at the whim of others.

Rose felt her lip tremble and turned her face away, staring in the direction of distant Burrow Mump, so that he could not see. She had dreamed again last night, dreamed of the ghostly warrior on his gray horse. This time as he lifted her onto his lap, he had bent and kissed her. And his mouth had been Gunnar's mouth.

He had even taken her dream now, stolen even that small solace.

"I am a mercenary." His voice sounded as usual, calm and controlled. But there was something more in it—a trace of urgency—that made her listen despite keeping her gaze fixed in the opposite direction.

"A mercenary has no land, Rose. He fights and is paid for it. I fight well—I am strong and well taught. I have my own band of loyal men who follow me. They trust me, and I do what I can to ease their lives."

"Except that you killed one of them, although you tell me that was pretense. Am I to believe every word you say?"

He shot her a sideways glance, but otherwise pretended he had not heard her. "Being a mercenary is what I do best, but no mercenary can live forever. I see my death, Rose, and it does not make me happy. One day I will be too slow to see the blade swing down, and that will be my end. Buried by strangers in a strange place."

She said nothing, but her body quivered with his words as if she, too, could see that final day. And sense the loss of him.

"This past year I have felt the painful need of something more. My own land, my own woman, and the children we can make together. I am tired of this mercenary life. I have much to give, Rose, and I want to give it for those who *mean* something to me, not some weak-chinned Norman baron, greedy for English land. When Radulf offered me Somerford, it seemed like the answer to my dreams."

He sounded sincere. If she had not known better, Rose would have believed him, mayhap even sympathized with him. But Rose did know better.

"And it did not occur to you, after Lord Radulf offered you Somerford Manor, that it already belonged to me? And that my people were perfectly happy with that arrangement?"

He hesitated. No doubt wondering whether to lie again, Rose supposed furiously. "The thought of having my own land tempted me. When I first came to Somerford Manor I could see myself biding there, and the people needed protecting—*I* could protect them. How was I to know whether you were to be trusted? You had sent for mercenaries behind Radulf's back—or so he said. You appeared to be in league with your knight, plotting against him. At worst, Radulf thought you were tight in Fitzmorton's hand, scheming with him to steal Crevitch. At best, you were a weak, easily led fool."

Rose looked down into the water and saw it not at all. Her vision was blurred by tears of rage.

"Arno asked Brother Mark to write the letter," she said through stiff lips. "I sealed it as he asked, when he told me what was in it. He lied about that, and then he must have sent the letter to Lord Fitzmorton. I suppose that makes me the 'easily led fool.' "

"Rose . . ."

"No! Go on, tell me the remainder. I'd like to hear more of your fairy tales."

His voice became even more matter-of-fact, as if he

had set himself a task and meant to see it through. "One of Radulf's men intercepted the letter. It bore your seal. He sent for me, and I went to Fitzmorton and made myself known—Miles was in the north then, or it never would have worked. When the letter arrived, I was given the job. I did not know what the plot consisted of at first, or even if there was a plot. But soon I understood it was Arno's idea entirely, and that you were innocent."

"And all this you kept to yourself and lied." Rose wondered how she could sound so calm—she felt hot and cold with her anger.

"I am telling the truth now."

She looked around sharply at that, hearing the smile in his voice. Jesu, he *was* smiling! A wry smile of self-mockery. Her anger turned icy, the extent of his betrayal growing larger with each remembered hurt. He had lied and lied again, he had taken her body and made her *want* him, he had let her begin to believe that she could trust him.

He had even promised to obey her—what were Gunnar Olafson's promises worth?

They were like water, trickling through her fingers.

Rose lifted her chin and took a breath. She was going to hurt him. Just as he had hurt her.

"My people do not need a man like you. You are worse than Miles de Vessey—at least he fights for what he believes in, whether that be good or bad. You fight for coin, and now you tell me you would steal my land on a whim. I can smell the blood on your hands, Captain. Honor? You do not even know what it is! Whatever becomes of me now, I will make it my life's ambition to stop you from becoming Somerford's lord."

He said nothing to that. His face was cold and closed, the line of his mouth straight and grim. He looked as if he had been carved from rock. Her words had struck home, then—good! Rose told herself she was very pleased. Perhaps he would finally realize how pointless it was to try and excuse himself to her—if that was what he was doing. She would never forgive him, never trust him, ever again. Aye, she was very pleased indeed . . .

Rose sank down further in the boat, and drearily watched as the island drew nearer.

Gunnar wondered what she was thinking, and then told himself he did not care. He *would* not care. Why did he need to regain her trust anyway? Believing in himself had always been enough before. Why did he need *her* to believe in him, too? It was childish, and Gunnar had never been that. He was a man, and a natural leader. She was right, there was blood on his hands, but in that he was no different from all the other fighting men in King William's England. She had said it to diminish him, set him on a level lower than her own.

It had worked.

He had felt diminished, for a brief time. Until he reminded himself that women were nothing more than a diversion from life's more serious pursuits. They gave his body release, nothing more.

Why should he care if Rose was hurt and embittered by what he had done?

Because her pain affected him.

It was as if she were sunlight, and she touched everything in his life. Without her, he knew his world would slip back into perpetual shadow.

Aye, well, you'd best get used to the darkness, for she does not want you and will never forgive you!

Gunnar was not vain, but neither could he play at false modesty and pretend women weren't attracted to him. He had never found himself in a situation where the woman he wanted didn't want him.

Until now.

By Odin, why did he have to choose the one woman who denied him!

"Gunnar."

Rose's soft voice saying his name brought him back with a jolt. He followed her gaze. They were much closer to the island now, and it looked as if they had a welcome. A dozen or more merefolk stood down upon the shore, some with weapons in hand, awaiting their arrival.

"When we touch land stay in the boat," Gunnar said calmly. "Do not be afraid. I can protect you."

"I am not afraid," she retorted, but her dark eyes were enormous. She was playing a part because she did not want to appear weak before him. He could understand that, he even admired her for it . . . as long as she did exactly as he told her.

The merefolk were small and wiry in stature, their hair very dark and their skin tanned and lined by the hard life they led on the island. These were the remnants of the old peoples, the Britons and the Celts, who had been driven into these marshes long ago by the arrival of the land hungry Angles and Saxons. The men carried spears, longbows and arrows, and the occasional sword. Nothing as well wrought as Fenrir—Gunnar knew he could kill half of them before they brought him down, and the rest after that.

A cluster of women and children were huddled farther up the gentle slope, on top of which stood rows of turf and sod huts. Smoke rose low over the flat rooftops, wafting down to the shore, and with it came the smell of food cooking.

Their boat bumped into the thin strip of reeds on the bank. Gunnar stepped out, giving a brief glance to Rose. "Stay there until I tell you so," he commanded. He did not wait for her answer—as with his men, he expected her unquestioning obedience—but turned to the mere-folk. His stance was easy and relaxed, legs apart, one hand resting on his sword hilt and the other loosely at his side. They were not to know, but it was his battle stance.

"We are from Somerford Manor," he said in English.

Their faces didn't change. Apart from the differences of situation and lifestyle, they were just as unfriendly and suspicious as the villagers of Somerford. Gunnar could not blame them for being distrustful, but he hoped that—unlike Rose—he would be able to persuade them to believe differently.

"This is Lady Rose." He nodded toward the boat. "Somerford was her manor, but now her lands have been stolen."

An older-looking man stepped forward. His dark eyes were mere slits through skin folded with wrinkles, his gray hair was long and straggly, and he had a strong presence despite his stooped shoulders. "Who has stolen her land? Is it the King's Sword? I had thought he claimed the land in the first place."

His English was strangely accented, but Gunnar, who had traveled far, had no trouble understanding it. "No, not Radulf, 'tis Fitzmorton who has stolen Somerford."

No one said a word, and yet it was as if a breeze had rippled through them. The elder alone spoke. "Lately

Fitzmorton's men have come into our Mere and eaten our fish and frightened our people," he said. "They stayed on some of the uninhabited islands, and then spread tales about us that are not true." The black eyes watched him expectantly, full of wily cunning.

Gunnar wondered what was expected of him. Disbelieving laughter? That was probably what Arno would have done; Gunnar knew better.

"There have been attacks made on Somerford village, and although your people have been blamed we know it was Fitzmorton's doing."

He smiled, and again Gunnar had the sensation of a silent wind stirring the group.

"What is he saying? His English is strange."

Gunnar came close to jumping with surprise. Her voice was right behind him, which meant that *she* was right behind him. He felt her hand press into his back, the touch of it impossibly cool.

"I told you to stay in the boat," he said harshly in French. It sounded like a reprimand—it *was* a reprimand.

The hand was removed. He could picture the look on her face, it would be all Lady Rose. "*I* am paying *you*, Captain, not the other way around."

Some mischievous demon made him say, "Last time we bargained, lady, you were paying me . . . only it was not with coin."

She drew in her breath with a hiss, but before she could prolong the argument, he began to repeat the elder's words to her. Before he had finished, she came out from her safe spot behind him, and only his hand on her arm prevented her from boldly walking right up to the merefolk.

"I will take Somerford back, and there will be peace once more for the villagers and the people of the Mere." She said it with complete sincerity. "But for now, just for a little while, until Radulf comes to our aid, we need shelter and food. Will you shelter us?"

The old man listened, his black eyes never leaving Rose, and then he turned and consulted with his people.

"You should have stayed in the boat," Gunnar said.

He felt her eyes on his profile, trying to read the emotion behind his face.

"I am not one of your mercenaries," she told him quietly. "I do as I think fit. Remember it."

His mouth curled. "I am yours to command, lady."

Rose didn't say anymore.

The elder turned to face Gunnar and Rose again. "We will shelter you for a day or so, but you cannot stay long. If you are fleeing Fitzmorton he will come after you and then he will kill all of us here on the zoy . . . the island."

"We understand that," Gunnar said. "We don't wish to put your people in danger."

His black gaze slid curiously over Gunnar. "*You* are not from Somerford."

"I am Gunnar Olafson," and Gunnar smiled as if he hadn't a care in the world. "I am Lady Rose's shield, her protector."

The elder nodded, although there was an answering half smile on his timeworn face. "I am Godenere. Come with me and I will show you where you can rest."

Rose swallowed another piece of her fish and sipped fresh, warm goat's milk from a wooden bowl. The inside of their burrowed hut was small and dark, and the smoke from the small fire in the middle of the room spiraled up through a hole in the turf roof. The furniture consisted of a couple of shelves on the wall, a bench, a stool, and a small table. The bed was on the ground, a mattress stuffed with sweet, dry foliage and covered in soft skins.

It was not much different from some of the Somerford village huts, and Rose knew she should not be surprised. Did it take a crisis like this to make her realize the merefolk were no different from their brethren on dry land? Certainly, if what Godenere had said was the truth, they were not her enemies.

It was Fitzmorton and his kind who were the enemy. They were the ones she should have been preparing herself against all along. But she had trusted Arno because he was Edric's friend, and in trusting him she had foolishly lost everything.

I will get it back. Lord Radulf will get Somerford Manor back.

Aye, he probably would, eventually. But how many people would die in the process? And what of the harvest, so close now? Would that be lost while powerful men squabbled? Aye, and the poor folk would suffer—it was always the way. And what of Rose, who had lost Somerford Manor in the first place?

No, Rose did not expect to be given a second chance.

Despondently she sipped more milk. The goats were penned at one end of the village. The village itself was built on the highest point of the island or, as the merefolk called it, the zoy. There were numerous cottages and huts, with ducks and geese roaming at will. Children had watched from doorways, big-eyed, as she and Gunnar had walked passed. It was probably Gunnar who fascinated them, she decided. So big, a giant with copper braids and storm-blue eyes, he was as out of place in the island village as a Viking ship in a duck pond.

Rose finished her fish and bent to examine uneasily a mound of green vegetable in another bowl. It looked unfamiliar, some sort of waterweed, mayhap. Certainly nothing she had ever eaten before.

"'Tis good, lady. Our children grow strong when they eat it."

Rose looked up. A woman—girl, really—was watching her with a faint, superior smile. Rose raised her eyebrows at Gunnar. "I think she is telling me to eat it up, but her English is so strange, I cannot be sure."

"Something like that," he agreed, in French. He was sitting in the shadows like a pagan god, his copper braids framing his handsome face. Rose wasn't surprised to see that blank, besotted look slip over the girl's pretty features. It was exactly the same expression she had seen on the faces of the women in her own hall—womankind were all alike, it seemed, when it came to Gunnar Olafson.

He murmured something in English to the girl, and she simpered as she collected the empty bowls. Rose knew she was staring but she could not seem to help it. The girl filled his cup with more milk before she left, turning for one last lingering glance. Outside there was a noisy burst of chatter. Another face peered into the hut, this one not so young or pretty, and then it was withdrawn and there was more laughter.

Rose, becoming seriously alarmed, was glad to hear Godenere's voice. She didn't completely understand his words, but he seemed to be telling the crowd to go away and allow the strangers some rest. The chatter and giggles faded away as the lust-struck women dispersed.

Rose's stomach felt pleasantly full, she was warm and, just now, safe from the threat of Miles and Arno and Fitzmorton. Suddenly the women lurking about their hut, eager for a glimpse of the mercenary, were almost amusing. She looked over to Gunnar and smirked.

"What is it?" He was lifting his bowl of milk and stopped, frowning back at her.

"You," Rose retorted. He narrowed his eyes at her, and that seemed even funnier. Was it really so simple to breach his legendary tranquillity? Or mayhap Gunnar Olafson had had a bad day.

For no sensible reason *that* made her laugh.

"Me?" He watched her giggling to herself, and his suspicion turned to bemusement. It was a rare day when Gunnar Olafson was the source of a woman's hilarity.

"The way they look at you—the women. You are like a giant flower, Gunnar, and they are the silly bees and butterflies that come to smell the scent and try and sip the nectar. You spoil them for all the other flowers in the field."

One of his eyebrows rose and he waited patiently while she pressed her fingers to her lips, trying to prevent the little spurts of laughter from escaping. This was madness, and she knew it, and yet the laughter was bubbling up inside her like a boiling pot, and try as she might, she could not keep it down. If Constance were here she'd tell Rose to take a deep breath.

Gunnar had leaned back, his hands folded comfortably behind his head. He appeared so relaxed, but Rose no longer believed it. It was pretense, another lie. A man like Gunnar Olafson would never be able to truly relax. She wondered how much longer it would be before another of the Mere women found an excuse to return. More milk? More fish? More of that nasty green seaweed?

She had to laugh again, but now her stomach was beginning to hurt.

"Are you jealous, Rose? Is that it?"

That stopped her. Sobered her instantly. Rose sat up and gulped in a deep breath of smoky air, wiping her streaming eyes with her sleeve. But the dried salt in the cloth stung them and they only watered the more.

"Hardly," she mocked, pressing her fingers to her eyes and blinking hard. "I am not such a simpleton as that, Captain."

"And what is wrong about admiring the way a man looks? Men admire women all the time." He had leaned forward slightly, and now there was a glint in his eyes that made her nervous.

Rose sniffed. "Is that what you call it? Admiration? The poor creatures would spin in circles if you asked them to!"

"And you would not?" he retorted, shifting closer. There was something in his voice, a warning, and Rose glanced at him sideways. "Well, lady?"

"No, I would not! Some women are more gullible than others. And I know that men are not to be trusted, Captain—if I did not know it before then I surely know it now. Men do not feel as women do, you see. Their hearts are colder, harder. Like the sword you wear strapped to your hip, men use their hearts to wound, Captain, and sometimes the wound is fatal."

Gunnar seemed puzzled by her intensity as he stared at her across the smoky firelit room. "I can see you truly believe every word you say. Is it a lesson, lady, taught to you when you were young?"

She paled but could not find a reply. She had given too much of herself away already.

His voice went on—a soft, mesmerizing murmur. "My father would lie down and die to protect my mother. He would fight an army to keep her safe. Is that not feeling deeply, lady?"

Was that true? Or was it another lie?

"Lord Radulf would howl like a wolf who has lost his mate if anything happened to his Lily. He told me once that she is his moon, that she lights his way. Is that not feeling deeply, lady?"

"You are twisting my words."

"How so? I am simply showing you that you are wrong. Maybe there are men like those you mention, but not all."

"You show me two men who care for their women," Rose retorted. "How many does that leave who do not?"

"And you judge all men by the actions of a few, lady."

Rose frowned at him, annoyed that he was smiling at her as if he had won the argument. He was wrong and she was right, and she knew it. That was all that mattered. So she shrugged her shoulder indifferently and said, "How can you understand? You are a man."

"Aye, I *am* a man," he repeated softly, and now there was danger in his voice. "And there are many things I understand." She watched him uncertainly as he shifted even closer. His hand closed, large and warm, upon her knee. "I understand how much you like me to touch you," he murmured.

She pushed his hand away. "'Tis not the same!"

"How so?" He was on his knees before her now, and she glared up into his face, but he was still smiling. Could he not see how much she hated him? "I know you like this," he murmured, his voice deep in his chest, and bending, set his lips to hers. The taste of him, the heat of him, was nearly her undoing.

"You are wrong," she whispered.

He chuckled softly, and opening his lips, kissed her long and deeply. Everything shifted. She felt as if her entire world narrowed until it was centered on Gunnar and his mouth on hers, his body against hers, hard and heavy. Rose moaned and slid her hands about his neck.

His hand found her breast, gently squeezing, and she arched against him. "I know how much you ache and burn, Rose. I understand, because I ache and burn, too."

She opened her eyes and stared at him, watchful, cautious, but intrigued despite her doubts. "Do you?" she asked, surprised at the breathlessness of her voice.

"Lady, you know I do." His mouth was against her cheek, her temple, her throat. He rolled to his side, carrying her with him, holding her firm against his body. "You have only to look at me, Rose, and I want you. You laugh and tell me those women think I am a flower, but lady, I would sup upon your nectar all day."

She laughed, she couldn't help it—the thought of Gunnar supping . . . But his eyes were dark and there was a tension in his smile she already knew.

He wanted her; he didn't lie about that.

She slid her hand down over the rigid muscles of his belly and closed her fingers over his manhood, where it strained eagerly against his breeches.

"You are very hard, Captain," she murmured. "Is that for me or do you plan to take the Mere women one by one?"

He choked, and then he had rolled over again, this time pinning her beneath him, one of his thighs pressed between hers, his hands either side of her face. "I want you," he said, and, bending his head, kissed her until her head was spinning. His fingers were determined as he lifted her skirts, slipping into her soft folds and finding her as eager as he. Rose tugged at the ties of his breeches and slid them down, freeing him. He lifted her hips and immediately drove deep into her, immersing himself in her, as if he could never get close enough.

"Rose," he groaned and withdrawing thrust again. She moved with him, her hair wild about her, her eyes blurred with desire and pleasure. Her hands slid under his tunic, finding the hard, smooth planes of his chest, and then his mouth was on hers again, taking her cries as she reached her peak, and giving her back his own ecstasy as he followed her to the top.

Stop this, stop it now!

Rose gasped and tried to pull away, straightening her clothing, her face flushed with anger and embarrassment and the knowledge that once again he had breached her ramparts. "No," she gasped, "no, I didn't want . . . I didn't mean . . ."

But Gunnar caught her hand, drawing her back against him, holding her to stillness while he gazed steadily into her eyes.

"There is just you and me," he said, like the calm in the storm that was tearing at her, making her head ache. "We are together in this, Rose. Trust me, lean on me. Let me be your shield, just for now. It is what I am good at. And I will hold you close and maybe, for once, *I* will not feel so alone."

He looked so sincere. As if he meant it. Rose suddenly wished with all her heart that he *did* mean it. Tears sprang into her eyes, but she wouldn't let them fall. Slowly, like an unwilling sacrifice, she relaxed against him. It felt good, so good . . .

Why not? she asked herself. Take what he offered without guilt or fear, and later, when Somerford was saved, she could end it.

End it? Just like that?

Yes! thought Rose. *I will end it . . . but for now I will take what he offers—and we will both be happy.*

She nodded her head almost brusquely, her decision made. He had been still, awaiting her answer. Now he brushed back her hair, and slowly began to kiss her. Soft, tender kisses that grew longer and more passionate, until kissing wasn't enough, and they lost themselves once more in an act, the meaning of which both of them denied.

Chapter 18

"Gunnar Olafson?" It was Godenere's voice from beyond the doorway in the shadows.

Light was fading from the day, and Rose had been asleep in the smoky darkness, lying in Gunnar's arms. They had not left the hut, and when food was brought to them, a crowd accompanied the meal and then faded away with the emptied dishes.

Rose's villagers believed the merefolk had tails in place of legs. Now Rose understood how it felt to be looked on as a freak.

"This is all to do with you," she had told Gunnar.

But he had looked at her and, smiling, shaken his head. "No, lady. 'Tis you they come to look at. Your beauty holds them spellbound. The goddess from the castle, that is you."

Rose had laughed, delighted with the compliment, even if she didn't believe it. She stretched up to kiss his rough cheek. The stubble was turning into a young beard, but it was so fair it was barely noticeable unless she was close, unless she brushed her fingers across his skin.

What was it about him that made her chest ache? This feeling inside her, this swelling of happiness and pain, of longing . . . It wasn't sensible to allow herself to be carried away on this wave of emotion. She would be much wiser to step back from him, hold herself aloof . . .

"Gunnar Olafson?"

Godenere's voice came again, more insistent.

Rose sat up, just as Gunnar got to his feet. He was still bare chested from their last bout of lovemaking, although he had pulled on his breeches. He was like a dream come true, thought Rose, and felt a spurt of jealousy as she thought of all those mere women drooling over him.

Gunnar stooped beneath the roofline to save cracking his head as he went to the doorway. The door itself was made of withy sticks twisted into a thick mat and fastened to the jamb with leather straps. He pushed the door aside and there was Godenere, bathed in the golden light of the setting sun, patiently waiting. Behind him . . .

Rose sighed. It was as she had feared. Behind Godenere was gathered what looked like the entire village.

Nervous suddenly, Rose, too, quickly got to her feet. She twisted her long dark hair back over her shoulder, brushing down her gown, smoothing her sleeves. Her body still tingled from Gunnar's touch, and ached pleasantly in places it had never ached before. She was untidy, her skin and clothing were salty, and she felt frighteningly vulnerable to the gaze of others.

She had always been quick before to hide that vulnerability under her lady-of-the-manor face, but here she had no authority. She might as well be a serf, a peasant at the whim of the great ones.

Coming up behind Gunnar, she placed her hand against his broad back. His skin was smooth, apart from the scars, the evidence of his dangerous life. She wanted to wrap her arms about him and breathe in his scent, press close and forget.

Gunnar glanced questioningly at her over his shoulder. Perhaps he read her need in her face, for he reached around and drew her to his side. She settled into the curve of his body, and his big hand came to rest on her hip as if it were the most natural thing in the world.

Godenere was saying something about Normans in his quick tongue. Gunnar answered him, his own voice low and measured, but Rose felt his body tense and knew the news wasn't good.

Behind Godenere, men, women, and children peered at the two of them, some curious, some stifling giggles, some suspicious. Rose couldn't blame them for the last. If she and Gunnar were bringing danger to this island by being there, it was better they left now.

Gunnar nodded to what Godenere was saying, his fingers smoothing thoughtfully over Rose's round hip. The warmth in her blood began to simmer. She kept herself still, trying to concentrate on the conversation between the two men, but the feel of his long fingers was distracting.

Suddenly Godenere nodded in Rose's direction. "This lady belongs to you?" he asked.

Rose understood that. She froze and dared not look at Gunnar. Was that how it seemed to these people? she asked herself bleakly. Did it already appear that she was Gunnar's woman, to do with as he pleased? As her father had made her mother his creature?

Gunnar was taking his time in replying, his hand had stilled on her hip. The crowd shifted forward curiously, the pretty serving girl to the front.

'Twas just as well she did not mean to cling to Gunnar Olafson forever, Rose thought crossly. How could she endure this every day? It would drive her to distraction . . .

"No." Gunnar smiled at the old man, and there was a hint of regret in his tone. "I am her man, that is all. But she does not belong to me, or any man."

Godenere looked doubtful. He said something to the watching crowd, and there was a questioning murmur. Some of the women sighed in disappointment. Rose felt her face heating up under their continued scrutiny, and was glad when Godenere and Gunnar finished their conversation, and she was able to retreat into the hut.

"What did he say?" she asked curiously, avoiding his eyes as she bent to warm her hands at the smoldering peat fire.

He crouched down beside her, the black breeches stretching deliciously over his thighs. His copper braids swung forward as he leaned toward her, and his voice was low. "They have seen Normans searching in the Mere. For us, they think—why else would they be here? Miles must have Somerford in his fist now, but he will not feel safe until he has killed me and taken you."

She turned and met his gaze. There was something hot and angry in his storm-blue eyes, a sense of terrible danger. But it was not a threat to her—it was Miles whom Gunnar meant to hurt.

He reached out and touched her cheek, his fingers gentle—it always surprised her how gentle he was, as if because his hands were used to wielding a sword, they could not do anything else. He had proved her wrong in that, at least.

"We are no longer safe here," he went on, and dropped his hand. The peat fire shifted, a piece falling out onto the floor beyond the stone trough, and he used his boot to push it back to safety.

"Then what will we do?" she ventured, watching the stirred peat flare before returning to its usual sulky smolder.

"Our presence puts these people in danger. If Miles and his men come upon us here, they will kill them for giving us shelter. Fitzmorton rules his lands by terror Rose. He isn't like Radulf, he isn't like you."

"I know what Fitzmorton is," she said quietly.

"Godenere wants to move us onto another island, a place where nobody lives. Then, if we are captured, no one can be punished for sheltering us."

"I see." Rose felt herself shrink with disappointment She had hoped that, somehow, they would be able to return to Somerford, regain what was lost. Now they must travel even farther into the bewildering Mere. Mayhap they would still be there when they were old and gray traipsing from island to island, an old exiled couple . . .

Gunnar interrupted her bleak vision.

"Godenere and I have made a plan."

"What sort of plan?" Rose felt her stomach clench Would she have to decide whether to trust him again? Jesu, why did it always come down to *trust*?

"Godenere will send some of his people to find the searching Normans. They will make up some tale about seeing us, and in the process let them know where we are hiding. When they come, we will be waiting for them. We will spring the trap and the victory will be ours."

"*We* will spring the trap?" she retorted, so close to him now that her breath stirred his hair. "I would very much like to fight Miles, but I cannot even lift your sword!"

He smiled, his eyes crinkling at the corners. "I swear you could wither them with one look, lady. But it will not be necessary. Godenere is willing to send a group of his men to fight with us."

"Godenere is willing to do this? For us?"

"You promised to bring them peace and security when you regain Somerford. They will never get that if Fitzmorton takes your manor."

That was true enough.

The idea had merit, but to deliberately set themselves up as bait in a snare . . . ? Rose sat silent, steadying her jumping nerves.

You have been through worse. And if it means we can be free of this present threat, then it must be considered worth the attempt.

"When must we go?"

Gunnar knelt beside her, not touching her, but so close she could feel his warmth. It was comforting, like the sun shining on a cold day. 'Twas a pity that soon he would be gone, and she would be alone once more.

"We must go soon."

Rose nodded. Suddenly she did not want to meet his eyes. The words came out of nowhere. "You said you were my man."

"Aye. 'Tis the truth, whether you believe it or not. I have pledged myself to obey you, Rose."

"I don't want—"

"I will win Somerford back for you. I swear this." Suddenly he bowed his head before her. "I swear it. I make it my vow, lady. Please believe me."

Reluctantly, Rose placed one shaking hand on his bowed head. His hair was as soft beneath her fingers as she had feared. There were hot tears on her cheeks, but she didn't remember crying them. She wanted to believe him so much, so very much. She longed to give herself over to him, to let everything go—like a taut rope cut free. But she could not. She had held herself apart for too long.

"Gunnar, please . . . I do not want you to do this. I am not your lady. I cannot be your lady. Ever."

" 'Ever' is a long time, Rose."

He looked at her through the fall of his copper hair, his blue eyes blazing. Surely he meant what he said, in this moment she almost believed him despite all she feared to the contrary.

And yet one part of her, stubborn and afraid, whispered caution.

"Aye," she said at last. "It is."

The Mere glowed in the dusk, mirroring the pink and orange and azure of the sky. Birds flew dark above and dragonflies glided low. The water shone, the reeds were fringes of black, and the boats slipped like ghosts through the secret channels and wider ponds.

There were four boats, twelve young men, who had come with them to help them hide from Fitzmorton and, if it came to it, to fight. Shaggy-haired, bearded, and reserved, they moved their craft with a certainty that came of having lived their entire lives in the Mere.

Twilight was turning to darkness, and biting insects

came out to feed on them. Rose pulled her cloak up over her head, covering her flesh as best she could. As she turned to see what lay ahead, she realized they were drawing closer to solid land. A knoll rose abruptly from the flat levels, towering above them.

Burrow Mump.

The place of her dreams.

Surely they could not be going there? And yet the boats moved relentlessly onward, closer and closer to that dark shape. The paddles so quiet, with only the softest splash. The air about them was warm, thick, the light was magical, and there before her lay the place of her dreams.

Was *this* a dream? Rose was no longer sure.

Suddenly the reeds seemed to stir around her, as if brushed by an unseen hand. She shivered.

"Rose?" It was Gunnar's voice.

"Is that where we are going?"

He glanced beyond her, at the rising bulk of the island. "Aye. Godenere said it was a place no one came to."

"Why is that?" She was whispering; somehow it seemed wrong not to whisper in this place. "Why does no one come here?"

"He said the ghosts of their ancient ones live here. The dead. It is their Valhalla. When Miles's men find us, they will help us to victory."

Rose held her breath as the boat came into the shore, brushing through the reeds in the shallows, bumping onto dry land. For a moment no one moved. There was no sound. Nothing.

The silence was inexpressibly eerie.

Gunnar climbed out and helped Rose to follow. As she stood, her cloak wrapped close about her, he pulled their boat high up onto the shore. The other men were also moving about, not speaking, quickly securing their boats and then moving off into the darkness.

Gunnar and Rose followed.

There was little that lived on Burrow Mump. A few small animals, perhaps. It felt deserted. The men lit a fire with the peat they had brought with them. It smoldered but soon grew hot. Rose sat within its comforting glow, leaning against Gunnar's side, her eyes half closed.

Out there on the Mere it was very dark; even the stars did not seem to shine very bright. The reeds rustled in the occasional cool breeze, but other than that the strange stillness remained. A breathless feeling, a waiting feeling.

About her, the men spoke in soft voices, and sometimes Gunnar nodded and sometimes he said something in return. Their voices lulled her, took the edge off her fears, and after a time she slept.

Rose was all alone in the night. Above her the moon shone down, but it was small and insignificant and so far away. She turned around, trying to get her bearings, searching for some landmark. That was when she saw the steep shoulder of the knoll against the stars, and realized, with a quick thud of her heart, that she was standing on Burrow Mump.

Her blood turned to ice. She tried to run, but as was the way in dreams, her legs were slow and stiff and would not work. And then the ground was opening up around her, and she could see a chamber, a deep passageway, spearing into the heart of the hillside.

Far, far down Rose heard the rumble of something stirring.

She was running in earnest now. Somehow she had gotten beyond Burrow Mump, and was out on the Mere. Her feet slipped on the muddy path, a biting pain in her side. Behind her a great whooshing of air came howling across the Levels, and with it a sound like a hundred voices roaring all at once.

The warriors had arisen from their underground world.

Rose lost a shoe. Gasping, her breath sobbing, she abandoned it and ran on. Suddenly before her was the solid bulk of Somerford Keep. A single light flickered in the solar window, beckoning her to safety. Nearly there, nearly there . . . She knew she should not, but she could not help it.

Rose glanced over her shoulder.

They were close. Oh, so close.

Ghostly horses with flowing tails and manes were galloping above the water. Warriors, their arms and chests gleaming, their long hair tangled by the gust of the fierce wind that had followed them from their underground home. They were bearing down on her.

Rose turned her face to Somerford Keep and struggled forward, even knowing it was useless. They were coming too quickly; she would never make it.

Rose sat up with a jerk. Gunnar was above her, a frown in his eyes. "Lady? You were dreaming."

Was she? Rose blinked up at him. It had seemed very real. The ghostly riders, the flight across the Mere. This time *her* warrior had not been there, just the ravening pack. Why was that? What did it mean?

She shivered and tried to sit up. She was, she realized, resting across his lap, and he was leaning back against the hull of one of the boats. Sleeping sitting up, if he was sleeping at all.

"What is it?" he asked her, not trying to stop her, watching her with that stillness that made her even more edgy. "What frightens you?"

Rose pushed her hair out of her eyes and blinked against the smoke of the fire. Peat did not roar and crackle like wood, it was a low fire, hot and sullen, and it lasted a long time.

" 'Tis this place," she said at last, her voice wavering despite her efforts to calm herself. Her skin was tingling with fright, the dream still very real. "Don't you feel it?"

Gunnar glanced about him, then drew his knee up and wrapped his arms about it. He smiled. "The ancient ones, do you mean? Are you afraid they will steal you away—"

"Don't!" she said sharply, and looked over her shoulder, as if afraid she would see the deep underground cavern, the waiting warriors.

Gunnar bit his lip. She was truly afraid. Who would have thought the indomitable Lady Rose would be frightened of old English bones? Her weakness gave him a sense of hope that perhaps she needed him after all. Gunnar had always thought of himself as a protector. It would please him greatly to be able to protect Rose. Even if it was only from evil fairy tales.

"I am not afraid," he said in his measured way. "Fenrir is proof against any danger, be it flesh and blood or spirit. He fights in both worlds."

"Fenrir," she repeated, eyes huge and dark in her white face.

"The great black Norse wolf. No chain could hold him. He would soon scatter your ancient ones."

She sighed and closed her eyes, but her body remained tense, unable to relax back into sleep.

"Come lady, you have more to fear from Miles than from this place," he chided her gently.

She opened her eyes and peered at him, as if trying to make out his expression in the fading light of the fire. "Do you believe we will defeat him, Gunnar? Will our trap work?"

"Of course."

"And Radulf will come and save my people?"

"He will."

She nodded, as if she were satisfied rather than relieved. Her mouth turned down, surprising him. She looked sad.

"You are not happy to hear this?"

Rose shook her head. "Oh yes, of course I am. I am very happy. It is just that . . . Radulf will not want me as his vassal after this. I will have to leave. My father may take me in."

She said it without expression, as if it meant nothing to her, but Gunnar felt the shiver beneath her pretense. Rose was terrified. The idea that someone, anyone, had hurt her, made her suffer, rose in him in a great wave. He could not contain it.

"Who has hurt you!" he burst out so loudly that she jumped.

"Shh, Gunnar, you will wake—"

He swallowed hard, but his fists were clenched on his knees and the muscles in his arms bunched and tightened. "Then what is wrong. Tell me, and I will be quiet."

She eyed him uneasily, but he kept the fierce look on his face, and after a moment the stiffness went out of her back and shoulders, and she bowed her head. It was a sign of capitulation, but he didn't understand what it was she had given up until she began to speak.

Her voice was soft and low. He had to lean forward to hear some of it, but he heard most, and it was enough. She told a tale not uncommon in those times, one he had heard before. Rose, the solemn little girl caught between the brutality of her father and the instability of her mother, suffering the taunts of a selfish brother. Never a child at all. Taking on adult responsibilities despite her tender years, willing to give away her own happiness for the sake of others, longing for love and never finding it. Edric, perhaps, had loved her, in his way. Arno had coveted her. Her people loved her, but that was the sort of love children felt for a parent.

She felt guilt, because she had tried to hold fast to Somerford when she should have gone at once to Radulf. Instead she had thought to hire mercenaries and buy herself time to escape her mess. She had feared that if Radulf was made aware of the situation he would replace her.

Probably she was right.

Radulf *would* replace her.

He looked up and found that she was watching him. She was regretting that she had opened herself up to this probing. Gunnar felt her unease and distrust shiver across his skin. And he felt the weight of the burden her words had laid upon him. She had not asked him to take it up, Rose would never do that, but he was willing. Gunnar was good at saving people, and if anyone needed saving at this moment, it was Lady Rose of Somerford Manor.

He was her man. He had told her so, and it was the truth. Now he had a chance to prove it.

But Gunnar had waited too long to give her his answer.

"It doesn't matter," she said abruptly, and lay down on her side by the fire, pulling her cloak over her. Containing herself, holding her emotion inside, curling tightly about it. "I can sleep now."

After a moment Gunnar also lay down, but he did not close his eyes. A wry smile tugged at his lips. His mother would laugh at him if she knew that he was contemplating giving up everything for the sake of a woman. He, the big strong mercenary captain, to whom women were weak creatures put on the land so that he could keep them safe and, when the urge was there, take them to his bed.

But he would never allow them into his heart.

And now it seemed as if one had found her way in there after all. Aye, he loved her. He had been like Fenrir, his Norse wolf, never chained, running free. Rose had chained him with his love for her, and he was glad of it.

He would do as he had promised, he would return Somerford to her, and then it would be her decision whether he left to continue his wanderings, or stayed by her side.

"Gunnar Olafson?"

Gunnar lifted his head and met the eyes of the boy crouched beside him. Barely old enough to grow a beard, thought Gunnar with a sigh, and yet brave enough to come with him and fight the Normans.

"Come," the boy said urgently, beckoning at him.

Gunnar climbed to his feet, careful not to disturb Rose. She lay in a heap, only the top of her head showing from beneath the cloak. The boy led him to a vantage point upon a rocky outcrop to one side of the knoll. From there they could see the Levels spread out before them in the early morning light.

Fitzmorton's men had fanned out, a dozen of them, some on foot and some in boats.

This was it, then. The fight he had been anticipating. A low hum of excitement started up inside him, and he rested his hand on Fenrir's hilt. *Soon, my friend*, he thought. *Soon*.

And by God and Odin, Miles would be sorry then that he had crossed Gunnar Olafson and the woman he loved.

"Rose?"

She blinked and looked up at him, smiling before she remembered herself. The smile became tentative, then faded altogether before his stern demeanor. She turned away from him and carefully eased her stiff and aching body from the hard ground, biting her lip so as not to groan aloud.

Who would have thought that she would miss her bed so much?

"Are you hungry?" he was asking her calmly, as if this were just another day. "There is salt fish and some bread and goat's cheese. We have to move quickly, Rose. Miles's men are out searching for us."

Rose was trying to imagine salt fish on a stomach already queasy with nerves and weariness, but his last words brought her up sharply and the fish was forgotten.

"We have made a plan, Rose. Tonight you will sleep at Somerford, that I promise you."

She tried to read him, but other than the fact that he believed what he said, she could see nothing. Last night, after her bad dream, she had been weak and foolish, and had told him about her father and mother. What had she hoped for? Sympathy? A pat on the head and a never-mind?

She wished now she had said nothing. Obviously it meant nothing to him, and why should it? He had pledged himself to her, but he did not love her. *My heart is my own to give.* Rose could understand why a man who must sell his sword for coin would want to keep his heart safe. Why he would need one thing at least to call his own.

Then why was there a wistful longing inside her, that somehow she could steal or beg or borrow his heart from him? If he loved her enough, would he stay by her always? Would he be Radulf to her Lily?

Rose tried to imagine a life where a man loved her like that. Despite her faults, or because of them. It made her dizzy, as if she had drunk too much strong mead.

Gunnar was watching her, waiting.

Miles's men were coming and they had no time for foolishness.

She knew then that he did not want a weak and feeble woman. He wanted strength and authority. She must be the lady of the manor again. For him, just for him.

"Thank you, Gunnar," she said at last, and lifted her chin proudly. "Now tell me what I must do."

* * *

Their narrow boat slid out into the open stretch of water, within clear sight of the searching Normans. There was a shout, but Gunnar was already turning the boat, with Rose clinging to the bow, back the way they had come. She turned to look, her eyes wide and dark and gleaming with excitement.

"They are very slow," she said, and a smile tugged at her mouth. "Ah, now they are in their boats, now they are following."

Gunnar paddled harder, edging between the tall reeds, ignoring the angry squawk as a bird crashed out of its shelter and took flight, the beating wings all but brushing his shoulder. He looked grim, determined—the man he had been the day he came to Somerford.

Behind them Fitzmorton's men huffed and puffed, paddling with more splash than finesse. Their loud and angry voices floated over the water. She looked again. Miles de Vessey was not there—of course not, he would not come on such a mission, he would send his henchmen to hunt his enemies down through the mud and water. Then, when they were tied and bound securely before him, he would finish them off.

"They are closing, Gunnar," she said anxiously.

"We are almost there." His chest was heaving with the effort of keeping up speed, one man against a dozen.

Burrow Mump flashed by on their left, and then they shot out into the wide, reed-fringed pond they had decided on for their trap. Gunnar speared the boat into a tall screen of reeds just as Fitzmorton's men entered the smooth water behind them. They were still paddling furiously in pursuit, and were more than halfway across the pool before they realized their error.

The mere men stood up, above the reeds, spears

raised, arrows aimed. Cursing, Fitzmorton's men attempted to turn their boats, desperately trying to find a way through. There was none. They were covered on all sides, and were at a disadvantage, being in their fragile boats in the middle of a deep pool. To their credit, when they realized it, they still raised their own weapons, preparing to fight it out.

Gunnar stood up.

"Give up!" he shouted. "We have double your number and more. Give up. What are you fighting for? Lord Radulf will come soon and take Somerford back and then he will kill you all. Give up now and your lives will be spared."

He was expecting some argument, a show of bravado at least, perhaps even a half-hearted fight. Instead the men looked about them at the strange merefolk and then back at Gunnar Olafson, confused, wavering.

"Gunnar!"

The voice came across the Levels, echoing against the rise of the island. It was a voice Gunnar knew well. Startled, he straightened and peered over the reeds. There was a man standing unsteadily in a boat, his head bare to the sunlight, a grin splitting his face.

Gunnar would have known that wild black hair anywhere.

"Ivo," he murmured. Then, with a shout, "Ivo!"

Ivo laughed, a low chuckle. "What are you doing to Radulf's men, Gunnar? I don't think you should kill them—Radulf might not like it."

Chapter 19

The gate was wide open.

Rose urged her horse forward, damping down the fear inside her, needing to see what was inside and yet frightened of what she would see. She hardly noticed the men riding with her. Ivo was close behind her and Gunnar was in front of her. The rest were strangers—Lord Radulf's men.

Ivo had told her the story. Radulf had set out for Somerford as soon as Alfred had arrived at Crevitch with Harold the miller and Millisent and Will.

Lily, told the bare bones of the facts, had given her husband a long, cool look and told him to mend his mess. Radulf had glowered back at her, but set off for Somerford immediately.

He had taken back the keep that same day. The easy victory had been a combination of the small army Radulf had taken with him, and the fact that Arno and Miles had not counted on Rose's people inside the keep working against them. Miles in particular had thought to conquer the English with fear and threats, but old Edward and his cohorts had used stealth, waiting until Radulf was close and then opening the gate to him.

After a brief and bloody battle, Somerford was won.

"Thank God for it," Radulf had allegedly said, when it was over. "I could not have faced my lady wife if I had lost."

Rose had smiled when Ivo told her that. "You are alive," she had added, looking him up and down. "I saw you die."

Ivo had laughed, his smile transforming his fierce features. "Aye, 'twas a trick. Didn't Gunnar tell you? We have used it before. I have returned to life more than once, lady."

Gunnar had told her, and she had said she believed him. Now, with the evidence before her eyes, she realized that she hadn't *really* believed him, not truly. Not until now.

She felt shamed by her mistrust, even remembering all the untruths he had told her. And then, as they approached the Somerford ramparts, she tried very hard not to feel anything at all.

"How many of my people have died?" she asked quietly of no one in particular.

Gunnar glanced at her over his shoulder. She wondered what it was he saw, for his usual tranquil expression wavered at the edges, and for a moment she saw tenderness in his eyes. It nearly undid her.

"Rose . . ."

"Lady Rose," she corrected him savagely, afraid he would make her cry. She could not cry, not when her people needed her strong.

His face stilled. Too late she wondered if her words might have stung his pride, made him feel the lesser man. And then he had turned away, and she was gazing at his broad back and the fall of his copper hair.

So it was they passed through the gate into the bailey.

It was quiet. Everywhere Rose looked there were armed men. But when her eyes had grown used to armor and helmets and grim expressions, she noticed that her own people were also there. They appeared a little shaken and unsure, but they had lived through other battles and they would heal.

They even managed a ragged cheer at the sight of her.

Rose felt tears sting her eyes and lifted a hand in salute. Turning her head, she searched for loved faces, praying that none was missing. There was old Edward, standing tall and proud, his wrinkled face grimy, a cut on his cheek, but still grinning.

"Lady Rose!" he shouted. "God bless our lady!"

Others took up the cry, and Rose bowed her head, tears trickling down her cheeks. If this was to be her last homecoming, it was surely special. One she would never forget no matter what came after.

The horses had drawn to a halt near the keep. Blindly, Rose tried to tug her foot from the stirrup, but a firm hand closed over her instep, freeing her. Warm fingers caught her about the waist, strong arms lifted her effortlessly to the ground. Through her tears and tangled hair she had a glimpse of searching blue eyes, but when she would have retained her clasp on his arm, Gunnar moved back, away from her.

Keeping his distance.

Rose swayed, momentarily distracted, lost in a way she had never felt before. It was not weakness, for she knew now she was strong. It was a sense of lack, as if a part of herself were now missing because he stood too far away.

Before she could grasp the significance of this, a cry shrilled through the noise and chatter about her.

"Lady! Dear lady!"

Constance was hobbling down the steps. Rose ran forward with open arms to hug her. It was only as she held those fragile bones in her strong arms that she realized the old woman had a black eye.

"They have hurt you," she gasped, her voice shaking with anger.

Constance chuckled. "I have had worse," she retorted with bravado, though her mouth trembled. "When that Miles found you had gone, he hit me, so I fell down and pretended to take a fit. They left me be after that, lady."

Rose put a hand to her lips, not knowing whether to laugh or cry. "But you are all right, Constance? Nothing is broken or—"

"No, lady, nothing is broken. I will live to see you give Somerford Manor an heir, you may be sure."

Rose shook her head, smiling.

"You should have seen Miles's face when he knew it was Lord Radulf coming," Constance went on, eyes gleaming with grim enjoyment. "I thought he'd piss his breeches!"

"Miles is gone?" Gunnar came and frowned down at her, his anger and disappointment palpable.

"Aye, Captain," Constance replied, eyeing him a little warily. "He escaped before Radulf took back the keep. Gone back to Fitzmorton his master, I'll be bound."

She glanced at Rose as she said it, and Rose saw the

concern in her face. The old woman was probably wondering if her lady would also be riding in that direction, before the sun had set that night.

Sweyn had followed Constance, and Reynard hovered behind them. Ethelred, his arm tied up in a makeshift bandage, looked pale but determined not to show he was hurt. When he stumbled and grimaced with pain, Ivo gave him an exasperated look and shoved him down onto a mounting block before he fell.

Gunnar was looking around him. "Where are the rest of Miles's men? There were at least twenty. Did they all escape?"

"Radulf trussed them up and sent them back to Crevitch. They are his proof, he says, when he sends word to the king. Fitzmorton will be out of favor when his treachery is known—Radulf is a king's favorite, after all. They found Steven trussed up beyond the woods. The boy was bruised but alive, but probably only because they meant to ransom him."

Gunnar nodded as if that made sense to him. "And Arno?" he added.

Ivo looked to Rose and away again. "Sir Arno was slain, Gunnar. There was courage in it. An honorable death. After Miles had left him, he fought like a berserker. 'Twas as if he preferred death to capture."

"Aye." Gunnar also looked at Rose, coolly assessing her expression. "He knew what awaited him if he was captured."

Rose closed her eyes against them both. *Arno, dead?* It was inconceivable. As if one of her family had died. Even though he had betrayed her, was a traitor, she could still pity him. She knew, when she thought of him in the days and weeks to come, that she would mourn the man she had once believed him to be.

"Lady?"

Gunnar was standing very close to her, still watching her. Did he think she was going to faint? Rose stiffened her back. "Aye, captain?" she said, as if they had never lain together, panting and gasping from their lovemaking. As if they were strangers again.

"Lord Radulf is here," he said quietly.

Rose had a sensation of the bailey tilting, and by sheer effort of will she made it right itself. She turned stiffly toward the keep. Radulf was indeed there. He stood in the doorway, watching her, waiting.

The moment she dreaded had come, then.

Rose walked toward him, the soles of her feet touching the earth as if it were unfamiliar to her. When she reached the bottom of the steps, she dipped low in a curtsy. He was her lord and she his vassal. She was in his hands and she knew it. Her future depended on the next few heartbeats.

"Lord Radulf," she said, breathless but proud.

"Lady Rose," he retorted, his voice low and husky but perfectly audible.

"Thank you for coming to our rescue, my lord. I—I am most grateful."

He made a sound that could have been a laugh. "Are you, Lady Rose? Come inside and we will discuss what has been happening here at Somerford and why you should have told me about it."

"Aye, my lord." She started up the steps, as if they weren't slipping and sliding about all over the place.

"And we will talk about your father, lady. Let us talk a little about him." His tone had turned menacing.

Rose froze, wavering, her foot half raised to take the next step. A hard, warm hand closed on her back, steadying her. She had not realized Gunnar was there until then. He stood behind her, like a shield, and she was very grateful.

"I knew nothing of his plans," she whispered, her throat raw with terror. "I have hated him all my life and now he would drag me into a plot of which I knew nothing. Please, my lord, believe me, I knew not what he and Arno were at!"

Radulf was watching her, considering her, his black eyes seeming to pierce her very skull.

"Her father?" Gunnar had come to stand beside her, as if he would share equally in her disgrace. "What is this talk of her father, Radulf?"

Radulf raised his brows, but he didn't take his gaze from Rose's face. "Will you tell him, lady, or will I? I have kept the truth to myself all this time, as you asked me to do after the marriage papers between you and Edric were signed. But now I think it is time to speak it aloud."

Rose swallowed, her eyes flickering to Gunnar's frowning, puzzled face. She had wanted to tell him in the Mere, but somehow there had not been the time. Or the moment.

No, that was not true. She had not trusted him. She had wanted to tell him, she had known she should tell him, but she had stopped herself from doing so. If she had accused him of telling lies, then she was equally accused.

"My father is Fitzmorton." She said it bleakly. "I am

his bastard daughter. He brought me from Normandy when my mother died, to use to further his ambitions. He and Lord Radulf thought to secure a peace through me. I would marry Edric, and Fitzmorton would not seek to steal Lord Radulf's land. A show of his good faith. But the truth was my father never valued me, so breaking his word and my heart meant little. Mayhap he always intended to betray me and Radulf when the chance came his way. When Edric died, he sought to control Somerford Manor through Arno, and when that did not work, he decided he would send Miles. And now Lord Radulf thinks I am in league with him, plotting to hand him Somerford, but 'tis not so. I hate him. I would rather die myself than let Fitzmorton take my lands."

Gunnar was staring back at her, his face blank, empty. There was no warmth in his eyes, there was nothing.

She was Fitzmorton's daughter.

How he must hate her.

"I cannot go back to him," she said quietly, speaking to him alone. "I really will die."

"Lady, you are very dramatic!" Radulf had come down the last few steps that separated them to take her hand. His fingers were warm, and they squeezed hers in an attempt at comfort. But Rose was too distressed to understand what he meant.

"Come," Radulf went on gently, "and we will talk. Gunnar? Will you come? We had a deal, did we not, my friend? And you have carried out your part of it, as I knew you would. I have a compromise to suggest . . ."

Gunnar was still looking at her. Rose knew very well what deal it was he had with Radulf. Radulf had offered him Somerford Manor in return for uncovering the plot. Strangely, aside from her fear for her own future and the pain of her loss, she was glad that her lands and her people would now be under Gunnar's care. She knew he would protect them with his life, and care for them as if they were his own flesh and blood. Beneath his handsome face and cold logic, he was a deeply honorable man.

She knew that at last, when it was too late. But still the acknowledgment lifted something dark from her heart. Rose took a deep breath and looked him in the eye, not knowing exactly what she meant to say, only that she could not be silent any longer . . .

But he didn't give her time to say anything. Gunnar turned to Radulf, drawing him a little away, murmuring in a low, serious tone. Rose stood, unwillingly left out and uneasy as to their conversation. It was about her, she knew it. They should not speak of her without giving her the chance to reply.

Just as she was about to step in and demand to hear, Radulf nodded brusquely and came back to her. Gunnar stayed where he was, one hand resting on his sword hilt, the other by his side, his strong legs slightly apart. It was a stance he adopted often, familiar now. But it was his eyes she stared into. They were very blue, and there was something shining in their depths like grief.

Her heart plummeted within her.

No, not that. Please, not that.

He turned away. He was striding down the steps and across the bailey, his men falling in wordlessly behind him. He was leaving; without a word to her he was going.

Shocked, Rose swung back to face Radulf, her whole body shaking.

"My lord! What—"

Radulf took her hands in his, holding her steady. His black eyes were intense, forcing her by the sheer strength of his will to heed his words.

"Lady Rose, you will retain Somerford Manor. I believe you were an innocent victim of this plot. Somerford is yours, you are my vassal still, but you must swear to me that you will never again fear to ask for my help."

She shook her head, overwhelmed by what he was saying. "But . . . Gunnar? I thought . . ."

"Gunnar Olafson has relinquished any rights he had to your manor. He has given them back to you. He tells me he made you a vow, lady. You were fortunate in your choice of mercenary, were you not?"

He was watching her closely, as if he sought something in her face. Rose managed a nod.

"Aye, my lord," she whispered, "I was most fortunate."

He smiled. "If you need help again, you will know where to seek it, won't you? I would not be adverse to you looking to Gunnar Olafson if you were ever in . . . need. I spoke just now of a compromise. I meant to suggest a partnership between the two of you, a joint ruling of Somerford Manor. Maybe, at some other time, we can speak of it again, hmm?"

The look he gave her was almost wicked. And then he had dismissed her, calling out for his horse, and turning to shout his goodbyes with a smile.

"I leave you enough men to protect Somerford from

your father's greedy gaze, lady! Now I must go home. Lily awaits."

"My lord. Of course, my lord . . ."

Rose stared after him, wondering what it all meant. Had he meant to give her hope where Gunnar was concerned, or was he threatening her? A partnership could mean many things. She never knew with Radulf, and she was too weary now to make sense of it. There was only one thought in her head, and it drove all others before it.

I want him back. Please, oh please, I want him back . . .

Is it really too late?

Her heart ached, but as she turned to her people the familiar mask slipped over her face. The lady of the manor. And her voice lifted, cool and authoritative.

"Listen to me, my people! We are safe from Lord Fitzmorton and his plot, but it is not just Lord Radulf and Captain Olafson who have saved us. I want to tell you of the merefolk and what their bravery has meant to us in these grave times . . ."

The dream slipped over her like a well-worn cloak.

Rose was alone on the Mere, Burrow Mump at her shoulder like a familiar black shadow. She was already running, knowing what would come, and they were behind her. The horde of men, roaring across the Levels, their passing flattening the reeds like a giant hand and making the water slap and hiss.

She screamed and made no sound.

Ahead of her lay Somerford Keep, a pale candle flickering in the window. The dark stones looked solid and safe, and yet Rose knew very well she could never reach it in time. She glanced behind her and the warriors were close. Their savage faces were set, their eyes fixed on her. She searched them, but saw no one she recognized.

Where was he? Why was he not there, riding before them?

Rose almost gave up then, and sank to her knees and awaited her fate.

But then she saw him.

He was coming toward her, but he was riding from the direction of Somerford Keep! The gray horse pounded across the Mere, tail and mane streaming. His copper hair was dulled by the moonlight, tangling in the roaring wind that came with the horde from Burrow Mump. He drew his sword and held it aloft, and then he swung it down, and it seemed as if it cleaved the very air in two.

Behind her, Rose heard the ghostly warriors give a terrible shriek.

The world shimmered and splintered about her, light flashing as though there were a great storm. Rose covered her head with her arms, expecting any moment to be swallowed into blackness. When she dared to look up again, there was only silence.

The warriors were gone, back to their cavern in the Mump.

Only he was there, her own warrior. Gunnar Olafson upon his gray horse, smiling down at her. When he stretched out his hand, she took it, and he lifted her onto the saddle before him.

"I am taking you home," he said.

"Lady?"

His breath was warm on her cheek; the familiar feel

of his body was pressed to hers. Rose blinked and opened her eyes, and it did not seem strange at all that Gunnar should be there in her bed. He had brought her home, hadn't he?

"Hmm." She sighed and curled her arms about his neck, nuzzling his jaw, enjoying the scratchy feel of it.

He stiffened and then relaxed, his hand smoothing back her sweet-scented hair. "Lady? I am come to say goodbye."

That got her attention.

Rose's eyes opened wide, and she leaned back to give him a startled glance. "Goodbye?" she repeated. Then, as if suddenly realizing where they were, she sat up, making space between them. "I cannot think. What do you here in my chamber?"

Gunnar sighed, and propped himself up on one elbow as if he belonged in her bed. "I did not mean to come here at all, but then I could not go without saying goodbye. We have work in the north, there has been a skirmish and Radulf wants us to travel to Lily's lands and—"

"You mean, go away?"

He gave her a long look. "Aye, Rose, that is what I said. We are going away. I will not see you again for—" But he shook his head, and his mouth turned grim. "I will not see you again."

She shook her head back and forth, several times. "No! I will not allow it. Radulf can send Ivo. You are needed here, Gunnar. Somerford . . . Somerford needs you. Even Radulf agrees with me on that!"

He blinked slowly, as if to give himself time to assimilate what she had just said.

"I know you gave up your rights to my lands, and I

am grateful. I don't know why you did it, but—"

"They were always yours, Rose. Besides, I did not take Somerford back for you as I promised. Radulf and Ivo did that. I was not worthy to take your lands anyway because my vow was not properly honored."

Rose stared at him. "But you did give me back Somerford! If it had not been for you, I would have lost everything. I would have been dead, or worse. My father would have given me to Miles, you know that, don't you? You saved me from that, Gunnar." Her voice wavered and stopped.

He shrugged, looking uncomfortable. "Maybe." He glanced at her sideways, still propped up on his elbow, his long body on the rumpled covers of her bed. "You are Fitzmorton's daughter," he said, as if that were an answer.

"Aye, his bastard daughter. It means nothing."

"You are the daughter of a powerful lord, lady. It means something."

Is that why he had left? Because he thought himself too lowly for her now? Rose could not bear it. Constance was right—there was more to a man than his blood relatives. There was what he was inside, what he did with his life, whether the travails he faced strengthened or diminished him.

Gunnar was strong, and he had come into her life and made her strong, too. But it was more than that. She loved him, she needed him. She was not her mother, pleading for Fitzmorton's cruel love. She was Lady Rose, and she loved a man who was her equal. Her complement. And if he should go from her now, then winning back Somerford would be a hollow victory.

Rose shook her head, and suddenly she was walking

toward him, her hands clenched into fists by her sides. "Gunnar, please, please don't leave me. Please don't go north. I want you . . . I need you here, with me. I cannot be the Lady of Somerford unless you are by my side. I am sick with longing for you. Stay with me and be my shield."

Still he said nothing, watching her. "Do you trust me?" he asked her quietly.

"Aye, I do. I will. I know now that what you told me was part of your mission for Radulf. You had to pretend. Lives depended on it. I understand that." She was gazing at him so earnestly. "You would never betray me, Gunnar."

"No, I would not," he vowed softly. He reached out and caught her hand with his fingers, drawing her onto the bed and into his arms. She went with a gasping laugh.

His body rolled onto hers, pinning her down. He was fully dressed, even down to his sword and his boots. She didn't care. He was her man, her warrior, and she loved him.

Rose tried the words out in her head and they sounded good. She tried them out loud.

"I love you, Gunnar."

He smiled slowly, his blue eyes blazing down at her. "I love you, too, lady."

"Then kiss me, Gunnar, for I can't wait any longer."

"But do you command me, Rose?"

She laughed, stretching up until her mouth brushed his. "Aye, I command you, Gunnar."

And so he did.